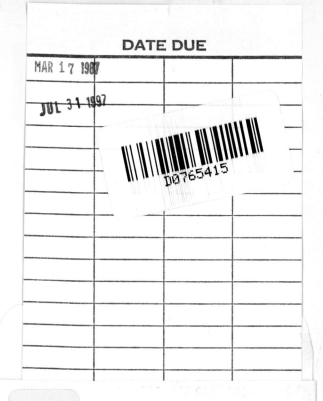

All but impossible?

# ALL BUT IMPOSSIBLE!

# *All But Impossible!*

An Anthology of
Locked Room & Impossible Crime Stories
by Members of the Mystery Writers of America

*Edited by Edward D. Hoch* 1930 -

**Ticknor & Fields**

New Haven and New York

1981

Designed by John O. C. McCrillis

**Library of Congress Cataloging in Publication Data**
Main entry under title:

All but impossible!

1. Detective and mystery stories, American. 2. Crime and criminals — Fiction. I. Hoch, Edward D., 1930–
II. Mystery Writers of America.
PS648.D4A43      813′.01′08      81-8718
ISBN 0-89919-045-6          AACR2

Printed in the United States of America

P 10 9 8 7 6 5 4 3 2 1

01/82 Midwest # 18629

To the Memory of
John Dickson Carr & Clayton Rawson
Who Contributed So Much to MWA
and to the Locked Room Story

# Contents

# Introduction

The locked room story has a long and noble history, going back to Poe's "The Murders in the Rue Morgue." It reached its peak in the Golden Age of detective fiction just prior to World War II, but a large number of mystery writers and fans still find a fascination with it. The crime in the sealed chamber, the impossible disappearance, the magical murder before scores of witnesses — these are the meat of the pure detective story. Today, when so many mysteries are merely crime or chase thrillers, a reader picking up a locked room or impossible crime tale can be assured of a real puzzle.

When I began work on this anthology it occurred to me that readers might be interested in a guide to the best locked room novels, to accompany this selection of short stories and novelettes. I asked a number of writers, editors, critics and fans in America, England and Sweden to give me a list of their favorite locked room or impossible crime novels — up to ten in number, arranged in order of preference. I ended up with seventeen lists including my own. Some could give me only two or three titles, while others had difficulty limiting their choice to ten. In all cases I awarded ten points to the first-place choice, nine to the second, and so on.

The panel of seventeen consisted of Robert Adey, Jack Adrian, Jacques Barzun, Jon L. Breen, Robert E. Briney, Jan Broberg, Frederick Dannay (Ellery Queen), Douglas G. Greene, Howard Haycraft, Edward D. Hoch, Marvin Lachman, Richard Levinson & William Link (a joint list), Francis M. Nevins, Jr., Otto Penzler, Bill Pronzini, Julian Symons, and Donald A. Yates. In all, they listed exactly fifty novels, though only twenty-one appeared on more than one list.

I am the first to admit my poll was informal and unscientific. Still, the results are interesting. Here is a list of our ten best, with the total number of points awarded to each book:

1. *The Three Coffins,* John Dickson          104 points
   Carr (1935) (British title: *The
   Hollow Man*)
2. *Rim of the Pit,* Hake Talbot (1944)        59 points
3. *The Mystery of the Yellow Room,*           57 points
   Gaston Leroux (1908)
4. *The Crooked Hinge,* John Dickson           55 points
   Carr (1938)
5. *The Judas Window,* Carter Dickson          51 points
   (John Dickson Carr) (1938)
6. *The Big Bow Mystery,* Israel               47 points
   Zangwill (1892)
7. *Death From a Top Hat,* Clayton             39 points
   Rawson (1938)
8. *The Chinese Orange Mystery,*               35 points
   Ellery Queen (1934)
9. *Nine Times Nine,* H. H. Holmes             30 points
   (Anthony Boucher) (1940)
10. *The Peacock Feather Murders,*             22 points
    Carter Dickson (John Dickson
    Carr) (1937) (British title: *The
    Ten Teacups*)

*The Three Coffins* was clearly far in front. It appeared on
twelve of the seventeen lists, and was in first place on seven
of them. And it's not too surprising that four of the top ten
books are by John Dickson Carr, long considered the master
of the locked room story. The early classics by Zangwill and
Leroux were fondly remembered, as were Golden Age books
by Rawson, Queen and Boucher. Perhaps the biggest surprise
on the list is the high position for *Rim of the Pit,* an excellent
book but one long out of print in America.

All ten of these books appeared on at least four lists. For
those interested in runners-up, the next five were on three
lists each:

11. *The King Is Dead,* Ellery Queen          20 points
    (1952)

12. *Through a Glass, Darkly,* Helen          19 points
    McCloy (1950)
13. *He Wouldn't Kill Patience,* Carter       18 points
    Dickson (John Dickson Carr)
    (1944)
14. (tie) *Too Many Magicians,* Randall       13 points
    Garrett (1967)
    *Invisible Green,* John Sladek            13 points
    (1977)

No other titles appeared on more than two lists or received more than ten points.

So much for novels about locked rooms and impossible crimes. What about short stories? At least two members of my panel suggested that locked rooms and impossible crimes work best in the short story length, and there's something to be said for that opinion. A look at the publication dates of the fifteen books listed above shows only two of them published after 1952 — yet most of the stories in this book first appeared after that date. If the locked room novel is in a decline, the locked room short story is still alive and well.

In choosing the stories for this book I have tried to show the various types of locked room/impossible crime problems and solutions, while still using tales which are first of all entertaining to read. As with all previous MWA anthologies, these stories have been contributed by their authors, with all proceeds going to the Mystery Writers of America. I wish to thank each of them, as well as the estates of John Dickson Carr and Clayton Rawson, for allowing me to use these stories.

I also wish to thank the authors, editors, critics and fans who participated in my locked room poll. And special thanks to my wife Patricia, who helped with many aspects of this book.

*Rochester, N.Y.*                                   EDWARD D. HOCH

# The Shadow of the Goat

**John Dickson Carr**

*The year 1926 was an important one in the development of the locked room/impossible crime story, though perhaps it didn't seem so at the time. The Golden Age of detective fiction was just getting under way, and many of its brightest stars had yet to be heard from. But at Haverford College in Pennsylvania young John Dickson Carr was editing a monthly literary magazine,* The Haverfordian. *In it appeared his earliest mysteries, recently discovered and collected by Douglas G. Greene. This story, his first real locked room tale, was also his first to use a series detective — the French sleuth Bencolin, who would reappear in three more short stories and five novels.*

IT WAS a thoughtful room, and tobacco smoke clung round the edges of the lamp. The two men who sat there were thoughtful, but that was not the only point of similarity between them. They had the same worried look of persons too much interested in other men's affairs. Sir John Landervorne had once come from that vague section of London known as Whitehall, and he had been possibly the only man in the city who might have given police orders to Scotland Yard. If M. Henri Bencolin was only one of France's eighty-six prefects of police, he was not the least important of them.

Fog had made London medieval again, a place of towers and footsteps and dim figures. It blurred the windows of the room in Fontain Court, the backwater of Fleet Street where the barristers sometimes walk in their ghostly wigs, swinging canes like swords. In the room the two men, sitting opposite each other with white shirt fronts bulging exactly alike, smoked similar cigars — Bencolin with his black beard, Landervorne's beard gray as the cigar ash. It gave one a weird feeling: picture of a detective at thirty, then a picture of him at sixty. Their eyes were somber.

"If you tell me your story," said Sir John, "you will have to tell it to Billy Garrick, because these are his rooms, and he will be in presently. But it will be safe; he was there last night too."

Bencolin nodded. He spoke rather wearily.

"I know it, my friend. Of course, I did not telephone you officially — I am not connected officially with the matter. Well! Last night near Worksop, in Nottinghamshire, M. Jules Fragneau was murdered. That is why I wanted to see you."

"Then," said the Englishman, "I shall have to tell you a story which will not interest you, unless you believe in sorcery. Because, you see, the only man who might have killed Fragneau walked through a pair of locked shutters at ten o'clock last night."

"The report is true, then. Oh, the devil!" Bencolin fretted.

"The report is fantastic, and true. I saw Cyril Merton go into a room that had only one door, which was bolted and which I was watching. The room had only one window, barred, with locked shutters. There was no fireplace, nor was there any secret means of egress; the walls were stone. Exactly that. It was a stone box. But I tell you Merton went into the place — and vanished. Lord Brandon and Garrick, who were with me when we searched it both before and after the disappearance, will verify what I say. Afterwards an even stranger thing occurred. For surely Merton killed Fragneau, and then he very nearly committed another murder, at which time I saw him evaporate before my eyes. That, my dear sir, is witchcraft, and,'' he added thoughtfully, "I am a sane man. At least, I think I am a sane man.''

M. Bencolin got up. Fog had crept in and mingled with the tobacco smoke; the Frenchman shivered. He looked small and shrunken, and very tired. With the cigar protruding ludicrously from his mouth, he began to wander about the room.

"My friend, I am beaten. Name of God!'' he said fiercely. "I am beaten! I thought that I had enough impossible riddles in my case. But unless we can prove he made a phantom of himself a third time, and got into a locked house, a poor stupid fellow named Fulke will be indicted for murder. Of course these events are connected! Tell me the whole story, please.''

Sir John sat back in his chair. His face was pinched with thought.

"Very well. There's a preface, you see, about Cyril Merton. Give Merton a wig and a sword, and he would be your seventeenth-century swashbuckler — but you must grant him a wig. For though he was tall, and rather strangely handsome with a thin luminous face in which you saw every emotion as through glass, the man's head was shaven. He had studied in Germany before he became an actor, and his ugly nature got him into duels with the saber, which left scars on his head. The scars were so hideous that hair only made them worse. So he kept his head shaven, criss-crossed white. But the beauty of his face, with the short dark beard, kept him from being ridiculous.

"He was our greatest actor. If you saw him in any of the old romantic plays you know the medieval soul of the man. He could turn himself into any sort of character; that was his genius. The man's hobby was sorcery and the deadly arts, in pursuit of which he had a library stuffed with forgotten books — the works of Hermes the Egyptian, Lillius, Geber, James Stuart, Cotton Mather, all of them. He belonged in a day when they burned such men.

"That was why he bought the place. Bell House is on a tract of ground that was once a part of Sherwood Forest, about thirty miles from where Fragneau lived. Bell House! You can see the tower of the bell lifted over the trees, with a hill of silver birches white in the moonlight, and the wind moving them. It was built when William the Norman darkened England with a hurricane of swords, and there are clanking ghosts in its halls. That was a dirty, snarling age — church and the devil frightening the soul out of people, big men in armor, faces caked with blood, butchering in nameless filth — the very bogey house of history. Why, the moat around Bell House is twenty feet deep.

"I have to tell you about a dinner Cyril Merton gave. There was the banquet hall, with pointed windows of painted glass, and the candles shining on them; I remember the white shirt fronts, the cigar smoke, the flashing teeth when people laughed. One gets a series of impressions in a shadowy place like that. For example, I remember the picture of Billy Garrick with Madeline — maybe because Madeline is my daughter — on the staircase after dinner; on the staircase under the dark portraits, and the candles. They are both yellow-haired, handsome as old Saxons. It was an absurd gesture on his part, but the place for it: he kissed her hand.

"They are in love, and I have an especial interest in Garrick for that reason. I was worried about him that evening. Billy is a nephew of Jules Fragneau. Because the old man had been rather more than his father, and made him his heir, Fragneau's enemies were Billy's enemies. Which was the reason why Merton, who hated Fragneau almost to the point of idiocy, never got along with the lad. He had been forced to invite him because Billy was my guest, and I was too close a neighbor to be omitted. For the same reason Billy had been forced to accept. All through the evening I felt uneasy.

"It all culminated in a foolish argument in the smoking room. The men had assembled there by a big blazing fireplace, with stags' heads, and all that. Having just come away from Madeline, Billy was in an exultant, swaggering mood. He smoked cigarettes and laughed at Merton, who was holding forth on his hobby of medieval magic against Lord Brandon and Mr. Julian Arbor. He was standing against the mantelpiece, black beard, shaven head, using that smile with which he argues.

" 'I was telling you,' said Merton, 'about the book of Gersault de Brilliers, published by Meroit, Paris, in 1697 'Contes du Diable,' with a subhead: 'Avec L'Histoire de L'Homme Qui Savait S'Evanouir.' One of the accounts deals with a man who walked into a locked room and vanished utterly. De Brilliers put it down to sorcery, which is possible. But a perfectly practicable kind of sorcery.'

"Mr. Julian Arbor protested. Arbor is a strange sort of English gentleman; doesn't at all object to helping out people who are financially in a hole — at tremendous interest. Just a polished form of moneylender. The man looks kindly, but he has a hard glaze on him like a tombstone. He protested gently: 'My dear fellow —'

" 'Bosh!' struck in Billy Garrick. 'Bosh, Merton!'

"It was a typical gathering, with a mass of stuffy landed proprietors who always have the look of just having eaten too much. Bald and florid and oratorical as the elder Pitt. Lord Brandon is one of these.

" 'This, sir,' observed Lord Brandon, 'strikes me as being a great deal of foolishness.' He waddled to the fire, waving his hands.

" 'Nevertheless, it happened,' the actor replied. 'It can happen again.'

"Billy was just a bit drunk. He protested furiously:

" 'Look here, Merton, you're usually so aloof that nobody contradicts you. And this grand superiority complex of yours

is making me tired! If you can stand there and talk solemn
stuff like that —'

" 'It can be done,' said Merton quietly. 'I can do it myself.'

"He was always one to play to an audience, and he enjoyed the consternation he created among that group of
squires, smiling at his cigar.

" 'You mean, Merton, that you can walk into a locked
room — a real locked room — and disappear?' asked Julian
Arbor.

" 'Trap doors!' snapped Billy instantly.

" 'There are no trap doors. I say that I can go into a stone
room here at the castle, have you lock doors and windows,
and I can vanish. Just that.'

" 'Bosh!' repeated Billy.

" 'See here,' said Merton, 'if you want my opinion, even
a host's opinion, your talk is damned impertinence.'

" 'And if you want mine,' said Billy, 'yours is damned
nonsense.'

"Merton was furious; the glass face lit like fire.

" 'We'll drop your gutter behavior for the present; it can
be argued later. Garrick, do you want to wager me a thousand pounds that I can't do what I say, eh?'

" 'Oh, I say!' cried Julian Arbor. 'Don't be a fool!' He
turned to Billy in alarm. 'Surely you won't — Merton, I refuse to allow —'

" 'What have you got to do with it?' demanded Billy, who
was angry too. 'Keep out of this, sir! Merton, I shall be glad
to see you make an ass of yourself. I accept your wager.'

" 'If Mr. Merton will allow me, I accept it too,' Lord
Brandon interposed.

"Merton laughed.

" 'Are there any other takers, gentlemen?' he said casually.''

Sir John paused. Bencolin had sat down, and was staring
at him. The Englishman lighted another cigar before he resumed.

"Well, the thing was fantastic, but it was done. Only Mr. Julian Arbor would not remain to see the wager carried out. He said he had to catch a night train for London, departing with somewhat jarring abruptness —"

"For *London?*" demanded Bencolin. "London? Pardon me; go on."

The words had been rather like a yelp. Sir John smiled.

"I was surprised, I must confess, but there were other matters on my mind. Merton was carrying off the affair with theatrical grace. We had to tell the ladies, who suspected some sort of joke, but insisted on following us. And yet the big halls, the weird unnaturalness of the place, got their nerves on edge; Madeline enjoyed it. The others began a shrill rush of talk, which gradually slowed and stopped like a run-down gramophone. Anything was better than the unnatural sound of those voices.

"Merton took us upstairs. We were a solemn company, parading the halls with candles. That castle was too big for us, and the moon was too far — it followed us along every hall, peering through the windows. Once Merton paused by a window, the silhouette of him with the moon behind his head; his face jumped suddenly out of the dark as he lighted a cigarette by the candleflame, and then it vanished. The silhouette contorted as though the man were dancing.

"He led us to an immense room, quite bare, so that you could see only the aimless candles moving under people's faces. At its far end was a door, which Merton threw open. It communicated with a flight of steps, walled with stone and having at the top another door. On the threshold Merton paused, with a kind of bluish glow behind him.

" 'This,' he said, 'is the room itself. I should prefer that the ladies did not enter. Come along, Lord Brandon, Sir John, Garrick too — examine it. I shall go in here. You will bolt the door at the bottom of the steps on the outside, and watch it. First go over this staircase to be sure there is no other exit.'

"Somebody laughed a bit nervously. Merton finished his

cigarette while we moved around the flight of steps. Then —"

"Wait!" Bencolin interrupted. "Please don't describe it; don't describe the room. I am going to see it, and I want to form my own impressions. It might lead me astray if I heard too many details. But one thing: was there a washstand in the place?"

Sir John's heavy eyes flashed open.

"Yes! Why do you ask? That washstand was a curious thing to see there. . . ."

"Go on, my friend."

"We will say, then, that the room was large and odd. Garrick, Lord Brandon and I went over every foot of it. Intact! A window in a big stone embrasure was firmly barred. We closed and locked the shutters. Then we pronounced ourselves satisfied, Lord Brandon red and puzzled. As we were going out, Merton stopped us. He stood by the table in the light of a lamp of blue glass, but only his absolutely pallid hand protruded from the shadow, toying with a little ebony figure of . . . a goat. Garrick, as tall and threatening as he, said: 'Anything more?'

" 'Lord Brandon,' Merton answered, ignoring him, 'I am doing a dangerous thing. If I make a mistake, if you have any cause to think that such is the case, at the end of fifteen minutes come up here instantly! You promise me that?'

"Brandon promised —"

"One moment," said the Frenchman. "Did you look in all the table drawers?"

"My dear fellow," Sir John returned petulantly, "a man can't hide in a table drawer, or escape through it."

"Of course not. Well?"

"The last thing I remember was Merton standing by the table, playing with the tiny goat's figure. It was as though he were deliberately trying to call our attention to that image."

"He was. He may have been trying to give you a clue."

"Oh, come! What do you mean by that?"

"I don't know; it merely struck me as curious. You went downstairs?"

"We went downstairs, yes. I bolted the lower door on the

outside. Then it began. We found that we had left all but two of the candles in Merton's room. There we were, a blundering, half-frightened crowd in a gulf of a place, candles tossing. Nervous laughter, figures moving about us. I had one of the lights, and kept it on my watch. Fifteen minutes — dragging. And women talking, and talking. But I never lost sight of the door, nor did Lord Brandon, who was standing in front of it. Somewhere in the house I thought I heard hurrying footsteps, and once the sound of water running. Finally there occurred the thing that broke our nerves like somebody jumping on you in the dark.

"It was an explosion, the terrific noise a pistol makes when it is fired indoors. Brandon and his following would have rushed the door even had not somebody shouted, 'Time's up!' The cry ripped into a screech of the bolt and a rush of feet up the stairs, but I remained in the background to make sure nobody slipped past those who entered. Nobody did! I went up slowly, examining the stairs, and joined the group at the door when I was certain of it —"

Suddenly Sir John crashed his fist down on the chair arm.

"Merton was gone! No one left the top door; the others stood guard while Brandon, Garrick and I searched the whole apartment. We were in a kind of frenzy. Shutters fastened, bars untouched; as a matter of fact, there was dust on the bars. No Merton, no hidden door. Some sort of weapon had been fired there, for a faint tang of powder was in the air, but we found no weapon. The blue glass lamp burned dully, fixing our eyes like a crucible, and a bit of smoke hovered over it like waving hands. . . But in spite of it all, I know that before we came nobody had either entered or left that door!"

*And, as later events proved, Sir John spoke the absolute truth.*

## II

Lamplight had made the thickening smoke in the room a yellow haze. Both Bencolin and Sir John Landervorne looked weirdly unnatural. Bencolin said:

"That statement, my friend, would be ridiculed in a court
of law. We can prove nothing on the man now — don't you
see? Under the circumstances of Fragneau's death, either the
man Fulke or myself, the only other occupants of his house,
must have killed him. Fragneau was stabbed about twelve
o'clock last night. Merton disappeared at ten, easily in time
for him to have gone thirty miles by motor. There is nothing
more inconspicuous than the driver of an automobile at night.
Now, then, at twelve-fifteen, or thereabouts, I telephoned
you at your home, because I knew that you lived close to
Merton. It was no burglar's work, because nothing had been
stolen at Fragneau's home; the only person who might have
killed Fragneau was Merton, and I wanted to check up on his
whereabouts instantly. There would be no possibility of his
servants lying as to his movements if I communicated with
*you*. Your butler told me that you were at Merton's, and had
not returned. I left a message for you to call —"

"At twelve-fifteen," interrupted the Englishman, "Madeline, Garrick and I were returning to my home. In that interval Merton had not appeared. The question being: if he was
perpetrating a joke, why did he not return? We waited two
hours before we reassured the servants and left. But in the
vicinity of one-thirty, Merton *did* come back. We will con-
nect that up with the story later. Tell me about Fragneau."

"The very devilish simplicity of it, my friend, is that I
have no story. You know Fragneau. His hobby was astron-
omy; I will not say astrology, because it was there that the
Merton-Fragneau feud began. Every time I have visited his
house he has shown me some new device to keep out bur-
glars. He had a big glass dome of an observatory on the roof,
an open place, so that in this fanatical fear of intruders there
was an iron fence, ten feet high and electrically charged,
around the entire roof. The house being small, every window
had its own protective fastening. On each of the two doors
was a lock for which no duplicate key could be made! Imagine it — the place was a fortress. Fulke, a big, awkward,
red-haired fellow, was his new servant. I remember his

wooden face at the door when I arrived, hair tilted over its side like a vivid wig — and the white-lit dome uncanny up against the night sky, with Fragneau's shadow flickering over it.

"Facts, these. At eleven o'clock Fragneau went over the place, adjusted all his devices, locked his doors. We had been talking, but he insisted on working in his laboratory as a nightly ritual. I was not interested, and went to my room to read. It overlooked the front stairs. At twelve I grew tired of reading, at which time I started for the observatory to bring him down for a final cigar. . . .

"Fragneau sat before the telescope with a stupid grin on his face. His chest was heavy with blood where he had been stabbed with a bone-handled knife a very few minutes before. The glare of light, the white-pointed face like a goat's, the yellow shaft protruding from his chest, all calm as sleep.

"I summoned Fulke; the house was searched, the doors and windows found locked. Neither of us had heard an intruder. We calmly went about questioning each other; then I put in two telephone messages, to you and to the local police. That is all, except for one point. At twelve-thirty a man rang the doorbell and asked to see Fragneau. . . . Once," added the Frenchman abruptly, "when I learned that Fulke was a new servant, I conceived a theory as to the assassination. Now it is all dark, considering what you say, unless . . ." He paused, and smiled.

"Unless what?"

"Unless, in a manner of speaking, Cyril Merton washed himself down the drain. To give you more than an indication —"

"Bencolin," demanded the Englishman, "are you insane? Great God!"

"Wait! Please wait! You would be insulted if I continued. My friend, I think the motive in this affair is money. Do you know who rang the doorbell half an hour after the murder? It was Mr. Julian Arbor."

## III

A gust of colder air blew in from the foggy corridor as the door opened. Bencolin was still straining forward, elbow on the table, the fingers of his hand crooked toward Sir John. And as a third figure, lean and tall in its greatcoat, came toward them, they had the appearance of people in a storm. The newcomer took off his hat, displaying eyes of a rather brilliant vivid blue in a face glistening like wax. The eyes struck Bencolin with the suddenness of rifle shots; they had a wretchéd, terrible appeal.

"Hello, Sir John," he said hoarsely, croaking with a cold. "This the M. Bencolin you came to see? My name's Garrick, sir. Well, every dragnet in England is out for that damned murdering — Start a fire, will you?"

He sat down, shivering, and threw off his coat. His arm was in a sling.

"I — I just left Madeline. She was crying. . . ."

There was an odd strained silence. Then Sir John got up blunderingly and began to heap wood in the fireplace.

"He didn't suffer," said Bencolin. "I mean . . ."

"I am glad to hear it," replied the young man. They did not see his face.

"My friend," the Frenchman began, "God willing, we will find Merton."

He paused, but the words had something like the ring of an oath. Then he looked at Garrick's arm. "The second victim! When did he attack?"

"It was about one-thirty. Sir, the thing is too incredible! Are you sure Merton is a *man?*"

"Steady!" warned Sir John.

"Well . . . I had gone to bed. It was bright moonlight in the room, hard and clear as glass. I was fuming about Merton, just drifting to sleep, when I heard someone cry out."

Sir John paused with a lighted match in his hand.

"I was at one window across the quadrangle," he interposed. "My room. I could not sleep. Then I saw a shadow move. The moon shone on a head that was perfectly white. Something began climbing the ivy toward a window on the second floor, and when I realized whose window, I knew who that person was. I could not help screaming to warn Garrick —''

"It saved my life," the other said calmly. "When I sat up in bed, a silhouette reared up over the windowsill, but I saw the white head. And then," he rushed on, "it came at a kind of bound, like a goat. The light from the open window was blocked as it got me; I felt the tangle of the bedclothes, the rip into my arm of a pain, blinding and sickish like ether. My arm began to grow hot, but I fought him. Somehow he tore away — Sir John, are you *sure* nobody left by the door?''

"I would swear to it. Listen, Bencolin, for your final riddle. After I cried out, I ran out of my room. In the central hallway I met Dorset, the butler who took your message. I didn't explain, but I told him to hurry outside and stop anybody who came out by a window. Don't you see? If we were in time, we had Merton trapped! Doors were banging open in the house, lights flashing on. When I reached Garrick's door the lights in the corridor were blazing. Behind the door was the furious wheezing and thudding of a fight; a chair clattered over; somebody began to run. The door was bolted, but it was flimsy wood. I battered it until the bolt ripped out. Billy almost ran into me — and before him there was a shadow. I switched on the lights, standing in the door, and for one instant the picture was hideous and sharp and motionless as waxworks. Billy, full white on the square of gray moonlight, with a sheet trailing him, his arm running red as though it were alive. The intruder was gone! We hunted the room over, after which I called to Dorset. He answered that nobody had left by the window.''

"He was going for the door!" Garrick cried excitedly. "Then you opened it in my face. And yet I touched him a moment before!''

Bencolin sat with his head between his hands; Sir John

was standing by the fireplace without moving, and held the charred curl of a match. Fog had seeped into the room until the lamplight was all but obscured.

## IV

Bencolin had not slept for twenty-four hours. If the man who had listened to the amazing recitals of Sir John Landervorne and Billy Garrick the night before had been neat, correct as a picture, then it was somewhat of an apparition which went stamping about Bell House the next day. Unshaven, with a battered hat stuck on his head like a helmet, the man resembled a conception of an early Goth. He had been seen early in the morning standing against a red tattered sky among the mists at the edge of the moat, and he was poking in the water with a walking stick.

This was no England of the sort called merrie, of Robin Hood and warm leaves and gray goose feather. It was stern as the Norman. And the work which presently occupied the constables under Bencolin's direction was sterner still. Through the November morning they were wading in the moat.

When, after a while, he entered the big silent house, there were only a few servants for him to question. Their employer had not returned, and yet they were fearful to leave. While he explored every dusty corner, he could hear the solemn tramp of feet. Finally he went upstairs to the tower room. It was there, in the afternoon, that those he had summoned found him.

The afternoon sun, an ugly rose color, shot across the room like a spotlight from the window embrasure. It rested on the closed door of a closet, which Bencolin had earlier in the day explored and found empty. In the middle of the apartment stood the table with its tiny goat's statue, so that the sun outlined on the closet door a monstrous figure of a goat. When Sir John Landervorne opened the door to the room, he saw only that shaft of light in shadows, beyond which was the glow of Bencolin's eternal cigar. The Englishman shuddered, fumbling at his beard.

"That you, Bencolin?" he asked. "Ugh! What a place! Shall we come in?"

"I see no reason," protested a voice behind him, "for dragging us up here from London! I told you everything you wanted to know last night." It was Julian Arbor, who pushed past Sir John; though he seemed angry, not a muscle in his big white face moved.

"The matter is serious," Bencolin responded. "Will the rest of you come in? Lord Brandon? Thank you. And Mr. Garrick. Who's that?" His nerves were jumpy, and he leaned suddenly out into the light at the sound of another voice.

"Madeline insisted —" said Sir John.

"I did!" a little voice confirmed him, laughing. The girl looked light as though she might be blown by a wind, with a sort of half beauty in her face that was rather better than loveliness. Whiteclad, she moved forward. "Mayn't I stay? You've promised us a solution, and I want to hear it."

"Sir John, this is impossible!" the Frenchman snapped.

"I won't go," said the girl. "I have as much right to be here as anyone."

Bencolin stared at her; at the sight of his face a movement went through the watchers. They knew why. In that room was terror.

"Merton is here!" said Bencolin.

"That was it — terror. Sir John began thickly, nervously.

"Go out, Madeline; please go out. My God, what are you saying?"

"He is here," went on the Frenchman, "he is in this room. Lord Brandon, stand in front of that door. The rest of you sit down, and whatever happens, do not move."

In the half darkness somebody stumbled a little. Bencolin had stepped in front of the window. Against the reddish light they saw his profile with the high hooked nose and bearded jaw. The energy had gone out of him; his shoulders were stooped, and he stared out thoughtfully into the sky.

"It's an odd case," he said. "It's the only case on record in which a man proves an alibi for his murderer. And it shows many curious things. For example, there is that appearance of Mr. Julian Arbor at Fragneau's house after the murder —''

"Look here," snapped Arbor, and he came into the light with his big white face intent. "I told you I was there, I admitted it. But what does that mean? It doesn't show that I killed Fragneau, if that's what you think! It doesn't show that I had any criminal intent —''

"Of course not," said the Frenchman, "but what does it show? I mean, you have been telling me what it doesn't show; now I ask you what it does show." He did not turn from the window, but he went on rapidly: "And what does the white head of this midnight prowler show?"

"Why, that it was Merton." Sir John stared at him oddly.

"You are wrong. The white head shows that it was *not* Merton."

"Then you say," Sir John cried, "that Merton did not stab Garrick?"

"Not at all. Merton did stab Garrick."

"Well, why didn't Merton come in the window, then?"

"Because he was dead," said Bencolin quietly.

There was a sudden silence like the stroke of a gong. They all looked at Bencolin as though he had gone mad and were gabbling calm nonsense.

"You will find Merton's body in the closet behind you, Sir John," continued the Frenchman. He turned full about, and he did not raise his voice when he spoke again, but it had a horrible sound of finality:

"Open the closet, Garrick. One of your victims is inside."

## V

Garrick stood looking stupidly before him, his hand moving in a tiny futile gesture. The others were perfectly motionless.

"We got his body out of the moat this morning," Bencolin said with dull flat monotony, "where you threw it. Open the door!"

A tiny space separated Garrick from collapse. He looked

down at his feet. There was a trickle of water crawling from under the door.

"I — can't," muttered Billy Garrick.

"Listen! You killed Fragneau."

"Yes. I killed Fragneau." The reply was mechanical. Sir John suddenly sat down, with his head between his hands.

"Shall I tell them how it happened?"

"No!"

"But I will, Garrick. You and Merton were in debt to Julian Arbor. You arranged this impersonation, you and Merton, so that by following your own example, Lord Brandon and others would wager five thousand pounds. Really, some sort of plot was obvious when I knew that no such book as 'Contes du Diable' exists! Julian Arbor did not know, which was why he protested against a wager in which either of you two must lose. You are exactly the same height as Merton — Sir John said so — and of his build. When he went to his room he put into effect the genius at impersonation that Sir John has mentioned. He shaved off his beard, he wore a wig which he had prepared in that table drawer, and cosmetic touches under the lights completed the effect. It was his genius! Remember: candlelight! Nobody could detect it. There might have been a slip only in the *voice,* but you had a cold, the same cold you have now, and hence it was easy. After the door had been bolted on the outside and Merton had completed his preparations, he went to the stairs and waited, flat against the wall by the lower door. On his way down he fired a blank cartridge, which was the one thing that would send the watchers flying pell-mell through the door. It was dark; Brandon had no candle, and could see nothing before or behind him except the lighted door at the top of the stairs. Those who came through the door felt only jostling bodies — Merton mingled with them and went upstairs again *as you.* You had already slipped down into the house and out of it; remember that Sir John did not see you from the time he left the tower room until after he had entered it again in search of Merton, and that he heard footsteps in the house. Nobody

was watching any door except the one behind which Merton
had locked himself. Nobody saw you go out. For the space
of the next three hours *Merton was yourself*.

"But you had a deeper motive when you connived with
Merton for this impersonation. Ostensibly it was a mere matter of winning the money bet by Lord Brandon and dividing
it; that was how you obtained Merton's assistance. Your real
motive was murder. Your real motive was in establishing an
alibi for your presence at Bell House while you motored to
Fragneau's home. Diabolical cleverness of it! You could not
conceivably be accused of the crime when all unknowingly
Merton had proved you to be at Bell House while Fragneau
was being killed. And you meant Merton to be accused of
the deed instead!" He turned to Sir John. "Think, my friend!
Who would be the only person in the world who would have
a key to that Fragneau house? Why, the man Fragneau
trusted, the man who was his heir! Did that never strike you
as logical? Fulke did not know, because Fulke was a new
servant, and I nearly overlooked the possibility because you,
Sir John, had sworn Garrick was at Bell House the entire
evening. Garrick needed money; therefore Fragneau, he reasoned, must die. The winning of a fortune, and Merton punished for the act. But because Merton had established his
alibi, Merton too must die, or otherwise the plan would be
revealed.

"What does he do? He lets himself into Fragneau's house,
kills him, and returns. Meanwhile Merton, masquerading as
Garrick, has been forced to go home with Sir John. He retires
immediately, lets himself out of the window, and goes back
to Bell House, where he has arranged to meet Garrick that
they may change identities again before daylight destroys the
complete reality of the make-up. At the edge of the moat
Garrick meets him. Ah, don't you see it? The struggle by the
water, where Merton, almost wresting the knife from Garrick
before the latter stabs him, wounds Garrick in the arm. Then
Merton's death, the sack filled with stones into which the
body is stuffed, the disappearance into the water. It is done!

For though police authorities might search Bell House for a living Merton, they would never search the moat for a dead one.

"Garrick, wounded, returns from Bell House to Sir John's residence. As he crosses the lawn Sir John sees him, but imagines very naturally that it is Merton, whom he has no grounds to suspect dead. Yellow hair in the moonlight makes an excellent 'white head'; try the effect of it for yourself. Garrick hears Sir John's warning cry; he knows that he is trapped unless . . .

"Then," cried the Frenchman, "what occurs to this master sorcerer? Why, Sir John has fancied that Merton is attacking him; why not pretend that such was the case, else otherwise Garrick could never explain the wound in his arm? It dovetailed perfectly! Garrick strips off his clothing, dons pajamas, and tears the bandage from his arm, allowing the blood to flow. Something like four minutes elapsed before Sir John came to the room. Garrick scuffles with himself in the dark, invents an ingenious story which is the only thing that will save him from discovery. Out of near catastrophe he has produced another attack that will be ascribed to Merton!"

## VI

The tensity had gone out of them all, and there remained only the ruin of tragedy. False emotional stimulant left a sickish after-feeling. Arbor and Sir John had moved away from Garrick. All the elaborate mummery that had been gone into seemed cheap and tawdry as a music hall illusion. Here was simply a felon.

Bencolin made a little gesture of weariness.

"Eh, bien!" he murmured. "You do not find it pleasant, you do not find it even clever. It upsets every beautiful tradition of a story; not only have we shattered our hero, but there is not enough of the theatrical in him to follow a story formula and kill himself. Because reality is infinitely more childish than the stories about it. Messieurs, you have lived an allegory. What do you make of it? And how do you ex-

plain the chance that made Mr. Arbor, irritated by this blind
wager of those who could not afford it, leave Bell House and
go to Fragneau's to demand recompense for his nephew's
debts?''

Rather absently Sir John put on his hat.

"Well . . ." he said without looking at Garrick. Lord
Brandon opened the door. He had not spoken. There was
nothing in his face but contempt.

Julian Arbor muttered, "You gutter rat!" somewhat incredulously. A constable had come into the darkling room
and was going toward Garrick. The latter's nerves were entirely gone; he had slid down to the floor, and Bencolin
thought he heard him moan just once. The Frenchman was
speaking softly:

"We should none of us fancy that we are devils. Merton
did, because he could take any form at will, like Satan, who
appeared at the witches' sabbath in the form of a goat (that
was why he kept calling your attention to the goat). . . .
Somewhere we people of the old school thought that there
was faith, and honor, and loyalty. We do not believe it now,
Sir John. We have seen the other side of youth. . . . It is
our last illusion, as the impersonation was Merton's. . . .
We do not think it now, Sir John. . . ."

It was almost dark in the room now. The others were all
at the door, except Madeline Landervorne. She had come up
steadily, and she was bending over the man on the floor, and
as she knelt, her eyes glittered with tears.

"Billy," she said, "I don't believe them. I don't believe
them!"

# The Little House at Croix-Rousse

### Georges Simenon

**(translated by Anthony Boucher)**

.

*This story was one of Georges Simenon's first mysteries, written in 1927 for a French magazine. To my knowledge, it is the only locked room tale among his hundreds of novels and stories.*

I HAD NEVER seen Joseph Leborgne at work before. I received something of a shock when I entered his room that day.

His blond hair, usually plastered down, was in complete disorder. The individual hairs, stiffened by brilliantine, stuck out all over his head. His face was pale and worn. Nervous twitches distorted his features.

He threw a grudging glare at me which almost drove me from the room. But since I could see that he was hunched over a diagram, my curiosity was stronger than my sensitivity. I advanced into the room and took off my hat and coat.

"A fine time you've picked!" he grumbled.

This was hardly encouraging. I stammered, "A tricky case?"

"That's putting it mildly. Look at that paper."

"It's the plan of a house? A small house?"

"The subtlety of your mind! A child of four could guess that. You know the Croix-Rousse district in Lyons?"

"I've passed through there."

"Good! This little house lies in one of the most deserted sections of the district — not a district, I might add, which is distinguished by its liveliness."

"What do these black crosses mean, in the garden and on the street?"

"Policemen."

"Good Lord! And the crosses mark where they've been killed?"

"Who said anything about dead policemen? The crosses indicate policemen who were on duty at these several spots on the night of the eighth-to-ninth. The cross that's heavier than the others is Corporal Manchard."

I dared not utter a word or move a muscle. I felt it wisest not to interrupt Leborgne, who was favoring the plan with the same furious glares which he had bestowed upon me.

"Well? Aren't you going to ask me *why* policemen were

22

stationed there — six of them, no less — on the night of the eighth-to-ninth? Or maybe you're going to pretend that you've figured it out?''

I said nothing.

"They were there because the Lyons police had received, the day before, the following letter:

*"Dr. Luigi Ceccioni will be murdered, at his home, on the night of the eighth-to-ninth instant."*

"And the doctor had been warned?" I asked at last.

"No! Since Ceccioni was an Italian exile and it seemed more than likely that the affair had political aspects, the police preferred to take their precautions without warning the party involved."

"And he was murdered anyway?"

"Patience! Dr. Ceccioni, fifty years of age, lived alone in this wretched little hovel. He kept house for himself and ate his evening meal every day in an Italian restaurant nearby. On the eighth he left home at seven o'clock, as usual, for the restaurant. And Corporal Manchard, one of the best police officers in France and a pupil, to boot, of the great Lyons criminologist Dr. Eugène Locard, searched the house from basement to attic. He proved to himself that no one was hidden there and that it was impossible to get in by any other means than the ordinary doors and windows visible from the outside. No subterranean passages nor any such hocus-pocus. Nothing out of a mystery novel . . . You understand?''

I was careful to say nothing, but Leborgne's vindictive tone seemed to accuse me of willfully interpolating hocus-pocus.

"No one in the house! Nothing to watch but two doors and three windows! A lesser man than Corporal Manchard would have been content to set up the watch with only himself and one policeman. But Manchard requisitioned five, one for each entrance, with himself to watch the watchers. At nine p.m. the shadow of the doctor appeared in the street. He re-entered his house, *absolutely alone*. His room was upstairs; a light went on in there promptly. And then the police vigil began. Not one of them dozed! Not one of them deserted his post! Not one of them lost sight of the precise point which he had been delegated to watch!

"Every fifteen minutes Manchard made the round of the group. Around three a.m. the petroleum lamp upstairs went out slowly, as though it had run out of fuel. The corporal hesitated. At last he decided to use his lock-picking gadget and go in. Upstairs, in the bedroom, seated — or rather half lying — on the edge of the bed was Dr. Luigi Ceccioni. His hands were clutched to his chest and he was dead. He was completely dressed, even to the cape which still hung over his shoulders. His hat had fallen to the floor. His underclothing and suit were saturated with blood and his hands were soaked in it. One bullet from a six-millimeter Browning had penetrated less than a centimeter above his heart."

I gazed at Joseph Leborgne with awe. I saw his lip tremble.

"No one had entered the house! No one had left!" he groaned. "I'll swear to that as though I'd stood guard myself: I know my Corporal Manchard. And don't go thinking that they found the revolver in the house. *There wasn't any revolver!* Not in sight and not hidden. Not in the fireplace, or even in the roof gutter. Not in the garden — not anywhere at all! In other words, a bullet was fired in a place where there was no one save the victim himself and where there was no firearm!

"As for the windows, they were closed and undamaged; a bullet fired from outside would have shattered the panes. Besides, a revolver doesn't carry far enough to have been fired from outside the range covered by the cordon of policemen. Look at the plan! Eat it up with your eyes! And you may restore some hope of life to poor Corporal Manchard, who has given up sleeping and looks upon himself virtually as a murderer."

I timidly ventured, "What do you know about Ceccioni?"

"That he used to be rich. That he's hardly practiced med-

icine at all, but rather devoted himself to politics — which
made it healthier for him to leave Italy.''

"Married? Bachelor?''

"Widower. One child, a son, at present studying in Argentina.''

"What did he live on in Lyons?''

"A little of everything and nothing. Indefinite subsidies
from his political colleagues. Occasional consultations, but
those chiefly *gratis* among the poor of the Italian colony.''

"Was anything stolen from the house?''

"Not a trace of any larcenous entry or of anything stolen.''

I don't know why, but at this moment I wanted to laugh.
It suddenly seemed to me that some master of mystification
had amused himself by presenting Joseph Leborgne with a
totally impossible problem, simply to give him a needed les-
son in modesty.

He noticed the broadening of my lips. Seizing the plan, he
crossed the room to plunge himself angrily into his armchair.

"Let me know when you've solved it!'' he snapped.

"I can certainly solve nothing before you,'' I said tact-
fully.

"Thanks,'' he observed.

I began to fill my pipe. I lit it, disregarding my companion's rage which was reaching the point of paroxysm.

"All I ask of you is that you sit quietly,'' he pronounced.
"And don't breathe so loudly,'' he added.

Ten minutes passed as unpleasantly as possible. Despite
myself, I called up the image of the plan, with the six black
crosses marking the policemen.

And the impossibility of this story, which had at first so
amused me, began to seem curiously disquieting.

After all, this was not a matter of psychology or of detective *flair,* but of pure geometry.

"This Manchard,'' I asked suddenly. "Has he ever served
as a subject for hypnotism?''

Joseph Leborgne did not even deign to answer that one.

"Did Ceccioni have many political enemies in Lyons?"
Leborgne shrugged.

"And it's been proved that the son *is* in Argentina?"

This time he merely took the pipe out of my mouth and tossed it on the mantelpiece.

"You have the names of all the policemen?"

He handed me a sheet of paper:

Jérôme Pallois, 28 married
Jean-Joseph Stockman, 31, single
Armand Dubois, 26, married
Hubert Trajanu, 43, divorced
Germain Garros, 32, married

I reread these lines three times. The names were in the order in which the men had been stationed around the building, starting from the left.

I was ready to accept the craziest notions. Desperately I exclaimed at last, "It *is* impossible!"

And I looked at Joseph Leborgne. A moment before his face had been pale, his eyes encircled, his lips bitter. Now, to my astonishment, I saw him smilingly head for a pot of jam.

As he passed a mirror he noticed himself and seemed scandalized by the incongruous contortions of his hair. He combed it meticulously. He adjusted the knot of his cravat.

Once again Joseph Leborgne was his habitual self. As he looked for a spoon with which to consume his horrible jam of leaves-of-God-knows-what, he favored me with a sarcastic smile.

"How simple it would always be to reach the truth if preconceived ideas did not falsify our judgment!" he sighed. "You have just said, 'It *is* impossible!' So therefore . . ."

I waited for him to contradict me. I'm used to that.

"So therefore," he went on, "it *is* impossible. Just so. And all that we needed to do from the very beginning was simply to admit the fact. There was no revolver in the house, no murderer hidden there. Very well: then there was no shot fired there."

"But then. . . ?"

"Then, very simply, Luigi Ceccioni arrived *with the bullet already in his chest.* I've every reason to believe that he fired the bullet himself. He was a doctor; he knew just where to aim — 'less than a centimeter above the heart,' you'll recall — so that the wound would not be *instantly* fatal, but would allow him to move about for a short time."

Joseph Leborgne closed his eyes.

"Imagine this poor hopeless man. He has only one son. The boy is studying abroad, but the father no longer has any money to send him. Ceccioni insures his life with the boy as beneficiary. His next step is to die — but somehow to die with no suspicion of suicide, or the insurance company will refuse to pay.

"By means of an anonymous letter he summons the police themselves as witnesses. They see him enter his house where there is no weapon and they find him dead several hours later.

"It was enough, once he was seated on his bed, to massage his chest, forcing the bullet to penetrate more deeply, at last to touch the heart . . ."

I let out an involuntary cry of pain. But Leborgne did not stir. He was no longer concerned with me.

It was not until a week later that he showed me a telegram from Corporal Manchard:

AUTOPSY REVEALS ECCHYMOSIS AROUND WOUNDS AND TRACES FINGER PRESSURE STOP DOCTOR AND SELF PUZZLED POSSIBLE CAUSE STOP REQUEST YOUR ADVICE IMMEDIATELY

"You answered?"

He looked at me reproachfully. "It requires both great courage and great imagination to massage oneself to death. Why should the poor man have done that in vain? The insurance company has a capital of four hundred million . . ."

# The Problem of the Emperor's Mushrooms

## James Yaffe

*James Yaffe was one of the first and youngest mystery writers to be discovered by* Ellery Queen's Mystery Magazine. *It's fitting that his earliest stories were ingenious impossible crime tales like this one, because* EQMM *has always been the prime showcase for such stories. (In fact, thirteen out of the twenty in this book had their first American publication there.) In an author's note to the following story, James Yaffe says, "I wrote this story over thirty-five years ago, when I was eighteen years old. It was part of a series about the same detective which I started writing when I was sixteen. I have published a dozen books since then, had a play produced on Broadway, and written a great many detective stories. The naivete of the prose, characterization, and social background in this piece of juvenilia make me blush, but I have to admit the plotting is not without ingenuity. In fact, it rather shocks me. What ever became of that clever teen-ager of thirty-five years ago? Why isn't he around to help me as I struggle with my plots today?"*

". . . In the midst of these distractions, Agrippina thought she had an opportunity to execute the black design which she had long since harbored in her breast, to kill the Emperor Claudius, her husband. Instruments of guilt were ready at her beck, but the choice of the poison was still to be considered: if quick and sudden in its operation, the treachery would be manifest; a slow corrosive would bring on a lingering death. In that case, the danger was that the conspiracy might in the interval be detected. . . . She resolved, therefore, to try a compound of new and exquisite ingredients, such as would make directly to the brain, yet not bring on immediate dissolution. . . . We are told by the writers of that day that a palatable dish of mushrooms was the vehicle of the poison. . . ."

— Tacitus, *The Annals,* Book XII

PAUL DAWN leaned back in the comfortable easy chair with a sigh of new and exquisite relaxation. After two weeks of intense work — until he had finally discovered how the ingenious Mrs. Cranfield was able to kill her artist protégé without disturbing the locked doors of his studio — the chief, and only member of the Homicide Squad's Department of Impossible Crimes was in the right mood for sloth. And in these peaceful surroundings — Professor Bottle's living room — he thought he could enjoy it. He sipped his coffee with the air of a contented pussycat lapping up its evening milk, while his gray-haired friend in the opposite chair looked on with satisfaction, and then, after a moment, broke the silence.

"How would you like to solve an impossible murder — ?" he began, but got no further.

Paul Dawn winced. "Oh, my God! Not *you,* Professor! Haven't I enough trouble with that middle-aged bloodhound, Inspector Fledge?"

Frederick A. Bottle, Professor of Ancient History, smiled

soothingly. "Believe me, Paul, I don't mean to disturb your present state of pleased paralysis. The impossible crime to which I refer can be investigated in the cozy comfort of this living room. It happens, you see, to be approximately two thousand years old."

Paul glared for a moment, his cup of coffee raised to his lips. "Don't you suppose the scent has become rather — cold by this time?" He finished the coffee in a gulp.

Bottle laughed. "Oh, rather. I don't expect you really to solve this affair, you know. Just thought you might be interested in it as a challenge. It's all about a dish of deadly mushrooms."

"Mushrooms! Professor, you're supposed to be an historian, not a chef."

"And so I am. Indeed, these mushrooms have roused the curiosity of a great many historians. They were the cause of at least one death and possibly more; they started one of the most despicable figures of human history on his career; they mark the direct beginning of the dissolution of the Roman Empire. Furthermore, they are the leading actors in what, so far as I know, is the only authentic impossible crime of historical significance."

Paul Dawn lit a cigarette and deftly produced a smoke ring. "Tell me about your Latin mushrooms," he said.

Frederick Bottle leaned forward and with a voice that managed to be dramatic without loss of restraint, began his story. "The Emperor Claudius, who died in the year 54 B.C., was a pompous, stupid man with too much power. He was the sort of ruler who, in his blundering naïveté, practically begged for assassination. . . ."

There was a knock on the living room door.

Something long and bony, wearing a thin face behind its spectacles, glowered sourly from the doorway. God, undecided whether to create a man or a woman, had somehow succeeded in creating neither. The creature in the doorway had a shape of sorts which only suggested femininity because it was draped in the conventional white uniform of a trained nurse; the creature had a voice which suggested a slamming door.

"Your wife is upset, Professor Bottle. She wants to see you right away."

Bottle sighed wearily. "I'm very busy. Tell Audrey I'll be up later this evening, Miss Poindexter."

"Your wife is not a well woman, Professor. She'll be all nerves tonight if you don't see her right now."

"Thank you, Miss Poindexter. That will do."

"I'll give her a sedative, then. But it won't calm her down." And so saying, Miss Poindexter turned abruptly and marched off.

"Audrey was always high-strung," Bottle said, getting up to shut the door. "But she's been much worse since her illness."

"I don't imagine the presence of that petrified Florence Nightingale would soothe anybody's nerves."

"Poindexter? I can't stand the woman myself, but Audrey seems to like her. And, of course, Poindexter does everything for her — dresses her, washes her, feeds her, even tastes all her food ahead of time to be sure it isn't too hot, or too salty, or something. But where was I?"

"The mushrooms of Emperor Claudius," Paul said. "An historical crossword puzzle which you have just challenged me to solve."

"Quite right." Bottle cleared his throat in his best professorial manner. "I explained to you already that Claudius was a weakling and a fool. There is an unflattering legend, dealing with his ascension to the Roman throne, that seems to substantiate this. According to his story, Claudius, who was living in the imperial palace at the time of the great purge in which the old ruler was killed, was found by the conspirators hiding behind the curtains in his mother's boudoir, and shivering for dear life. As luck would have it, the conspirators had just been worrying about whom to put on the throne now that the old emperor was dead; and here was Claudius, with the blood of emperors in his veins and not too many brains in his head; in short, the perfect puppet ruler. So they gave him the crown.

"Claudius ruled with a none too firm hand for more than a dozen years, mainly occupying himself with books of philosophy and food. When he became emperor, he had been married to a certain Messalina; she bored him, however, and he soon disposed of her — by offhandedly accusing her of adultery and having her publicly executed — and he remarried, this time with his own niece, the lovely and unscrupulous Agrippina."

"The study of Roman history," said Paul Dawn, "must play hell with a person's moral sense."

"It doesn't though," said Bottle. "Historians are really the most moral souls in the world. People like Claudius and Agrippina always seem so very far off —" And for a brief moment there was something like a very far off look in the professor's eyes. "But I must get on with the story. Agrippina was a young woman of great ingenuity and even greater ambition. As an encouragement to her ambition, she had a son by a previous marriage, a perfectly despicable youth, but she adored him and hoped to make him emperor. The boy's name — perhaps you've heard of him — was Nero.

"You can see, of course, how the idea of murdering Claudius occurred quite naturally to Agrippina. Perhaps, in fact, she had intended to murder him from the moment she agreed to marry him. This, indeed, is what Tacitus believed, when he described the incident in his *Annals;* but Tacitus is always far more entertaining than accurate. Be that as it may, the idea of killing Claudius and placing Nero on the throne began with Agrippina and soon developed into an organized conspiracy, with an incalculable number of important personages involved in it. Roman conspiracies are really quite astonishing, Paul. Practically everybody at court always seems to know about them beforehand, including the emperor's closest advisers, his friends, his family, and sometimes the emperor himself.

"The rest of the story is simple and gruesome. In the traditional Roman manner, Agrippina decided to kill Claudius by the use of poison. She hesitated at first over what poison to use: it could not work too quickly, or she might betray herself; nor could it work too slowly — the emperor might save himself. She finally hit upon a happy medium, a kind of poison which, as we know from fairly reliable sources, was supposed to begin taking effect on the victim within thirty minutes, usually less, and kill within twenty-four hours.''

Paul asked lazily, between smoke rings, "Do you know its name?''

"Impossible to tell.'' Bottle shrugged. "It might be any number of concoctions. If only Tacitus had described the death of Claudius in more detail, we might perhaps be able to diagnose the poison from the symptoms. This is one of those countless historical mysteries that can never be solved.''

"I wonder,'' Paul said softly. "But go ahead with the unpleasant details.''

"It's all very horrible. A notorious dealer in poisons, a woman named Locusta, was hired by Agrippina to prepare the mixture. Locusta, an odious creature, evidently operated a thriving business in moderately-priced murder, for Tacitus, in writing of her, informs us that she was 'reserved among the instruments of state to serve the purposes of dark ambition.' The poison was then administered to Claudius in a dish of succulent mushrooms, one of his favorite foods. He ate heartily, and soon began to feel ill. Agrippina was nervous, however, as she watched his illness, and determined to finish him off immediately, instead of waiting the full twenty-four hours for his death. She called in the emperor's most trusted physician, Xenophon — who naturally was also involved in the plot. Pretending to help Claudius unload his stomach, Xenophon swabbed his throat with a feather, a common medical practice of the day. This feather, however, was dipped in a few drops of deadly poison. Claudius, already weak from the effects of the poisoned mushrooms, went into convulsions and died violently and almost instantly.''

Paul Dawn nodded thoughtfully. "Pleasantly bloodthirsty," he said. "But I hardly understand why you mention it to me at all. There's no impossible crime involved in this.''

"I'm not finished yet," said Bottle with an enigmatic smile. "I haven't told you about Halotus, the emperor's poison-taster.''

"You interest me. Go on.''

"The institution of the poison-taster was, as you may know, a common one among the Roman emperors and lords. Nearly every important Roman of the time lived constantly in fear of his life, and came to expect death from almost any source. Consequently, he kept by him at all times a poison-taster whose job it was to partake of small portions of all his food and drink before he did so himself. If there was any poison in the food, the taster would indicate its presence.''

"And how would the taster indicate its presence?''

"By dying! The important citizen would then order a new meal.''

"And, I trust, a new poison-taster.''

"Correct. Claudius was perhaps the most nervous, most frightened, most suspicious of all the emperors. He kept his poison-taster near him every minute of the day. This taster was a man named Halotus, mentioned briefly by Tacitus, in *The Annals*. Other sources tell us a good deal about Claudius's dread of poison. His routine was something like this: before every meal, he would watch carefully as Halotus tasted all his food; then he always waited not a few minutes but exactly one hour before tasting any of it himself, with Halotus by his side every moment; finally, if Halotus felt no ill effects at the end of the hour, Claudius would eat freely.''

"He didn't," Paul observed, "enjoy many hot meals that way.''

"He didn't care. He was worried more about remaining

alive to enjoy the cold ones. And that brings us directly to
the impossible crime. When the poisoned mushrooms were
served to Claudius, Halotus, his poison-taster, must have
eaten a portion of them first. At the end of thirty minutes, he
should have felt and looked quite ill; at the end of an hour,
he should have looked even more ill. Why, then, did Claudius go ahead and eat those mushrooms, when quite obviously they had just poisoned his human guinea-pig? Or, to
put it the other way around, *how was it possible that the
same mushrooms which poisoned Claudius should have left
his poison-taster completely unharmed?* The answer, of
course, is that it's impossible, the first impossible murder in
history. Well, Paul, two thousand years have passed since
then, and it's about time somebody solved it!''

Blissfully unconscious of poisoned Roman emperors and
puzzled New York detectives, an aesthetic smoke ring floated
dreamily towards the clouds. No shutters slammed, no hinges
squeaked in Professor Frederick Bottle's living room, and no
sinister storms raged wildly outside; and yet, this seemed to
Paul Dawn's mind a perfect atmosphere for slamming shutters, squeaking hinges, and raging storms. He had developed
a habit lately, which irritated him deeply, of transforming
every setting that he encountered in real life into the kind of
unreal, fairy-tale setting he might encounter in a detective
story. And curiously, the more he concentrated on the emperor's magical mushrooms, the more he felt like a character
of fiction. It was a damned nuisance.

"Murder," he said slowly, "is a cozy affair really, inti-
mate, personal, and eminently social. Like the theatre or political democracy, murder can only flourish in a highly organized and closed society. That's why I feel uncomfortable
trying to solve a murder at such a great distance."

"You'd like to be able to question the suspects, is that it?
Study their reactions? Probe their characters?"

"Don't be absurd. I never study the reactions of my suspects; it's a fruitless and frustrating occupation. Suspects can
have all sorts of reactions; they can turn reactions on and off

like water in a faucet; they can look innocent, guilty, frightened, and calm with amazing versatility. No, I prefer contemporary murders, Professor, because having solved a case, I am always sure that I will be able to check my solution with the truth and find out whether or not I was right."

Bottle nodded his head knowingly. "You're vain, that's what! You don't like the idea of a case where there can be no glory and no gloating after it's all over. You're just annoyed because you won't be able to show the murderer how clever you've been!"

"That may be," Paul admitted. "On the other hand, perhaps I'll get the chance after all. But I want you to tell me more about the people involved in this ancient mystery. It is essential that I become more intimately acquainted with Claudius, Agrippina, Xenophon, and Halotus."

"Very well, then: the Emperor Claudius." Bottle waited for a moment, then began thoughtfully. "More than anything else, I think that Claudius resembled a nervous old woman. A hypochondriac, a coward, and a fop, he pampered himself excessively and spent more time on the comfort of his body than the care of his country. He was vain and stupid, but he also possessed to a great extent the single positive quality that seems to have characterized every one of the so-called 'bad emperors.' He was cruel. The story of his disposal of Messalina, his first wife, is not a pretty one; Tacitus makes it quite clear that Claudius, in spite of his personal squeamishness, had thrown his share of enemies to the lions."

"Hypochondriac, Professor? How can you be sure of that?"

"I can't, of course. But it seems logical, doesn't it? Claudius was supposed to be a man of robust, sturdy proportions, stocky and well-fed and glowing with health; and yet, we constantly read about his weak nerves and his migraine headaches and his sudden illnesses, most of them brought on by the most trivial causes. What more probable than for him to be a hypochondriac? But let me tell you about his wife, for she was a much more forceful and admirable individual."

"Indeed? You admire the murderous Agrippina?"

"Yes, I do, in a way. She strikes me with a firm, power-ful, masculine effect, a woman of great will and strength, of iron character and subtle intellect, despicable as she may have been according to all moral standards."

Paul Dawn made a face. "Personally, she revolts me. So do all deliberate killers."

"To be sure. Don't forget, though, that the Roman citizen was a great deal more tolerant of deliberate murder than we are today. He had to be, or else he would have gone about condemning ninety per cent of his friends and relations. In any event, the ingenuity of Agrippina's murder is enough to command the highest respect."

"Tell me more about Agrippina."

"What more can I tell? Assuming her to be a murderess, it is difficult to understand the dominant factor in her char-acter: what was it that led her to kill her husband? Lust for power? A simple desire to rule the country through her son? Not very likely, for after all she ruled the country anyway, through Claudius. Was she prompted, then, by an extraordi-nary affection of mother for offspring? According to an old legend, Agrippina was warned by an oracle, before Nero's birth, that her son would grow up to become emperor and to kill his mother; and she was supposed to have answered that she didn't care what happened to her so long as her son be-came emperor. Then, of course, there's the possibility, which I rather fancy myself, that she killed Claudius because she couldn't stand living with him any longer. What do you think, Paul?"

"I think absolutely nothing. I feel, however, altogether too much."

"Not very lucid, are you? I'll tell you about Halotus, the poison-taster, and Xenophon, the physician."

"Unnecessary," said Paul Dawn, "I already know why Claudius died while his poison-taster remained alive. Your two-thousand-year-old mystery is solved. As a matter of fact," he continued, "it's more than solved."

Professor Bottle leaned forward eagerly. "How do you mean that?"

"There are two possible solutions," said Paul. "Both of them are equally plausible. Both of them are equally dramatic. Perhaps both of them are equally correct.

"The first solution hinges on the nature of the poison that was placed in the mushrooms; or rather, I should say, on the nature of the poison that was *not* placed in the mushrooms. But I ought to start at the beginning with the two all-important facts. You said that Claudius was a suspicious and frightened hypochondriac. You also made it clear that Claudius fell ill because of the mushrooms, but that he was actually killed, not by the poisoned mushrooms, but by the poisoned feather. Suppose you wanted to kill a suspicious hypochondriac with a poisoned feather, Professor: in what way could you convince your suspicious and frightened victim that he might safely allow you to stick that feather down his throat?"

"Impossible," said Bottle. "If he was very suspicious, he would never let me stick anything down his throat."

"Oh, yes, he would, Professor, if you took advantage of his hypochondria — if he believed, as Claudius was tricked into believing, *that he had already been poisoned and that your feather was the only means of saving his life!*

"Of course, you now understand what happened. The mushrooms were served to Claudius *without any poison in them at all.* Halotus tasted them in Claudius's presence; an hour passed, after which, since nothing had happened to his poison-taster, Claudius felt no qualms about eating the mushrooms himself. But as soon as he finished the last mushroom, Halotus must have suddenly begun to groan and writhe about and double up as if he had been poisoned. It was all an elaborate act, of course. Halotus had been bribed by Agrippina to pretend at the right moment that he was poisoned. The purpose? To make Claudius, who had just finished his mushrooms, believe that he too was poisoned! This was no difficult feat, since Claudius was a hypochondriac, and could easily be convinced of his own illness. And, once convinced

that he too was dying, Claudius could also be convinced that
the only cure would be for Xenophon to swab his throat with
a feather. The impossible murder was thus made possible,
Professor, by the very precautions with which Claudius
hoped to prevent it.''

Curiously enough, Professor Bottle hardly seemed elated.
''That's all?'' he asked. ''That's how it was done?''

''That's one solution,'' said Paul Dawn. ''But there's a
second one. Are you sure you'd care to hear it?''

''Definitely. There may be great historical value in this.''

''I doubt it.'' Paul sighed and shook his head almost sadly.
''I am a plumber,'' he said, ''and I want to commit a murder;
I will probably kill my man with a water pipe. I am a car-
penter, and I want to commit a murder; I will most likely
knock out my victim's brains with a hammer. I am a detec-
tive-story writer, and I want to commit a murder; I will undoubtedly model it after one of my own plots. I am Paul
Dawn, and I want to commit a murder; I will assuredly de-
vise an impossible crime. Suppose, then, that I am a professor of ancient history, and I want to commit a murder. Will
I not go back to ancient history for my inspiration?''

Professor Bottle tightened his grip on the arms of his chair.
He said nothing, but he seemed to be trembling.

Paul Dawn went on in a calm, relentless voice. ''The murder of Claudius is interesting, no doubt, but after all, there is
so little information to be had on the subject, so little really
reliable evidence, that to try and solve it at all seems a foolish waste of time. Why, then, did you go out of your way to
ask my help in solving it? And why did you falsify and dec-
orate the facts? Why such careful and detailed analysis of the
characters of Claudius and Agrippina when there is nothing
known for certain about the characters of Claudius and
Agrippina?''

Paul leaned forward and his voice grew louder. ''A strange
thing about Claudius and Agrippina — at least, about the two
people that I met tonight under those names. What was Claudius? A nervous, suspicious, vain, and irritating hypochon-

driac — just like the woman in bed upstairs! And what was
Agrippina? A brilliant, subtle, forceful, even heroic figure,
wronged and persecuted, a justified killer — just like the
man who sits across from me at this moment! There is no
difference, no difference in the world — except that the
sexes are switched around; and even then, there is no difference, for Claudius 'resembled a nervous old woman,' and
Agrippina produced a 'firm, masculine effect.' And where, it
may be asked, is Halotus, the poison-taster? Where else but
upstairs, stern and unapproachable in a white nurse's uniform, tasting all of 'Claudius's' food ahead of time, 'to be
sure it isn't too hot, or too salty, or something'?

"My God!" Paul cried, rising to his feet with sudden fury.
"Did you invite me here tonight *to plan your wife's murder?*"

Bottle said nothing at first, but finally, "I'm sorry," in a
low voice, "very sorry."

"And how useless it all was! You thought the two situa-
tions were parallel. You thought the solution to Agrippina's
crime would give you the key to your own. But how helpless
you are! They're not really the same at all. The old murder,
the murder of Claudius, depended entirely on the role of
Xenophon and his poisoned feather. But this is the twentieth
century A.D.! How did you expect to use a poisoned
feather?"

"I don't know what I expected. It was just an idea. It was
stupid of me."

Suddenly Paul Dawn fell back in his chair and began to
laugh. He laughed loud and long, and could hardly get out
his words. "What did I tell you? What did I say about the
historian's moral sense? Pour me a drink, Professor, something strong, and let's forget the whole thing!"

Bottle was still bewildered, still stunned. "I don't understand. Why are you so happy?"

"Am I happy? I was thinking how lucky I am to be a
member of the Homicide Squad — a mild and moral profession, where we only meet the nicest people. . . ."

# From Another World

## Clayton Rawson

*This story by Clayton Rawson, first published in 1948, has become an anthology favorite — though this is its first appearance in an MWA volume. The story was a direct result of the friendly rivalry that existed between Rawson and John Dickson Carr. Rawson challenged Carr to solve a murder in a truly "sealed" room — a room in which even the edges of the doors and windows had been sealed with paper tape from the inside. Carr was first with his solution and it appeared in the 1944 Carter Dickson novel* He Wouldn't Kill Patience. *Four years later Rawson's solution appeared in this story. The two solutions were quite different and equally good. More than that, they gave a clue to the ways in which two different writers approached the same problem.*

IT WAS undoubtedly one of the world's strangest rooms. The old-fashioned rolltop desk, the battered typewriter, and the steel filing cabinet indicated that it was an office. There was even a calendar memo pad, a pen and pencil set, and an overflowing ashtray on the desk, but any resemblance to any other office stopped right there.

The desk top also held a pair of handcuffs, half a dozen billiard balls, a shiny nickel-plated revolver, one celluloid egg, several decks of playing cards, a bright green silk handkerchief, and a stack of unopened mail. In one corner of the room stood a large, galvanized-iron milk can with a strait jacket lying on its top. A feathered devil mask from the upper Congo leered down from the wall and the entire opposite wall was papered with a Ringling Bros. and Barnum & Bailey twenty-four sheet poster.

A loose-jointed dummy figure of a small boy with popeyes and violently red hair lay on the filing cabinet together with a skull and a fishbowl filled with paper flowers. And in the cabinet's bottom drawer, which was partly open and lined with paper, there was one half-eaten carrot and a twinkly-nosed, live white rabbit.

A pile of magazines, topped by a French journal, *l'Illusioniste,* was stacked precariously on a chair, and a large bookcase tried vainly to hold an even larger flood of books that overflowed and formed dusty stalagmites growing up from the floor—books whose authors would have been startled at the company they kept. Shaw's *Saint Joan* was sandwiched between Rowan's *Story of the Secret Service* and the *Memoirs of Robert Houdin.* Arthur Machen, Dr. Hans Gross, William Blake, Sir James Jeans, Rebecca West, Robert Louis Stevenson, and Ernest Hemingway were bounded on either side by Devol's *Forty Years a Gambler on the Mississippi* and Reginald Scot's *Discoverie of Witchcraft.*

The merchandise in the shop beyond the office had a similar surrealist quality, but the inscription on the glass of the outer door, although equally strange, did manage to supply an explanation. It read: *Miracles For Sale* — THE MAGIC SHOP, *A. Merlini, Prop.*

And that gentleman, naturally, was just as unusual as his place of business. For one thing, he hadn't put a foot in it, to my knowledge, in at least a week. When he finally did reappear, I found him at the desk sleepily and somewhat glumly eying the unopened mail.

He greeted me as though he hadn't seen another human being in at least a month, and the swivel chair creaked as he settled back in it, put his long legs up on the desk, and yawned. Then he indicated the card bearing his business slogan — NOTHING IS IMPOSSIBLE — which was tacked on the wall.

"I may have to take that sign down," he said lazily. "I've just met a theatrical producer, a scene designer, and a playwright all of whom are quite impossible. They came in here a week before opening night and asked me to supply several small items mentioned in the script. In one scene a character said 'Begone!' and the stage directions read: 'The genie and his six dancing girl slaves vanish instantly.' Later an elephant, complete with howdah and princess, disappeared the same way. I had to figure out how to manage all that and cook up a few assorted miracles for the big scene in heaven, too. Then I spent thirty-six hours in bed. And I'm still half asleep." He grinned wryly and added, "Ross, if you want anything that is not a stock item, you can whistle for it."

"I don't want a miracle," I said. "Just an interview. What do you know about ESP and PK?"

"Too much," he said. "You're doing another magazine article?"

"Yes. And I've spent the last week with a queer assortment of characters, too — half a dozen psychologists, some professional gamblers, a nuclear physicist, the secretary of the Psychical Research Society, and a neurologist. I've got an appointment in half an hour with a millionaire, and after that I want to hear what you think of it."

"You interviewed Dr. Rhine at Duke University, of course?"

I nodded. "Sure. He started it all. He says he's proved conclusively that there really are such things as telepathy, mind reading, clairvoyance, X-ray vision, and probably crystal gazing as well. He wraps it all up in one package and calls it ESP — meaning extrasensory perception."

"That," Merlini said, "is not the half of it. His psychokinesis, or PK for short, is positively miraculous — and frightening." The magician pulled several issues of the *Journal of Parapsychology* from the stack of magazines and upset the whole pile. "If the conclusions Rhine has published here are correct — if there really is a tangible mental force that can not only reach out and influence the movements of dice but exert its mysterious control over other physical objects as well — then he has completely upset the apple cart of modern psychology and punctured a whole library of general scientific theory as well."

"He's already upset me," I said. "I tried to use PK in a crap game Saturday night. I lost sixty-eight bucks."

My skepticism didn't disturb Merlini. He went right on, gloomier than ever. "If Rhine is right, his ESP and PK have reopened the Pandora's box in which science thought it had forever sealed voodoo and witchcraft and enough other practices of primitive magic to make your hair stand on end. And *you're* growling about losing a few dollars —"

Behind me a hearty, familiar voice said, "I haven't got anything to worry about except a homicidal maniac who has killed three people in the last two days and left absolutely no clues. But can I come in?"

Inspector Homer Gavigan of the New York City Police Department stood in the doorway, his blue eyes twinkling frostily.

Merlini, liking the Cassandra role he was playing, said, "Sure. I've been waiting for you. But don't think that PK won't give you a splitting headache, too. All a murderer would have to do to commit the perfect crime — and a

locked room one at that — would be to exert his psychoki-
netic mental force from a distance against the gun trigger.''
He pointed at the revolver on the desk. ''Like this —''

Gavigan and I both saw the trigger, with no finger on it,
move.

*Bang!*

The gun's report was like a thunderclap in the small room.
I knew well enough that it was only a stage prop and the
cartridge a blank, but I jumped a foot. So did Gavigan.

''Look, dammit!'' the inspector exploded, ''how did
you —''

The Great Merlini grinned. He was fully awake now and
enjoying himself hugely. ''No,'' he said, ''that wasn't PK,
luckily. Just ordinary run-of-the-mill conjuring. The Rising
Cards and the Talking Skull are both sometimes operated the
same way. You can have the secret at the usual catalogue
price of —''

Like most policemen Gavigan had a healthy respect for
firearms and he was still jumpy. ''I don't want to buy either
of them,'' he growled. ''Do we have a date for dinner — or
don't we? I'm starved.''

''We do,'' Merlini said, pulling his long, lean self up out
of the chair and reaching for his coat. ''Can you join us,
Ross?''

I shook my head. ''Not this time. I've got a date just now
with Andrew Drake.''

In the elevator Merlini gave me an odd look and asked,
''Andrew Drake? What has he got to do with ESP and PK?''

''What doesn't he have something to do with?'' I replied.
''Six months ago it was the Drake Plan to Outlaw War; he
tried to take over the U.N. single-handed. Two months ago
he announced he was setting up a $15-million research foun-
dation to find a cancer cure in six months. 'Polish it off like
we did the atom bomb,' he says. 'Put in enough money, and
you can accomplish anything.' Now he's head over heels in
ESP with some Yoga mixed in. 'Unleash the power of the
human mind and solve all our problems.' Just like that.''

"So that's what he's up to," Merlini said as we came out on to Forty-second Street, a block from Times Square, to face a bitterly cold January wind. "I wondered."

Then, as he followed Gavigan into the official car that waited and left me shivering on the curb, he threw a last cryptic sentence over his shoulder.

"When Drake mentions Rosa Rhys," he said, "you might warn him that he's heading for trouble."

Merlini didn't know how right he was. If any of us had had any clairvoyant ability at all, I wouldn't have taken a cab up to Drake's; all three of us would have gone — in Gavigan's car and with the siren going full blast.

As it was, I stepped out all alone in front of the big Ninety-eighth Street house just off Riverside Drive. It was a sixty-year-old mansion built in the tortured style that had been the height of architectural fashion in the 1880's but was now a smoke-blackened monstrosity as coldly depressing as the weather.

I nearly froze both ears just getting across the pavement and up the steps, where I found a doctor with his finger glued — or frozen perhaps — to the bell push. A doctor? No, it wasn't ESP; a copy of the *AMA Journal* stuck out of his overcoat pocket, and his left hand carried the customary small black case. But he didn't have the medical man's usual clinical detachment. This doctor was jumpy as hell.

When I asked, "Anything wrong?" his head jerked around, and his pale blue eyes gave me a startled look. He was a thin, well-dressed man in his early forties.

"Yes," he said crisply. "I'm afraid so." He jabbed a long forefinger at the bell again just as the door opened.

At first I didn't recognize the girl who looked out at us When I had seen her by daylight earlier in the week, I had tagged her as in the brainy-but-a-bit-plain category, a judgment I revised somewhat now, considering what the Charles hair-do and Hattie Carnegie dress did for her.

"Oh, hello, doctor," she said. "Come in."

The doctor began talking even before he crossed the threshold. "Your father, Elinor — is he still in the study?"

"Yes, I think so. But what —"

She stopped because he was already gone, running down the hall toward a door at its end. He rattled the doorknob, then rapped loudly.

"Mr. Drake! Let me in!"

The girl looked puzzled, then frightened. Her dark eyes met mine for an instant, and then her high heels clicked on the polished floor as she too ran down the hall. I didn't wait to be invited. I followed.

The doctor's knuckles rapped again on the door. "Miss Rhys!" he called. "It's Dr. Garrett. Unlock the door!"

There was no answer.

Garrett tried the doorknob once more, then threw his shoulder against the door. It didn't move.

"Elinor, do you have a key? We must get in there — quickly!"

She said, "No. Father has the only keys. Why don't they answer? What's wrong?"

"I don't know," Garrett said. "Your father phoned me just now. He was in pain. He said, *'Hurry! I need you. I'm'* " — the doctor hesitated, watching the girl; then he finished " *'— dying.'* After that — no answer." Garrett turned to me. "You've got more weight than I have. Think you can break this door in?"

I looked at it. The door seemed solid enough, but it was an old house and the wood around the screws that held the lock might give. "I don't know," I said. "I'll try."

Elinor Drake moved to one side and the doctor stepped behind me. I threw myself against the door twice and the second time felt it move a bit. Then I hit it hard. Just as the door gave way I heard the tearing sound of paper.

But before I could discover what caused that, my attention was held by more urgent matters. I found myself staring at a green-shaded desk lamp, the room's only source of light, at the overturned phone on the desk top, and at the sprawled

shape that lay on the floor in front of the desk. A coppery
highlight glinted on a letter opener near the man's feet. Its
blade was discolored with a dark wet stain.

Dr. Garrett said, "Elinor, you stay out," as he moved past
me to the body and bent over it. One of his hands lifted
Andrew Drake's right eyelid, the other felt his wrist.

I have never heard a ghost speak but the sound that came
then was exactly what I would expect — a low, quivering
moan shot with pain. I jerked around and saw a glimmer of
white move in the darkness on my left.

Behind me, Elinor's whisper, a tense thread of sound,
said, "Lights," as she clicked the switch by the door. The
glow from the ceiling fixture overhead banished both the
darkness and the specter — but what remained was almost as
unlikely. A chair lay overturned on the carpet, next to a small
table that stood in the center of the room. In a second chair,
slumped forward with her head resting on the tabletop, was
the body of a woman.

She was young, dark-haired, rather good-looking, and had
an excellent figure. This latter fact was instantly apparent because — and I had to look twice before I could believe what
I saw — she wore a brief, skin-tight, one-piece bathing suit.
Nothing else.

Elinor's eyes were still on the sprawled shape on the foor.
"Father. He's — dead?"

Garrett nodded slowly and stood up.

I heard the quick intake of her breath but she made no
other sound. Then Garrett strode quickly across to the woman
at the table.

"Unconscious," he said after a moment. "Apparently a
blow on the head — but she's beginning to come out of it."
He looked again at the knife on the floor. "We'll have to
call the police."

I hardly heard him. I was wondering why the room was so
bare. The hall outside and the living room that opened off it
were furnished with the stiff, formal ostentation of the overly
rich. But Drake's study, by contrast, was as sparsely fur-

nished as a cell in a Trappist monastery. Except for the desk, the small table, the two chairs, and a three-leaf folding screen that stood in one corner, it contained no other furniture. There were no pictures on the wlls, no papers, and although there were shelves for them, no books. There wasn't even a blotter or pen on the desk top. Nothing but the phone, desk lamp and, strangely enough, a roll of gummed paper tape.

But I only glanced at these things briefly. It was the large casement window in the wall behind the desk that held my attention — a dark rectangle beyond which, like a scattered handful of bright jewels, were the lights of New Jersey and, above them, frosty pinpoints of stars shining coldly in a black sky.

The odd thing was that the window's center line, where its two halves joined, was criss-crossed by two-foot strips of brown paper tape pasted to the glass. The window was, quite literally, sealed shut. It was then that I remembered the sound of tearing paper as the lock had given way and the door had come open.

I turned. Elinor still stood there — motionless. And on the inside of the door and on the jamb were more of the paper strips. Four were torn in half, two others had been pulled loose from the wall and hung curled from the door's edge.

At that moment a brisk, energetic voice came from the hall. "How come you leave the front door standing wide open on the coldest day in —"

Elinor turned to face a broad-shouldered young man with wavy hair, hand-painted tie, and a completely self-assured manner. She said, "Paul!" then took one stumbling step and was in his arms.

He blinked at her. "Hey! What's wrong?" Then he saw what lay on the floor by the desk. His self-confidence sagged.

Dr. Garrett moved to the door. "Kendrick," he said, "take Elinor out of here. I'll —"

"No!" It was Elinor's voice. She straightened up, turned suddenly and started into the room.

But Paul caught her. "Where are you going?"

She tried to pull away from him. "I'm going to phone the police." Her eyes followed the trail of bloodstains that led from the body across the beige carpet to the overturned chair and the woman at the table. "She — killed him."

That was when I started for the phone myself. But I hadn't taken more than two steps when the woman in the bathing suit let out a hair-raising shriek.

She was gripping the table with both hands, her eyes fixed on Drake's body with the rigid unblinking stare of a figure carved from stone. Then, suddenly, her body trembled all over, and she opened her mouth again — But Garrett got there first.

He slapped her on the side of the face — hard.

It stopped the scream, but the horror still filled her round dark eyes and she still stared at the body as though it were some demon straight from hell.

"Hysteria," Garrett said. Then seeing me start again toward the phone, "Get an ambulance, too." And when he spoke to Paul Kendrick this time, it was an order. "And get Elinor out of here — quickly!"

Elinor Drake was looking at the girl in the bathing suit with wide, puzzled eyes. "She — she killed him. Why?"

Paul nodded. He turned Elinor around gently but swiftly and led her out.

The cops usually find too many fingerprints on a phone, none of them any good because they are superimposed on each other. But I handled the receiver carefully just the same, picking it up by one end. When headquarters answered, I gave the operator the facts fast, then asked him to locate Inspector Gavigan and have him call me back. I gave Drake's number.

As I talked I watched Dr. Garrett open his black case and take out a hypodermic syringe. He started to apply it to the woman's arm just as I hung up.

"What's that, doc?" I asked.

"Sedative. Otherwise she'll be screaming again in a minute."

The girl didn't seem to feel the needle as it went in.

Then, noticing two bright spots of color on the table, I went across to examine them closely and felt more than ever as though I had stepped straight into a surrealist painting. I was looking at two rounded conical shapes each about two inches in length. Both were striped like candy canes, one in maroon against a white background, the other in thinner brilliant red stripes against an opalescent amber.

"Did Drake," I asked, "collect seashells, too?"

"No." Garrett scowled in a worried way at the shells. "But I once did. These are mollusks, but not from the sea. *Cochlostyla,* a tree snail. Habitat: the Philippines." He turned his scowl from the shells to me. "By the way, just who are you?"

"The name is Ross Harte." I added that I had had an appointment to interview Drake for a magazine article and then asked, "Why is this room sealed as it is? Why is this girl dressed only in —"

Apparently, like many medical men, Garrett took a dim view of reporters. "I'll make my statement," he said a bit stiffly, "to the police."

They arrived a moment later. Two uniformed prowl-car cops first, then the precinct boys and after that, at intervals, the homicide squad, an ambulance intern, a fingerprint man and photographer, the medical examiner, an assistant D.A. and later, because a millionaire rates more attention than the victim of a Harlem stabbing, the D.A. himself, and an assistant chief inspector even looked in for a few minutes.

Of the earlier arrivals the only familiar face was that of the homicide squad's Lieutenant Doran — a hard-boiled, coldly efficient, no-nonsense cop who had so little use for reporters that I suspected he had once been bitten by one.

At Dr. Garrett's suggestion, which the intern seconded, the girl in the bathing suit was taken, under guard, to the nearest hospital. Then Garrett and I were put on ice, also under guard, in the living room. Another detective ushered Paul Kendrick into the room a moment later.

He scowled at Dr. Garrett. "We all thought Rosa Rhys
was bad medicine. But I never expected anything like this.
Why would *she* want to kill him? It doesn't make sense."

"Self-defense?" I suggested. "Could he have made a pass
at her and —"

Kendrick shook his head emphatically. "Not that gal. She
was making a fast play for the old man — and his money. A
pass would have been just what she wanted." He turned to
Garrett. "What were they doing in there — more ESP experiments?"

The doctor laid his overcoat neatly over the back of an
ornate Spanish chair. His voice sounded tired and defeated.
"No. They had gone beyond that. I told him that she was a
fraud, but you know how Drake was — always so absolutely
confident that he couldn't be wrong about anything. He said
he'd put her through a test that would convince all of us."

"Of what?" I asked. "What was it she claimed she could
do?"

The detective at the door moved forward. "My orders,"
he said, "are that you're not to talk about what happened
until after the lieutenant has taken your statements. Make it
easy for me, will you?"

That made it difficult for us. Any other conversational subject just then seemed pointless. We sat there silent and uncomfortable. But somehow the nervous tension that had been
in our voices was still there — a foreboding, ghostly presence waiting with us for what was to happen next.

A half hour later, although it seemed many times that long,
Garrett was taken out for questioning, then Kendrick. And
later I got the nod. I saw Elinor Drake, a small, lonely figure
in the big hall, moving slowly up the wide stairs. Doran and
the police stenographer who waited for me in the stately dining room with its heavy crystal chandelier looked out of
place. But the lieutenant didn't feel ill at ease; his questions
were as coldly efficient as a surgeon's knife.

I tried to insert a query of my own now and then, but soon

gave that up. Doran ignored all such attempts as completely as if they didn't exist. Then, just as he dismissed me, the phone rang. Doran answered, listened, scowled and then held the receiver out to me. "For you," he said.

I heard Merlini's voice. "My ESP isn't working so well today, Ross. Drake is dead. I get that much. But just what happened up there, anyway?"

"ESP my eye," I told him. "If you were a mind reader you'd have been up here long ago. It's a sealed room — in spades. The sealed room to end all sealed rooms."

I saw Doran start forward as if to object. "Merlini," I said quickly, "is Inspector Gavigan still with you?" I lifted the receiver from my ear and let Doran hear the "Yes" that came back.

Merlini's voice went on. "Did you say sealed room? The flash from headquarters didn't mention that. They said an arrest had already been made. It sounded like a routine case."

"Headquarters," I replied, "has no imagination. Or else Doran has been keeping things from them. It isn't even a routine sealed room. Listen. A woman comes to Drake's house on the coldest January day since 1812 dressed only in a bathing suit. She goes with him into his study. They seal the window and door on the inside with gummed paper tape. Then she stabs him with a paper knife. Before he dies, he knocks her out, then manages to get to the phone and send out an SOS.

"She's obviously crazy; she has to be to commit murder under those circumstances. But Drake wasn't crazy. A bit eccentric maybe, but not nuts. So why would he lock himself in so carefully with a homicidal maniac? If headquarters thinks that's routine I'll —" Then I interrupted myself. There was too much silence on the other end of the wire. "Merlini! Are you still there?"

"Yes," his voice said slowly, "I'm still here. Headquarters was much too brief. They didn't tell us her name. But I know it now."

Then, abruptly, I felt as if I had stepped off into some
fourth-dimensional hole in space and had dropped on to some
other nightmare planet.

Merlini's voice, completely serious, was saying, "Ross,
did the police find a silver denarius from the time of the Cae-
sars in that room? Or a freshly picked rose, a string of
Buddhist prayer beads, perhaps a bit of damp seaweed?"

I didn't say anything. I couldn't.

After a moment, Merlini added, "So — they did. What
was it?"

"Shells," I said dazedly, still quite unconvinced that any
conversation could sound like this. "Philippine tree snail
shells. Why, in the name of —"

Merlini cut in hastily. "Tell Doran that Gavigan and I will
be there in ten minutes. Sit tight and keep your eyes open."

"Merlini!" I objected frantically; "if you hang up without —"

"The shells explain the bathing suit, Ross, and make it
clear why the room was sealed. But they also introduce an
element that Gavigan and Doran and the D.A. and the commissioner are not going to like at all. I don't like it myself.
It's even more frightening as a murder method than PK."

He hesitated a moment, then let me have both barrels.

"Those shells suggest that Drake's death might have been
caused by even stranger forces — evil and evanescent
ones — from another world!"

My acquaintance with a police inspector cut no ice with
Doran; he ordered me right back into the living room.

I heard a siren announce the arrival of Gavigan's car
shortly after, but it was a long hour later before Doran came
in and said, "The inspector wants to see all of you — in the
study."

As I moved with the others out into the hall I saw Merlini
waiting for me.

"It's about time," I growled at him. "Another ten minutes
and you'd have found me DOA, too — from suspense."

"Sorry you had to cool your heels," he said, "but Gavigan is being difficult. As predicted, he doesn't like the earful Doran has been giving him. Neither do I." The dryly ironic good humor that was almost always in his voice was absent. He was unusually sober.

"Don't build it up," I said. "I've had all the mystery I can stand. Just give me answers. First, why did you tell me to warn Drake about Rosa Rhys?"

I didn't expect murder, if that's what you're thinking," he replied. "Drake was elaborating on some of Rhine's original experiments aimed at discovering whether ESP operates more efficiently when the subject is in a trance state. Rosa is a medium."

"Oh, so that's it. She and Drake were holding a séance?"

Merlini nodded. "Yes. The Psychical Research Society is extremely interested in ESP and PK. It's given them a new lease on life. And I knew they had recommended Rosa, whom they had previously investigated, to Drake."

"And what about the Roman coins, roses, Buddhist prayer beads — and snail shells? Why the bathing suit and how does that explain why the room was sealed?"

But Doran, holding the study door open, interrupted before he could reply.

"Hurry it up!" he ordered.

Going into that room now was like walking on to a brightly lighted stage. A powerful electric bulb of almost floodlight brilliance had been inserted in the ceiling fixture and its harsh white glare made the room more barren and cell-like than ever. Even Inspector Gavigan seemed to have taken on a menacing air. Perhaps it was the black mask of shadow that his hat brim threw down across the upper part of his face; or it may have been the carefully intent way he watched us as we came in.

Doran did the introductions. "Miss Drake, Miss Potter, Paul Kendrick, Dr. Walter Garrett."

I looked at the middle-aged woman whose gayly frilled, altogether feminine hat contrasted oddly with her angular figure, her prim determined mouth, and the chilly glance of complete disapproval with which she regarded Gavigan.

"How," I whispered to Merlini, "did Isabelle Potter, the secretary of the Psychical Research Society, get here?"

"She came with Rosa," he answered. "The police found her upstairs reading a copy of Tyrrell's *Study of Apparitions*." Merlini smiled faintly. "She and Doran don't get along."

"They wouldn't," I said. "They talk different languages. When I interviewed her, I got a travelogue on the other world — complete with lantern slides."

Inspector Gavigan wasted no time. "Miss Drake," he began, "I understand the medical foundation for cancer research your father thought of endowing was originally your idea."

The girl glanced once at the stains on the carpet, then kept her dark eyes steadily on Gavigan. "Yes," she said slowly, "it was."

"Are you interested in psychical research?"

Elinor frowned. "No."

"Did you object when your father began holding séances with Miss Rhys?"

She shook her head. "That would only have made him more determined."

Gavigan turned to Kendrick. "Did you?"

"Me?" Paul lifted his brows. "I didn't know him well enough for that. Don't think he liked me much, anyway. But why a man like Drake would waste his time —"

"And you, doctor?"

"Did I object?" Garrett seemed surprised. "Naturally. No one but a neurotic middle-aged woman would take a séance seriously."

Miss Potter resented that one. "Dr. Garrett," she said icily, "Sir Oliver Lodge was not a neurotic woman, nor Sir William Crookes, nor Professor Zoëllner, nor —"

"But they were all senile," Garrett replied just as icily. "And as for ESP, no neurologist of any standing admits any such possibility. They leave such things to you and your society, Miss Potter — and to the Sunday supplements.''

She gave the doctor a look that would have split an atom, and Gavigan, seeing the danger of a chain reaction if this sort of dialogue were allowed to continue, broke in quickly.

"Miss Potter. You introduced Miss Rhys to Mr. Drake and he was conducting ESP experiments with her. Is that correct?"

"Miss Potter's voice was still dangerously radioactive. "It is. And their results were most gratifying and important. Of course, neither you nor Dr. Garrett would understand —''

"And then," Garret⁺ cut in, "they both led him on into an investigation of Miss Rhys's psychic specialty — apports."
He pronounced the last word with extreme distaste.

Inspector Gavigan scowled, glanced at Merlini, and the latter promptly produced a definition. "An apport," he said, "from the French *apporter,* to bring, is any physical object supernormally brought into a séance room — from nowhere usually or from some impossible distance. Miss Rhys on previous occasions, according to the Psychical Society's *Journal,* has apported such objects as Roman coins, roses, beads, and seaweed.''

"She is the greatest apport medium," Miss Potter declared somewhat belligerently, "since Charles Bailey.''

"Then she's good," Merlini said. "Bailey was an apport medium whom Conan Doyle considered bona fide. He produced birds, Oriental plants, small animals, and on one occasion a young shark eighteen inches long which he claimed his spirit guide had whisked instantly via the astral plane from the Indian Ocean and projected, still damp and very much alive, into the séance room.''

"So," I said, "that's why this room was sealed. To make absolutely certain that no one could open the door or window in the dark and help Rosa by introducing —''

"Of course," Garrett added. "Obviously there could be no apports if adequate precautions were taken. Drake also moved a lot of his things out of the study and inventoried every object that remained. He also suggested, since I was so skeptical, that I be the one to make certain that Miss Rhys carried nothing into the room on her person. I gave her a most complete physical examination — in a bedroom upstairs. Then she put on one of Miss Drake's bathing suits."

"Did you come down to the study with her and Drake?" Gavigan asked.

The doctor frowned. "No. I had objected to Miss Potter's presence at the séance and Miss Rhys countered by objecting to mine."

"She was quite right," Miss Potter said. "The presence of an unbeliever like yourself would prevent even the strongest psychic forces from making themselves manifest."

"I have no doubt of that,". Garrett replied stiffly. "It's the usual excuse, as I told Drake. He tried to get her to let me attend but she refused flatly. So I went back to my office down the street. Drake's phone call came a half hour or so later."

"And yet" — Gavigan eyed the two brightly colored shells on the table — "in spite of all your precautions she produced two of these."

Garrett nodded. "Yes, I know. But the answer is fairly obvious now. She hid them somewhere in the hall outside on her arrival and then secretly picked them up again on her way in here."

Elinor frowned. "I'm afraid not, doctor. Father thought of that and asked me to go down with them to the study. He held one of her hands and I held the other."

Gavigan scowled. Miss Potter beamed.

"Did you go in with them?" Merlini asked.

She shook her head. "No. Only as far as the door. They went in and I heard it lock behind them. I stood there for a moment or two and heard Father begin pasting the tape on the door. Then I went back to my room to dress. I was expecting Paul."

Inspector Gavigan turned to Miss Potter. "You remained upstairs?"

"Yes," she replied in a tone that dared him to deny it. "I did."

Gavigan looked at Elinor. "Paul said a moment ago that your father didn't like him. Why not?"

"Paul exaggerates," the girl said quickly. "Father didn't dislike him. He was just — well, a bit difficult where my men friends were concerned."

"He thought they were all after his money," Kendrick added. "But at the rate he was endowing medical foundations and psychic societies —"

Miss Potter objected. "Mr. Drake did *not* endow the Psychical Society."

"But he was seriously considering it," Garrett said. "Miss Rhys — and Miss Potter — were selling him on the theory that illness is only a mental state due to a psychic imbalance, whatever that is."

"They won't sell me on that," Elinor said, and then turned suddenly on Miss Potter, her voice trembling. "If it weren't for you and your idiotic foolishness Father wouldn't have been — killed." Then to Gavigan, "We've told all this before, to the lieutenant. Is it quite necessary —"

The inspector glanced at Merlini, then said, "I think that will be all for now. Okay, Doran, take them back. But none of them are to leave yet."

When they had gone, he turned to Merlini. "Well, I asked the questions you wanted me to, but I still think it was a waste of time. Rosa Rhys killed Drake. Anything else is impossible."

"What about Kendrick's cabdriver?" Merlini asked. "Have your men located him yet?"

Gavigan's scowl, practically standard operating procedure by now, grew darker. "Yes. Kendrick's definitely out. He entered the cab on the other side of town at just about the time Drake was sealing this room and he was apparently still in it, crossing Central Park, at the time Drake was killed."

"So," I commented, "he's the only one with an alibi."

Gavigan lifted his eyebrows. "The only one? Except for

Rosa Rhys they *all* have alibis The sealed room takes care of that.''

"Yes," Merlini said quietly, "but the people with alibis also have motives while the one person who could have killed Drake has none."

"She did it," the inspector answered. "So she's got a motive, and we'll find it."

"I wish I were as confident of that as you are," Merlini said. "Under the circumstances you'll be able to get a conviction without showing motive, but if you don't find one, it will always bother you."

"Maybe," Gavigan admitted, "but that won't be as bad as trying to believe what she says happened in this room."

That was news to me. "You've talked to Rosa?" I asked.

"One of the boys did," Gavigan said sourly. "At the hospital. She's already preparing an insanity defense."

"But why," Merlini asked, "is she still hysterical with fright? Could it be that she's scared because she really believes her story — because something like that really did happen in here?"

"Look," I said impatiently, "is it top secret or will somebody tell me what she says happened?"

Gavigan glowered at Merlini. "Are you going to stand there and tell me that you think Rosa Rhys actually believes —"

It was my question that Merlini answered. He walked to the table in the center of the room. "She says that after Drake sealed the window and door, the lights were turned off and she and Drake sat opposite each other at this table. His back was toward the desk, hers toward that screen in the corner. Drake held her hands. They waited. Finally she felt the psychic forces gathering around her — and then, out of nowhere, the two shells dropped onto the table one after the other. Drake got up, turned on the desk light, and came back to the table. A moment later it happened."

The magician paused for a moment, regarding the bare, empty room with a frown. "Drake," he continued, "was examining the shells, quite excited and pleased about their appearance when suddenly, Rosa says, she heard a movement behind her. She saw Drake look up and then stare incredulously over her shoulder.'' Merlini spread his hands. "And that's all she remembers. Something hit her. When she came to, she found herself staring at the blood on the floor and at Drake's body.''

Gavigan was apparently remembering Merlini's demonstration with the gun in his office. "If you,'' he warned acidly, "so much as try to hint that one of the people outside this room projected some mental force that knocked Rosa out and then caused the knife to stab Drake —''

"You know,'' Merlini said, "I half expected Miss Potter would suggest that. But her theory is even more disturbing.'' He looked at me. "She says that the benign spirits which Rosa usually evoked were overcome by some malign and evil entity whose astral substance materialized momentarily, killed Drake, then returned to the other world from which it came.''

"She's a mental case, too,'' Gavigan said disgustedly. "They have to be crazy if they expect anyone to believe any such —''

"That,'' Merlini said quietly, "may be another reason Rosa is scared to death. Perhaps she believes it but knows you won't. In her shoes, I'd be scared, too.'' He frowned. "The difficulty is the knife.''

Gavigan blinked. "The knife? What's difficult about that?''

"If I killed Drake,'' Merlini replied, "and wanted appearances to suggest that psychic forces were responsible, you wouldn't have found a weapon in this room that made it look as if I were guilty. I would have done a little de-apporting and made it disappear. As it is now, even if the knife was propelled supernaturally, Rosa takes the rap.''

"And how,'' Gavigan demanded, "would you make the knife disappear if you were dressed, as she was, in practically nothing?'' Then, with sudden suspicion, he added,

"Are you suggesting that there's a way she could have done that — and that you think she's not guilty because she didn't?"

Merlini lifted one of the shells from the table and placed it in the center of his left palm. His right hand covered it for a brief moment, then moved away. The shell was no longer there; it had vanished as silently and as easily as a ghost. Merlini turned both hands palms outward; both were unmistakably empty.

"Yes," he said, "she could have made the knife disappear, if she had wanted to. The same way she produced the two shells." He made a reaching gesture with his right hand and the missing shell reappeared suddenly at his fingertips.

Gavigan looked annoyed and relieved at the same time. "So," he said, "you do know how she got those shells in here. I want to hear it. Right now."

But Gavigan had to wait.

At that moment a torpedo hit the water-tight circumstantial case against Rosa Rhys and detonated with a roar.

Doran, who had answered the phone a moment before, was swearing profusely. He was staring at the receiver he held as though it were a live cobra he had picked up by mistake.

"It — it's Doc Hess," he said in a dazed tone. "He just started the autopsy and thought we'd like to know that the point of the murder knife struck a rib and broke off. He just dug out a triangular pointed piece of — steel."

For several seconds after that there wasn't a sound. Then Merlini spoke.

"Gentlemen of the jury. Exhibit A, the paper knife with which my esteemed opponent, the district attorney, claims Rosa Rhys stabbed Andrew Drake, is a copper alloy — and its point, as you can see, is quite intact. The defense rests."

Doran swore again. "Drake's inventory lists that letter opener but that's all. There is no other knife in this room. I'm positive of that."

Gavigan jabbed a thick forefinger at me. "Ross, Dr. Garrett was in here before the police arrived. And Miss Drake and Kendrick."

I shook my head. "Sorry. There was no knife near the door and neither Elinor nor Paul came more than a foot into the room. Dr. Garrett examined Drake and Rosa, but I was watching him, and I'll testify that unless he's as expert at sleight of hand as Merlini, he didn't pick up a thing."

Doran was not convinced. "Look, buddy. Unless Doc Hess has gone crazy too, there was a knife and it's not here now. So somebody took it out." He turned to the detective who stood at the door. "Tom," he said, "have the boys frisk all those people. Get a policewoman for Miss Drake and Potter and search the bedroom where they've been waiting. The living room, too."

Then I had a brainstorm. "You know," I said, "if Elinor is covering up for someone—if three people came in here for the séance instead of two as she says — the third could have killed Drake and then gone out, with the knife. And the paper tape could have been —" I stopped.

"— pasted on the door *after* the murderer left?" Merlini finished. "By Rosa? That would mean she framed herself."

"Besides," Gavigan growled, "the boys fumed all those paper strips. There are fingerprints all over them. All Drake's."

Merlini said, "Doran, I suggest that you phone the hospital and have Rosa searched, too."

The lieutenant blinked. "But she was practically naked. How in blazes could she carry a knife out of here unnoticed?"

Gavigan faced Merlini, scowling. "What did you mean when you said a moment ago that she could have got rid of the knife the same way she produced those shells?"

"If it was a clasp knife," Merlini explained, "she could have used the same method other apport mediums have employed to conceal small objects under test conditions."

"But dammit!" Doran exploded. "The only place Garrett didn't look was in her stomach!"

Merlini grinned. "I know. That was his error. Rosa is a regurgitating medium, like Helen Duncan, in whose stomach the English investigator, Harry Price, found a hidden ghost — a balled-up length of cheesecloth fastened with a safety pin which showed up when he X-rayed her. X-rays of Rosa seem indicated, too. And search her hospital room and the ambulance that took her over."

"Okay, Doran," Gavigan ordered. "Do it."

I saw an objection. "Now *you've* got Rosa framing herself, too," I said. "If she swallowed the murder knife, why should she put blood on the letter opener? That makes no sense at all."

"None of this does," Gavigan complained.

"I know," Merlini answered. "One knife was bad. Two are much worse. And although X-rays of Rosa before the séance would have shown shells, I predict they won't show a knife. If they do, then Rosa needs a psychiatric examination as well."

"Don't worry," Gavigan said gloomily. "She'll get one. Her attorney will see to that. And they'll prove she's crazier than a bedbug without half trying. But if that knife isn't in her —" His voice died.

"Then you'll never convict her," Merlini finished.

"If that happens," the inspector said ominously, "you're going to have to explain where that knife came from, how it really disappeared, and where it is now."

Merlini's view was even gloomier. "It'll be much worse than that. We'll also have an appearing and vanishing murderer to explain: someone who entered a sealed room, killed Drake, put blood on the paper knife to incriminate Rosa, then vanished just as neatly as any of Miss Potter's ghosts — into thin air."

And Merlini's prediction came true.

The X-ray plates didn't show the slightest trace of a knife. And it wasn't in Rosa's hospital room or in the ambulance. Nor on Garrett, Paul, Elinor Drake, Isabelle Potter, nor, as Doran discovered, on myself. The Drake house was a mess by the time the boys got through taking it apart — but no knife with a broken point was found anywhere. And it was shown beyond doubt that there were no trapdoors or sliding panels in the study; the door and window were the only exits.

Inspector Gavigan glowered every time the phone rang. The commissioner had already phoned twice and without mincing words expressed his dissatisfaction with the way things were going.

And Merlini, stretched out in Drake's chair, his heels up on the desk top, his eyes closed, seemed to have gone into a trance.

"Blast it!" Gavigan said. "Rosa Rhys got that knife out of here somehow. She had to! Merlini, are you going to admit that she knows a trick or two you don't?"

The magician didn't answer for a moment. Then he opened one eye. "No," he said slowly, "not just yet." He took his feet off the desk and sat up straight. "You know," he said, "if we don't accept the theory of the murderer from beyond, then Ross must be right after all. Elinor Drake's statement to the contrary, there must have been a third person in this room when that séance began.

"Okay," Gavigan said, "we'll forget Miss Drake's testimony for the moment. At least that gets him into the room. Then what?"

"I don't know," Merlini said. He took the roll of gummed paper tape from the desk, tore off a two-foot length, crossed the room and pasted it across the door and jamb, sealing us in. "Suppose I'm the killer," he said. "I knock Rosa out first, then stab Drake —"

He paused.

Gavigan was not enthusiastic. "You put the murder knife in your pocket, not noticing that the point is broken. You put blood on the paper knife to incriminate Rosa. And then —" He waited. "Well, go on."

"Then," Merlini said, "I get out of here." He scowled at the sealed door and at the window. "I've escaped from handcuffs, strait jackets, milk cans filled with water, packing cases that have been nailed shut. I know the methods Houdini used to break out of safes and jail cells. But I feel like he did when a shrewd old turnkey shut him in a cell in Scotland one time and the lock — a type he'd overcome many times before — failed to budge. No matter how he tried or what he did, the bolt wouldn't move. He was sweating blood because he knew that if he failed, his laboriously built-up reputation as the escape king would be blown to bits. And then —" Merlini blinked. "And then —" This time he came to a full stop, staring at the door.

Suddenly he blinked. "Shades of Hermann, Kellar, Thurston — and Houdini! So that's it!"

Grinning broadly, he turned to Gavigan. "We will now pass a miracle and chase all the ghosts back into their tombs. If you'll get those people in here —"

"You know how the vanishing man vanished?" I asked.

"Yes. It's someone who has been just as canny as that Scotch jailer, and I know who."

Gavigan said, "It's about time." Then he walked across the room and pulled the door open, tearing the paper strip in half as he did so.

Merlini, watching him, grinned again. "The method by which magicians let their audiences fool themselves — the simplest and yet most effective principle of deception in the whole book — and it nearly took me in!"

Elinor Drake's eyes still avoided the stains on the floor. Paul, beside her, puffed nervously on a cigarette, and Dr. Garrett looked drawn and tired. But not the irrepressible Potter. She seemed fresh as a daisy.

"This room," she said to no one in particular, "will become more famous in psychic annals than the home of the Fox sisters at Lilydale."

Quickly, before she could elaborate on that, Merlini cut in. "Miss Potter doesn't believe that Rosa Rhys killed Drake. Neither do I. But the psychic force she says is responsible didn't emanate from another world. It was conjured up out of nothing by someone who was — who had to be — here in this room when Drake died. Someone whom Drake himself asked to be here.''

He moved into the center of the room as he spoke and faced them.

"Drake would never have convinced anyone that Rosa could do what she claimed without a witness. So he gave someone a key — someone who came into this room *before* Drake and Rosa and Elinor came downstairs.''

The four people watched him without moving — almost, I thought, without breathing.

"That person hid behind that screen and then, after Rosa produced the apports, knocked her out, killed Drake, and left Rosa to face the music.''

"All we have to do,'' Merlini went on, "is show who it was that Drake selected as a witness.'' He pointed a lean forefinger at Isabelle Potter. "If Drake discovered how Rosa produced the shells and realized she was a fraud, you might have killed him to prevent an exposure and save face for yourself and the society; and you might have then framed Rosa in revenge for having deceived you. But Drake would never have chosen you. Your testimony wouldn't have convinced any of the others. No. Drake would have picked one of the skeptics—someone he was certain could never be accused of assisting the medium.''

He faced Elinor. "You said that you accompanied Rosa and your father to the study door and saw them go in alone. We haven't asked Miss Rhys yet, but I think she'll confirm it. You couldn't expect to lie about that and make it stick as long as Rosa could and would contradict you.''

I saw Doran move forward silently, closing in.

"And Paul Kendrick,'' Merlini went on, "is the only one of you who has an alibi that does not depend on the sealed room. That leaves the most skeptical one of the three — the man whose testimony would by far carry the greatest weight.

"It leaves you, Dr. Garrett. The man who is so certain that there are no ghosts is the man who conjured one up!''

Merlini played the scene down; he knew that the content of what he said was dramatic enough. But Garrett's voice was even calmer. He shook his head slowly.

"I am afraid that I can't agree. You have no reason to assume that it must be one of us and no one else. But I would like to hear how you think I or anyone else could have walked out of this room leaving it sealed as it was found."

"That," Merlini said, "is the simplest answer of all. You walked out, but you didn't leave the room sealed. You see, *it was not found that way!*"

I felt as if I were suddenly floating in space.

"But look —" I began.

Merlini ignored me. "The vanishing murderer was a trick. But magic is not, as most people believe, only a matter of gimmicks and trapdoors and mirrors. Its real secret lies deeper than a mere deception of the senses; the magician uses a far more important, more basic weapon — the psychological deception of the mind. *Don't believe everything you see* is excellent advice; but there's a better rule: don't believe everything you *think.*"

"Are you trying to tell me," I said incredulously, "that this room wasn't sealed at all? That I just thought it was?"

Merlini kept watching Garrett. "Yes. It's as simple as that. And there was no visual deception at all. It was, like PK, entirely mental. You saw things exactly as they were, but you didn't realize that the visual appearance could be interpreted two ways. Let me ask you a question. When you break into a room the door of which has been sealed with paper tape on the inside, do you find yourself still in a sealed room?"

"No," I said, "of course not. The paper has been torn."

"And if you break into a room that had been sealed but from which someone has *already gone out,* tearing the seals — what then?"

"The paper," I said, "is still torn. The appearance is —"

"— *exactly the same!*" Merlini finished.

He let that soak in a moment, then continued. "When you saw the taped window, and then the torn paper on the door, you made a false assumption — you jumped naturally, but much too quickly, to a wrong conclusion. We all did. We assumed that it was you who had torn the paper when you broke in. Actually, it was Dr. Garrett who tore the paper — when he went out!"

Garrett's voice was a shade less steady now. "You forget that Andrew Drake phoned me —"

Merlini shook his head. "I'm afraid we only have your own statement for that. You overturned the phone and placed Drake's body near it. Then you walked out, returned to your office where you got rid of the knife — probably a surgical instrument which you couldn't leave behind because it might have been traced to you."

Doran, hearing this, whispered a rapid order to the detec-tive stationed at the door.

"Then," Merlini continued, "you came back immediately to ring the front-door bell. You said Drake had called you, partly because it was good misdirection; it made it appear that you were elsewhere when he died. But equally impor-tant, it gave you the excuse you needed to break in and find the body without delay — *before Rosa Rhys should regain consciousness and see that the room was no longer sealed!*"

I hated to do it. Merlini was so pleased with the neat way he was tying up all the loose ends. But I had to.

"Merlini," I said. "I'm afraid there is one little thing you don't know. When I smashed the door open, I heard the pa-per tape tear!"

I have seldom seen the Great Merlini surprised, but that did it. He couldn't have looked more astonished if lightning had struck him.

"You — you *what?*"

Elinor Drake said, "I heard it, too."

Garrett added, "And I."

It stopped Merlini cold for a moment, but only a moment.

"Then that's more misdirection. It has to be." He hesitated, then suddenly looked at Doran. "Lieutenant, get the doctor's overcoat, will you?"

Garrett spoke to the inspector. "This is nonsense. What possible reason could I have for —"

"Your motive was a curious one, doctor," Merlini said. "One that few murderers —"

Merlini stopped as he took the overcoat Doran brought in and removed from its pocket the copy of the AMA *Journal* I had noticed there earlier. He started to open it, then lifted an eyebrow at something he saw on the contents listing.

"I see," he said, and then read: *"A Survey of the Uses of Radioactive Traces in Cancer Research* by Walter M. Garrett, M.D. So that's your special interest?" The magician turned to Elinor Drake. "Who was to head the $15-million foundation for cancer research, Miss Drake?"

The girl didn't need to reply. The answer was in her eyes as she stared at Garrett.

Merlini went on. "You were hidden behind the screen in the corner, doctor. And Rosa Rhys, in spite of all the precautions, successfully produced the apports. You saw the effect that had on Drake, knew Rosa had won, and that Drake was thoroughly hooked. And the thought of seeing all that money wasted on psychical research when it could be put to so much better use in really important medical research made you boil. Any medical man would hate to see that happen, and most of the rest of us, too.

"But we don't all have the coldly rational, scientific attitude you do, and we wouldn't all have realized so quickly that there was one very simple but drastic way to prevent it — murder. You are much too rational. You believe that one man's life is less important than the good his death might bring, and you believed that sufficiently to act upon it. The knife was there, all too handy, in your little black case. And so — Drake died. Am I right, doctor?"

Doran didn't like this as a motive. "He's still a killer," he objected. "And he tried to frame Rosa, didn't he?"

Merlini said, "Do you want to answer that, doctor?"

Garrett hesitated, then glanced at the magazine Merlini still held. His voice was tired. "You are also much too rational." He turned to Doran. "Rosa Rhys was a cheap fraud who capitalized on superstition. The world would be a much better place without such people."

"And what about your getting that job as the head of the medical foundation?" Doran was still unconvinced. "I don't suppose that had anything to do with your reasons for killing Drake?"

The doctor made no answer. And I couldn't tell if it was because Doran was right or because he knew that Doran would not believe him.

He turned to Merlini instead. "The fact still remains that the cancer foundation has been made possible. The only difference is that now two men rather than one pay with their lives."

"A completely rational attitude," Merlini said, "does have its advantages if it allows you to contemplate your own death with so little emotion."

Gavigan wasn't as cynical about Garrett's motives as Doran, but his police training objected. "He took the law into his own hands. If everyone did that, we'd all have to go armed for self-protection. Merlini, why did Ross think he heard paper tearing when he opened that door?"

"He did hear it," Merlini said. Then he turned to me. "Dr. Garrett stood behind you and Miss Drake when you broke in the door, didn't he?"

I nodded. "Yes."

Merlini opened the medical journal and riffled through it. Half a dozen loose pages, their serrated edges showing where they had been torn in half, fluttered to the floor.

Merlini said, "You would have made an excellent magician, doctor. Your deception was not visual, it was auditory.''

"That," Gavigan said, "tears it."

Later I had one further question to ask Merlini.

"You didn't explain how Houdini got out of that Scottish jail, nor how it helped you solve the enigma of the unsealed door."

Merlini lifted an empty hand, plucked a lighted cigarette from thin air and puffed at it, grinning.

"Houdini made the same false assumption. When he leaned exhaustedly against the cell door, completely baffled by his failure to overcome the lock, the door suddenly swung open and he fell into the corridor. The old Scot, you see, hadn't locked it at all!''

# *Through a Glass, Darkly*

## Helen McCloy

*Though lack of space prevents us from publishing any of the impossible crime or locked room novels listed in my introduction, we can do the next best thing. Here is the original short story version of Helen McCloy's* Through a Glass, Darkly, *published two years before the novel's appearance in 1950.*

IN HER own mind Mrs. Lightfoot thought of the whole matter as "that unfortunate affair of Faustina Crayle." Characteristically she did not try to find out what had actually happened. She showed little curiosity and no fear. Whether the peculiar gossip about Faustina Crayle was based on malicious lying or hysterical hallucination, its effect was equally damaging to the Brereton School. That was the only thing that mattered to a headmistress as single-minded as Mrs. Lightfoot.

By the end of the week she was comfortably sure she would never hear the name Crayle again. And then, that bright October morning, when she was just settled in the study with her morning mail, Arlene brought her that dreadful visiting card:

> ### Dr. Basil Willing
>
> *Medical Assistant to the District Attorney*
> *of New York County*

The man, Willing, did not look like her idea of a man who held a political appointment in New York. He entered the room with easy, not ungraceful deliberation. He had the lean figure and sun-browned skin that come from living outdoors. Yet the wide brow and deep-set eyes gave his face a stamp of thoughtfulness. Those eyes were more alert, direct, and disturbing than any she had ever seen.

"Dr. Willing?" Mrs. Lightfoot held his card fastidiously between thumb and forefinger. "This is Massachusetts, not New York. And I fail to see how anything at Brereton can interest the district attorney or his medical assistant."

"That happened to be the only card I had with me," returned Basil. "I rarely use it. The district attorney's office plays only a small part in my working life. I'm a doctor of medicine, specializing in psychiatry. And I've come to see you because Faustina Crayle consulted me. My sister-in-law,

Mrs. Paul Willing, employed her as a governess two years ago."

Mrs. Lightfoot could be blunt when necessary. "Just what do you want?"

Basil met this with equal bluntness. "To know why your art teacher, Faustina Crayle, was dismissed after five weeks' employment, without warning or reason given, even though, under her contract, you had to pay her a year's salary for the five weeks."

So Faustina hadn't told him the truth. Or . . . could it be she didn't know the truth herself?

"I've ruled out any defect in teaching method or scholarship, appearance or deportment," Basil was saying. "My sister-in-law would not have employed Miss Crayle if she had any fault so obvious and you wouldn't hesitate to have called such a fault to her attention. What remains? Something libelous that you suspect and can't prove. One of our old friends dipsomania, kleptomania, or nymphomania. Lesbianism is always with us. And now there's communism. Miss Crayle might have concealed any one of these *gaucheries* from my sister-in-law since Miss Crayle did not live with the Paul Willings. She was only in their apartment for a few hours each day."

Mrs. Lightfoot lifted her eyes. "It was none of those things."

Basil saw with surprise that she was genuinely moved. He realized that it was a rare thing for such a woman to feel strong emotion. "What was it, Mrs. Lightfoot? I think you owe it to Miss Crayle to let her know. You've made it almost impossible for her to get another position as a teacher. People talk. And then . . . two curious incidents occurred, just as Miss Crayle was leaving, which she herself cannot explain. She met two pupils on the stairs, girls of thirteen — Barbara Vining and Diana Chase. She said their faces were 'bland as milk' and a pair of light voices fluted demurely: 'Good-bye, Miss Crayle!' But when she had passed them, a sound followed her down the stairwell — a faint, thin giggle, shrill

and tiny as the laughter the Japanese attribute to mice. . . In
the lower hall Miss Crayle passed one of the maids, Arlene
Murphy. Her behavior was even more extraordinary. She
shrank back, with dilated eyes, as if she were afraid of Miss
Crayle."

Mrs. Lightfoot was beaten. "I suppose I'll have to tell
you."

He studied her face. "Why are you afraid to tell me?"

Her answer startled him. "Because you won't believe me.
You'd better hear it from some of the eye-witnesses. We'll
start with Arlene." She pressed a bell on the wall beside her.

The maid was as young as the graduating class at Brereton — probably eighteen, at the most twenty. Under a white
apron, she wore a gray chambray dress, high-necked, long-
sleeved, full-skirted. Mrs. Lightfoot had won the battle for
low heels and no cosmetics, but Arlene had carried two other
hotly contested points — flesh-colored stockings and no cap.

"Come in and shut the door, Arlene. Will you please re-
peat to Dr. Willing what you told me about Miss Crayle?"

"Yes, ma'am, but you said not to tell anybody!"

"I'm releasing you from that promise, just this once."

Arlene turned vacant, brown eyes on Basil. Her brows
were hairless. This gave her face a singularly naked look.
Some glandular deficiency, he suspected. She was breathing
through her mouth and that made her look stupid.

"I was upstairs, turning down beds for the night," said
Arlene. "When I got through, I started down the backstairs.
It was getting dark, but it was still light enough to see the
steps. Those backstairs are enclosed, but there's two windows. I saw Miss Crayle coming up the stair, toward me. I
thought it was a bit odd for her to be using the back stairs
instead of the front. I says: 'Good evening, Miss.' But she
didn't answer. She didn't even look at me. She just went on
up to the second floor. That was kinda queer 'cause she was
always polite to everybody. But even then I didn't think
much about it until I went on down into the kitchen and
. . ." Arlene paused to swallow. "There was Miss Crayle."

The girl's hands were trembling. Her eyes searched Basil's face for some sign of disbelief. "Honest, sir, she couldn't have got back to the kitchen by way of the upper hall, the front stairs, the dining room, or the pantry. Not in the little time it took me to finish going down the back stairs to the kitchen. She just couldn't, even if she'd run."

"What was Miss Crayle doing in the kitchen?" asked Basil.

"She had some flowers she'd just got in the garden. She was fixing a vase with water at the table by the sink."

"Were the two dressed exactly the same way? The one on the stair and the one in the kitchen?"

"Like as two peas. Brown felt hat. Bluish gray coat. Covert, I think they call it. No fur, no real style at all. And brown shoes. The kind with no tongues and criss-cross laces they call 'ghillies.' And some old pigskin gloves she always used for gardening."

"Did the hat have a brim?"

"Uh-huh. I mean, yes, sir."

"Did you see Miss Crayle's face on the backstairs?"

"Yes, sir. I didn't look at her particular. No reason why I should. And the hat brim was down over her eyes. But I saw her nose and mouth and chin. I'd swear it was her."

"Did you speak to Miss Crayle in the kitchen?"

"Soon as I got my breath, I says: 'Lord, miss, you give me a turn! I coulda sworn I just passed you on the stair, comin' down.' She smiled and said: 'You musta been mistaken, Arlene. I been in the west garden the last half hour. I only just come into the house and I haven't been upstairs yet.' Well, sir, you know how it is. Something like that happens and you think: 'What the —' I mean: 'Oh, well, I musta been mistaken.' And that's the end of it . . . if nothing more happens. But this time — well, that was just the beginning. In a week or so there was stories going all over the school about Miss Crayle and —"

Mrs. Lightfoot interrupted. "That will do, Arlene. Thank

you. And will you please ask Miss Vining and Miss Chase
to come to my study immediately?"

"Goethe," said Basil, as the door shut. "The gray suit
with gilt edging. Emilie Sagée. And *The Tale of Tod La-
praik*. The *doppelganger* of the Germans. The *ka* of the
Egyptians. The double of English folk lore. You see a figure,
solid, three dimensional, brightly colored, moving and obeying all the laws of optics. Its clothing or posture is vaguely
familiar. It turns its head and — you are looking at yourself.
A perfect mirror-image of yourself, only — there is no mirror. And that frightens you. For tradition tells you that he
who sees his own double must die."

"Only if he sees it face to face," amended Mrs. Lightfoot.
"The history of the *doppelganger* legend is very curious.
Lately I've begun to wonder if the atmosphere could act as a
mirror under certain conditions, something like a mirage but
reflecting only one person . . ."

A light tap fell on the door. Two little girls about thirteen
entered the study and curtsied to Basil when Mrs. Lightfoot
introduced them as Barbara Vining and Diana Chase.

The drab masculinity of the Brereton uniform merely
heightened by contrast the delicate, feminine coloring of Barbara Vining — pink and white skin, silver-gold hair, and
eyes the misty blue of star sapphires. The line of her lips was
so subtly turned that even in repose they seemed to quiver on
the edge of suppressed laughter.

The same uniform brought out all that was plain and dull
in Diana Chase: the straight, mouse-colored hair; the
pinched, white face; the forlorn mouth. Only the eyes, a clear
hazel, showed a sly spark of potential mischief.

They listened gravely as Mrs. Lightfoot explained what
she wanted. "Barbara, suppose you tell Dr. Willing what
happened. Diana, you may correct Barbara if she makes any
mistake."

"Yes, Mrs. Lightfoot." The faint pink in Barbara's cheeks
warmed to rose. Obviously she enjoyed being the centre of

the stage. "We two were in the writing room on the ground floor. I was writing my brother, Raymond, and Diana was writing her mother. All the other girls were down at the basketball field and most of the teachers. But she was outside the middle window — Miss Crayle. It was a French window, standing open, so I could see her plainly. She'd set her easel up in the middle of the lawn and she was sketching in water colors. She was wearing a blue coat but no hat. It was fun watching the quick, sure way she handled her brush."

"You've forgotten the armchair," put in Diana.

"Armchair? Oh . . ." Barbara turned back to Basil. "There was an armchair in that room with a slip-cover in Delft blue. We called it 'Miss Crayle's chair' because she sat there so often. I rather expected her to come in and sit in that chair when she was through painting and then — it happened." Barbara's voice faded, suddenly shy.

Diana took over. "I looked up and saw that Miss Crayle had come in without my hearing her. She was sitting in the blue armchair, her hands loose in her lap, her head resting against the back. She didn't seem to notice me, so I went on writing. After a while, I looked up again. She was still in the armchair. But that time my eyes wandered over to the window and . . ." Diana lost her nerve. "You tell him, Babs."

"Miss Crayle was still sketching outside the window?" suggested Basil.

"I suppose Mrs. Lightfoot told you." Barbara looked at him sharply. "I heard Di gasp, so I looked up and saw her staring at two Miss Crayles — one in the armchair, in the room with us; the other on the lawn, outside the window. The one in the chair was perfectly still. The one outside the window was moving. Only . . ." Barbara's voice wavered. "I told you how quick and sure her motions were? Well, after we saw the figure in the chair, the figure outside the window was — slower. Every movement was sort of languid and weighted. Like a slow-motion picture."

"Made me think of a sleepwalker," added Diana.

"What was the light like?"

"Bright sunlight on the lawn," answered Barbara. "So bright the shades were drawn halfway down inside."

"It was pretty awful," went on Diana. "Sitting there, the two of us, alone in the room with that — that thing in the armchair. And the real Miss Crayle outside painting in that slow, unnatural way. Afterward, I thought of all sorts of things we might have done. Like trying to touch the thing in the chair. Or calling to Miss Crayle from the window and waking her from her — her trance or whatever it was. But at the time — well, I was just too frightened to think or move."

"I sat there and told myself it wasn't happening," said Barbara. "Only it was. I suppose it only lasted a minute or so. It seemed like a hundred years. Then the figure in the chair got up and went into the hall without a sound. The door was standing open and it seemed to melt into the shadows beyond. We sat there about three seconds. Then we ran to the door. There was no one in sight. So we went back to the window but — Miss Crayle had gone. . . ."

When they were alone, Mrs. Lightfoot looked at Basil "Was a practical woman ever confronted with such a fantastic problem? Six girls have been withdrawn from Brereton already. That's why Miss Crayle had to go."

"But Barbara and Diana are still here. Didn't they write their parents about this?"

"Barbara has no parents — only a brother, a rather light-hearted young man of twenty-six who doesn't take his duties as guardian too seriously. Diana's parents are divorced. The father lives with a second wife in California. The mother is chiefly occupied in nursing her grievances against the father and nagging the courts to increase her alimony. Neither is greatly concerned with Diana. She's been a pupil here since her seventh year. Barbara only came to us this Fall. She's been going to a day school in New York."

Basil studied the intelligent face under the sleek mound of dark hair flecked with gray. "What is your own opinion?"

A hint of defiance crept into Mrs. Lightfoot's voice. "I am a modern woman, Dr. Willing. That means I was born without faith in religion and I have lost faith in science. I don't understand the theories of Messrs. Planck and Einstein, but I grasp enough to realize that the world of matter may be a world of appearances — that even our own bodies are a part of this dance of electrons. What's behind it, we don't know. How does my mind act on my body when I decide to move my arm? Neither psychology nor physiology can tell me . . .

"By what trick could Faustina Crayle create the illusion of her double? And why? She gained nothing. It cost her a job. She may be an unconscious trickster — an hysteric with impulses to amaze and frighten people, impulses that she can't control because she is not aware of them herself. That might explain why she played such a trick, but not how.

"There is a third possibility. Suppose Faustina Crayle is . . . abnormal in a way that modern science will not acknowledge?"

If Mrs. Lightfoot feared an outburst of that outraged skepticism that is a sure sign of hidden credulity — the fool's fear of being fooled — she had misjudged her man. "Did anyone else see Miss Crayle's double? Besides two girls of thirteen and a maid of nineteen or twenty?"

Mrs. Lightfoot caught the implication. "There was one other witness — middle-aged, sober, reasonably shrewd and observant. Myself."

After a moment, she went on: "I had a dinner engagement outside the school that evening. I came out of my room about six. A pair of sconces are always lighted in the upper hall at that hour. Each has a hundred-watt bulb under a small shade. Their light extends to the first landing of the front stair. Below that landing the stair was in shadow this particular evening, for Arlene had neglected to turn on the ceiling light in the lower hall. I started down the stair with one hand on the balustrade, moving slowly because my dress had a long, full skirt. As I reached the first landing, someone, one in greater

haste, brushed past me without a word of apology and I saw
that it was Miss Crayle.

"She didn't actually jostle me, but I felt the drafty dis-
placement of air that you feel when anyone passes closely
and swiftly. And her ungloved hand brushed my arm where
the skin was bare between my cuff and my glove. That contact was inhumanly cold. I remember thinking: *she must have
been outdoors* . . . I didn't see her face as she passed. But
I recognized her back — the brown hat and the blue covert
coat, the only outdoor clothes she had except a winter coat
still in storage. I was irritated by her rudeness. Manners are
important at Brereton. I raised my voice, making it crisp and
peremptory: 'Miss Crayle!'

" 'Yes, Mrs. Lightfoot?'

"Dr. Willing, that answering voice came from the upstairs
hall, above me, and I could still see Miss Crayle's back moving into the shadows of the lower hall, below me. I looked
up. Faustina Crayle was standing at the head of the stairs, in
the full light of the upper hall, wearing the brown hat and
blue coat. Her eyes, bright with life and intelligence, looked
into mine, and she spoke again: 'You called me, Mrs. Lightfoot?' I looked down. There was nothing in the lower hall
then — nothing but shadows. I said: 'I thought you passed
me just now on the stair. I didn't know you were just behind
me.' She answered: 'That's rather odd. You were going
down so slowly and I was in such a hurry to get the evening
mail that my first impulse was to slip past you on the stair.
But I didn't because I realized how rude that would be.'

"So she'd had the unrealized intention. . . . I recalled
how often a sleepwalker will carry out an intention previously suppressed in his waking state. Suppose that uncen-
sored, autonomous action of the unconscious mind in sleep-
walking could be pushed a little further? Suppose that the
unconscious mind could project some form of itself outside
the body? Not a material form, but a visible one. Just as
mirror-reflections and rainbows are visible and even photo-
graphable though materially neither one exists. Or suppose a

case of split personality where the secondary personality gathers enough vital energy to project that sort of visible yet immaterial image of itself . . .

"I assure you it took all the nerve I had to go on down that stair into the darkness and turn on the light in the lower hall. There was no one — except Arlene coming into the drawing-room from the dining room. 'Did you meet anyone just now?' I asked her. She shook her head: 'No, ma'am. I haven't seen a soul.' "

"No wonder you didn't dare tell Faustina Crayle why you wished her to leave!" Basil's glance strayed to the lawn outside the window where the autumn breeze tumbled the dead leaves and pounced on them in erratic starts and sallies like an invisible kitten.

"She would have thought me mad. Do you?"

"No. A conformist skepticism is a pretty cheap commodity. He who accepts the incredulities of his time without question is as naive as he who accepts its credulities." Basil's eyes returned to Mrs. Lightfoot. "You spoke of a drafty sensation when the double passed. Any sound? Swish of air? Rustle of clothing?"

"No sound at all."

"Footfalls?"

"No, but that would be so in any case. The stair carpet is thick and soft."

"Every human body carries some faint odor or combination of odors," mused Basil. "Face powder, lipstick, hair tonic, permanent wave lotion, or shaving lotion. Iodine or some other medicine. The breath odors — food, wine, tobacco. And the clothing odors — mothballs, shoe polish, dry cleaning fluids, Russian leather, or Harris tweed. Finally there are those body odors the soap advertisements worry us about. You are one witness who was close enough to touch the double, however briefly. Did you notice any odor, however faint or fleeting?"

Mrs. Lightfoot shook her head emphatically. "There was no odor, Dr. Willing, unless I missed it."

"I doubt that." He glanced toward a row of flower pots on the window sill. "Only a woman with keen senses would enjoy a fragrance as delicate as rose geranium or lemon verbena."

Mrs. Lightfoot smiled. "I even use lemon verbena on my handkerchief. My one really gaudy vice, but a French firm puts out an essence of *verveine* I can't resist. It's supposed to be an after-shaving lotion for men, so I'm probably the only woman in the world who uses it."

"Did Miss Crayle use any perfume habitually?"

"Lavender. She always used it on her hair."

"No hint of lavender about the double?"

"No." Mrs. Lightfoot's smile became ironic. "You wouldn't expect a reflection in a mirror to have an odor, would you?"

Basil picked up his hat and driving gloves. "Why did this double of Miss Crayle appear only at Brereton? Didn't Miss Crayle teach at another school last year? A place in Virginia called Maidstone?"

Mrs. Lightfoot looked at him grimly. "I hadn't meant to tell you. Mollie Maidstone is a friend of mine and I got the truth out of her a few days ago, under pledge of secrecy, but . . . Miss Crayle left Maidstone last year under precisely the same conditions that she is now leaving Brereton."

The apartment house stood between Lexington Avenue and the river. Basil passed through a door flanked by copper tubs planted with ivy to a self-service elevator and pressed the button marked Penthouse. In a vestibule on the top floor he lifted a knocker and chimes rang. The young woman who opened the door was tall for her sex, but slenderly fashioned with frail wrists and ankles, tapering hands and narrow, high-arched feet. Her hair was a pale tan, almost a biscuit color, so fine and soft that it had no shape or sleekness, but floated about her small head in a thistledown halo, stirring gently with each movement she made. The long face was sallow and earnest, the lips thin, the nose prominent and rather sharp. She led the way to a terrace. The sun had just set. Beyond the parapet the peaks and valleys of the mountainous city shimmered insubstantially in a silver haze.

Basil offered cigarettes. She shook her head impatiently. He lit one for himself. "Miss Crayle, do you know the German legend of the *doppelganger?*"

Tears gathered in the cloudy blue eyes. She covered her face with her hands. "Dr. Willing, what am I going to do?"

"Then you do know. Why didn't you tell me before you sent me to Mrs. Lightfoot?"

"Would you have believed me? I don't know anything . . . except what people said about me at Maidstone." Her hands dropped. She turned toward him, apparently unconscious of reddened eyelids. "Now I suppose it's happened again at Brereton. Mrs. Lightfoot wouldn't tell me, but I thought she might tell you — a psychiatrist, working with the district attorney in New York . . ."

Basil told her all he had learned at Brereton. "Is that the sort of thing that happened at Maidstone?"

He caught a hint of lavender as Faustina dabbed at her eyes with a handkerchief. "Pretty much. Maidstone is quite like Brereton. Only in Virginia instead of Massachusetts. The girls don't wear uniforms but it's strict in other ways. No male visitors except Sunday and so on. After I'd been there a week I knew I was being watched and talked about. Other teachers refused my little invitations for tea or shopping. Even the servants waited on me grudgingly. I took it for hostility. Now I believe it was fear. In my fourth week I got a note from Miss Maidstone. Dismissal with a check for a year's services. I took the note to her study. She was quite emotional about the whole thing. She even wrote me a letter of recommendation. That got me the job at Brereton afterward. You see, though she had to keep it secret because of her school, Miss Maidstone has dabbled in psychic research. She took books out of a locked cupboard and read me about other 'doubles' that had been reported to various research societies in Europe. She didn't suspect me of fraud. For that very reason she would not keep me at Maidstone.''

"Do you believe in this yourself?''

Faustina smiled bitterly. "I know I'm not a fraud. You don't know that, of course. But I do. And I can't see how or why anyone else should play such a trick on me. What remains? When you've lost your job twice because of a thing, you don't think it's just imagination . . . I'm like Madame du Deffand. I don't believe in it, but I'm afraid of it.''

"Of what?''

"Of this . . . thing. Suppose I were to see it myself? I've had just one glimpse, on the front stair at Brereton. All I saw was the back of a figure, dressed in clothes like mine, brushing past Mrs. Lightfoot. That could be anyone who looked like me and wore similar clothes. Even if I were to see a face resembling mine, at a distance, in a dim light — that could be illusion or trickery, a face resembling mine by chance or made up deliberately to look like mine. But if I should suddenly come upon a face close at hand, in a clear light, and recognize it as my own face in every small detail — I believe I should die. Because that couldn't be faked.''

"How often was the double seen at Maidstone?''

"Three times. On the front lawn while I was asleep upstairs. On an upstairs sleeping porch while I was teaching a class in a downstairs room. And once it passed an open door while I stood inside the door with another teacher.''

Basil crushed the stub of his cigarette in an ashtray. "Miss Crayle, is there anyone who has reason to hate you? Or who would benefit by your death?''

"No one I know of. I have no family. My mother died when I was six and I don't remember my father.''

"Any property?''

"A small cottage at Seabright on the Jersey coast, left to me by my mother. And some jewelry. Just trinkets, I suppose, for my mother was not a wealthy woman. Mr. Watkins, the lawyer, is going to have it appraised for me.''

"Who gets the jewelry and the cottage when you die?"

"I'm leaving the cottage to a school friend. I'm not supposed to inherit the jewelry until my thirtieth birthday."

"What becomes of the jewelry if you die before then?"

"I really don't recall." The colorless brows knitted. "There was something in the will about that."

"Better give me the name and address of your lawyer . . . Septimus Watkins? He manages half the big trust funds in New York." Basil rose to go. "Are you staying here long?"

"I'm leaving this evening. The friends who live here will be back tonight. They just lent me the place for this weekend. I need rest. And privacy. So I thought I'd go down to the cottage at Seabright."

"Don't." Basil looked up sharply. "Go to a hotel. The biggest, brightest, noisiest hotel you can find. And let me know where you are as soon as you're settled. . . ."

When Basil arrived, Septimus Watkins was just leaving his office. He laid hat and gloves and silver-topped malacca stick back on his desk and sat down without removing his topcoat. While Basil was talking, Watkins's bleak glance traveled toward the window view of Old Trinity, dark and dwarfish among higher buildings. "The whole business sounds like adolescent humor to me."

"Who inherits the jewelry if Miss Crayle dies before thirty?"

"Dr. Willing, I know your reputation. I believe you'll be discreet. So I'll tell you as much as I can. For that is the quickest way to disabuse your mind of the preposterous idea that anything threatens Miss Crayle. That unfortunate girl, Faustina, is illegitimate." Watkins's small, close smile seemed to savor the lubricities of the past, safely sterilized by time. "Did you ever hear of Rosa Diamond? She was the daughter of a man who wrote hymns and lived in Philadelphia. She had red hair. In the nineties she ran away from home — first New York, then Paris. There she became a star of the *demi-monde* — one of those fabulous courtesans Balzac describes in such rich detail. A provincial American girl, she learned from her lovers to speak and write perfect French, to understand music and art and letters. It's hard to make your generation understand such hetaerae. Only Paris and Athens in certain periods have produced them.''

"Wasn't she co-respondent in a divorce case of the 1900's?''

"In 1912. A corporation lawyer of New York wanted a divorce without accusing his wife. Rosa Diamond was so notorious that he had only to go to Paris and be seen once, driving in the Bois with her in an open carriage, to obtain his divorce. That single drive was considered adequate proof of adultery. It was said that he paid Rosa Diamond a thousand dollars and that they parted at her door without his even kissing her fingertips. But they met again and . . . Faustina Crayle is their daughter. Rosa knew her trade. She was to have been simply a convenience. Instead she altered the whole course of his life. He fell in love with her . . .''

Again came the little smile of reminiscent salacity. "He brought her back to America. He gave her a town house in Manhattan and a seaside cottage in New Jersey at Seabright. But he didn't marry her. Such men didn't marry such women in those days.''

"And that is the origin of that meagre, bloodless girl!'' Basil thought of the flat chest, the narrow flanks. "Does she know?''

"I've tried to keep it from her, as her parents wished. Several times she has asked me if she were illegitimate. I lied, but I'm afraid she didn't believe me. . . . It was in 1918 when Rosa was forty-three that she gave birth to Faustina. The father already had a legitimate heir by his divorced wife. He was in his fifties then and knew he had not long to live — a heart condition which Faustina has inherited. He wanted to provide for the little girl without unpleasant publicity which might affect her future. To avoid mentioning Rosa or Faustina in his will, he gave Rosa a collection of handsome jewels which had belonged to his mother. There was another fund to put Faustina through school, but the jewels — sold at a fair price, with the proceeds invested judiciously —would give her a tidy income for life — say, ten thousand a year in 1918 and even more today. The value of Faustina's jewels has appreciated in the last thirty years, while, unhappily, the crash of 1929 wiped out the fortune left to the legitimate heir. That young man shot himself leaving two minor heirs, legitimate grandchildren of Faustina's father, who have less money than she today."

"But if Faustina dies before the age of thirty, the jewels revert to these children of her natural half-brother?"

"There was some bad feeling when the grandfather gave family jewels to Rosa Diamond and she developed a sense of guilt about it. According to her will, Faustina inherits the jewels at thirty but if Faustina dies before thirty, I, as executor, must dispose of the jewels according to instructions in a sealed envelope deposited with me, which can be opened only after Faustina's death and in the presence of a probate judge. Rosa herself told me this envelope contains instructions to give the jewels to the legitimate heirs. The sealed envelope was a device she contrived so that her will could be read to Faustina without Faustina learning the name of her natural half-brother or suspecting their relationship. That name I cannot reveal, even to you, Dr. Willing. It would betray a trust to revive such an old, unhappy scandal."

"Do the legitimate heirs know about Rosa's will and the sealed instructions?"

"Naturally. The family knew from the beginning what had become of their jewels. When they asked me if there was any legal way to recover the jewels, I convinced them there was not, by explaining exactly what disposition Rosa had made of them."

"Did you mention Faustina Crayle by name?"

"I believe I did. Why not?"

Wearily, Basil rose to take his leave. "Tell me one more thing: has either of these legitimate heirs any connection with the Maidstone School? Or Brereton?"

"I must decline to answer that."

It was full night when Basil reached the narrow brownstone house on lower Park Avenue where he had lived so many years. Before the war he had regarded it as a poor substitute for his father's home in Baltimore. Now, after years overseas, this was his home and always would be. He loved the river of cars flowing uptown at office-closing-time, the soft bloom of curtained lamplight in the low, old-fashioned houses on either side of the wide street, the glitter of the Grand Central building against velvety blue darkness, the whisper of tires, the ring of heels and the nip of frost in the air which announced winter and a new season of gaiety.

Juniper met him in the vestibule. "Some folks waitin' in the library."

Basil went up a flight of stairs to the long, white-paneled "library" that was also living-room and study. Juniper had drawn wine-colored curtains and lighted lamps. At the sound of Basil's step a young man turned swiftly toward the door. The lamplight found golden highlights in the ash-blond hair, cut close to his small head. "Dr. Willing? Forgive this intrusion, but the matter is urgent. I am Raymond Vining, Barbara's brother. It was Mrs. Lightfoot who suggested that we should see you. This is Dr. Willing — Mrs. Chase, Diana's mother. And my *fiancée*, Miss Aitchison."

The women were shadows beyond the lamplight. Basil pressed the chandelier switch. Mrs. Chase had kept the tilted nose, chubby cheeks, and rounded chin of youth, but there were deep lines scored on either side of the mouth. The bright, reddish brown hair was as patently artificial as the tomato-red of her lips. She was dressed with ostentation — dark mink, black velvet, and diamonds. Miss Aitchison was a ripe beauty of eighteen or twenty with splendid dark eyes, golden skin, and fruity, red lips, set off by a neat brown suit

and a vivid scarf of burnt orange. Basil paused as he caught
the ghost of a familiar fragrance — lemon verbena. But he
could not tell which of the three had brought it into the room.

"Do you think I should withdraw Diana from the school?"
demanded Mrs. Chase.

"I can't advise you about that." Basil realized she was the
sort of woman who tries to unload any responsibility on the
nearest man.

"At least you can tell us what has been happening there!"

"All sorts of odd things happen at schools," drawled Miss
Aitchison insolently, her legs crossed, a cigarette smoking in
one gloved hand.

Basil seized the opening. "You went to Brereton?"

"No, I'm Maidstone and —"

Raymond Vining interrupted. "Dr. Willing, just what did
happen? Was it hysteria? Or fraud?"

Basil turned to look at Vining. He had Barbara's fresh
pink and white skin, and her eyes, the misty blue of star
sapphires. He had her lips — the line so subtly turned that
even in repose it seemed to quiver on the edge of laughter.
He had the attenuated face and figure Victorian novelists
called "aristocratic." Basil had seen the same traits too often
in the families of farmers and factory workers to accept the
odd biological belief that the human bone structure can be
altered in a few generations by property and leisure.

"Was Miss Crayle an agent?" went on Vining. "Or a victim?"

Basil took a book from his shelves. "Here is something
that is supposed to have happened in Livonia in 1845. It's
been published in various versions by Robert Dale Owen, by
Aksakoff, by Flammarion." He began to read aloud. It was
almost the same story as Faustina's. Only the girl's school
was at Volmar, fifty-eight miles from Riga, and the girl was
a French teacher from Dijon, Emilie Sagée, fair, gentle, aged
thirty-two. Two identical figures were seen simultaneously by
an embroidery class of forty-two girls — one appearing for
several minutes in a chair in the classroom while the other

could be seen gathering flowers in the garden outside the window. As long as the appearance remained in the chair, the girl outside moved "slowly and heavily like a person overcome with fatigue." There were other appearances, even more curious, until finally all but twelve of the forty-three girls were withdrawn by their parents and Mademoiselle Sagée was dismissed. She wept and cried: "This is the nineteenth time since my sixteenth year that I have lost a position because of this!" From that moment, when she walked out of the Neuwelcke School, she vanished from history. What became of her, no one knows. But in 1895 Flammarion looked at the birth records in Dijon for 1813 — the year of Mademoiselle Sagée's birth if she were thirty-two in 1845. There was no Sagée. But on January 13, 1813 an infant girl named Octavie Saget was born and, of course, Saget is pronounced precisely the same as Sagée in French. In the record after that name appeared the significant words *illegitimate*.

"There is one striking point about all this," concluded Basil. "The exact parallel between the two cases. In some details the Crayle case is a plagiarism of the Sagée case."

"Except for the illegitimacy," murmured Vining.

"So what?" said Miss Aitchison rudely.

"Someone who wishes to injure Miss Crayle has read the story of Mademoiselle Sagée and adapted it to that purpose. But that isn't the worst. According to tradition, she who sees her own double must die. Miss Crayle lives in fear of seeing the figure herself. This haunting by a double is a constant threat of death to her — psychologically on the same plane as threatening, anonymous letters. It could end in insanity, suicide — even murder."

"How could anyone fake the thing?" cried Vining. "Mirrors?"

"Not when Miss Crayle was painting on the lawn and the double was sitting in an armchair inside the house."

"Alice . . ." Vining turned to Miss Aitchison. "I'm going to take Barbara out of that school. Wouldn't you?"

"I suppose so." Miss Aitchison looked bored.

"You're right!" Mrs. Chase would always join the majority with enthusiasm. "I'm going to take Diana away the first thing tomorrow. . . ."

After dinner Basil called Assistant Chief Inspector Foyle at his Flatbush home. "Nothing we can do tonight," said Foyle, when Basil had outlined facts and conjectures. "You told her to go to a big hotel. Couldn't be any hocus-pocus there. Tomorrow I'll see this Watkins character at his office. If I busted in on his home tonight, it would be twice as difficult . . ."

It was six forty-five A.M. when the telephone rang beside the bed. "Dr. Willing?" Mrs. Lightfoot's voice roused him. "I'm sorry to disturb you, but a policeman just called me from New Jersey. Faustina Crayle is dead."

Basil met an early train from Massachusetts at Grand Central and took Mrs. Lightfoot to breakfast in the station. Then he drove her to Centre Street.

"After you phoned this morning I got what dope I could from the New Jersey State Police," said Foyle to Basil. "No evidence of suicide — let alone murder. Not even accident. Just natural death from heart failure. You told me yourself Watkins said her heart was weak."

"I wonder how many people he told . . ." muttered Basil.

"She didn't go to a hotel," added Foyle. "Her friends at the penthouse say Miss Crayle got a phone call that changed her mind about that. She went down to this seaside cottage she'd inherited. Her body could have lain there for weeks if the caretaker hadn't happened to pass the house around three A.M., coming home from a covered-dish supper at the church there. She saw a light and notified the state police. They found the front door ajar, Miss Crayle's key still in the lock outside, and her key-ring dangling. Just one light inside — a lamp in the hall. There's a couple of little parlors to the right of the hall with a pair of transparent glass doors between. Miss Crayle was lying prone in the middle of the first parlor, her head toward the glass doors, still wearing hat, coat and gloves, her purse and dressing-case beside her. Nothing in the room disarranged. No money taken. The Jersey cops found a taxi-driver who drove her from the station to the cottage and left her there around eleven fifty. The doctor says she must have been dead by midnight at the latest.

"It's plain what happened. She unlocked the door and left it ajar with her key in the lock while she stepped inside to switch on a few lights. What every woman does when she enters an empty house alone at night. Before she got any farther than the first parlor, her heart just stopped."

"Did you check alibis?" asked Basil.

"Oh, sure. Mrs. Chase was with a supper party from eleven P.M. to three thirty A.M. Miss Aitchison and Vining were at the Crane Club. Bartender remembers their coming in together at ten P.M. and leaving together at one thirty A.M."

"Anything else?"

"Well . . ." Foyle hesitated. "It's pretty silly. You know how superstitious hayseeds are. One of the yokels down at this place, Seabright, declares he passed Faustina Crayle walking along a backroad at three thirty A.M. He didn't know it when he testified, but that was after the cops had found her dead body. . . ."

In the car Basil glanced at Mrs. Lightfoot. "I'm going to Seabright."

"May I go with you? I'm beginning to feel responsible for Miss Crayle. If I hadn't turned her out so summarily . . ."

Miss Crayle's cottage was three miles beyond the village, between pinewoods and sea — white clapboarding with shutters and door of grayish green. Though the road was unfrequented, Russian olive, bayberry, and scrub pine had been cultivated to mask the windows. A ragged lawn sloped up to the crest of a dune covered with poverty grass. There was no one in sight but the front door was unlatched. "Would police be so careless?" murmured Basil.

Mrs. Lightfoot followed him inside reluctantly. "Dr. Willing, could a . . . a double survive the death of the personality that projected it? Even for a few hours?"

He wasn't listening. He was looking at the hall — white woodwork, white wallpaper flecked with green. A lamp stood on a telephone table in the curve of the stair. Basil examined the bulb — one hundred watts. The only light in the hall. It would illuminate the hall itself brilliantly, but the light would be low, ceiling and upper wall remaining in shadow. Some radiance would spill through the wide archway into the parlor on the right but it would still be low, and the second parlor, beyond the transparent glass doors, would be lost in shadows. Basil stepped into the first parlor. He pressed a light switch beside the archway. No light came. The bulbs in the ceiling fixture looked smoky. Probably dead.

The second parlor could be reached only by way of the first. The two were almost exactly alike. Each had white woodwork and a bay window at the far end with frilly, white curtains and green upholstered seat. Each had a rug of faded-rose color, slipcovers splashed with roses the same shade, and leaves of faded green. Only close inspection showed a difference in such details as the color of ashtrays and the arrangement of chairs.

"Monotonous," said Basil. "Two rooms in the same colors."

"It would be worse if they were decorated in contrasting colors," retorted Mrs. Lightfoot. "That would make both rooms look smaller by dividing them. Just as a woman in contrasting blouse and skirt looks shorter than a woman in a dress all one color. This way the eye travels from one room to the other without a break and you get the effect of one long room even with the glass doors closed."

"Why doors at all? Why not one big room?"

Mrs. Lightfoot glanced about her. "There's no radiator. Probably no furnace in a summer cottage like this. But with the glass doors closed, this first parlor is small enough to be heated by a portable stove, electric or oil."

Basil walked down the room to the glass doors. "What do you make of these marks?" They were minute scratches on the wooden frames that separated each small transparent glass pane from the others.

"It's hard to paint the wooden frames without smearing the glass," suggested Mrs. Lightfoot. "Amateur painters often cut a piece of cardboard the same size as the pane and fit it inside the frame over the glass while they're painting. Afterward you have to pry out the cardboard. This painter seems to have used a needle."

"It wasn't a painter. Those scratches were made after the paint was dry and —"

"What's that?" exclaimed Mrs. Lightfoot. "It sounds like footfalls upstairs!"

"It is," agreed Basil calmly. "I've been listening to them for some time."

The footfalls were coming downstairs. There was no attempt at stealth. The heels rang clear and unafraid on each step. Then came a sudden pause. Basil visualized a figure arrested in motion by sight of the front door, which he had left wide open. The footfalls resumed with a certain caution. In the hall archway appeared the large, formidable figure of Septimus Watkins.

"Dr. Willing!" Surprise seemed to master indignation. "I trust you've learned enough from the local police to accept as I do their statement that Miss Crayle's death was perfectly natural. As I mentioned yesterday, her heart —" His voice wavered, stopped. All three listened to the sound of other footfalls — younger, fleeter — running down the stair.

"So you didn't come alone?" Basil moved toward the arch. The footfalls ceased as abruptly as they had begun.

Basil was the first to speak. "I'm glad Alice Aitchison told me she went to Maidstone."

Raymond Vining moved forward. With him came a faint scent of lemon verbena. "What has that to do with . . .?"

"Your murdering your grandfather's illegitimate daughter, Faustina Crayle? Everything."

"Don't say a word, Ray!" called Watkins. "I'll get you the best criminal lawyer money can buy!"

Basil spoke as if thinking aloud. "Alice Aitchison must have known or guessed the truth. Enough to charge her as accessory? Probably, since, as your wife, she would share the money you got from the sale of Faustina's jewels when you received them. And Barbara? She's only thirteen, but she's intelligent. She may have guessed —"

"No!" Vining shouted. "Alice didn't know and neither did Barbara! You can charge me but you can't charge them! I won't let you!"

"Why, that's a confession!" gasped Mrs. Lightfoot.

Not until the drive back to New York did Basil have a chance to give her the details: "I suspected Vining the moment I saw his close family resemblance to Faustina, his grandfather's daughter. He was the only person involved who was physically able to impersonate her double, even under favorable conditions. Both Vining and Faustina had the attenuated "aristocratic" figure — narrow flanks, finely cut wrists and ankles, tapering hands, slender, high-arched feet. In woman's dress, his figure would look like hers. And in a dim light at a fair distance his face could pass for hers. Both had the "aristocratic" small head and long, oval face, the prominent nose and thin lips. Both were the ash-blond type, with cloudy blue eyes like star sapphires. Rachel face powder would make Vining's fresh pink skin as sallow as Faustina's. He was actor enough to subdue the mocking expression of his lips to Faustina's look of wistful seriousness. Especially when his face was shaded by a wide hatbrim.

"He discovered the resemblance when Alice Aitchison was at Maidstone a year ago. He wanted to break the strict rule against male visitors on any day but Sunday. He was in love and he wanted to visit her at any time of day or night he pleased. So he used a trick as old as pagan Rome. Remember how the intrusion of young Clodius, dressed as a woman, at a ceremony deigned for women only, caused Caesar to divorce the wife that wasn't above suspicion? Like Clodius, Vining was young, slight, beardless. He could pass as one girl among many girls if he wore a girl's clothing and kept at a distance from others in a dim light. But he didn't pass as one girl among many. He was mistaken for a particular girl — one of the young teachers, Faustina Crayle. Miss Maidstone kept her books on psychic research under lock and key, but they were there. Trust some of the girls to get hold of the key and read about the *doppelganger* myth. Stories of a mysterious 'double' began to crystallize around Faustina. Alice Aitchison would report the fact to Vining with great glee for she would have noticed his resemblance to Faustina and she would realize how the stories had started. But Vining himself would know why that resemblance existed. Thanks to Watkins, he knew all there was to know about his grandfather's natural daughter and he was in a position to recognize that rather unusual name — Faustina Crayle. He made a point of seeing Faustina for himself. He saw how strong the family resemblance was though the difference in sex, and therefore in dress, made it unapparent to the casual observer. All this gave him the idea for a unique method of murder that would not leave any mark on Faustina's body or even require his presence at the moment of her death.

"When she went to Brereton, he sent his little sister Barbara to the same school as an unconscious spy, reporting to him quite innocently all that went on inside the school. The front and back stairs and the French windows at Brereton made it fairly easy for him to slip in and out of the building, especially when most people who saw him at a distance mistook him for Faustina who had a right there. For his more startling effects he chose his witnesses carefully — a stupid, suggestible young servant and two flighty little girls of thirteen, one his own sister who wouldn't give him away if she ever guessed the truth. I think his meeting with you on the stair was an accident. You were too shrewd an observer for him to seek you deliberately. But there were bound to be some accidents. He made the best of that one, slipping through the drawing-room and out a French window, just before Arlene came in from the dining room. He let his hand brush your arm purposely because he knew his hand was icy cold — he had just come in from outside — and he knew that coldness would be almost as effective as the filmy, unreal texture of the Sagée double's touch which he couldn't imitate. At Brereton he appeared in a coat and hat copied exactly from Faustina's and reproduced one striking incident from the case of Emilie Sagée — slow motions during the appearance of her double. Presumably he did this by drugging something Faustina ate or drank, timed to affect her at the moment he appeared as her double.

"No wonder Faustina herself came to believe in the double and fear it. That was how he killed her — with her own fear. He knew the plan of the Seabright cottage — it had belonged to his grandfather. He knew about the two parlors which were the same size and shape, with bay windows facing each other at opposite ends, and the pair of glass doors between the two rooms. Watkins could tell him they were still decorated in the same colors. The rest was simple. He went down to Seabright in Faustina's absence. He obtained mirrors the same size and shape as the panes of glass in the pair of doors and fitted a mirror over each pane, inside the wooden frame. He put dead bulbs in the ceiling fixture of the first parlor. That was all. Except the telephone call to Faustina last night. He would introduce himself as one of the mysterious family she had wondered about for so long and make an appointment to meet her at her own house that same night. He could tell her things about Watkins and her mother that would make his identification convincing. Then he went off to the Crane Club with Alice Aitchison to establish an alibi.

"At eleven fifty Faustina let herself into the dark, empty cottage with a latchkey, leaving it in the door while she snapped on the hall light. It was chance that she stepped into the first parlor next. But she was bound to enter it sooner or later that evening and when she did — only one thing could happen. She would press the ceiling switch beside the hall archway. No light would come on since the bulbs were dead. A movement would draw her eyes to the pair of doors, now mirrored. Whose movement? Her own, reflected there. *But she wouldn't know it was a reflection!* She would believe with absolute conviction that there was transparent glass in those doors and that she was looking *through* it. There was nothing to tell her in that first, swift glance that she was look-ing at the first parlor reflected in a mirror, instead of the second parlor viewed through glass — remember, both rooms were alike in shape and color and the low, irregular light from the single lamp in the hall was deceptive by the time it reached the mirrors in the pair of doors.

"You see what happened? *Faustina's own reflection killed her!* She had a weak heart. For over a year her mind had been subjected to intensive psychological preparation for belief in the *doppelganger*. As she said: *when you've lost your job twice because of a thing, you don't think it's just imagination.* She toppled face down, frightened to death by the oldest, the simplest of all illusions — her own reflection. She lay dead of terror when there was nothing to terrify anyone — merely a mirror imaging the prone body of a dead girl.

"Vining had to remove the mirrors before the body was found. He went down to Seabright to do that after he'd given Faustina ample time to die. He wore woman's dress for the last time. He might not have been seen at all. As it happened he was seen and mistaken once again for Faustina. When the police checked the time and found 'Faustina' had been 'seen' after she was dead, only one thing could happen. The story of Faustina's double became the story of Faustina's ghost and the police would write the whole thing off as village superstition.

"As Faustina's double, Vining tricked the eye adroitly. No doubt he wore rubber-soled shoes to trick the ear as well, for the double never made a sound. His cold hand even tricked your sense of touch. But there was one grosser, more primordial sense he didn't trick — smell."

"But the double had no odor at all!" objected Mrs. Lightfoot.

"That's the point. Every human body has some odor. Yet you said the double had none. Did that mean it really was inhuman? Or was there some condition that would make one body seem odorless to another? There is just one such condition: when two bodies have the same odor — for example, when they are both using the same perfume. A nonsmoker kissing a smoker is keenly aware of nicotine fumes. Two smokers kissing will each believe the other has a clean breath because neither detects the odor.

"You used lemon verbena. So I knew, after my first talk with you, that *Faustina's double was someone who also used lemon verbena.* Any other odor you would have noticed — except your own. Faustina herself used lavender water. You told me so and I noticed it when I was with her. So the double couldn't be Faustina herself. That narrowed my search considerably. I wanted someone who looked like Faustina, someone who used lemon verbena, someone who had connections with both Maidstone and Brereton, someone who had a motive for injuring or destroying Faustina. Vining alone met all those conditions. When I entered my own library last night I caught a hint of lemon verbena. I wasn't sure which of the three was using it — Mrs. Chase, Miss Aitchison, or Vining. But Vining was the most likely since he was the only man among them and you had told me it was a man's lotion. Today, the moment he came downstairs, I noticed it again. I suppose lemon verbena was such an ingrained habit with him that he forgot to suppress it when he was impersonating the double.''

"You've solved the mystery of Faustina Crayle," said Mrs. Lightfoot. "But what about the mystery of Emilie Sagée?''

Basil slowed for a sharp curve, then accelerated. "That is a mystery that we must always see through a glass, darkly . . .''

# Snowball in July

## Ellery Queen

*Though he's not generally thought of as a locked room writer, Ellery Queen has produced four novels and more than a dozen short stories and radio plays which deal with impossible crime of one sort or another. This is one of his best, about a jewel robber, a missing witness, and a vanishing train.*

A T PLAYFUL moments Diamond Jim Grady liked to refer to himself as a magician, a claim no one disputed — least of all the police. Grady's specialty was jewel robbery at gunpoint, a branch of felonious vaudeville which he had elevated to an art form. His heists were miracles of advance information, timing, teamwork, and deception. And once he got his hands on the loot it vanished with the speed of light, to be seen no more in the shape the manufacturing jeweler had wrought.

Grady's most spectacular trick was keeping himself and his fellow artists out of jail. He would drill his small company without mercy in the wisdom of keeping their mugs covered, their mitts gloved, and their traps shut while on stage. There was rarely a slip in his performances; when one occurred, the slipping assistant disappeared. As Diamond Jim reasonably pointed out, "What witness can identify a slob that ain't here?"

Grady might have gone on forever collecting other people's pretties and driving the law and insurance companies mad, but he pulled one trick too many.

In explanation it is necessary to peep into Diamond Jim's love life. Lizbet had been his big moment for two years and ten months — a slim eye-stopper as golden and glittery as any choice piece in his collection. Now, in underworld society a romantic attachment of almost three years' duration is equivalent to an epic passion, and Lizbet may be forgiven the folly of having developed delusions of permanence. Unfortunately, that was not all she developed; include an appetite for pizza pies and French ice cream, and along with it her figure. So one night, when Grady's bloated eye cased the dainty anatomy of Maybellene, pivot girl of the Club Swahili line, that was all for Lizbet.

One of Grady's staff, a lovelorn lapidary who could grind an ax as well as a diamond, tipped Lizbet the bad news from a phone booth in the Swahili men's room even as Diamond Jim prepared toothily to escort Maybellene home.

Lizbet was revolted at the perfidy of man. She also realized that unless she lammed with great rapidity her life was not worth the crummiest bangle on the junk counter of the nearest Five-and-Dime. She knew far, far too many of Diamond Jim's professional secrets; she even knew where a couple of bodies — of ex-slobs — were buried.

So Lizbet took barely the time to grab an old summer mink and a fistful of unaltered mementos from Grady's latest personal appearance before she did an impromptu vanishing act of her own.

Immediately Lizbet became the most popular girl in town. Everybody wanted her, especially the police and Grady. The smart money, doping past performances strictly, was on Grady, but this time the smart money took a pratfall. Lizbet was not in town at all. She was in Canada, where — according to every Royal Northwest movie Lizbet had ever seen — the Mounties were large and incorruptible and a girl could think without worrying about stopping a shiv in her back. Having thought, Lizbet slung the summer mink about her plump shoulders, taxied to the nearest police station, and demanded protection and immunity in exchange for a pledge to take the witness stand back home and talk herself, if need be, into lockjaw.

And she insisted on being ushered into a cell while Montreal got in touch with New York.

The long distance negotiations took twenty-four hours — just long enough for the news to leak out and inundate the front pages of the New York newspapers.

"So now Grady knows where she is," fumed Inspector Queen. He was on special assignment in charge of the case. "He'll go for her sure. She told Piggott and Hesse when they flew up to Montreal that she can even drape a first-degree murder rap around Grady's fat neck."

"Me," said Sergeant Velie gloomily, "I wouldn't give a plugged horse car token for that dame's chances of getting back to New York with a whole hide."

"What is he, a jet pilot?" asked Ellery. "Fly her down."

"She won't fly — has a fear of heights," snapped his father. "It's on the level, Ellery. Lizbet's the only girl friend Grady ever had who turned down a penthouse."

"Train or car, then," said Ellery. "What's the hassle?"

"A train he'd make hash out of," said Sergeant Velie, "and a car he'd hijack some truck to run off the road into a nice thousand-foot hole."

"You're romancing."

"Maestro, you don't know Grady!"

"Then you're tackling this hind end to," said Ellery negligently. "Dad, have Grady and his gang picked up on some charge and locked in a cell. By the time they're sprung this woman can be safe on ice somewhere in Manhattan."

"On ice is where she'll wind up," said Sergeant Velie.

When Ellery found that Diamond Jim had anticipated interference and disappeared with his entire company, including Maybellene, a more respectful glint came into his eye.

"Let's pull a trick or two of our own. Grady will assume that you'll get Lizbet to New York as quickly as possible. He knows she won't fly and that you wouldn't risk the long car trip. So he'll figure she'll be brought down by rail. Since the fastest way by rail is a through express, it's the crack Montreal train he'll be gunning for. Does he know Piggott and Hesse by sight?"

"Let's say he does," said Inspector Queen, perking up notwithstanding the heat, "and I see what you mean. I'll fly Johnson and Goldberg up there along with a policewoman of Lizbet's build and general appearance. Piggott and Hesse take the policewoman onto the Special, heavily veiled, while Goldie and Johnson hustle Lizbet onto a slow train —"

"You think this Houdini plays with potsies?" demanded Sergeant Velie. "You got to do better than that, my masters."

"Oh, come, Sergeant, he's only flesh and blood," said Ellery soothingly. "Anyway, we're going to do better than that. To befuddle him completely, somewhere along the route we'll have her taken off and complete the trip by automobile.

In fact, Dad, we'll take her off ourselves — the three of us. Feel better, Velie?''

But the Sergeant shook his head. "You don't know Grady.''

So Detectives Goldberg and Johnson and an ex-chorus girl named Policewoman Bruusgaard flew to Montreal, and at the zero hour Detectives Piggott and Hesse ostentatiously spirited Policewoman Bruusgaard — veiled and sweltering in Lizbet's own mink — into a drawing room on the Canadian Limited. Thirty minutes after the Limited rolled out of the terminal Detectives Johnson and Goldberg, attired as North Country backwoodsmen and lugging battered suitcases, swaggered behind Lizbet into the smoking car of a sooty, suffocating all-coach local-express entitled laughingly in the timetables The Snowball. Lizbet was in dowdy clothes, her coiffure was now blue-black, and her streaming face, scrubbed clean of heavy makeup, seemed a sucker's bet to fool even Grady — so many wrinkles and crow's-feet showed.

And the game was en route.

For on a sizzling hot morning in July two unmarked squad cars set out from Center Street, Manhattan, for upstate New York. In one rode the Queens and Sergeant Velie, in the other six large detectives.

The Sergeant drove lugubriously. "It won't work," he predicted. "He operates practically by radar. And he can spot and grease an itchy palm from nine miles up. I tell you Grady's got this up his sleeve right now.''

"You croak like a witch doctor with bellyache," remarked Inspector Queen, squirming in his damp clothes. "Just remember, Velie, if we don't get to Wapaug with time to spare —''

Wapaug was a whistle stop on the C. & N.Y. Railroad. It consisted of several simmering coal piles, a straggly single street, and a roasted-looking cubby of a station. The two cars drove up to the brown little building and the Inspector and Ellery went inside. No one was in the hotbox of a waiting room but an elderly man wearing sleeve garters and an eye-shade who was poking viciously at the innards of a paralyzed electric fan.

"What's with The Snowball?"

"Number 113? On time, mister."

"And she's due —?"

"10:18."

"Three minutes," said Ellery. "Let's go."

The cars had drawn up close, one at each end of the platform. Two of the six detectives were leaning exhaustedly against an empty handtruck. Otherwise, the baked platform was deserted.

They all squinted north.

10:18 came. 10:18 went.

At 10:20 they were still squinting north.

The stationmaster was in the doorway now, also squinting north.

"Hey!" rasped Inspector Queen, swatting a mosquito. "Where was that train on time last?"

"At Grove Junction." The stationmaster peered up the tracks, which looked as if they had just come out of a blast furnace. "Where the yards and roundhouse are. It's the all-train stop two stations north."

"Train 113 stops at the next station north, too, doesn't she? Marmion? Did you get a report on her from Marmion?"

"I was just gonna check, mister."

They followed him back into the hotbox and the elderly man put on his slippery headphones and got busy with the telegraph key. "Marmion stationmaster says she pulled in and out on time. Left Marmion 10:12."

"On time at Marmion," said Ellery, "and it's only a six-minute run from Marmion to Wapaug —" He wiped his neck.

"Funny," fretted his father. It was now 10:22. "How could she lose four minutes on a six-minute run? Even on this railroad?"

"Somethin's wrong," said the stationmaster, blowing the sweat off his eyeshade band. He turned suddenly to his key.

The Queens went back to the platform to stare up the local track toward Marmion. After a moment Ellery hurried back into the waiting room.

"Stationmaster, could she have switched to the express track at Marmion and gone right through Wapaug without stopping?" He knew the answer in advance, since they had driven along the railroad for miles in their approach to Wapaug; but his brains were frying.

"Nothin's gone through southbound on these tracks since 7:38 this mornin'."

Ellery hurried out again, fingering his collar. His father was sprinting up the platform toward the squad car. The two detectives had already rejoined their mates in the other car and it was roaring up the highway, headed north.

"Come on!" shouted Inspector Queen. Ellery barely made it before Sergeant Velie sent the car rocketing toward the road. "Somehow Grady got onto the trick — a smear, a leak! He's waylaid The Snowball between here and Marmion!"

They kept watching the ties. The automobile road paralleled the railroad at a distance of barely twenty feet, with nothing between but gravel.

And there was no sign of a passenger train, in motion or standing still, wrecked or whole. Or of a freight, or even a handcar. Headed south — or, for that matter, headed north.

They almost shot through Marmion before they realized that they had covered the entire distance between the two stations. The other car was parked below the weathered eaves of an even smaller shed than the one at Wapaug. As they twisted back in reverse, four of the detectives burst out of the little station.

"She left Marmion at 10:12, all right, Inspector!" yelled one. "Stationmaster says we're crazy. We must have missed it!"

The two cars raced back toward Wapaug.

Inspector Queen glared at the rails flashing alongside. "Missed it? A whole passenger train? Velie, slow down!"

"That Grady," moaned Sergeant Velie.

Ellery almost devoured a knuckle, saying nothing. He kept staring at the glittering rails. They winked back, jeering. It was remarkable how straight this stretch of track between Marmion and Wapaug was, how uncluttered by scenery. Not a tree or building beside the right of way. No water anywhere — not so much as a rain puddle. No curves, no grades; no siding, spur line, tunnel, bridge. Not a gully, gorge, or ravine. And no sign of wreckage. . . . The rails stretched, perfect and unburdened, along the floor of the valley. For all the concealment or trickery possible, they might have been a series of parallel lines drawn with a ruler on a sheet of blank paper.

And there was Wapaug's roasted little station again.

And no Snowball.

The Inspector's voice cracked. "She pulls into Grove Junction on time. She gets to Marmion on time. She pulls out of Marmion on time. But she doesn't show up at Wapaug. Then she's got to be between Marmion and Wapaug! What's wrong with that?" He challenged them, hopefully, to find something wrong with it.

Sergeant Velie accepted. "Only one thing," he said in a hollow voice. "She ain't."

That did it. "I suppose Grady's palmed it!" screamed his superior. "That train's between Marmion and Wapaug somewhere, and I'm going to find it or — or buy me a ouija board!"

So back they went to Marmion, driving along the railroad at ten miles per hour. And then they turned around and crept Wapaugward again, to shuffle into the waiting room and look piteously at the stationmaster. But that railroad man was sitting in his private oven mopping his chafed forehead and blinking at the shimmering valley through his north window.

No one said a word for some time.

When the word came, everyone leaped. "Stationmaster!" said Ellery. "Get your Marmion man on the key again. Find out if, after leaving Marmion at 10:12, *The Snowball didn't turn back.*"

"Back?" The elderly man brightened "Sure!" He seized his telegraph key.

"That's it, Ellery!" cried Inspector Queen. "She left Marmion southbound all right, but then she backed up north *past* Marmion again for a repair, and I'll bet she's in the Grove Junction yards or roundhouse right now!"

"Grove Junction says," whispered the stationmaster, "that she ain't in their yards or roundhouse and never was — just went through on time. And Marmion says 113 pulled out southbound and didn't come back."

All were silent once more.

Then the Inspector slapped at a dive-bombing squadron of bluebottle flies, hopping on one foot and howling, "But how can a whole train disappear? Snowball! Snowball in July! What did Grady do, melt her down for ice water?"

"And drank her," said Sergeant Velie, licking his lips.

"Wait," said Ellery. "Wait . . . I know where The Snowball is!" He scuttled toward the door. "And if I'm right we'd better hurry — or kiss Lizbet goodbye!"

"But *where?*" implored Inspector Queen as the two cars flashed north again, toward Marmion.

"Down Grady's gullet," shouted the Sergeant, wrestling his wheel.

"That's what he wanted us to think," shouted Ellery in reply. "Faster, Sergeant! Train leaves Marmion and never shows up at the next station south, where we're waiting to take Lizbet off. Vanishes without a trace. Between Marmion and Wapaug there's nothing at all to explain what could have happened to her — no bridge to fall from, no water or ravine to fall into, no tunnel to hide in, no anything — just a

straight line on flat bare country. Marvelous illusion. Only
the same facts that give it the appearance of magic also explain it. . . . No, Velie, don't slow down," Ellery yelled as
the dreary little Marmion station came into view. "Keep
going north — *past* Marmion!"

"North past Marmion?" said his father, bewildered. "But
the train came *through* Marmion, Ellery, then headed
south . . ."

"The Snowball's nowhere south of Marmion, is it? And
from the facts it's a physical impossibility for her to be anywhere south of Marmion. So she *isn't* south of Marmion,
Dad. *She never went through Marmion at all.*"

"But the Marmion stationmaster said —"

"What Grady bribed him to say! It was all a trick to keep
us running around in circles between Marmion and Wapaug,
while Grady and his gang held up the train *between Marmion
and Grove Junction!* Isn't that gunfire up ahead? We're still
in time!"

And there, four miles north of Marmion, where the valley
entered the foothills, cowered The Snowball, frozen to the
spot. A huge trailer-truck dumped athwart the local tracks
had stopped her, and judging from the gun flashes the train
was under bombardment of half a dozen bandits hidden in
the woods nearby.

Two figures, one lying still and the other crawling toward
the woods dragging a leg, told them that the battle was not
one-sided. From two of the shattered windows of a railroad
car a stream of bullets poured into the woods. What Grady
& Co. had not known was that Northwoodsmen Goldberg
and Johnson had carried in their battered suitcases two sub-
machine guns and a large supply of ammunition.

When the carful of New York detectives broke out their
arsenal and cut loose, the Grady gang dropped their weapons
and trudged out with their arms held high . . .

Ellery and Inspector Queen found Lizbet on the floor of
the smoking car with assorted recumbent passengers, in a litter of hot cartridge shells, while Detectives Johnson and

Goldberg prepared rather shakily to enjoy a couple of king-size cigarettes.

"You all right, young woman?" asked the Inspector anxiously. "Anything I can get you?"

Lizbet looked up out of a mess of dyed hair, gunsmoke, sweat, and tears. "You said it, pop — that witness chair!"

# The Newtonian Egg

**Peter Godfrey**

*Peter Godfrey, a South African writer and journalist who now resides in England, has long been fascinated with impossible crimes and Chesterton-like paradox in his short stories. This one about an impossible poisoning features an especially small "locked room" — an egg!*

THE DYING MAN," said Hal Brooke, "ate a hearty wedding breakfast."

On the other side of the room Kurtz, also with a tray on his knees, sneered. He said: "It's a funny thing about this disease. You can feel on top of the world one minute, and be knocking at the pearly gates the next. Even if you are getting married this afternoon, you could pop off just as well today as any other day." He grinned. "Maybe the excitement will make it even more likely. You know, I've been thinking about it for the last few minutes — trying to imagine which would be the most appropriate moment for you to kick the bucket. At first I thought during the ceremony . . . but there's a much better time."

"Yes?"

"Yes. In that fraction of a second before the final consummation. Although, of course, almost any time today would still be poetically satisfying."

Brooke said softly: "You love me very much, don't you, Kurtzie?"

In the third bed, Winton moved his bandaged wrists, moaned and cursed. "Shut up," he said. "Shut up. We've got to die — we know that. But why keep talking about it? Why talk?"

"Winton," said Kurtz, "doesn't like talk. Oh, no. He prefers action — only he bungles his actions. When you managed to steal that scalpel, Winton, why didn't you just cut your throat and have done with it? Didn't you realise the nurses would be bound to discover your cut wrists before anything serious happened? Or did you just go through the motions, with some half-witted idea of gaining sympathy?"

"I should have used it on you," said Winton. "It would have stopped your infernal talking."

"Minds," said Brooke. "Funny things. Look at yours, Kurtz. A good brain, education and experience behind it, a capacity to think constructively when you choose. Only, you don't choose. You prefer to twist and distort into the meanest, most personal, ugliest channels you can conceive. A real mental prostitution. And then there's you, Winton — no real mind at all, only a few cockeyed emotions. No intelligence. Just a sort of blind stretching forward to satisfy the need of the moment.''

Winton said: ''What do you know about what goes on in my mind? What about the scalpel? Could you have got one, Mr Genius?''

''If I wanted one,'' said Brooke, ''I'd get one. And if I wanted to use it, I'd use it properly. I don't know how you got it, Winton, but I'm pretty certain it was by accident. And I'm not running down your lack of mind through malice. Oh no. You're the luckiest of the three of us. When you go, you've got so very little to lose.''

Winton cursed. He repeated: ''How do you know what I think about?''

''I don't — except by inference. But let's find out. Take this boiled egg, for instance. Here, let me hold it in my hand. Now, look at it, and tell me what you think.''

As Winton hesitated, Kurtz laughed from his bed. ''Come on, Winton, I want to hear this, too.''

''It's just . . . an egg,'' said Winton. ''Laid by a hen, on a farm somewhere. And boiled here in the kitchen.''

''And brought to me, warm and white and unbroken,'' said Brooke. ''I know. That's how your mind works. But this egg tells my mind a lot more.''

''Like what?''

''Oh, many things . . . It reminds me, for instance, of Isaac Newton, of his discoveries — the law of gravitation — and from there, of space and time and the universe, of Einstein and relativity. And it reminds me on the other side, of pre-Newtonian science, of the theories of transmutation of metals; and I see that Newton is the link, and the two sides of the chain meet again today in the atom physicists.''

''You're talking nonsense,'' said Winton. ''What has an egg to do with Isaac Newton?''

''Ah, so you haven't even heard *that* story? Let me tell it to you — maybe it will provide some consolation for you. It shows how even great minds have their moments of aberration . . . You see, a friend once came into Newton's kitchen, and there was the savant holding an egg in the palm of his hand — like this — staring at it in utter concentration — and on the stove next to him his watch boiled merrily in a pot of water.''

Again, Kurtz laughed. Winton looked at Brooke uncertainly. He said: "You're still talking in the air . . .''

But Brooke was warming to his theme. "The human mind,'' he said, "what a magnificent mechanism! Properly applied, it creates miracles. Nothing, basically, is impossible —''

"Except us.'' In his triumph Winton spat. "What about us? All the best brains in science, all working on us, and they can't help. None of them can help.''

Kurtz said: "All the same, Brooke's right. One day they'll find a cure. Maybe the day after you die, Winton. Or the day before. That's why your scalpel idea was so completely and utterly foolish.''

"They still need data,'' said Brooke. "Sorry. I should have been more explicit. I should have said nothing is basically impossible when all the facts are known. Do you ever read detective stories?''

Winton said: "Trash.''

"Not all of them. I'm thinking of a particular story, written by a man who's now dead — Jacques Futrelle. A magnificent story called *The Problem of Cell 13*. Futrelle's hero is a man he calls The Thinking Machine. He claimed that if he were locked in the condemned cell under the usual conditions, with nothing except his own magnificent mental equipment, he would *think* himself out. And he did, Winton, he did.''

"In a story, yes. Anything's possible in a story. '

"Logic is the common denominator between good fiction and life. That's why I say your scalpel idea was clumsy.

There are so many easier, more ingenious methods. Now, if
I wanted to get rid of myself —''

"No," said Kurtz. "I don't like suicide — not even used
as an example. Rather, assume that you were planning to kill
Winton. Or better still, that I wanted to kill you. Much truer
to life.''

"All right, we'll say you want to kill me. And that you
use your mind in the way you ought to use it. You'll pick
something commonplace and apparently innocent, like — like
this egg here. Yes, the egg's a good idea. First, you lay your
hands on some virulent poison — if Winton could find a
scalpel, you most certainly could find some poison. And you
would work out a method of getting the poison inside the
unbroken shell of the egg . . .''

Winton said: "That's an impossibility, Brooke, a complete
impossibility.''

"It is? That's what they said about The Thinking Machine
and his guarded cell. And there's another angle, too — also
from detective fiction. In a book called *The Three Coffins* one
of the modern masters of detective fiction, John Dickson
Carr, had his chief character giving a lecture on how to commit murder in a hermetically sealed room. If I remember cor-
rectly, there were three main methods, each with dozens of
variations. And all perfectly possible — remember that,
Winton. And if a murderer can get into a sealed room, commit a murder and disappear, he could also get into a sealed
egg. The same principles apply. And the egg could be
brought to me, like this one, through the normal innocent
channels, and I could crack the shell, as I'm doing now,
scoop up the egg — yes, do all the natural things, absolutely
unsuspecting, put the spoon in my mouth, and die.''

He put the spoonful of egg into his mouth.

And died.


"Mr le Roux," said Nurse Metter, and then: "No, I can't
call you that. Hal has told me so much about you. I'm going

to call you Rolf, and you must call me Doris. I can't go on calling my husband's best friend by his surname, can I?"

"Definitely not." The brown eyes twinkled, and behind the beard the full lips curved in a smile. "I would have liked to have come earlier, but Hal's letter didn't give me much time. Still, I suppose I'll have a chance for a chat with him before the ceremony?"

"Of course. The padre won't get here until after lunch, and you can see Hal as soon as he's finished his breakfast. He's in Ward 3, just down the passage. You can follow me in when I go to fetch the trays. They'll be ringing for me any second now."

Rolf thought of the letter from Hal in his pocket. And he thought: "Nice girl. If only Hal could live his normal span . . ."

The girl must have seen something of his mental images. "I'm afraid I'm just a little bit nervous," she said. "You see, it's not every day . . ."

She turned as the buzzer behind her sounded, and Rolf noticed that the number 3 had dropped in the indicator. But the buzzer kept on, urgently, insistently.

"Oh," said Doris Metter. "Something's wrong!"

She whirled past Rolf, moved in long-limbed strides down the passage. He came after her. Just inside the door of Ward 3 she paused momentarily, clutching her throat with one hand.

The contorted body of Hal Brooke sprawled in a half-sitting position on the bed, knees drawn up and twisted as though from a violent spasm. There was a thin line of froth on his lips.

Doris Metter said "Oh" again; she ran forward, stumbled over the tray and crockery on the floor, struggled back to her feet, and threw herself sobbing on the breast of the corpse on the bed.

Rolf le Roux said to the man in the bed opposite: "Keep ringing the bell." He put his hands on Doris Metter's shoulders, and gently drew her away. While doing so, he caught the elusive smell, bent over the body to make more certain. When hc straightened again, his face was very grave.

Another nurse came to the door of the ward, hesitated only long enough to call out down the passage, and hurried forward. She caught the sobbing figure of Doris Metter in her arms and started to lead her gently from the room. They were only halfway to the door when the young doctor came in, took in the significance of the scene, and went to the living before the dead. He spoke quickly, consolingly; gave crisp instructions to the other nurses. Only then he came to look at the body.

He said to Rolf: "You're Mr le Roux, of course. Hal told me all about you. I'm Randall." And then: "This must have been a bad shock for you. Tragic, under the circumstances. But you must remember it could be expected to happen at any time."

Rolf's eyes were hard and implacable. "Smell his lips," he said.

Randall looked at him for a long second, then bent over the body. His expression also changed. He said: "I see."

The man in the bed opposite shook his head, as though to clear it. "Poison," he said conversationally. "And it was suicide, you know, even though it probably doesn't look like it. Brooke was talking about suicide just before it happened."

The third patient sat up in bed, waved a bandaged wrist. "You're a liar, Kurtz. He was talking about you killing him."

"Here," said Randall, suspiciously, "what's all this?"

"I'll tell you," said Kurtz. "I think I remember almost every word of the conversation. And don't interrupt until I've finished, Winton. You can say all you want to, then." Rapidly he sketched out the conversation. "Is that right?"

"That's right," said Winton grudgingly.

Dr Randall grimly got down on hands and knees, sniffed over the shattered egg that was lying on the floor, looked up, and nodded.

"And the egg," said Rolf, "was opened by Brooke? Is that all that happened?"

"That's all," said Winton.

Randall started to say: "There's no way of getting potassium cyanide into an unbroken —" He stopped, because Kurtz was shaking with laughter.

"Poor old Winton and his literal mind," said Kurtz. "How Brooke would have loved to hear him now! Of course something else happened, but something so casual and commonplace that Winton would never think of mentioning it."

"And that was?"

"Brooke cracked the egg, and took the spoonful to his mouth, and he was talking all the time. But between these two actions he did something else. He took the salt-cellar from the cruet, poured a quantity on the surface of the egg, and mixed it in with the spoon. And only then did he take his mouthful."

"You mean," asked Randall, "the salt . . . ?" But while he was still speaking, Rolf was already on the floor, searching among the debris of the fallen tray.

"There it is," said Winton, "still lying on the bed."

Randall picked it up off the counterpane, unscrewed the top, and held the body of the container to his nose. He took one of the white grains, smelled it again to make sure, and touched it with his tongue. "No," he said, "this is ordinary table salt."

"So," said Kurtz, and looked quizzically at Rolf le Roux.

But Rolf said, almost to himself, "The timing . . ." and then, "How long did it take? I mean everything — from the moment the nurse left the breakfast trays to the moment she came back in answer to your ring?"

"Four or five minutes," said Kurtz.

"No," said Winton. "Longer than that. Say eight or nine."

"And all the time you both stayed in bed? You did not move?"

"I stayed in bed," said Winton. "But I don't know about

Kurtz. I was too busy looking at Brooke to notice what Kurtz did."

Kurtz smiled. "I stayed in bed, too." He looked at Rolf. "You know, Brooke was a real admirer of yours. He advertised you — the great Sherlock of the Cape Town C.I.D. It's rather interesting to watch you now — standing there, baffled over Newton's egg."

"Not Newton's egg," said Rolf. "Newton's apple.'"

Except for the corpse, he was alone in the Ward. Kurtz and Winton had been searched and taken out. Dr Randall had gone down the passage to telephone the police post at Bossiesfontein. He pulled the letter out of his pocket and read it again.

Dear Rolf,

If you ask me how I am, I will tell you that I am dying very nicely, thank you. Which is in direct contrast to the two other unfortunates in this ward. We all three are under sentence of death with intestinal T.B.; but, speaking strictly for myself, once you get accustomed to the feeling of general malaise and the knowledge that any given morning — if you will forgive the Irishism — you may wake up to find yourself dead, you can find some compensations, even in the valley of the shadow.

In my own case, I am delighted to find that my wits have never been so sharp and crystal-clear and — now hold on to your malodorous pipe — I am also getting married.

Don't get a shock — it's all perfectly feasible and natural. I've checked with the quacks here, and read up all the authorities myself just to make sure, and this is certain — the disease, in the form I have it, is neither contagious nor infectious nor transmissible by heredity. Only fatal. And think of this, Rolf — I can still partially cheat death if I have a child.

And I'm *going* to have that child. It's all arranged. One of the doctors here by the name of Randall pulled strings — particularly decent of him because I think he's got a soft spot for Doris himself. (Oh, yes, of course, I should have told you — the girl is a nurse here, Doris Metter.) Anyway, he's doing everything possible. After the ceremony, we move straight into a private ward. Doris has been examined, too, and is 100 per cent healthy.

I know this all sounds like cold-blooded stud arrangements, but I may not have the time to waste on tact and social graces. I want a child, and I want a healthy child — one that has a chance to make better use of its life than I have.

Doris not only understands, she shares my urge. Last night she told me why. You see, she had an elder brother she worshipped, and he also died of an incurable disease — haemophilia — at the age of fourteen. I suppose there is basically some sort of Freudian identification in her mind between me and her brother, and she feels that in our child — and it'll be a son for sure — she'll have me and her brother too. But that's not entirely the whole story for either of us. You see, oldtimer, we're really in love. The ceremony is on Tuesday — and don't you dare send me your congratulations by letter. I want to hear them verbally, direct from the labyrinths of your beard. If you catch a train from Cape Town on Sunday night, you should be here on the morning of the marriage, the lucky day.

More when I see you in the flesh —

Hal.

Not the letter of a suicide, thought Rolf. And yet, in three days much could happen. The half-life he was living, the twisted motives . . .

To decide definitely, there were many other things to be found out. Access to poisons, for instance. Opportunity, generally. More facts were needed, new angles. Sometimes, looked at from a different direction, the impossible became obvious . . . and he owed it to Hal to make absolutely sure.

Rolf found Dr Randall sitting at the desk in the office along the passage. He asked: "Have you contacted the police?"

"No," said Randall. "I was . . . well, to tell the truth, I was waiting for you. I wanted to have a talk."

"Yes?"

"I . . . Look here, *must* I call the police? Won't you forget about the poison — let me sign a death certificate? What good will it do with the police prying around, badgering Dor — Nurse Metter? What for? Isn't it enough that Hal's dead, without him also being branded a suicide? Isn't it really better my way?"

Rolf said: "Maybe it would be . . . easier. But what if it was not suicide? Would you want his murderer to go scot-free?"

Randall was deeply upset. "Don't forget he was a doomed man in any case. And who could have killed him? Kurtz? Winton? Also doomed men. Is it worthwhile putting all this further torture on an innocent girl?"

"Hal Brooke was my friend," said Rolf. He sat for a moment, with his eyes far away. "For his sake, and if I were *sure* . . . but I first have to be sure, you understand. We can wait two hours, and after that I promise you I will make up my mind."

"Thank you, Mr le Roux. And if I can help in any way . . . ?"

"First, I'd like to know where the poison could have come from."

"In all probability from this room. From that closet over there."

"Locked?"

"Well, yes — but actually the lock slips if you give a sharp jerk on the door. We should have had it repaired, of course, only . . . well, it's just been neglected."

Rolf was staring at the serried bottles and jars on the shelf. He located the tiny potassium cyanide container, and scratched his beard contemplatively. He said: "One thing I don't understand . . . there are poisons here, yes, but there are also harmless drugs. Isn't it unusual to keep them together?''

"Not if you realise that, being so far from town, we dispense most of our own medicines, and that this room is our dispensary.''

"Even so, isn't potassium cyanide rather a strange drug to have here?''

"No. It's a common drug in a T.B. hospital. It's used in making up a very effective cough mixture. A tiny quantity, of course — the basis is a minim two drops to eight ounces of other ingredients.''

"I see. And so it is perfectly possible for one of the patients to walk in here, if he knows about the room, jerk open the locked cupboard, and remove a quantity of poison? Could it be done unseen?''

"Definitely. It was from this room, we think, that Winton stole the scalpel with which he tried to commit suicide. But it would have to be done late at night. During the day, if I'm not here, there's a nurse on duty.''

"Have you actually noticed that anything here was interfered with at any time?''

"No. I can honestly say I've *seen* nothing . . .''

"But?''

"Well, when I came and sat down here just now, I had a feeling that there was something wrong, something out of place. Just a *vague* feeling . . .''

She lay on the bed in the darkened room, and if she had been weeping the atmosphere of tragedy would have seemed less.

"There's nothing to talk about,'' she said. ''It's just . . . horrible. And I don't think you would understand.''

"Perhaps I would,'' said Rolf. ''He was my friend, you know. And he wrote me all about the situation. Let *me* talk, rather. You can tell me whether I am right . . . You see, I know what he wanted — how he felt about having a child. And how you felt. And it seems to me that, even though you loved him, the horror is not so much Hal dying. You knew it would happen, and you were prepared for it. No, the horror in your mind is that the child will never be born, that Hal will not live again in your child, that you have nothing of him left . . .''

She started to cry — hoarse, racking sobs. ''Yes,'' she said, ''yes.'' And then: ''I couldn't even give him his last wish.'' She heaved convulsively in her sobbing ''I had a brother once —'' and then gave herself over to a paroxysm of grief. After a while she quieted. ''He wanted a child so badly. That's the irony of it. So badly that . . . and his face, when he heard from Dr Randall that I had been examined, that there was nothing wrong with me, that I could have his son, a healthy son . . . That was all he had left in life, Rolf.''

He waited for her, then he asked: ''When you brought him his tray in the morning, was there anything about it that was *different*?''

''No,'' she said. ''It was his usual breakfast. A soft-boiled egg and coffee.''

''And the others in the ward — did they also have boiled eggs?''

''No. Kurtz's egg was fried, and Winton had an omelette.''

''Was Hal's egg in any way cracked?''

''No. It was just an egg. I gave the order in the kitchen, and a few minutes later took the three trays in.''

''And after that?''

''I had more trays to carry to other wards. And then I heard that you were here, and I came to speak to you. You know . . . the rest.''

''Yes. But tell me this — from the time you took Hal his tray to the moment we went back to the ward, how long do you think it was?''

''A long time,'' she said. ''At least twenty-five minutes.''

Rolf le Roux came back to the dispensary, sat down at the desk, and put his head in his hands. Motive, he thought, that was the key . . . the motive for suicide — or murder. And he thought again of that last conversation in the ward, the dying man's lecture on Jacques Futrelle and John Dickson Carr. A sealed egg, yes, and Isaac Newton . . . looking at the egg while the watch boiled . .  the law of gravitation . . .

Because his thoughts were travelling in circles he opened his eyes, emptied his mind, and looked around the room.

And looking, he felt what the doctor had experienced before him, the vague unease that a pattern was wrong, that something was out of position. And right in front of his eyes, on the bookshelf above the desk he saw what it was.

The huge volumes of the *British Encyclopaedia of Medical Practice* Volumes 1, 2, 3, 4, 5, 7, 6, 8 — volumes 7,6. One out of place. Which?

The index of volume 7 told him nothing. He turned to volume 6. Gout, granuloma, guinea-worm disease, haemetemesis, haemophilia. He remembered Hal's letter.

Page 123. Definition: An hereditary disease, only affecting males. Prognosis: grave. A fatal illness, and generally fatal in childhood. Females cannot have it, but they do transmit it to male offspring. *And Doris's brother had died of haemophilia.* That meant the disease had been transmitted through her mother. And if Doris herself had a *male* child it would . . . No, that wasn't quite right. Her male child *might* have haemophilia. Not would.

I know something about genetics, thought Rolf, and yet I very nearly made that mistake. A layman reading the first paragraphs and then skipping over the formulae beneath would almost certainly fall into the mental trap, be *sure* that if Doris bore a boy it would certainly be a haemophiliac.

Here was a motive. Yes, for suicide. If Hal, with his searching curiosity had crept in here last night, had looked at the book — how would he have reacted? The poison closet so handy . . . but where would he keep it? What would he use as a container? Would he, with his tidy mind, have destroyed himself without warning Doris of the peril of her blood?

And besides, it was a motive for murder too. Randall, in love with Doris, fond of Hal . . . Suppose he only heard last night that her brother had died of the disease. Suppose he came here to check the truth, and he knew about Hal's urge for the child, and Doris's . . . Might he not have resolved to kill to save her future misery? He had been anxious enough to sign a death certificate . . . No. Not a doctor. Such reasoning would be incredible for a doctor.

Could it be something else, something apart from this, some motive pointing the finger at Kurtz or Winton?

The truth . . .

He saw it. And the room whirled.

Isaac Newton, he thought. How it all came back to him. The talk about the egg . . . and then the proof that Kurtz had actually named the murder weapon. The saltcellar. Because if a man took salt from a cruet stand, when finished he would most likely replace the cellar in the cruet. Especially if he were eating off the limited surfaces of a tray. Or he would put it on the tray. And in his death paroxysms, if the cruet, the tray, everything fell to the floor, then the saltcellar would also fall. Like Newton's apple, obeying the law of gravitation. And if the saltcellar were found on the bed, then someone must have put it there. Or rather, put an *innocent* saltcellar on the bed —

*After gaining possession of the poisoned one.*

And then there was the final irrefutable psychological proof: the perception of time.

Newton and his egg again. A subtlety — the great man's mind was wandering into absent-minded reverie, because although he was staring at what he thought was his watch, he wasn't really seeing it. His mind was wandering because he knew that if he concentrated on his watch *the egg would seem to take longer to boil.*

Kurtz said four or five minutes; Winton said eight or nine.

But Doris Metter thought it was twenty-five minutes. *Because she had been waiting for it to happen.*

And Rolf saw her again, in the cold light of his mind, stumble over the tray on the floor, rise to her feet, weep on the breast of the corpse. And the actions formed two clear patterns. Picking up the poisoned saltcellar, putting down the innocent one.

But he saw also another image. He saw her, last night, the night before her wedding day, standing in the dispensary, picking up the medical book on a curious impulse, reading, and having her whole world collapse in a few lines. And he saw into her mind, too, into the torment and chaos, crystallising in the soul-tearing illogic of her resolution. In his ears again he heard her voice, bubbling through her tears: "I couldn't even give him his last wish, Rolf — not even his last wish."

Rolf de Roux stood up, slowly and heavily, and he walked along the corridor until he met Dr Randall, and he said: "I have made a mistake. You may sign the death certificate."

# The Triple-Lock'd Room

## Lillian de la Torre

*Here's one of Lillian de la Torre's historical mysteries
about Dr. Sam: Johnson. As usual with this fine series,
the problem and its solution have their roots in the literature, history, and art of the Johnsonian age.*

THE AFFAIR of the triple-lock'd room began as an affair of gallantry, and ended as an affair of mystery and horror. The scene of the tragedy was commonplace enough, being the staymaker's house where I lodged near Piccadilly. The *dramatis personae* all lodged there. The strange knot of Jamaicans had the parlour floor. Sanry the drunken rope-dancer pigged it in the attick. The two-pair-of-stairs floor was divided between James Bruce the Abyssinian traveller and your humble servant, James Boswell younger of Auchinleck, advocate, amateur of crime, and friend to the great Sam: Johnson.

Everybody snubbed the rope-dancer; Bruce the traveller snubbed everybody but the Jamaican lady; and the Jamaican lady snubbed nobody. 'Twas pleasant to attend her levee of mornings before I set out on my daily ramble. On a memorable day in that summer of 1775, Dr. Sam: Johnson was my companion in the lady's chamber.

Her name was Mrs. Winwood. She was newly come to London from the plantations to set up for a lady of fashion, and her *boudoir* lacked no detail of the *ton*. 'Twas all in the Chinese taste. The four-poster bed was richly canopied in China damask. Mr. Chippendale's Chinese chairs were everywhere. There was plenty of red and gold lacquer. An ornate cabinet held ivory knickknacks. Gold dragons two feet high writhed up the japanned coal-box and coiled about its brass handles. The fire-place had a brass fender, and for the summer a fan of white paper in the grate. A Gothick book with gilded margins lay open on a marquetry table, though I seriously doubted whether Mistress Winwood could read its crabbed black-letter. Next it a small Benares coffer, open, revealed a blaze of jewelry within.

We had the field to ourselves, save for the lady's fashionable menagerie of creatures. A motley paraqueet pranced on a carven stand. A snubby creature of the canine kind blinked on a silken cushion, half-closing contemptuous eyes in a sooty face.

" 'Tis a picture," cried I, surveying the scene, "from the pencil of Mr. Hogarth!"

"Aye," assented Dr. Johnson, "it shall be called *The Lady's Toilette-table.*"

Indeed only my burly friend himself in his old snuff-brown suit was out of drawing as he sat oscillating upon one of the Chippendale chairs, causing the chair to creak ominously and the Jamaican lady to flinch.

'Twas the sweetest little pink-and-gold pocket Venus ever I saw, sitting at her toilette-table among a confusion of patch-boxes and ribbands, her mask, her fan, her stay-lace, her pomander, lying lost in the litter. She wore a sacque of willow-green tissue, frothing with lace about a bosom more revealed than hid. There were diamonds at throat, wrist, and bosom. The waves of her dusky hair were piled high. She wore a patch like a half-moon beside one liquid black eye, and a patch like a star at the edge of the tiny, perfect pout of her mouth. Her skin glowed like a golden peach. She smiled upon us with pursed lips, making a mouth like a kiss. I could have been her knight-errant.

Much I envied the tiny black page who leaned at her knee. Not that the little savage appreciated his position; for though gorgeous in cloth-of-gold caftan and turban plumed and jewelled, he bore in his ugly brown face a timeless sorrow.

"Sure 'tis a Lilliputian philosopher," remarked Dr. Sam: Johnson, scanning the impassive face.

"A pygmy Nestor —" I concurred.

Johnson quoted:

> *"Klagge tai ge petontai ep' okeanoio rhoaon,*
> *Andrasi Pygmaioisi phonon kai kera pherousai."*

"O, Lord, Sir, spare us your Greek!" cried I. "What does this little animal understand of Homer's works?"

"Little enough, I'll wager. What would you give, my lad," bending to place his great paw on the small cloth-of-gold shoulder, "what would you give to learn about Homer?"

The dark eyes blinked.

"Pompey give what he have, sah," piped the page.

Dr. Johnson was much pleased with his answer.

"Sir," said he to me, "a desire of knowledge is the natural feeling of mankind; and every human being, whose mind is not debauched, will be willing to give all that he has to get knowledge."

I doubt whether either Pompey or his mistress understood this discourse. Dr. Johnson, however, whose good sense keeps pace with his benevolence, omitted to gratify Pompey with an account of the Greek poet. He gratified him rather with a thing more to the purpose, namely sixpence; and the lady, pleased, patted the small golden shoulder.

Standing at her back, her waiting-woman glowered and muttered. Sure never had pocket Venus a stranger Abigail. She was a powerful mulatto, not tall but wide, with watchful black eyes in a broad ugly face. Above her narrow furrowed brow she had twisted a clout of red marked with tortuous figures of black. Her red stuff gown strained with muscles as her arms moved. With an angry jerk she fastened a brilliant pin like a coach-and-four in the lady's tower of curls, and said something between her teeth to the little brown page. He shrank against the lady.

"Ma'am," says Dr. Sam: Johnson bluntly, ignoring this by-play, "you've not brought me hither to discuss Homer. Pray what is it that disquiets you?"

Mistress Winwood gave him a level look.

"I will tell you," said she. "You must know that I went with the company of comedians to Jamaica. I was much admired in both comedy and tragedy, and thus I formed many — friendships —" said the lady delicately, "and received many a gift of jewels, before I married. My husband was a rich planter of Montego Bay, and 'twas his pleasure to adorn me with still handsomer jewels of his own providing. He bought me my mulatto woman, whom you see here, and nothing was wanting that would satisfy me. But alas, within short months, the sultry vapours of Jamaica had carried off my beloved Mr. Winwood, and I was left to mourn."

A tear stole down the golden cheek.

"There was naught left for me but to leave the scene of my sorrow and begin life anew. I realized my holdings. I took my jewels, and Hannah her little son, and hither came we — to find," the comedian inclined gracefully in my direction, "friendship and consolation in Mr. Boswell."

This was fast progress! I returned the inclination, with a smile into which I infused as much meaning as I could.

"What's this to the purpose?" growled Johnson.

"Why, Sir, the jewels. They lie there," she nodded towards the Benares coffer, "and I go in fear for jewels and life together."

"How so, ma'am?"

"Look. I found under my pillow last night — *this.*"

Dr. Sam: Johnson looked with contempt on the strange toy she displayed. 'Twas nothing so fearsome, being most like a shuttlecock, made of white feathers bound together with long dark hair. The bunch protruded from a little sack of yellow leather, stuck with seven pins.

"Foh," said Dr. Johnson. "This is a child's toy; this is one of Pompey's amusements. Come here, boy."

Pompey, idly whisking flies by the window, looked around, and began to approach. When he saw the white feather toy he stood stock still, and would approach no further.

"Come on, boy. Acknowledge your property."

Pompey put his little black hands behind him.

"No, sah. Not Pompey's."

He backed into the chimney-corner. As the rusty wig and the glossy black head bent together over the feathered shuttlecock, the jewelled turban sought diversion. First he tried the pug-dog's temper, who shewed ugly teeth. Then he reached up and pulled the paraqueet's tail-feathers. For that he got a sharp jab in his small brown finger, and one crimson drop started. Savagely he bit at the torn place with his sharp white teeth, and his eyes rolled in anger. The next thing I knew, he had bundled the paraqueet, chain and all, into the Chinese box, and slammed the slanting lid. Then ensued such a clanking and squawking as brought the lady from her shuttlecock and the mulatto from the toilette-table. Mistress Winwood released the indignant bird, which sat on her finger croaking. Hannah gave the erring page a box o' the ear that staggered him, and then dragged him screaming into the backward regions.

As his cries faded, peace returned. Mistress Winwood set the paraqueet back on his perch and refastened the chain. Dr. Johnson returned his attention to the shuttlecock.

" 'Twas under my pillow," the lady told him, "and I found it there in the morning. And last night after I blew out my candle, something outside tried to lift the hook on my door. I cried out, and it went away."

"Let us look at this door-fastening." Dr. Sam: Johnson heaved his great bulk erect and lumbered to the door. The lady followed him, and I followed her.

'Twas the slightest of hooks, that fell into a loop of metal affixed to the jamb.

" 'Twill never do, ma'am," says my ingenious friend. "Any knife-blade can lift it from without. We'll fix you bolts above and below, that shall repel intruders and make you and your jewels safe."

"Let it be as you wish," said the lady. "Yet I trust no lock nor bolt, I. Pray, Mr. Boswell, take upon you to watch my door from without, that nobody enters to do me harm."

The lady put forth this unreasonable request with so ravishing a smile, I had no heart to refuse; though in truth I had preferred to be a watcher 'tother side of the bolt.

"Then I'll join you," cried Dr. Johnson, reading my mind, "to preserve the proprieties."

"Damn your proprieties!" cried I inwardly.

As we stood thus clustered about the door, a mighty rap-ping upon the other side of the panel startled us. We gave ground.

"Enter," said Mistress Winwood.

Whereupon, ducking under the door-frame, in marched quite the tallest man I had ever seen without first paying a fee. 'Twas James Bruce, the Abyssinian traveller, who lodged in the second floor front. He stood a magnificent seven feet.

'Twas my first view of my fellow-lodger. Mistress Winwood made him known to us, and he bowed without a word. His presence in the lady's chamber, seven feet tall and handsome as a god, boded little good to the suit of James Boswell, five feet odd and indifferent pretty. I seated myself sullenly.

The seven-foot Scotchman chose a dubious Chippendale chair, and sat mum. We sat as mum, and tried to freeze him. But the lady shone upon him. Under her smile and her wide-eyed interest, he thawed indeed, and began to regale us with wonders. I saw Dr. Sam: Johnson shift and mutter uneasily at the romantick traveller's story. We must needs hear of the fabled lyre of the antient Egyptians —

"There's one liar the less in Egypt," muttered Dr. Johnson *sotto voce,* "now that you're returned to London—"

Unearing, the fabulous traveller fabled on, of the Abyssinians, who cut their steaks from the living cow, and the Watussi, a race of giants, who absolutely looked down their noses at a mere seven feet, and the Wambutti —

"Who," burst in Johnson, unable to brook more wonders, "have no doubt their heads beneath their shoulders, as Mandeville fabled before you. Sir, your servant, I've had enough of romantick extravagance, so I'll e'en take my leave. Ma'am, yours, and we'll wait upon you after supper."

Perforce I made my bow, and left the giant master of the field.

As we mounted to my lodging above, we encountered the

rope-dancer. He was running, absolutely running, down the balustrade. The man had the feet of a fly. When he saw me, he came to a halt by dropping lightly to the landing. He seized me by the lappet and breathed alcoholic fumes in my face.

"Pray, Mr. Boswell," he whined, "a trifle till Monday; for then I'll be *flush* of the *cole,* I assure 'ee, 'tis Hoxham Fair, and I'll dance on the rope again."

I looked at the narrow keel of a face, the rough wigless head, the closeset darting eyes, and liked him ill.

"Be off," said I, "for I've nothing on me."

"Then I know who has," replied he insolently, "where there's a little fellow-feeling too for a poor mountebank —"

And he danced off down the stair on his long shoeless toes. I heard him clatter at the Jamaican actress's door. So, Mr. Abyssinian traveller, I reflected sourly, where's your tête-à-tête now?

'Twas the rope-dancer, after all, who held the field. He was still there when we returned after supper, wigless and unbuttoned, working his long unshod feet on the fender and drinking tea from a flowery saucer. He pulled a long face when he saw us, and rose unwillingly to go. As he strolled to the door he jingled a pocketful, as if to flaunt the success of his errand. At the door he turned with his hand on the latch. He gave the Jamaican lady a servile congee, included us in an insolent nod, and drew the door softly to.

"Poor man," said Mistress Winwood, "the life of the stroller is thorny."

We in our turn drank tea from flowery saucers. Then we gave the lady into the broad black hands of Hannah, who dighted her for bed while we waited in the passage.

When the pug and the paraqueet had been turned out, and the black woman had retired to her pallet, it came our turn. Quietly we entered the chamber. How my heart beat as the tinkling voice greeted us from the shadow of the Chinese damask bed-curtains. The lady lay on the pillow, pallid as her linens, in a cloud of black hair. Her night-rail was another froth of lace, held with a diamond brooch.

"Have no fear, ma'am," says Dr. Sam: Johnson, "for here's what shall make all secure."

From his capacious pocket he dragged two stout bolts, and we proceeded to affix them on either side the hook, half-way up and half-way down the stout wooden door.

"Now, ma'am," says he, "with your permission I'll e'en make fast the window —"

"There's no need," says she, "for the wall falls sheer."

"Here's a balcony," said Dr. Johnson, peering out into the summer moonlight.

"That only a fly could come at," replied Mistress Winwood, "on that smooth brick wall."

"Then we'll lock out the flies," said Dr. Johnson firmly, and swung the catch tight.

"And pray, Dr. Johnson," whispered the lady, shamefaced, "look under the bed."

We looked under the bed. No desperado lurked there. But Dr. Johnson advanced the candle, and from a murky corner picked up some small object. On our knees on the Chinese rug we scanned it. 'Twas another shuttlecock. Dr. Johnson shook his head over it, and hastily concealed it from the lady in his capacious pocket.

"Nothing," said he to Mistress Winwood; "but we'll give the rest of the chamber a turnout."

We looked in the wardrobe. Nothing but the lady's silken gowns, breathing otto. We looked up the chimney. Nothing but soot. We looked into every corner that might conceal a man. Nothing but candle-shadows.

"All's safe, ma'am," said Dr. Johnson. "Do you hook and bolt after us, and your citadel is triple-lock'd."

"Good night," whispered she.

I bowed in the dark, not daring to approach and kiss her hand, and we took our leave.

Behind us we heard the hook fall into place and bolts ram home.

There was a damask sofa in the shadowy hall, and there we sat ourselves. The line of light under the door died as the lady blew out her candle. The house was still a while.

Besides me Dr. Sam: Johnson yawned mightily.

"This is a sleeveless errand," muttered he. "We have eased the lady's mind; let us ease ourselves with a bed. Nothing can come at Mistress Winwood through yonder triple-lock'd door. Come, let us go up."

'Twas my secret hope that through the triple-lock'd door, if I but waited long enough, would come the lady seeking the solace of my presence.

"Do you go up," said I.

"You'll come with me," said my stern mentor, "for a rake-helly young dog."

I could but laugh, and follow. We stole to the house-door, and opened it gently. I thought at the far end of the passage a door was eased open, but I could not be sure. We drew the door to, and mounted the stair.

My coat and waistcoat were off, and I was attacking my breeches-buttons, when I heard Mistress Winwood scream. In my shirt as I was I ran down the stair, and Dr. Sam: Johnson lumbered behind. As I ran the screaming ceased abruptly, to be succeeded by a silence more sinister yet. I ran down the long hall, thrust aside the mulatto woman where she stood dumbly shaking the door-handle, and flung myself against the panels.

We had done our work too well. The three locks held. Dr. Johnson added his great strength to mine, but to no purpose. If one lock gave, the others held it in line.

In a moment the seven-foot Scotchman ran in in his shirt-sleeves. In another moment the shoeless rope-dancer joined us, fully sober and fully cloathed, with his hair on end. We all four rushed at the door. It was too stout.

"Fetch the axe!" cried Dr. Johnson.

"Fetch a rope!" cried the mountebank. "If a rope be stretched from yonder tree opposite my window, I'll engage to walk across and so in at Mistress Windwood's casement."

" 'Tis lock'd."

"A window may be smashed."

"A door may be smashed. Fetch the axe."

"Do you wield the axe. I'll adventure by the rope."

"Do so," cried the Abyssinian traveller. "I've what shall assist you, which I used in climbing the Mountains of the Moon. 'Tis as it were a grappling-hook, which shall carry your rope from the ground to the balcony, and so a man may swarm up like a monkey."

"Do you break in like a monkey," cried Dr. Sam: Johnson contemptuously, "I'll break in like a man. Where's the axe?"

The explorer and the rope-dancer rushed off. The mulatto was dispatched backwards for the axe. We once more put our shoulder to the stout panels. In vain. At last we desisted and wiped our brows.

At that instant we heard from within the tinkle of breaking glass, and then the window creaked up. Another long moment, and we heard the three locks released. The door opened, and the mountebank stood before us. He was whiter than his ruffles.

"Mistress Winwood is dead," said he.

We stepped sombrely in. The mountebank touched flame to the candles. James Bruce hauled himself over the sill and entered; his shoes crunched on the broken glass of the window.

The Jamaican lady lay dead in her bed. A carving knife was buried to the hilt in the disordered laces of her night-rail. Save for that disorder, the room was as we left it.

"This is the work of the devil himself!" cried the mountebank, going green as he took in the situation. He looked fearfully behind him at our shadows wavering on the wall. "The window was lock'd tight; I had to break it. The door was hooked and double-bolted; you heard me lift the hook and undo the twin bolts. How could anything human do this, and make its way out again?"

A horrible cry, as from the Tartarian Lake, broke out be-

hind us. With jangled nerves I forced my head to turn. The
mulatto stood in the doorway with the axe in her hand. As I
looked at her she dropped the axe and fell to the floor by the
bedside.

"Damballa Oueddo!" she cried. "Ezilee! Ogoun Badagris!"

"These are devils she calls on!" cried the rope-dancer.
"This woman it is that has called up fiends to do this devil's
work!"

"This is devil's work," said Dr. Johnson heavily, "and
the devil is flown through the triple-lock'd door; or it is
man's work — and the man is still here."

With one consent we fell to searching. The mulatto woman
ignored us, and pursued her own strange rites. She cut a tress
of the shadowy hair, and bound it around her wrist. She
traced on the floor, in powder, designs I could not fathom.
When the designs were complete, and muttered over, she set
about kindling a fire. Dr. Johnson did not check her; he had
already got soot on his venerable brow assuring himself there
was still nothing else up the chimney. Backward she went for
coals. I stared at her strength; she heaved the hod in, filled,
as easily as she carried it out. It must have held a quarter-
chaldron.

Hunched over the grate she struck flint and steel. The paper fan blazed; she blew up the coals. When she had a good
glow, she laid aside the bellows and, crouching over the
flame, she began to mutter. Again she called upon Damballa
and Ogoun Badagris, rocking herself from side to side.

Our search was over. We had repeated in every detail our
search of one short hour before; and as before, had found
nothing. We stood to watch the woman's curious proceed-
ings.

"What do you do, good woman?" enquired Bruce curiously.

"I find the murderer. I see him in the flame."

"This is a rank superstition!" cried Dr. Johnson.

"Sir," said Bruce, "it may be; but I have seen in Africa such things as have made me wonder. What do you see, good woman?"

"I see a man. He comes down like a juju from the sky. He breaks the window, and turns back the bolt, and enters the room. I see him approach my lady. She screams. He strikes. Ah!"

The woman hid her face and wailed. The rope-dancer turned to Bruce.

"Your balcony is directly above. How easy to descend —"

"And break the glass?" Bruce caught him up. "*You* broke the glass. I saw you do it."

"And we heard you!" cried I.

"Perhaps Mistress Winwood admitted him," said the rope-dancer.

"If you were a gentleman," I cried hotly, "I'd call you to account for such a word!"

"Nay," said Bruce coolly, "let him prate. If the lady let me in, who let me out after the lady lay dead? Who shot the bolts after me? Robin Goodfellow belike? Or was it done by enchantment?"

"Why," said I slowly, "there's a way to shoot bolts from without. 'Tis done with packthread, and they shewed in court how it was done when they tried Sarah Malcolm."

"And the hook?"

"There must be a way for that too."

"And so," said Bruce with his cold smile, "you came running, and found me at the door with a handful of pack-thread!"

"We did not, Sir," owned Dr. Johnson. "Enough of this. This is matter for Bow Street. Let the watch be called."

I bellowed "Pompey!" into the hall. The rope-dancer at the broken window was bawling "Watch!"

"The child is too little," protested Hannah. "He will get lost."

The child in question came trotting down the hall to cut

her short. He was in his little shirt-tail, rubbing his eyes as he trotted along.

"Pompey here, sah."

A shout from the rope-dancer ended the matter. The watch had heard, and was even now upon the stair. Another moment, and in came the watchman in his antient coat to the heels, with his flapped hat, his lanthorn, and his staff. He saw at once how things stood, and acted decisively. First he opened the coffer of jewels.

"They are all there," said Hannah. "Nothing is missing."

Then he bellowed for his mate, and they took us all up.

They took us up! — me, James Boswell Esq: of Auchinleck, James Bruce the Abyssinian traveller, and Dr. Sam: Johnson the great lexicographer!

I would have made indignant proclamation of our names and qualities, but Dr. Johnson checked me with a look. The great man preferred to spend the night in the round-house with an unemployed rope-dancer and two Jamaican slaves!

So to the round-house we went. As we paraded on the pavement, I saw in the moonlight the rope dangling from the balcony, by which the rope-dancer had ascended. The great grappling-hook was plain to see, caught over the balcony rail. It had three prongs, and a ball to throw it by.

Late ramblers must have stared at the strange procession. As was his unhappy wont, Dr. Sam: Johnson lurched along muttering to himself, and touching the posts of the footway as he passed. The rope-dancer's narrow feet skimmed along without shoes; he seemed oblivious of the uneven paving-blocks. The mulatto woman slouched and mumbled. James Bruce the Abyssinian traveller strode along like a king. At first little Pompey trotted along behind like a puppy; but after a while Mr. Bruce took pity on his short legs and hoisted him to a towering shoulder.

Thus, each wrapped in who knows what thoughts, our ill-assorted company came to the round-house, and passed within. 'Twas an unfriendly structure of old brick and stone. I cannot say what amenities were provided in the forward

chamber for the refreshing of the watch. We were thrust into
the detention hold. A stale smell insulted our nostrils. Stark
stone was rough under foot; the walls were bare. A rough
deal table held the center; long benches lined the walls. Narrow windows interposed bars between us and the moonlight.
Sixpence to the watch brought us an exiguous farthing dip,
which did little to dispel the gloom of the place. As if from
far away came the rumble of coach-wheels and the cries of
roysterers between taverns.

'Twas an uneasy place to spend the night, most like some
antient tower in the wastes of Africa. As if it had been so,
Abyssinian Bruce laid himself stoically down like an old
campaigner. The rope-dancer paced like a tiger on his noiseless unshod feet. The mulatto woman sat and stared; her Lilliputian philosopher curled himself up like a dog in the corner. 'Twas our luck that we had the place to ourselves. I
stared up at the full moon through the barred window.

"Unravel me this, Sir," said I to my learned friend, seated
bolt upright on the bench. "If 'twas not the devil, who was
it?"

"One of these," he replied softly. "One of these.
Watch."

"Watch for what?"

"Let 'em smoulder, they'll smoak themselves," said he.

The staymaker's lodgers smouldered as the moon swung
over the sky. The rope-dancer kept up his noiseless pacing.
Hannah sat rigid, and muttered. Curled in his corner Pompey
slept the sleep of childhood, and stretched on the bench the
imperturbable explorer slept like a child too. My friend and
I waked, and heard nothing. The moon was waning as Dr.
Johnson leaned towards me and said in a loud whisper:

" 'Tis taedious to wait, but soon now we'll have this murderer."

"How so?"

"Why, I can tell you how," boomed my friend with unnecessary loudness. "You must know, this knifehandle was

of an exotick wood, which stains the hand. The stain deepens
as time passes. This murderer will be caught, my friend, *red-
handed.*''

The rope-dancer resumed his steady pacing. Hannah
swayed and muttered. Silence thickened.

A moment later my friend nudged me sharply, and I followed his gaze. Outlined against the narrow window was the
mulatto woman. By the uncertain light of the moon she was
staring intently at the palms of her hands.

"Never fear," said Dr. Johnson to me in his bull's mutter,
"we'll be cleared before the face of the magistrate. Trust me,
this murderer cannot escape. There's a diamond missing,
d'ye see; I missed it from the lady's night-rail though Hannah
did not. The murderer carries it on his person; and when he's
searched, 'tis all up with him.''

The rope-dancer stopped his pacing, and stood stock still.
The mulatto woman stiffened. The Abyssinian traveller lay
like the dead. Then the mulatto woman began to mutter between her teeth, angrily, without stopping. Pompey in his
corner slept unstirring. Suddenly the woman's wrath fell
upon the hapless page. She hauled him out from under the
bench, and addressed her biting patois to him. The little page
answered placatingly, but the woman was not to be placated.
Words brought blows; she shook him till his teeth rattled,
and then blows rained about his shoulders, till Dr. Johnson
was fain to step between them.

"Nay, ma'am, enough," said he, shielding the hapless
victim.

The woman gave over, and Pompey crept sobbing away
from her under the bench. Gradually his sobs died away, and
once more silence fell.

The rope-dancer tired of his pacing. Clutching his wild elf-
locks in both hands, he sank to the bench beside Bruce. The
traveller breathed heavily, and the rope-dancer bent over
him, feeling his heart, before resuming his pacing. Suddenly
Dr. Johnson spoke aloud.

"Mr. Bruce! Oblige me by handing me the diamond brooch which is in your left-hand waistcoat pocket."

Bruce came out of sleep standing up.

"I have taken no diamond brooch."

"Pray, Sir, don't quibble. The brooch is in your left-hand waistcoat pocket."

Bruce put up his heavy brows, and turned out the pocket. There was a flash of light in the moon as the diamond brooch fell to the stone floor.

"Sir," said Bruce steadily, "I give you my word of honour as a gentleman, I neither stabbed this unfortunate lady, nor stole her diamond brooch, which I now see for the first time."

"I believe you," cried I, "for 'tis clear this rope-dancer *planted* it on you, 'tis he that stabbed the lady for her jewels."

"Never believe it," said Bruce; "how did the poor man enter that triple-lock'd room and leave all lock'd again behind him?"

"Somebody did," said I, "that's plain to a demonstration."

"Why," says Dr. Johnson, "the rope-dancer did; he broke the window and turned the latch and so entered."

"I'll confess," cried the wretched rope-dancer. "I did indeed take the brooch — the lady was dead, she needed it no more, and my need was sore — but as God sees me, I never laid a finger on her, for she was good to me in my need."

He sank to the bench, and sobbed.

For a space there was no noise but his heavy gasping. Bruce composed himself again to slumber. The mulatto woman sat in sullen silence. Once the door creaked on its hinges, and we thought the watch had come for us; but nothing appeared at the crack, and the door creaked to again.

Suddenly from without there was an outcry. The heavy shouting of the watch and their thudding footsteps changed in the sound of blows and screams of pain. Then the door

jerked open, and the watchman shoved a small figure through
the door in a heap. 'Twas Pompey. We had not seen his
evasion, for he had slipped through noiselessly on his belly,
most like some little reptile. He returned sobbing and cring-
ing, and holding his head, which rang with the watchmen's
blows.

My merciful friend picked up the small shaking form, and
set him on his knee.

"Never cry, Pompey," said he.

"She beat me," sobbed Pompey.

"Never mind," said Dr. Sam: Johnson slowly; his long
shapely fingers gently stroked the small brown cheek.

"And they beat me," added Pompey, and wept afresh.

"Be comforted," said Dr. Johnson. "Do thou stay by me,
I'll tell thee a story. I'll tell thee of —"

He seemed to cast about for some suitable narrative. Memory suggested his choice.

"I'll tell thee of Homer, as I promised," said he, and repeated some lines in Greek; the round-house rang with his
sonorous voice.

I thought the little savage ever less likely to be entertained
with Greek.

"Which is to say," said Dr. Johnson, "in the words of
Alexander Pope:

> *"With shouts the Trojans, rushing from afar,*
> *Proclaim their motions, and provoke the war:*
> *So when inclement winters vex the plain*
> *With piercing frosts, or thick-descending rain,*
> *To warmer seas the cranes embodied fly,*
> *With noise, and order, through the midway sky;*
> *To pygmy nations wounds and death they bring,*
> *And all the war descends upon the wing.*

"But you are not to suppose," Dr. Johnson instructed his
unlikely pupil, "that these bird-contests ever happened, for
'tis only a fable."

"Nay, Sir," struck in the Abyssinian traveller, "there you are out, for in Africa —"

"Tut, Sir, a crane's but a bird, even in Africa."

"In Africa, Sir —"

The door was pushed roughly open, and the watch were there.

"You must come along to Bow Street," said the leader.

"Not I," said Dr. Sam: Johnson, "but you may take the murderer."

His powerful arms clamped like a vise upon the tiny figure in his lap.

The metamorphosis was astounding. One moment the small figure was nestled trustingly and innocently against the great shoulder. The next, it was a small fury, writhing, scratching, and biting, and cursing steadily in a strong new voice, in patios, African, and surprisingly good English. Then the mulatto woman struck like a fury, and we had all we could do to hold her off.

"Do you mean to tell me," I demanded incredulously, "that that small child stabbed his mistress?"

We sat at breakfast at the Mitre Tavern. Hannah and Pompey had been committed to Newgate, and now 'twas time to refresh ourselves after the fatigues of the night. Sombre James Bruce ate sparingly of bread and cheese; the hungry rope-dancer stuffed himself with buttock of beef; Dr. Johnson called for a cut of cold veal pye, and ate with relish.

"'Tis no small child," said Dr. Johnson, "but a grown man, a very dangerous desperado cast in Lilliputian mould."

Boswell: "Yet his mother —"

Johnson: "Foh, Hannah is not his mother."

"Of that you may be sure," said Abyssinian Bruce, "for they are of different races."

Johnson: "Hannah is his accomplice; and in all probability his mistress, for there is no human freak so freakish but he may find a woman to love him. They have confessed it, 'twas a deep-laid plot to come to England and be free; for 'tis known among the slaves, since the case of Sommersett three years since, that the slave is free the moment he sets foot on the free soil of England. So the new-bought slave-woman palms off her paramour as her child, and Mistress Winwood brings them hither. Now they will tarry with her only so long as will serve to prepare a refuge, and then steal the jewels and make off. Vigilance detected the first attempt —"

Boswell: "What part did the shuttlecock play?"

Bruce: "'Twas a sleepy charm; I have seen such things in my travels."

Johnson snapped his finger at the dawdling waiter, and more veal pye came on the run.

"So, Sir," said he, loading a mouthful, "a new plot was necessitated. Being unable to enter from without, Hannah bethought herself to hide her tiny accomplice in the lock'd room —"

Boswell: "Where: We searched the place."

Johnson: "We searched for a man. Had we been searching for a child, we would have looked in the coal-box, and found him."

Boswell: "What a risque!"

Johnson: "No risque at all, though he were caught there — simply another childish prank. He played his part well."

Boswell: "'Twas a mad risque to make the attempt the very night we were to watch."

Johnson: "They did not know of it. The plan was concerted, by chance, in their absence, and carried out after the woman was withdrawn. Concealed in the coal-box, Pompey heard us affix the bolts; but he doubted not he could draw them easily enough, and so make off. The bolted-door mystification was no part of his scheam."

Boswell: "Yet what folly, to set so weak an arm to assassination."

Johnson: "'Tis not so weak an arm, as I found when I tried to hold him. Nor was assassination intended; he was but to snatch the gems, and make off. But Mistress Winwood waked and screamed, and in panick he silenced her. He had no time to unlock the triple locks; he must hide again. Then indeed was he in danger, had he been discovered; but he could do no other. Soon enough his accomplice's wit taught her how to carry the coal-box out of danger without being suspected.''

Boswell (*thoughtfully*): "I made sure that the rope-dancer had done it by trickery. Say the scream was counterfeited, the lady but drugged within. Then the man who enters her smashed window in sight of witnesses may privily stab her before he opens the door and admits —"

The rope-dancer threw down the great bone he was gnawing, leaped to his shoeless feet, and hauled me up by the cravat.

"Ha' done," he cried roughly, "or gentleman or no you'll fight me."

James Bruce pulled him down on the bench with one great hand.

"With me so close on your heels," said he calmly, "Dr. Johnson knew better. Pray, Dr. Johnson, how did you smoak Pompey's imposture?"

"Well, Sir," replied Dr. Johnson as I settled my ruffles and the rope-dancer glowered upon his bone, "as we sat in the round-house, I tried one trick and another to learn the truth. I put forth the fable of the knife that stains the hand; and Hannah must needs examine her hands. Then she had been handling the knife. 'Twas no fable that a gem was missing. When I said so, it brought confusion, for there was guilt in two hearts. Our friend here thought to get clear of the gem, thrust in his matted poll; I was watching, and I saw the attempt. Hannah thought her accomplice was seeking to cheat her of part of the swag, and swinged him soundly for it. When Hannah turned against him, Pompey thought best to take to his heels before anger brought betrayal. And 'twas thus he betrayed himself."

"How so?"

"I took pity on a beaten child, took him on my knee, and patted his cheek. There is no mistaking a man's cheek that has gone a day without the razor. At first my mind could

scarce believe what my fingers told me. But I began to rec-
ollect what historians tell us, how Augustus had his dwarf,
and Constantine had one no bigger than a partridge; Mark
Antony had one under two feet in height, and Domitian assembled them by troops; Catherine de Medici bred the little
creatures. Why not then a waiting dwarf in Mistress Winwood's household?''

"What erudition, Sir!" cried Bruce.

"Aye," said I slyly, "on the part of *The Universal Magazine,* whence all these antient instances come."

"'Twas then clear," went on Johnson, ignoring me with
grandeur, "whose arm had the nerve for the deed, and whose
frame was small enough to hide safely in a room we searched.
I held him amused till the watch came; I assure you 'twas a
strange experience, reciting Homer while I held a dangerous
murderer on my knee."

"'Twas an interposition of Providence," said the rope-
dancer.

"Which found a learned instrument," said Abyssinian
Bruce, bowing to my ingenious friend. "Yet in one thing,
Dr. Johnson, you are out. Pompey is no freak of nature, but
a member of the race of pygmies that inhabit the African
forest. Whether they battle the cranes, I will not say; but had
you listened, instead of shouting me down, you would have
heard what report speaks of the race of the Wambutti, the
African pygmy, a race stunted, but clever, adroit, and strong.
Now, Sir, the Wambutti —"

"You, Sir," cried Dr. Johnson, cutting the discourse
short, "may have heard travellers' tales of the pygmies; but
*I,* Sir, (swelling) *I* am the man who caught one alive."

[This bit of fiction began with such a blackamoor page as Hogarth drew in *Marriage
à la Mode,* accreting the fictitious Jamaicans and the real African Traveller as it
developed.]

# The Brazen Locked Room

**Isaac Asimov**

*Here's a brief change of pace as we approach the mid-point of our book — a delightful fantasy by Isaac Asimov about a pact with the devil.*

COME, COME," said Shapur quite politely, considering that he was a demon. "You are wasting my time. And your own, too, I might add, since you have only half an hour left." And his tail twitched.

"It's *not* dematerialization?" asked Isidore Wellby thoughtfully.

"I have already said it is not," said Shapur.

For the hundredth time, Wellby looked at the unbroken bronze that surrounded him on all sides. The demon had taken unholy pleasure (what other kind indeed?) in pointing out that the floor, ceiling and four walls were featureless, two-foot-thick slabs of bronze, welded seamlessly together.

It was the ultimate locked room and Wellby had but another half hour to get out, while the demon watched with an expression of gathering anticipation.

It had been ten years previously (to the day, naturally) that Isidore Wellby had signed up.

"We pay you in advance," said Shapur persuasively. "Ten years of anything you want, within reason, and then you're a demon. You're one of us, with a new name of demonic potency, and many privileges beside. You'll hardly know you're damned. And if you don't sign, you may end up in the fire, anyway, just in the ordinary course of things. You never know. . . . Here, look at me. I'm not doing too badly. I signed up, had my ten years and here I am. Not bad."

"Why so anxious for me to sign then, if I might be damned anyway?" asked Wellby.

"It's not so easy to recruit hell's cadre," said the demon, with a frank shrug that made the faint odor of sulfur dioxide in the air a trifle stronger. "Everyone wishes to gamble on ending in Heaven. It's a poor gamble, but there it is. I think *you're* too sensible for that. But meanwhile we have more damned souls than we know what to do with and a growing shortage at the administrative end."

Wellby, having just left the army and finding himself with nothing much to show for it but a limp and a farewell letter from a girl he somehow still loved, pricked his finger, and signed.

Of course, he read the small print first. A certain amount of demonic power would be deposited to his account upon signature in blood. He would not know in detail how one manipulated those powers, or even the nature of all of them, but he would nevertheless find his wishes fulfilled in such a way that they would seem to have come about through perfectly normal mechanisms.

Naturally, no wish might be fulfilled which would interfere with the higher aims and purposes of human history. Wellby had raised his eyebrows at that.

Shapur coughed. "A precaution imposed upon us by — uh — Above. You are reasonable. The limitation won't interfere with you."

Wellby said. "There seems to be a catch clause, too."

"A kind of one, yes. After all, we have to check your aptitude for the position. It states, as you see, that you will be required to perform a task for us at the conclusion of your ten years, one your demonic powers will make it quite possible for you to do. We can't tell you the nature of the task now, but you will have ten years to study the nature of your powers. Look upon the whole thing as an entrance qualification."

"And if I don't pass the test, what then?"

"In that case," said the demon, "you will be only an ordinary damned soul after all." And because he was a demon, his eyes glowed smokily at the thought and his clawed fingers twitched as though he felt them already deep in the other's vitals. But he added suavely. "Come, now, the test will be a simple one. We would rather have you as a cadre than as just another chore on our hands."

Wellby, with sad thoughts of his unattainable loved one, cared little enough at the moment for what would happen after ten years and he signed.

Yet the ten years passed quickly enough. Isidore Wellby was always reasonable, as the demon had predicted, and things worked well. Wellby accepted a position and because he was always at the right spot at the right time and always said the right thing to the right man, he was quickly promoted to a position of great authority.

Investments he made invariably paid off and, what was more gratifying still, his girl came back to him most sincerely repentant and most satisfactorily adoring.

His marriage was a happy one and was blessed with four children, two boys and two girls, all bright and reasonably well behaved. At the end of ten years, he was at the height of his authority, reputation and wealth, while his wife, if anything, had grown more beautiful as she had matured.

And ten years (to the day, naturally) after the making of the compact, he woke to find himself, not in his bedroom, but in a horrible bronze chamber of the most appalling solidity, with no company other than an eager demon.

"You have only to get out, and you will be one of us," said Shapur. "It can be done fairly and logically by using your demonic powers, provided you know exactly what it is you're doing. You should, by now."

"My wife and children will be very disturbed at my disappearance," said Wellby, with the beginning of regrets.

"They will find your dead body," said the demon consolingly. "You will seem to have died of a heart attack and you will have a beautiful funeral. The minister will consign you to Heaven and we will not disillusion him or those who listen to him. Now, come, Wellby, you have till noon."

Wellby, having unconsciously steeled himself for this moment for ten years, was less panic-stricken than he might have been. He looked about speculatively. "Is this room perfectly enclosed? No trick openings?"

"No openings anywhere in the walls, floor or ceiling," said the demon, with a professional delight in his handiwork. "Or at the boundaries of any of those surfaces, for that matter. Are you giving up?"

"No, no. Just give me time."

Wellby thought very hard. There seemed no sign of closeness in the room. There was even a feeling of moving air. The air might be entering the room by dematerializing across the walls. Perhaps the demon had entered by dematerialization and perhaps Wellby himself might leave in that manner. He asked.

The demon grinned. "Dematerialization is not one of your powers. Nor did I myself use it in entering."

"You're sure now?"

"The room is my own creation," said the demon smugly, "and especially constructed for you."

"And you entered from outside?"

"I did."

"With reasonable demonic powers which I possess, too?"

"Exactly. Come, let us be precise. You cannot move through matter but you can move in any dimension by a mere effort of will. You can move up, down, right, left, obliquely and so on, but you cannot move through matter in any way."

Wellby kept on thinking, and Shapur kept on pointing out the utter immovable solidity of the bronze walls, floor and ceiling; their unbroken ultimacy.

It seemed obvious to Wellby that Shapur, however much he might believe in the necessity for recruiting cadre, was barely restraining his demonic delight at possibly having an ordinary damned soul to amuse himself with.

"At least," said Wellby, with a sorrowful attempt at philosophy, "I'll have ten happy years to look back on. Surely that's a consolation, even for a damned soul in hell."

"Not at all," said the demon. "Hell would not be hell, if you were allowed consolations. Everything anyone gains on Earth by pacts with the devil, as in your case (or my own, for that matter), is exactly what one might have gained without such a pact if one had worked industriously and in full trust in — uh — Above. That is what makes all such bargains so truly demonic." And the demon laughed with a kind of cheerful howl

Wellby said indignantly. "You mean my wife would have returned to me even if I had never signed your contract."

"She might have," said Shapur. "Whatever happens is the will of — uh — Above, you know. We ourselves can do nothing to alter that."

The chagrin of that moment must have sharpened Wellby's wits for it was then that he vanished, leaving the room empty, except for a surprised demon. And surprise turned to absolute fury when the demon looked at the contract with Wellby which he had, until that moment, been holding in his hand for final action, one way or the other.

It was ten years (to the day, naturally) after Isidore Wellby had signed his pact with Shapur, that the demon entered Wellby's office and said, most angrily, "Look here —"

Wellby looked up from his work, astonished. "Who are you?"

"You know very well who I am," said Shapur.

"Not at all," said Wellby.

The demon looked sharply at the man. "I see you are telling the truth, but I can't make out the details." He promptly flooded Wellby's mind with the events of the last ten years.

Wellby said. "Oh, yes I can explain, of course, but are you sure we will not be interrupted?"

"We won't be," said the demon grimly.

"I sat in that closed bronze room," said Wellby, "and —"

"Never mind that," said the demon hastily. "I want to know —"

"Please. Let me tell this my way."

The demon clamped his jaws and fairly exuded sulfur dioxide till Wellby coughed and looked pained.

Wellby said, "If you'll move off a bit. Thank you. . . . Now I sat in that closed bronze room and remembered how you kept stressing the absolute unbrokenness of the four walls, the floor and the ceiling. I wondered: why did you specify? What else was there beside walls, floor and ceiling.

You had defined a completely enclosed three-dimensional space.

"And that was it: three-dimensional. The room was not closed in the fourth dimension. It did not exist indefinitely in the past. You said you had created it for me. So if one traveled into the past, one would find oneself at a point in time, eventually when the room did not exist and then one would be out of the room.

"What's more, you *had* said I could move in any dimension, and time may certainly be viewed as a dimension. In any case, as soon as I decided to move toward the past, I found myself living backward at a tremendous rate and suddenly there was no bronze around me anywhere."

Shapur cried in anguish, "I can guess all that. You couldn't have escaped any other way. It's this contract of yours that I'm concerned about. If you're not an ordinary damned soul, very well, it's part of the game. But you must be at least one of *us,* one of the cadre: it's what you were paid for, and if I don't deliver you down below, I will be in enormous trouble."

Wellby shrugged his shoulders. "I'm sorry for you, of course, but I can't help you. You must have created the bronze room immediately after I placed my signature on the paper, for when I burst out of the room, I found myself just at the point in time at which I was making the bargain with you. There you were again: there I was; you were pushing the contract toward me, together with a stylus with which I might prick my finger. To be sure, as I had moved back in time, my memory of what was becoming the future faded out, but not, apparently, quite entirely. As you pushed the contract at me, I felt uneasy. I didn't quite remember the future, but I felt uneasy. So I didn't sign. I turned you down flat."

Shapur ground his teeth. "I might have known. If probability patterns affected demons, I would have shifted with you into this new if-world. As it is, all I can say is that you have lost the ten happy years we paid you with. That is one consolation. And we'll get you in the end. That is another.''

"Well, now,'' said Wellby, "are there consolations in hell? Through the ten years I have now lived, I knew nothing of what I might have obtained. But now that you've put the memory of the ten-years-that-might-have-been into my mind, I recall that, in the bronze room, you told me that demonic agreements could give nothing that could not be obtained by industry and trust in Above. I have been industrious and I have trusted.''

Wellby's eyes fell upon the photograph of his beautiful wife and four beautiful children, then traveled about the tasteful luxuriance of his office. "And I may even escape hell altogether. That, too, is beyond *your* power to decide.''

And the demon, with a horrible shriek, vanished forever.

# The Martian Crown Jewels

**Poul Anderson**

*Poul Anderson is one of several writers who have successfully combined science fiction with the detective story. Here he not only presents us with a fascinating locked room problem aboard a robot spaceship but also gives us a pastiche of Sherlock Holmes himself in the character of the detective Syaloch.*

THE SIGNAL was picked up when the ship was still a quarter million miles away, and recorded voices summoned the technicians. There was no haste, for the ZX28749, otherwise called the *Jane Brackney,* was right on schedule; but landing an unmanned spaceship is always a delicate operation. Men and machines prepared to receive her as she came down, but the control crew had the first order of business.

Yamagata, Steinmann, and Ramanowitz were in the GCA tower, with Hollyday standing by for an emergency. If the circuits *should* fail — they never had, but a thousand tons of cargo and nuclear-powered vessel, crashing into the port, could empty Phobos of human life. So Hollyday watched over a set of spare assemblies, ready to plug in whatever might be required.

Yamagata's thin fingers danced over the radar dials. His eyes were intent on the screen. "Got her," he said. Steinmann made a distance reading and Ramanowitz took the velocity off the Dopplerscope. A brief session with a computer showed the figures to be almost as predicted.

"Might as well relax," said Yamagata, taking out a cigarette. "She won't be in control range for a while yet."

His eyes roved over the crowded room and out its window. From the tower he had a view of the spaceport: unimpressive, most of its shops and sheds and living quarters being underground. The smooth concrete field was chopped off by the curvature of the tiny satellite. It always faced Mars, and the station was on the far side, but he could remember how the planet hung enormous over the opposite hemisphere, soft ruddy disc blurred with thin air, hazy greenish-brown mottlings of heath and farmland. Though Phobos was clothed in vacuum, you couldn't see the hard stars of space: the sun and the floodlamps were too bright.

There was a knock on the door. Hollyday went over, almost drifting in the ghostly gravity, and opened it. "Nobody allowed in here during a landing," he said. Hollyday was a stocky blond man with a pleasant, open countenance, and his tone was less peremptory than his words.

"Police." The newcomer, muscular, round-faced, and earnest, was in plain clothes, tunic and pajama pants, which was expected; everyone in the tiny settlement knew Inspector Gregg. But he was packing a gun, which was not usual, and looked harried.

Yamagata peered out again and saw the port's four constables down on the field in official spacesuits, watching the ground crew. They carried weapons. "What's the matter?" he asked.

"Nothing . . . I hope." Gregg came in and tried to smile. "But the *Jane* has a very unusual cargo this trip."

"Hm?" Ramanowitz's eyes lit up in his broad plump visage. "Why weren't we told?"

"That was deliberate. Secrecy. The Martian crown jewels are aboard." Gregg fumbled a cigarette from his tunic.

Hollyday and Steinmann nodded at each other. Yamagata whistled. "On a robot ship?" he asked.

"Uh-huh. A robot ship is the one form of transportation from which they could not be stolen. There were three attempts made when they went to Earth on a regular liner, and I hate to think how many while they were at the British Museum. One guard lost his life. Now my boys are going to remove them before anyone else touches that ship and scoot 'em right down to Sabaeus."

"How much are they worth?" wondered Ramanowitz.

"Oh . . . they could be fenced on Earth for maybe half a billion UN dollars," said Gregg. "But the thief would do better to make the Martians pay to get them back . . . no, Earth would have to, I suppose, since it's our responsibility." He blew nervous clouds. "The jewels were secretly put on the *Jane,* last thing before she left on her regular run. I wasn't even told till a special messenger on this week's liner gave·me the word. Not a chance for any thief to know they're here, till they're safely back on Mars. And that'll be *safe!*"

Ramanowitz shuddered. All the planets knew what guarded the vaults at Sabaeus.

"Some people did know, all along," said Yamagata thoughtfully. "I mean the loading crew back at Earth."

"Uh-huh, there is that." Gregg smiled. "Several of them have quit since then, the messenger said, but of course, there's always a big turnover among spacejacks — they're a restless bunch." His gaze drifted across Steinmann and Hollyday, both of whom had last worked at Earth Station and come to Mars a few ships back. The liners went on a hyperbolic path and arrived in a couple of weeks; the robot ships followed the more leisurely and economical Hohmann A orbit and needed 258 days. A man who knew what ship was carrying the jewels could leave Earth, get to Mars well ahead of the cargo, and snap up a job here — Phobos was always shorthanded.

"Don't look at me!" said Steinmann, laughing. "Chuck and I knew about this — of course — but we were under security restrictions. Haven't told a soul."

"Yeah. I'd have known it if you had," nodded Gregg. "Gossip travels fast here. Don't resent this, please, but I'm here to see that none of you boys leaves this tower till the jewels are aboard our own boat."

"Oh, well. It'll mean overtime pay."

"If I want to get rich fast, I'll stick to prospecting," added Hollyday.

"When are you going to quit running around with that Geiger in your free time?" asked Yamagata. "Phobos is nothing but iron and granite."

"I have my own ideas about that," said Hollyday stoutly.

"Hell, everybody needs a hobby on this God-forsaken clod," declared Ramanowitz. "I might try for those sparklers myself, just for the excitement —" He stopped abruptly, aware of Gregg's eyes.

"All right," snapped Yamagata. "Here we go. Inspector, please stand back out of the way, and for your life's sake don't interrupt us."

The *Jane* was drifting in, her velocity on the carefully pre-calculated orbit almost identical with that of Phobos. Almost, but not quite — there had been the inevitable small disturb-ing factors, which the remote-controlled jets had to compen-sate, and then there was the business of landing her. The team got a fix and were frantically busy.

In free fall, the *Jane* approached within a thousand miles of Phobos — a spheroid 500 feet in radius, big and massivē, but lost against the incredible bulk of the satellite. And yet Phobos is an insignificant airless pill, negligible even beside its seventh-rate planet. Astronomical magnitudes are simply and literally incomprehensible.

When the ship was close enough, the radio directed her gyros to rotate her, very, very gently, until her pickup an-tenna was pointing directly at the field. Then her jets were cut in, a mere whisper of thrust. She was nearly above the spaceport, her path tangential to the moon's curvature. After a moment Yamagata slapped the keys hard, and the rockets blasted furiously, a visible red streak up in the sky. He cut them again, checked his data, and gave a milder blast.

"Okay," he grunted. "Let's bring her in."

Her velocity relative to Phobos's orbit and rotation was now zero, and she was falling. Yamagata slewed her around till the jets were pointing vertically down. Then he sat back and mopped his face while Ramanowitz took over; the job was too nerve-stretching for one man to perform in its en-tirety. Ramanowitz sweated the awkward mass to within a few yards of the cradle. Steinmann finished the task, easing her into the berth like an egg into a cup. He cut the jets and there was silence.

"Whew! Chuck, how about a drink?" Yamagata held out unsteady fingers and regarded them with an impersonal stare.

Hollyday smiled and fetched a bottle. It went happily around. Gregg declined. His eyes were locked to the field, where a technician was checking for radioactivity. The ver-dict was clean, and he saw his constables come soaring over the concrete, to surround the great ship with guns. One of them went up, opened the manhatch, and slipped inside.

It seemed a very long while before he emerged. Then he came running. Gregg cursed and thumbed the tower's radio board. "Hey, there! Ybarra! What's the matter?"

The helmet set shuddered a reply: "Señor . .    Señor Inspector . . . . the crown jewels are gone."

Sabaeus is, of course, a purely human name for the old city nestled in the Martian tropics, at the juncture of the "canals" Phison and Euphrates. Terrestrial mouths simply cannot form the syllables of High Chlannach, though rough approximations are possible. Nor did humans ever build a town exclusively of towers broader at the top than the base, or inhabit one for twenty thousand years. If they had, though, they would have encouraged an eager tourist influx; but Martians prefer more dignified ways of making a dollar, even if their parsimonious fame has long replaced that of Scotchmen. The result is that though interplanetary trade is brisk and Phobos a treaty port, a human is still a rare sight in Sabaeus.

Hurrying down the avenues between the stone mushrooms, Gregg felt conspicuous. He was glad the airsuit muffled him. Not that the grave Martians stared; they varkled, which is worse.

The Street of Those Who Prepare Nourishment in Ovens is a quiet one, given over to handicrafters, philosophers, and residential apartments. You won't see a courtship dance or a parade of the Lesser Halberdiers on it: nothing more exciting than a continuous four-day argument on the relativistic nature of the null class or an occasional gunfight. The latter are due to the planet's most renowned private detective, who nests here.

Gregg always found it eerie to be on Mars, under the cold deep-blue sky and shrunken sun, among noises muffled by the thin oxygen-deficient air. But for Syaloch he had a good deal of affection, and when he had gone up the ladder and shaken the rattle outside the second-floor apartment and had been admitted, it was like escaping from nightmare.

"Ah, Krech!" The investigator laid down the stringed instrument on which he had been playing and towered gauntly over his visitor. "An unexbectet bleassure to see hyou. Come in, my tear chab, to come in." He was proud of his English — but simple misspellings will not convey the whistling, clicking Martian accent. Gregg had long ago fallen into the habit of translating it into a human pronunciation as he listened.

The Inspector felt a cautious way into the high, narrow room. The glowsnakes which illuminated it after dark were coiled asleep on the stone floor, in a litter of papers, specimens, and weapons; rusty sand covered the sills of the Gothic windows. Syaloch was not neat except in his own person. In one corner was a small chemical laboratory. The rest of the walls were taken up with shelves, the criminological literature of three planets — Martian books, Terrestrial micros, Venusian talking stones. At one place, patriotically, the glyphs representing the reigning Nest-mother had been punched out with bullets. An Earthling could not sit on the trapezelike native furniture, but Syaloch had courteously provided chairs and tubs as well; his clientèle was also triplanetary. Gregg found a scarred Duncan Phyfe and lowered himself, breathing heavily into his oxygen tubes.

"I take it you are here on official but confidential business." Syaloch got out a big-bowled pipe. Martians have happily adopted tobacco, though in their atmosphere it must include potassium permanganate. Gregg was thankful he didn't have to breathe the blue fog.

He started. "How the hell do you know that?"

"Elementary, my dear fellow. Your manner is most agitated, and I know nothing but a crisis in your profession would cause that in a good stolid bachelor. Yet you come to me rather than the Homeostatic Corps . . . so it must be a delicate affair."

Gregg laughed wryly. He himself could not read any Martian's expression — what corresponds to a smile or a snarl on a totally non-human face? But this overgrown stork —

No. To compare the species of different planets is merely to betray the limitations of language. Syaloch was a seven-foot biped of vaguely storklike appearance. But the lean, crested, red-beaked head at the end of the sinuous neck was too large, the yellow eyes too deep; the white feathers were more like a penguin's than a flying bird's, save at the blue-plumed tail; instead of wings there were skinny red arms ending in four-fingered hands. And the overall posture was too erect for a bird.

Gregg jerked back to awareness. God in Heaven! The city lay gray and quiet; the sun was slipping westward over the farmlands of Sinus Sabaeus and the desert of the Aeria; he could just make out the rumble of a treadmill cart passing beneath the windows — and he sat here with a story which could blow the Solar System apart!

His hands, gloved against the chill, twisted together. "Yes, it's confidential, all right. If you can solve this case, you can just about name your own fee." The gleam in Syaloch's eyes made him regret that, but he stumbled on: "One thing, though. Just how do you feel about us Earthlings?"

"I have no prejudices. It is the brain that counts, not whether it is covered by feathers or hair or bony plates."

"No, I realize that. But some Martians resent us. We do disrupt an old way of life — we can't help it, if we're to trade with you —"

"*K'teh.* The trade is on the whole beneficial. Your fuel and machinery — and tobacco, yesss — for our kantz and snull. Also, we were getting too . . . stale. And of course space travel has added a whole new dimension to criminology. Yes, I favor Earth."

"Then you'll help us? And keep quiet about something which could provoke your planetary federation into kicking us off Phobos?"

The third eyelids closed, making the long-beaked face a mask. "I give no promises yet, Gregg."

"Well . . . damn it, all right, I'll have to take the chance." The policeman swallowed hard. "You know about your crown jewels, of course."

"They were lent to Earth for exhibit and scientific study."

"After years of negotiation. There's no more priceless relic on all Mars — and you were an old civilization when we were hunting mammoths. All right. They've been stolen."

Syaloch opened his eyes, but his only other movement was to nod.

"They were put on a robot ship at Earth Station. They were gone when that ship reached Phobos. We've damn near ripped the boat apart trying to find them — we did take the other cargo to pieces, bit by bit — and they aren't there!"

Syaloch rekindled his pipe, an elaborate flint-and-steel process on a world where matches won't burn. Only when it was drawing well did he suggest: "Is it possible the ship was boarded en route?"

"No. It isn't possible. Every spacecraft in the System is registered, and its whereabouts are known at any time. Furthermore, imagine trying to find a speck in hundreds of millions of cubic miles, and match velocities with it . . . no vessel ever built could carry that much fuel. And mind you, it was never announced that the jewels were going back this way. Only the UN police and the Earth Station crew *could* know till the ship had actually left — by which time it'd be too late to catch her."

"Most interesting." Syaloch puffed hard.

"If word of this gets out," said Gregg miserably, "you can guess the results. I suppose we'd still have a few friends left in your Parliament —"

"In the House of Actives, yesss . . . a few. Not in the House of Philosophers, which is of course the upper chamber."

"It could mean a twenty-year hiatus in Earth-Mars traffic — maybe a permanent breaking off of relations. Damn it, Syaloch, you've *got* to find those stones!"

"Hm-m-m. I pray your pardon. This requires thought." The Martian picked up his crooked instrument and plucked a few tentative chords. Gregg sighed and attempted to relax. He knew the Chlannach temperament; he'd have to listen to an hour of minor-key caterwauling.

The colorless sunset was past, night had fallen with the unnerving Martian swiftness, and the glowsnakes were emitting blue radiance when Syaloch put down the demifiddle.

"I fear I shall have to visit Phobos in person," he said. "There are too many unknowns for analysis, and it is never well to theorize before all the data have been gathered." A bony hand clapped Gregg's shoulder. "Come, come, old chap. I am really most grateful to you. Life was becoming infernally dull. Now, as my famous Terrestrial predecessor would say, the game's afoot . . . and a very big game indeed!"

A Martian in an Earthlike atmosphere is not much hampered, needing only an hour in a compression chamber and a filter on his beak to eliminate excess oxygen and moisture. Syaloch walked freely about the port clad in filter, pipe, and *tirstokr* cap, grumbling to himself at the heat and humidity. He noticed that all the humans but Gregg were reserved, almost fearful, as they watched him — they were sitting on a secret which could unleash red murder.

He donned a spacesuit and went out to inspect the *Jane Brackney*. The vessel had been shunted aside to make room for later arrivals, and stood by a raw crag at the edge of the field, glimmering in the hard spatial sunlight. Gregg and Yamagata were with him.

"I say, you *have* been thorough," remarked the detective. "The outer skin is quite stripped off."

The spheroid resembled an egg which had tangled with a waffle iron: an intersecting grid of girders and braces above a thin aluminum hide. The jets, hatches, and radio mast were the only breaks in the checkerboard pattern, whose depth was about a foot and whose squares were a yard across at the "equator."

Yamagata laughed in a strained fashion. "No. The cops fluoroscoped every inch of her, but that's the way these cargo ships always look. They never land on Earth, you know, or any place where there's air, so streamlining would be unnecessary. And since nobody is aboard in transit, we don't have to worry about insulation or air-tightness. Perishables are stowed in sealed compartments."

"I see. Now where were the crown jewels kept?"

"They were supposed to be in a cupboard near the gyros," said Gregg. "They were in a locked box, about six inches high, six inches wide, and a foot long." He shook his head, finding it hard to believe that so small a box could contain so much potential death.

"Ah . . . but *were* they placed there?"

"I radioed Earth and got a full account," said Gregg. "The ship was loaded as usual at the satellite station, then shoved a quarter mile away till it was time for her to leave — to get her out of the way, you understand. She was still in the same free-fall orbit, attached by a light cable — perfectly standard practice. At the last minute, without anyone being told beforehand, the crown jewels were brought up from Earth and stashed aboard."

"By a special policeman, I presume?"

"No. Only licensed technicians are allowed to board a ship in orbit, unless there's a life-and-death emergency. One of the regular station crew — fellow named Carter — was told where to put them. He was watched by the cops as he pulled himself along the cable and in through the manhatch." Gregg pointed to a small door near the radio mast. "He came out, closed it, and returned on the cable. The police immediately searched him and his spacesuit, just in case, and he positively did not have the jewels. There was no reason to suspect him of anything — good steady worker — though I'll admit he's disappeared since then. The *Jane* blasted a few minutes late and her jets were watched till they cut off and she went into free fall. And that's the last anyone saw of her till she got here — without the jewels.''

"And right on orbit,'' added Yamagata. ''If by some freak she had been boarded, it would have thrown her off enough for us to notice as she came in. Transference of momentum between her and the other ship.''

"I see.'' Behind his faceplate, Syaloch's beak cut a sharp black curve across heaven. ''Now then, Gregg, were the jewels actually in the box when it was delivered?''

"At Earth Station, you mean? Oh, yes. There are four UN Chief Inspectors involved, and HQ says they're absolutely above suspicion. When I sent back word of the theft, they insisted on having their own quarters and so on searched, and went under scop voluntarily.''

"And your own constables on Phobos?''

"Same thing,'' said the policeman grimly. ''I've slapped on an embargo — nobody but me has left this settlement since the loss was discovered. I've had every room and tunnel and warehouse searched.'' He tried to scratch his head, a frustrating attempt when one is in a spacesuit. ''I can't maintain those restrictions much longer. Ships are coming in and the consignees want their freight.''

"*Hnachla.* That puts us under a time limit, then.'' Syaloch nodded to himself. ''Do you know, this is a fascinating variation of the old locked room problem. A robot ship in transit is a locked room in the most classic sense.'' He drifted off into a reverie.

Gregg stared bleakly across the savage horizon, naked rock tumbling away under his feet, and then back over the field. Odd how tricky your vision became in airlessness, even when you had bright lights. That fellow crossing the field there, under the full glare of sun and floodlamps, was merely a stipple of shadow and luminance . . . what the devil was he doing, tying a shoe of all things? No, he was walking quite normally —

"I'd like to put everyone on Phobos under scop," said Gregg with a violent note, "but the law won't allow it unless the suspect volunteers — and only my own men have volunteered."

"Quite rightly, my dear fellow," said Syaloch. "One should at least have the privilege of privacy in his own skull. And it would make the investigation unbearably crude."

"I don't give a fertilizing damn how crude it is," snapped Gregg. "I just want that box with the crown jewels safe inside."

"Tut-tut! Impatience has been the ruin of many a promising young police officer, as I seem to recall my spiritual ancestor of Earth pointing out to a Scotland Yard man who — hm — may even have been a physical ancestor of yours, Gregg. It seems we must try another approach. Are there any people on Phobos who might have known the jewels were aboard this ship?"

"Yes. Two men only. I've pretty well established that they never broke security and told anyone else till the secret was out."

"And who are they?"

"Technicians, Hollyday and Steinmann. They were working at Earth Station when the *Jane* was loaded. They quit soon after — not at the same time — and came here by liner and got jobs. You can bet that *their* quarters have been searched!"

"Perhaps," murmured Syaloch, "it would be worthwhile to interview the gentlemen in question."

Steinmann, a thin redhead, wore truculence like a mantle; Hollyday merely looked worried. It was no evidence of guilt — everyone had been rubbed raw of late. They sat in the police office, with Gregg behind the desk and Syaloch leaning against the wall, smoking and regarding them with unreadable yellow eyes.

"Damn it, I've·told this over and over till I'm sick of it!' Steinmann knotted his fists and gave the Martian a bloodshot stare. "I never touched the things and I don't know who did. Hasn't any man a right to change jobs?"

"Please," said the detective mildly. "The better you help the sooner we can finish this work. I take it you were acquainted with the man who actually put the box aboard the ship?"

"Sure. Everybody knew John Carter. Everybody knows everybody else on a satellite station." The Earthman stuck out his jaw. "That's why none of us'll take scop. We won't blab out all our thoughts to guys we see fifty times a day. We'd go nuts!"

"I never made such a request," said Syaloch.

"Carter was quite a good friend of mine," volunteered Hollyday.

"Uh-huh," grunted Gregg. "And he quit too, about the same time you fellows did, and went Earthside and hasn't been seen since. HQ told me you and he were thick. What'd you talk about?"

"The usual." Hollyday shrugged. "Wine, women, and song. I haven't heard from him since I left Earth."

"Who says Carter stole the box?" demanded Steinmann. "He just got tired of living in space and quit his job. He *couldn't* have stolen the jewels — he was searched, remember?"

"Could he have hidden it somewhere for a friend to get at this end?" inquired Syaloch.

"Hidden it? Where? Those ships don't have secret compartments." Steinmann spoke wearily. "And he was only aboard the *Jane* a few minutes, just long enough to put the box where he was supposed to." His eyes smoldered at Gregg. "Let's face it: the only people anywhere along the line who ever had a chance to lift it were our own dear cops."

The Inspector reddened and half rose. "Look here, you —"

"We've got *your* word that you're innocent," growled Steinmann. "Why should it be any better than mine?"

Syaloch waved both men back. "If you please. Brawls are unphilosophic." His beak opened and clattered, the Martian equivalent of a smile. "Has either of you, perhaps, a theory? I am open to all ideas."

There was a stillness. Then Hollyday mumbled: "Yes. I have one."

Syaloch hooded his eyes and puffed quietly, waiting.

Hollyday's grin was shaky. "Only if I'm right, you'll never see those jewels again."

Gregg sputtered.

"I've been around the Solar System a lot," said Hollyday. "It gets lonesome out in space. You never know how big and lonesome it is till you've been there, all by yourself. And I've done just that — I'm an amateur uranium prospector, not a lucky one so far. I can't believe we know everything about the universe, or that there's only vacuum between the planets."

"Are you talking about the cobblies?" snorted Gregg.

"Go ahead and call it superstition. But if you're in space long enough . . . well, somehow, you *know*. There are beings out there — gas beings, radiation beings, whatever you want to imagine, there's *something* living in space."

"And what use would a box of jewels be to a cobbly?"

Hollyday spread his hands. "How can I tell? Maybe we bother them, scooting through their own dark kingdom with our little rockets. Stealing the crown jewels would be a good way to disrupt the Mars trade, wouldn't it?"

Only Syaloch's pipe broke the inward-pressing silence. But its burbling seemed quite irreverent.

"Well —" Gregg fumbled helplessly with a meteoric paperweight. "Well, Mr. Syaloch, do you want to ask any more questions?"

"Only one." The third lids rolled back, and coldness looked out at Steinmann. "If you please, my good man, what is your hobby?"

"Huh? Chess. I play chess. What's it to you?" Steinmann lowered his head and glared sullenly.

"Nothing else?"

"What else is there?"

Syaloch glanced at the Inspector, who nodded confirmation, and then replied gently:

"I see. Thank you. Perhaps we can have a game sometime. I have some small skill of my own. That is all for now, gentlemen."

They left, moving like things of dream through the low gravity.

"Well?" Gregg's eyes pleaded with Syaloch. "What next?"

"Very little. I think . . . yesss, while I am here I should like to watch the technicians at work. In my profession, one needs a broad knowledge of all occupations."

Gregg sighed.

Ramanowitz showed the guest around. The *Kim Brackney* was in and being unloaded. They threaded through a hive of spacesuited men.

"The cops are going to have to raise that embargo soon," said Ramanowitz. "Either that or admit why they've clamped it on. Our warehouses are busting."

"It would be politic to do so," nodded Syaloch. "Ah, tell me . . . is this equipment standard for all stations?"

"Oh, you mean what the boys are wearing and carrying around? Sure. Same issue everywhere."

"May I inspect it more closely?"

"Hm?" *Lord, deliver me from visiting firemen!* thought Ramanowitz. He waved a mechanic over to him. "Mr. Syaloch would like you to explain your outfit," he said with ponderous sarcasm.

"Sure. Regular spacesuit here, reinforced at the seams." The gauntleted hands moved about, pointing. "Heating coils powered from this capacitance battery. Ten-hour air supply in the tanks. These buckles, you snap your tools into them, so they won't drift around in free fall. This little can at my belt holds paint that I spray out through this nozzle."

"Why must spaceships be painted?" asked Syaloch. "There is nothing to corrode the metal."

"Well, sir, we just call it paint. It's really gunk, to seal any leaks in the hull till we can install a new plate, or to mark any other kind of damage. Meteor punctures and so on." The mechanic pressed a trigger and a thin, almost invisible stream jetted out, solidifying as it hit the ground.

"But it cannot readily be seen, can it?" objected the Martian. "I, at least, find it difficult to see clearly in airlessness."

"That's right, Light doesn't diffuse, so . . . well, anyhow, the stuff is radioactive — not enough to be dangerous, just enough so that the repair crew can spot the place with a Geiger counter."

"I understand. What is the half-life?"

"Oh, I'm not sure. Six months, maybe? It's supposed to remain detectable for a year."

"Thank you." Syaloch stalked off. Ramanowitz had to jump to keep up with those long legs.

"Do you think Carter may have hid the box in his paint can?" suggested the human.

"No, hardly. The can is too small, and I assume he was searched thoroughly." Syaloch stopped and bowed. "You have been very kind and patient, Mr. Ramanowitz. I am finished now, and can find the Inspector myself."

"What for?"

"To tell him he can lift the embargo, of course." Syaloch made a harsh sibilance. "And then I must get the next boat to Mars. If I hurry, I can attend the concert in Sabaeus tonight." His voice grew dreamy. "They will be premiering Hanyech's *Variations on a Theme by Mendelssohn,* transcribed to the Royal Chlannach scale. It should be most unusual."

It was three days afterward that the letter came. Syaloch excused himsef and kept an illustrious client squatting while he read it. Then he nodded to the other Martian. "You will be interested to know, sir, that the Estimable Diadems have arrived at Phobos and are being returned at this moment.''

The client, a Cabinet Minister from the House of Actives, blinked. ''Pardon, Freehatched Syaloch, but what have you to do with that?''

''Oh . . . I am a friend of the Featherless police chief. He thought I might like to know.''

*''Hraa.* Were you not on Phobos recently?''

''A minor case.'' The detective folded the letter carefully, sprinkled it with salt, and ate it. Martians are fond of paper, especially official Earth stationary with high rag content. ''Now, sir, you were saying —?''

The parliamentarian responded absently. He would not dream of violating privacy — no, never — but if he had X-ray vision he would have read:

''Dear Syaloch,

''You were absolutely right. Your locked room problem is solved. We've got the jewels back, everything is in fine shape, and the same boat which brings you this letter will deliver them to the vaults. It's too bad the public can never know the facts — two planets ought to be grateful to you — but I'll supply that much thanks all by myself, and insist that any bill you care to send be paid in full. Even if the Assembly had to make a special appropriation, which I'm afraid it will.

''I admit your idea of lifting the embargo at once looked pretty wild to me, but it worked. I had our boys out, of course, scouring Phobos with Geigers, but Hollyday found the box before we did. Which saved us a lot of trouble, to be sure. I arrested him as he came back into the settlement, and he had the box among his ore samples. He has confessed, and you were right all along the line.

''What was that thing you quoted at me, the saying of that Earthman you admire so much? 'When you have eliminated the impossible, whatever remains, however improbable, must be true.' Something like that. It certainly applies to this case.

''As you decided, the box must have been taken to the

ship at Earth Station and left there — no other possibility existed. Carter figured it out in half a minute when he was ordered to take the thing out and put it aboard the *Jane*. He went inside, all right, but still had the box when he emerged. In that uncertain light nobody saw him put it 'down' between four girders right next to the hatch. Or as you remarked, if the jewels are not *in* the ship, and yet not *away* from the ship, they must be *on* the ship. Gravitation would hold them in place. When the *Jane* blasted off, acceleration pressure slid the box back, but of course the waffle-iron pattern kept it from being lost; it fetched up against the after rib and stayed there. All the way to Mars! But the ship's gravity held it securely enough even in free fall, since both were on the same orbit.

"Hollyday says that Carter told him all about it. Carter couldn't go to Mars himself without being suspected and watched every minute once the jewels were discovered missing. He needed a confederate. Hollyday went to Phobos and took up prospecting as a cover for the search he'd later be making for the jewels.

"As you showed me, when the ship was within a thousand miles of this dock, Phobos gravity would be stronger than her own. Every spacejack knows that the robot ships don't start decelerating till they're quite close; that they are then almost straight above the surface; and that the side with the radio mast and manhatch — the side on which Carter had placed the box — is rotated around to face the station. The centrifugal force of rotation threw the box away from the ship, and was in a direction toward Phobos rather than away from it. Carter knew that this rotation is slow and easy, so the force wasn't enough to accelerate the box to escape velocity and lose it in space. It would have to fall down toward the satellite. Phobos Station being on the side opposite Mars, there was no danger that the loot would keep going till it hit the planet.

"So the crown jewels tumbled onto Phobos, just as you deduced. Of course Carter had given the box a quick radioactive spray as he laid it in place, and Hollyday used that to track it down among all those rocks and crevices. In point of fact, it's path curved clear around this moon, so it landed about five miles from the station.

"Steinmann has been after me to know why you quizzed him about his hobby. You forgot to tell me that, but I figured it out for myself and told him. He or Hollyday had to be involved, since nobody else knew about the cargo, and the guilty person had to have some excuse to go out and look for the box. Chess playing doesn't furnish that kind of alibi. Am I right? At least, my deduction proves I've been studying the same canon you go by. Incidentally, Steinmann asks if you'd care to take him on the next time he has planet leave.

"Hollyday knows where Carter is hiding, and we've radioed the information back to Earth. Trouble is, we can't prosecute either of them without admitting the facts. Oh, well, there are such things as blacklists.

"Will have to close this now to make the boat. I'll be seeing you soon — not professionally, I hope!

Admiring regards,<br>Inspector Gregg

But as it happened, the Cabinet minister did not possess X-ray eyes. He dismissed unprofitable speculation and outlined his problem. Somebody, somewhere in Sabaeus, was farniking the krats, and there was an alarming zaksnautry among the hyukus. It sounded to Syaloch like an interesting case.

# The Day the Children Vanished

## Hugh Pentecost

*Hugh Pentecost is another prolific author who has written, to my knowledge, only this single mystery that qualifies as an impossible crime. It deals with a vanishing school bus and was mentioned in several news accounts when an actual school bus was hijacked in California a few years back.*

ON A BRIGHT, clear winter's afternoon the nine children in the town of Clayton who traveled each day to the Regional School in Lakeview disappeared from the face of the earth, along with the bus in which they traveled and its driver, as completely as if they had been sucked up into outer space by some monstrous interplanetary vacuum cleaner.

Actually, in the time of hysteria which followed the disappearance, this theory was put forward by some distraught citizen of Clayton, and not a few people, completely stumped for an explanation, gave consideration to it.

There was, of course, nothing interplanetary or supernatural about the disappearance of nine children, one adult, and a special-bodied station wagon which was used as a school bus. It was the result of callous human villainy. But, because there was no possible explanation for it, it assumed all the aspects of black magic in the minds of tortured parents and a bewildered citizenry.

Clayton is seven miles from Lakeview. Clayton is a rapidly growing quarry town. Lakeview, considerably larger and with a long history of planning for growth, recently built a new school. It was agreed between the boards of education of the two towns that nine children living at the east end of Clayton should be sent to the Lakeview School where there was adequate space and teaching staff. It was to be just a temporary expedient.

Since there were only nine children, they did not send one of the big, forty-eight-passenger school buses to get them. A nine-passenger station wagon was acquired, properly painted and marked as a school bus, and Jerry Mahoney, a mechanic in the East Clayton Garage, was hired to make the two trips each day with the children.

Jerry Mahoney was well liked and respected. He had been a mechanic in the Air Force during his tour of duty in the armed services. He was a wizard with engines. He was engaged to be married to Elizabeth Deering, who worked in the

Clayton Bank and was one of Clayton's choice picks. They were both nice people, responsible people.

The disappearance of the station wagon, the nine children and Jerry Mahoney took place on a two-mile stretch of road where disappearance was impossible. It was called the "dugway," and it wound along the side of the lake. Heavy wire guard rails protected the road from the lake for the full two miles. There was not a gap in it anywhere.

The ground on the other side of the road rose abruptly upward into thousands of acres of mountain woodlands, so thickly grown that not even a tractor could have made its way up any part of it except for a few yards of deserted road that led to an abandoned quarry. Even over this old road nothing could have passed without leaving a trail of torn brush and broken saplings.

At the Lakeview end of the dugway was a filling station owned by old Jake Nugent. On the afternoon of the disappearance the bus, with Jerry Mahoney at the wheel and his carload of kids laughing and shouting at each other, stopped at old man Nugent's. Jerry Mahoney had brought the old man a special delivery letter from the post office, thus saving the RFD driver from making a special trip. Jerry and old Jake exchanged greetings, the old man signed the receipt for his letter — which was from his son in Chicago asking for a loan of fifty dollars — and Jerry drove off into the dugway with his cargo of kids.

At the Clayton end of the dugway was Joe Gorman's Diner, and one of the children in Jerry's bus was Peter Gorman, Joe's son. The Diner was Jerry's first stop coming out of the dugway with his cargo of kids.

It was four-thirty in the afternoon when Joe Gorman realized that the bus was nearly three-quarters of an hour late. Worried, he called the school in Lakeview and was told by Miss Bromfield, the principal, that the bus had left on schedule.

"He may have had a flat, or something," Miss Bromfield suggested.

This was one of seven calls Miss Bromfield was to get in the next half hour, all inquiring about the bus. Nine children; seven families.

Joe Gorman was the first to do anything about it seriously. He called Jake Nugent's filling station to ask about the bus, and old Jake told him it had gone through from his place on schedule. So something had happened to Jerry and his busload of kids in the dugway. Joe got out his jeep and headed through the dugway toward Lakeview. He got all the way to Jake Nugent's without seeing the bus or passing anyone coming the other way.

Jake Nugent was a shrewd old gent, in complete possession of all his faculties. He didn't drink. When he said he had seen the bus — that it had stopped to deliver him his letter — and that he had watched it drive off into the dugway, you had to believe it. Cold sweat broke out on Joe Gorman's face as he listened. The dugway had a tendency to be icy. He had noticed coming over that it hadn't been sanded. Joe hadn't been looking for a major tragedy. But if the bus had skidded, gone through the guard rail . . .

He used Jake's phone to call the Dicklers in Clayton. The Dicklers' two children, Dorothy and Donald, were part of Jerry's load and they were the next stop after Joe's Diner. The Dicklers were already alarmed because their children hadn't appeared.

Joe didn't offer any theories. He was scared, though. He called the trooper barracks in Lakeview and told them about the missing bus. They didn't take it too seriously, but said they'd send a man out.

Joe headed back for Clayton. This time his heart was a lump in his throat. He drove slowly, staring at every inch of the wire guard rails. There was not a break anywhere, not a broken or bent post. The bus simply couldn't have skidded over the embankment into the lake without smashing through the wire guard rail.

Joe Gorman felt better when he came out at his diner at the Clayton end. He felt better, but he felt dizzy. Five min-

utes later Trooper Teliski came whizzing through from Lakeview and stopped his car.

"What's the gag?" he asked Joe.

Joe tried to light a cigarette and his hands were shaking so
badly he couldn't make it. Teliski snapped on his lighter and
held it out. Joe dragged smoke deep into his lungs.

"Look," he said. "The bus started through the dugway at
the regular time." He told about Jerry's stop at Nugent's.
"It never came out this end."

A nerve twitched in Teliski's cheek. "The lake," he said.

Joe shook his head. "I — I thought of that, right off. I
just came through ahead of you — looking. Not a break in
the guard rail anywhere. Not a scratch. Not a bent post. The
bus didn't go into the lake. I'll stake my life on that."

"Then what else?" Teliski asked. "It couldn't go up the
mountain."

"I know," Joe said, and the two men stared at each other.

"It's some kind of a joke," Teliski said.

"What kind of a joke? It's no joke to me — or the Dicklers. I talked to them."

"Maybe they had permission to go to a special movie or
something," Teliski said.

"Without notifying the parents? Miss Bromfield would
have told me, anyway. I talked to her. Listen, Teliski. The
bus went into the dugway and it didn't come out. It's not in
the dugway now, and it didn't go into the lake."

Teliski was silent for a moment, and then he spoke with a
solid attempt at common sense. "It didn't come out this
end," he said. "We'll check back on that guard rail, but let's
say you're right. It didn't skid into the lake. It couldn't go
up the mountain. So where does that leave us?"

"Going nuts!" Joe said.

"It leaves us with only one answer. The station wagon
never went into the dugway."

Joe Gorman nodded. "That's logic," he said. "But why
would Jake Nugent lie? Jerry's an hour and three-quarters
late now. If he didn't go in the dugway, where is he? Where

*could* he go? Why hasn't he telephoned if everything is okay?''

A car drove up and stopped. A man got out and came running toward them. It was Karl Dickler, father of two of the missing children. "Thank God you're here, Teliski. What happened?''

"Some kind of gag," Teliski said. "We can't figure it out. The bus never came through the dugway.''

"But it did!'' Karl Dickler said.

"It never came out this end,'' Joe Gorman said. "I was watching for Pete, naturally.''

"But it did come through!'' Dickler said. "I passed them myself on the way to Lakeview. They were about half a mile this way from Jake Nugent's. I saw them! I waved at my own kids!''

The three men stared at each other.

"It never came out this end,'' Joe Gorman said, in a choked voice.

Dickler swayed and reached out to the trooper to steady himself. "The lake!'' he whispered.

But they were not in the lake. Joe Gorman's survey proved accurate; no broken wire, no bent post, not even a scratch . . .

It was nearly dark when the search began. Troopers, the families of the children, the selectmen, the sheriff and twenty-five or thirty volunteer deputies, a hundred or more school friends of the missing children.

The lake was definitely out. Not only was the guard rail intact, but the lake was frozen over with about an inch of ice. There wasn't a break in the smooth surface of the ice anywhere along the two miles of shore bordering the dugway.

Men and women and children swarmed the woods on the other side of the road, knowing all the time it was useless. The road was called the "dugway" because it had been dug out of the side of the mountain. There was a gravel bank about seven feet high running almost unbrokenly along that

side of the road. There was the one old abandoned trail leading to the quarry. It was clear, after walking the first ten
yards of it, that no car had come that way. It couldn't.

A hundred phone calls were made to surrounding towns
and villages. No one had seen the station wagon, the children
or Jerry Mahoney. The impossible had to be faced.

The bus had gone into the dugway and it hadn't come out.
It hadn't skidded into the lake and it hadn't climbed the im-
penetrable brush of the mountain. It was just gone! Vanished
into thin air! . . .

Everyone was deeply concerned for and sympathetic with
the Dicklers, and Joe Gorman, and the Williams, the Trents,
the Ishams, the Nortons, and the Jennings, parents of the
missing children. Nobody thought much about Jerry Mahoney's family, or his girl.

It wasn't reasonable, but as the evening wore on and not
one speck of evidence was found or one reasonable theory
advanced, people began to talk about Jerry Mahoney. He was
the driver. The bus had to have been driven somewhere. It
couldn't navigate without Jerry Mahoney at the wheel. Jerry
was the only adult involved. However it had been worked —
this disappearance — Jerry must have had a hand in it.

It didn't matter that, until an hour ago, Jerry had been
respected, trusted, liked. Their children were gone and Jerry
had taken them somewhere. Why? Ransom. They would all
get ransom letters in the morning, they said. A mass kidnaping. Jerry had the kids somewhere. There weren't any rich
kids in Clayton so he was going to demand ransom from all
seven families.

So Jerry Mahoney became a villain because there was no
one else to suspect. Nobody stopped to think that Jerry's father and Jerry's girl might be as anxious about his absence as
the others were about the missing children.

At nine-thirty Sergeant Mason and Trooper Teliski of the
State Police, George Peabody, the sheriff, and a dozen men
of the community including Joe Gorman and Karl Dickler
stormed into the living room of Jerry Mahoney's house where

an old man with silvery white hair sat in an overstuffed armchair with Elizabeth Deering, Jerry's fiancée, huddled on the
floor beside him, her face buried on his knees, weeping.

The old man wore a rather sharply cut gray flannel suit, a
bright scarlet vest with brass buttons and a green necktie that
must have been designed for a St. Patrick's Day parade. As
he stroked the girl's blond hair, the light from the lamp reflected glittering shafts from a square-cut diamond in a heavy
gold setting he wore on his little finger. He looked up at
Sergeant Mason and his small army of followers, and his
blue eyes stopped twinkling as he saw the stern look on the
Sergeant's face.

"All right, Pat," Sergeant Mason said. "What's Jerry
done with those kids?" Pat Mahoney's pale blue eyes met
the Sergeant's stare steadily. Then crinkles of mirth appeared
at the corners of his eyes and mouth.

"I'd like to ask you something before I try to answer
that," Pat Mahoney said.

"Well?"

"Have you stopped beating your wife, Sergeant?" Pat Mahoney asked. His cackle of laughter was the only sound in
the room . . .

There are those who are old enough to remember the days
when Mahoney and Faye were listed about fourth on a bill of
eight star acts all around the Keith-Orpheum vaudeville circuit. Pat Mahoney was an Irish comic with dancing feet, and
Nora Faye — Mrs. Mahoney to you — could match him at
dancing and had the soprano voice of an angel.

Like so many people in show business, Pat was a blus-
terer, a boaster, a name dropper, but with it all a solid professional who would practice for hours a day to perfect a new
routine, never missed an entrance in forty years, and up to
the day young Jerry was born in a cheap hotel in Grand Rap-
ids, Michigan, had given away half what he earned to dead
beats and hopeless failures.

The diamond ring he wore today had been in and out of a

hundred hock shops. It had been the basis of his and Nora's security for more years than he liked to remember.

If you were left alone with Pat for more than five minutes, he went back to the old days — to the people he had idolized, like Sophie Tucker, and Smith and Dale, and Williams and Wolfus, and Joe Jackson. He'd known them all, played on the same bills with them all. "But," he would tell you, and a strange radiance would come into the pale blue eyes, "the greatest of them all was Nora Faye — Mrs. Mahoney to you."

Once he was started on his Nora, there was no way of stopping Pat Mahoney. He told of her talents as a singer and dancer, but in the end it was a saga of endless patience, of kindness and understanding, of love for a fat-headed, vain little Irish comic, of tenderness as a mother, and finally of clear-eyed courage in the face of stark tragedy.

Mahoney and Faye had never played the Palace, the Broadway goal of all vaudevillians. Pat had worked on a dozen acts that would crack the ice and finally he'd made it.

"We'd come out in cowboy suits, all covered with jewels, and jeweled guns, and jeweled boots, and we'd do a little soft shoe routine, and then suddenly all the lights would go out and only the jewels would show — they were made special for that — and we'd go into a fast routine, pulling the guns, and twirling and juggling them, and the roof would fall in! Oh, we tried it out of town, and our agent finally got us the booking at the Palace we'd always dreamed of."

There'd be a long silence then, and Pat would take a gaudy handkerchief from his hip pocket and blow his nose with a kind of angry violence. "I can show you the costumes still. They're packed away in a trunk in the attic. Just the way we wore them — me and Nora — the last time we ever played. Atlantic City it was. And she came off after the act with the cheers still ringing in our ears, and down she went on the floor of the dressing room, writhing in pain.

"Then she told me. It had been getting worse for months.

She didn't want me to know. The doctor had told her straight out. She'd only a few months she could count on. She'd never said a word to me — working toward the Palace — knowing I'd dreamed of it. And only three weeks after that — she left us. Me and Jerry — she left us. We were standing by her bed when she left — and the last words she spoke were to Jerry. 'Take care of Pat,' she says to him. 'He'll be helpless without someone to take care of him.' And then she smiled at me, and all the years were in that smile.''

And then, wherever he happened to be when he told the story, Pat Mahoney would wipe the back of his hand across his eyes and say: "If you'll excuse me, I think I'll be going home. . . .''

Nobody laughed when Pat pulled the old courtroom wheeze about "have you stopped beating your wife" on Sergeant Mason. Pat looked past the Sergeant at Trooper Teliski, and Joe Gorman, and Karl Dickler, and Mr. and Mrs. Jennings, whose two daughters were in the missing bus, and George Peabody, the fat, wheezing sheriff.

"The question I asked you, Sergeant," he said, "makes just as much sense as the one you asked me. You asked me what Nora's boy has done with those kids. There's no answer to that question. Do I hear you saying, 'I know what you must be feeling, Pat Mahoney, and you, Elizabeth Deering? And is there anything we can do for you in this hour of your terrible anxiety?' I don't hear you saying that, Sergeant.''

"I'm sorry, Pat," Mason said. "Those kids are missing. Jerry had to take them somewhere.''

"No!" Liz Deering cried. "You all know Jerry better than that!''

They didn't, it seemed, but they could be forgiven. You can't confront people with the inexplicable without frightening them and throwing them off balance. You can't endanger their children and expect a sane reaction. They muttered angrily, and old Pat saw the tortured faces of Joe Gorman and Karl Dickler and the swollen red eyes of Mrs. Jennings.

"Has he talked in any way queerly to you, Pat?" Mason asked. "Has he acted normal of late?"

"Nora's boy is the most normal boy you ever met," Pat Mahoney said. "You know that, Sergeant. Why, you've known him since he was a child."

Mrs. Jennings screamed out: "He'd protect his son. Naturally he'd protect his son. But he's stolen our children!"

"The Pied Piper rides again," Pat Mahoney said.

"Make him talk!" Mrs. Jennings cried, and the crowd around her muttered louder.

"When did you last see Jerry, Pat?"

"Breakfast," Pat said. "He has his lunch at Joe Gorman's Diner." The corner of his mouth twitched. "He should have been home for dinner long ago."

"Did he have a need for money?" Mason asked.

"Money? He was a man respected — until now — wasn't he? He was a man with a fine girl in love with him, wasn't he? What need would he have for money?"

"Make him answer sensibly!" Mrs. Jennings pleaded in a despairing voice.

Joe Gorman stepped forward. "Pat, maybe Jerry got sick all of a sudden. It's happened to men who saw action overseas. Maybe you saw signs of something and wouldn't want to tell of it. But my Pete was on that bus, and Karl's two, and Mrs. Jennings' two. We're nowhere, Pat — so if you can tell us anything! Our kids were on that bus!"

Pat Mahoney's eyes, as he listened to Joe Gorman, filled with pain. "My kid is on that bus, too, Joe," he said.

They all stared at him, some with hatred. And then, in the distance, they heard the wail of a siren. The troopers' car was coming from Lakeview, hell-bent.

"Maybe it's news!" someone shouted.

"News!"

And they all went stumbling out of the house to meet the approaching car — all but Elizabeth Deering, who stayed behind, clinging to the old man.

"I don't understand it," she said, her voice shaken. "They think he's harmed their children, Pat! Why? Why would they think he'd do such a thing? Why?"

Old Pat's eyes had a faraway look in them. "Did I ever tell you about The Great Thurston?" he asked. "Greatest magic act I ever saw."

"Pat!" Elizabeth said, her eyes widening in horror.

"First time I ever caught his act was in Sioux City," Pat said. "He came out in a flowing cape, and a silk hat, and he . . ."

Dear God, he's losing his reason, Elizabeth Deering told herself. Let the news be good! Let them be found safe!

Outside the siren drew close.

The police car with its wailing siren carried news, but it was not the sort the people of Clayton were hoping to hear.

It was reassuring to know that within a few hours of the tragedy the entire area was alerted, that the moment daylight came a fleet of army helicopters would cover the area for hundreds of miles around, that a five-state alarm was out for the missing station wagon and its passengers, and that the Attorney General had sent the best man on his staff to direct and coordinate the search.

Top officials, viewing the case coldly and untouched by the hysteria of personal involvement, had a theory. Of course there had to be a rational explanation of the disappearance of the bus, and Clyde Haviland, tall, stoop-shouldered, scholarly looking investigator from the Attorney General's office, was ordered to produce that explanation as soon as possible upon his arrival in Clayton. But beyond that, officials had no doubt as to the reason for the disappearance: this was a mass kidnaping; something novel in the annals of crime.

Since none of the families involved had means, Haviland and his superiors were convinced the next move in this strange charade would be a demand on the whole community to pay ransom for the children. The FBI was alerted to be ready to act the moment there was any indication of involvement across state lines.

While mothers wept and the menfolk grumbled angrily that Jerry Mahoney, the driver, was at the bottom of this, officialdom worked calmly and efficiently. The Air Force turned over its complete data on Technical Sergeant Jerry Mahoney to the FBI. Men who had known Jerry in the service were waked from their sleep or pulled out of restaurants or theaters to be questioned. Had he ever said anything that would indicate he might move into a world of violence? Did his medical history contain any record of mental illness?

Sitting at a desk in the town hall, Clyde Haviland reported on some of this to George Peabody, the sheriff, the town's three selectmen, Sergeant Mason and a couple of other troopers. Haviland, carefully polishing his shell-rimmed glasses, was a quiet, reassuring sort of man. He had a fine reputation in the state. He was not an unfamiliar figure to people in Clayton because he had solved a particularly brutal murder in the neighboring town of Johnsville, and his investigation had brought him in and out of Clayton for several weeks.

"So far," he said, with a faint smile, "the report on Jerry Mahoney is quite extraordinary."

"In what way?" Sergeant Mason asked, eager for the scent of blood.

"Model citizen," Haviland said. "No one has a bad word for him. No bad temper. Never held grudges. Never chiseled. Saves his money. His savings account in the Clayton bank would surprise some of you. On the face of it, this is the last person in the world to suspect."

"There has to be a first time for everything," Karl Dickler said. He was a selectman as well as one of the bereaved parents.

"It's going down toward zero tonight," George Peabody, the sheriff, said, glumly. "If those kids are out anywhere —"

"They're one hell of a long way from here by now, if you ask me," Sergeant Mason said.

Haviland looked at him, his eyes unblinking behind the lenses of his glasses. "Except that they never came out of the dugway."

"Nobody saw them," Mason said. "But they're not there so they did come out."

"They didn't come out," Joe Gorman said. "I was watching for them from the window of my diner at this end."

"That was the three seconds you were getting something out of the icebox in your pantry," Mason said.

"And I suppose everyone else along Main Street had his head in a closet at just that time!" Joe Gorman said.

"Or someone reached down out of the heavens and snatched that station wagon up into space," Haviland said. He was looking at Peabody's pudgy face as he spoke, and something he saw there made him add quickly: "I'm kidding, of course."

Peabody laughed nervously. "It's the only good explanation we've had so far."

Karl Dickler put his hand up to his cheek. There was a nerve there that had started to twitch, regularly as the tick of a clock. "I like Jerry. I'd give the same kind of report on him you've been getting, Mr. Haviland. But you can't pass up the facts. I'd have said he'd defend those kids with his life. But did he? And the old man — his father. He won't answer questions directly. There's something queer about him. Damn it, Mr. Haviland, my kids are — out there, somewhere!" He waved toward the frost-coated window panes.

"Every highway within two hundred miles of here is being patrolled, Mr. Dickler," Haviland said. "If they'd driven straight away from here in daylight — granting Mason is right and everybody was in a closet when the station wagon went through town — they'd have been seen a hundred times after they left Clayton. There isn't one report of anyone having seen the station wagon with the school-bus markings." Haviland paused to light a cigarette. His tapering fingers were nicotine stained.

"If you'd ever investigated a crime, Mr. Dickler, you'd know we usually are swamped with calls from people who think they've seen the wanted man. A bus — a busload of kids. Somebody *had* to see it! But there isn't even a crackpot report. If there was some place he could have stayed under cover — and don't tell me, I know there isn't — and started moving after dark, he might get some distance. But alarms are out everywhere. He couldn't travel five miles now without being trapped.''

"We've told ourselves all these things for hours!'' Dickler said, pinching savagely at his twitching cheek. "What are you going to *do,* Haviland?''

"Unless we're all wrong,'' Haviland said, "we're going to hear from the kidnapers soon. Tonight — or maybe in the morning — by mail, or phone or in some unexpected way. But we'll hear. They'll demand money. What other purpose can there be? Once we hear, we'll have to start to play it by ear. That's the way those cases are.''

"Meanwhile you just sit here and wait!'' Dickler said, a kind of despair rising in his voice. "What am I going to say to my wife?''

"I think all the parents of the children should go home. You may be the one the kidnapers contact. It may be your child they put on the phone to convince you the kids are safe.'' Haviland said. "As soon as it's daylight —''

"You think the kids *are* safe?'' Dickler cried out.

Haviland stared at the distraught father for a minute. Then he spoke, gently. "What kind of assurance could I give you, Mr. Dickler? Even if I tried, you wouldn't believe me. People who play this kind of game are without feelings, not rational. When you fight them, you have to walk quietly. If you scare them, God knows what to expect. That's why I urge you all to go home and wait.'' He dropped his cigarette on the floor and heeled it out. "And pray,'' he said . . .

Elizabeth Deering, Jerry Mahoney's girl, was sick with anxiety. Jerry was foremost in her mind; Jerry, missing with the children; Jerry, worse than that, suspected by his friends. But on top of that was old Pat Mahoney.

He hadn't made the slightest sense since the angry crowd had left his house. He had talked on endlessly about the old days in vaudeville. He seemed obsessed with the memory of the first time he had seen The Great Thurston in Sioux City. He remembered card tricks, and sawing the lady in half, and his wife Nora's childish delight in being completely bewildered. He seemed to remember everything he had seen the great man do.

Elizabeth tried, but she could not bring Pat back to the present. The tragedy seemed to have tipped him right out of the world of reason. She was partly relieved when she heard firm steps on the front porch. The other part of her, when she saw Sergeant Mason and the tall stranger, was the fear that they had news — bad news about Jerry.

Mason was less aggressive than he had been on his first visit. He introduced Haviland and said they wanted to talk to Pat. Elizabeth took them back into the living room where old Pat still sat in the overstuffed armchair.

Mason introduced Haviland. "Mr. Haviland is a special investigator from the Attorney General's office, Pat."

Pat's eyes brightened. "Say, you're the fellow that solved that murder over in Johnsville, aren't you?" he said. "Smart piece of work."

"Thanks," Haviland said. He looked at Pat, astonished at his gaudy vest and tie and the glittering diamond on his finger. He had been prepared for Pat, but not adequately.

"Sit down," Pat said. "Maybe Liz would make us some coffee if we asked her pretty."

Mason nodded to Liz, who went out into the kitchen. He followed her to tell her there was no news. Haviland sat down on the couch next to Pat, stretched out his long legs and offered Pat a cigarette.

"Don't smoke," Pat said. "Never really liked anything but cigars. Nora hated the smell of 'em. So what was I to do? You go to vaudeville in the old days, Mr. Haviland?"

"When I was a kid," Haviland said, lighting a cigarette.

"I never had the pleasure of seeing you, though, Mr. Mahoney."

"Call me Pat," Pat said. "Everyone does. I was nothing, Mr. Haviland. Just a third-rate song-and-dance man. But Nora — well, if you ever saw my Nora . . ."

Haviland waited for him to go on, but Pat seemed lost in his precious memories.

"You must be very worried about your son, Pat," he said.

For a fractional moment the mask of pleasant incompetence seemed to be stripped from Pat's face. "Wouldn't you be?" he asked, harshly. Then, almost instantly, the mask was fitted back into place, and old Pat gave his cackling laugh. "You got theories, Mr. Haviland? How're you going to handle this case?"

"I think," Haviland said, conversationally, "the children and your son have been kidnaped. I think we'll hear from the kidnapers soon. I think, in all probability, the whole town will be asked to get up a large ransom."

Pat nodded. "I'll chip in this diamond ring," he said. "It's got Jerry out of trouble more than once."

Haviland's eyes narrowed. "He's been in trouble before?"

"His main trouble was his Pop," Pat said. "Sometimes there wasn't enough to eat. But we could always raise eating money on this ring." He turned his bright, laughing eyes directly on Haviland. "You figured out how the bus disappeared?"

"No," Haviland said.

"Of course it doesn't really matter, does it?" Pat said.

"Well, if we knew —" Haviland said.

"It wouldn't really matter," Pat said. "It's what's going to happen now that matters."

"You mean the demand for money?"

"If that's what's going to happen," Pat said. The cackling laugh suddenly grated on Haviland's nerves. The old joker did know something!

"You have a different theory, Pat?" Haviland asked, keeping his exasperation out of his voice.

"You ever see The Great Thurston on the Keith-Orpheum circuit?" Pat asked.

"I'm afraid not," Haviland said.

"Greatest magic act I ever saw," Pat said. "Better than Houdini. Better than anyone. I first saw him in Sioux City —"

"About the case here, Pat," Haviland interrupted. "You have a theory?"

"I got no theory," Pat said. "But I know what's going to happen."

Haviland leaned forward. "What's going to happen?"

"One of two things," Pat said. "Everybody in this town is going to be looking for that station wagon in the lake, where they know it isn't, and they're going to be looking for it in the woods, where they know it isn't. That's one thing that may happen. The other thing is, they buy this theory of yours, Mr. Haviland — and it's a good theory, mind you — and they all stay home and wait to hear something. There's one same result from both things, isn't there?"

"Same result?"

"Sure. Nobody in Clayton goes to work. The quarries don't operate. The small businesses will shut down. People will be looking and people will be waiting . . ."

"So?"

"So what good will that do anyone?" Pat asked.

Haviland ground out his cigarette in an ash tray. "It won't do anyone any good. The quarry owners will lose some money. The small businesses will lose some money."

"Not much point in it, is there?" Pat said, grinning.

Haviland rose. He'd had about enough. Mason and Elizabeth were coming back from the kitchen with coffee. "There isn't much point to anything you're saying, Mr. Mahoney."

Pat's eyes twinkled. "You said you never saw The Great Thurston, didn't you?"

"I never saw him," Haviland said.

"Well, we'll see. If they're supposed to stay home and wait, they'll stay home and wait. If they're supposed to be

out searching, they'll be out searching. Ah, coffee! Smells
real good. Pull up a chair, Sergeant. By the way, Mr. Haviland, I'll make you a bet," Pat said.

"I'm not a betting man," Haviland said.

"Oh, just a manner-of-speaking bet," Pat said. "I'll make
you a bet that tomorrow morning they'll be out searching.
I'll make you a bet that even if you order them to stay home
and wait, they'll be out searching."

"Look here, Pat, if you know something . . ."

A dreamy look came into Pat's eyes. "Nora was so taken
with The Great Thurston that time in Sioux City I went
around to see him afterwards. I thought maybe he'd show me
how to do a few simple tricks. I pretended it was for Nora,
but really I thought we might use 'em in our act. He wouldn't
tell me anything — that is, not about any of his tricks. But
he told me the whole principle of his business."

"Sugar?" Elizabeth asked Haviland. Poor old man, she
thought.

"The principle is," Pat said, "to make your audience
think only what you want them to think, and see only what
you want them to see." Pat's eyes brightened. "Which reminds me, there's something I'd like to have you see, Mr.
Haviland."

Haviland gulped his coffee. Somehow he felt mesmerized
by the old man. Pat was at the foot of the stairs, beckoning.
Haviland followed.

Elizabeth looked at Mason and there were tears in her
eyes. "It's thrown him completely off base," she said. "You
know what he's going to show Mr. Haviland?" Sergeant Mason shook his head.

"A cowboy suit!" Elizabeth said, and dropped down on
the couch, crying softly. "He's going to show him a cowboy
suit."

And she was right. Haviland found himself in the attic, his
head bowed to keep him from bumping into the sloping
beams. Old Pat had opened a wardrobe trunk and, with the
gesture of a waiter taking the silver lid off a tomato surprise,

revealed two cowboy suits, one hanging neatly on each side of the trunk — Nora's and his. Chaps, shirt, vest, boots, Stetsons, and gun belts — all studded with stage jewelry.

". . . and when the lights went out," Pat was saying, "all you could see was these jew jaws, sparkling. And we'd take out the guns . . ." And suddenly Pat had the two jeweled six-shooters in his hands, twirling and spinning them. "In the old days I could draw these guns and twirl 'em into position faster than Jesse James!"

The spell was broken for Haviland. The old guy was cuckoo. "I enjoyed seeing them, Mr. Mahoney," he said. "But now, I'm afraid I've got to get back . . ."

As soon as dawn broke, Haviland had Sergeant Mason and Sheriff George Peabody take him out to the scene of the disappearance. Everyone else was at home, waiting to hear from the kidnapers. It had been a terrible night for the whole town, a night filled with forebodings and dark imaginings. Haviland covered every inch of the two-mile stretch of the dugway. You couldn't get away from the facts. There was no way for it to have happened — but it had happened.

About eight-thirty he was back in Clayton in Joe's Diner, stamping his feet to warm them and waiting eagerly for eggs and toast to go with his steaming cup of black coffee. All the parents had been checked. There'd been no phone calls, no notes slipped under doors, nothing in the early-morning mail.

Haviland never got his breakfast. Trooper Teliski came charging into the diner just as Joe Gorman was taking the eggs off the grill. Teliski, a healthy young man, was white as parchment, and the words came out of him in a kind of choking sob. "We've found 'em," he said. "Or at least we know where they are. Helicopters spotted 'em. I just finished passing the word in town."

Joe Gorman dropped the plate of eggs on the floor behind the counter. Haviland spun around on his counter stool. Just looking at Teliski made the hair rise on the back of his neck.

"The old quarry off the dugway," Teliski said, and gulped for air. "No sign of the bus. It didn't drive up there. But the kids." Teliski steadied himself on the counter. "School-books," he said. "A couple of coats — lying on the edge of the quarry. And in the quarry — more of the same. A red beret belonging to one of the kids —"

"Peter!" Joe Gorman cried out.

Haviland headed for the door. The main street of Clayton was frightening to see. People ran out of houses, screaming at each other, heading crazily toward the dugway. Those who went for their cars scattered the people in front of them. There was no order — only blind panic.

Haviland stood on the curb outside the diner, ice in his veins. He looked down the street to where old Pat Mahoney lived, just in time to see a wildly weeping woman pick up a stone and throw it through the front window of Pat's house.

"Come on — what's the matter with you?" Teliski shouted from behind the wheel of the State Police car.

Haviland stood where he was, frozen, staring at the broken window of Pat Mahoney's house. The abandoned quarry, he knew, was sixty feet deep, full to within six feet of the top with icy water fed in by constantly bubbling springs.

A fire engine roared past. They were going to try to pump out the quarry. It would be like bailing out the Atlantic Ocean with a tea cup.

"Haviland!" Teliski called desperately.

Haviland still stared at Pat Mahoney's house. A cackling old voice rang in his ears. "I'll make you a bet, Mr. Havi-land. I'll make you a bet that even if you order them to stay at home and wait, they'll be out searching."

Rage such as he had never known flooded the ice out of Haviland's veins. So Pat had known! The old codger had known *last night!*

Haviland had never witnessed anything like the scene at the quarry.

The old road, long since overgrown, which ran about 200

yards in from the dugway to the quarry, had been trampled
down as if by a herd of buffalo.

Within three-quarters of an hour of the news reaching
town, it seemed as if everyone from Clayton and half the
population of Lakeview had arrived at the quarry's edge.

One of the very first army helicopters which had taken to
the air at dawn had spotted the clothes and books at the edge
of the abandoned stone pit.

The pilot had dropped down close enough to identify the
strange objects and radioed immediately to State Police. The
stampede had followed.

Haviland was trained to be objective in the face of tragedy,
but he found himself torn to pieces by what he saw. Women
crowded forward, screaming, trying to examine the articles
of clothing and the books. Maybe not all the children were in
this icy grave. It was only the hope of desperation. No one
really believed it. It seemed, as Trooper Teliski had said, to
be the work of a maniac.

Haviland collected as many facts about the quarry as he
could from a shaken Sheriff Peabody.

"Marble's always been Clayton's business," Peabody
said. "Half the big buildings in New York have got their
marble out of Clayton quarries. This was one of the first
quarries opened up by the Clayton Marble Company nearly
sixty years ago. When they started up new ones, this one was
abandoned."

In spite of the cold, Peabody was sweating. He wiped the
sleeve of his plaid hunting shirt across his face. "Sixty feet
down, and sheer walls," he said. "They took the blocks out
at ten-foot levels, so there is a little ledge about every ten
feet going down. A kid couldn't climb out of it if it was
empty."

Haviland glanced over at the fire engine which had started
to pump water from the quarry. "Not much use in that," he
said.

"The springs are feeding it faster than they can pump it
out," Peabody said. "There's no use telling them. They got

to feel they're doing something." The fat sheriff's mouth set in a grim slit. "Why would Jerry Mahoney do a thing like this? *Why?* I guess you can only say the old man is a little crazy, and the son has gone off his rocker too."

"There are some things that don't fit," Haviland said. He noticed his own hands weren't steady as he lit a cigarette. The hysterical shrieking of one of the women near the edge of the quarry grated on his nerves. "Where is the station wagon?"

"He must have driven up here and — and done what he did to the kids," Peabody said. "Then waited till after dark to make a getaway."

"But you searched this part of the woods before dark last night," Haviland said.

"We missed it somehow, that's all," Peabody said, stubbornly.

"A nine-passenger station wagon is pretty hard to miss," Haviland said.

"So we missed it," Peabody said. "God knows how, but we missed it." He shook his head. "I suppose the only thing that'll work here is grappling hooks. They're sending a crane over from one of the active quarries. Take an hour or more to get it here. Nobody'll leave here till the hooks have scraped the bottom of that place and they've brought up the kids."

Unless, Haviland thought to himself, the lynching spirit gets into them. He was thinking of an old man in a red vest and a green necktie and a diamond twinkling on his little finger. He was thinking of a broken window pane — and of the way he'd seen mobs act before in his time.

Someone gripped the sleeve of Haviland's coat and he looked down into the horror-struck face of Elizabeth Deering, Jerry Mahoney's girl.

"It's true then," she whispered. She swayed on her feet, holding tight to Haviland for support.

"It's true they found some things belonging to the kids," he said. "That's all that's true at the moment, Miss Deering." He was a little astonished by his own words. He realized that, instinctively, he was not believing everything that he saw in front of him. "This whole area was searched last night before dark," he said. "No one found any schoolbooks or coats or berets then. No one saw the station wagon."

"What's the use of talking that way?" Peabody said. His eyes were narrowed, staring at Liz Deering. "I don't want to believe what I see either, Mr. Haviland. But I got to." The next words came out of the fat man with a bitterness that stung like a whiplash. "Maybe you're the only one in Clayton that's lucky, Liz. You found out he was a homicidal maniac in time — before you got married to him."

"Please, George!" the girl cried. "How can you believe —"

"What can anyone believe but that?" Peabody said, and turned away.

Liz Deering clung to Haviland, sobbing. The tall man stared over her head at the hundreds of people grouped around the quarry's edge. He was reminded of a mine disaster he had seen once in Pennsylvania: a whole town waiting at the head of the mine shaft for the dead to be brought to the surface.

"Let's get out of here," he said to Liz Deering, with sudden energy. . .

Clayton was a dead town. Stores were closed. Joe's Diner was closed. The railroad station agent was on the job, handling dozens of telegrams that were coming in from friends and relatives of the parents of the missing children. The two girls in the telephone office, across the street from the bank, were at their posts.

Old Mr. Granger, a teller in the bank, and one of the stenographers were all of the bank staff that had stayed on the job. Old Mr. Granger was preparing the payroll for the Clayton Marble Company. He didn't know whether the truck from the company's offices with the two guards would show up for the money or not.

Nothing else was working on schedule today. Even the hotel down the street had shut up shop. One or two salesmen had driven into town, heard the news, and gone off down the dugway toward the scene of the tragedy. A few very old people tottered in and out the front doors of houses, looking anxiously down Main Street toward the dugway. Even the clinic was closed. The town's doctors and nurses had all gone to the scene of the disaster.

Down the street a piece of newspaper had been taped over the hole in Pat Mahoney's front window. Pat Mahoney sat in the big overstuffed armchair in his living room. He rocked slowly back and forth, staring at an open scrapbook spread across his knees. A big black headline from a show-business paper was pasted across the top.

MAHONEY AND FAYE
BOFFO BUFFALO

Under it were pictures of Pat and Nora in their jeweled cowboy suits, their six-shooters drawn, pointing straight at the camera. There was a description of the act, the dance in the dark with only the jewels showing and the six-shooters spouting flame. "Most original number of its kind seen in years," a Buffalo critic had written. "The ever popular Mahoney and Faye have added something to their familiar routines that should please theater audiences from coast to coast. We are not surprised to hear that they have been booked into the Palace."

Pat closed the scrapbook and put it down on the floor beside him. From the inside pocket of his jacket he took a wallet. It bulged with papers and cards. He was an honorary Elk, honorary police chief of Wichita in 1927, a Friar, a Lamb.

Carefully protected by an isinglass guard were some snapshots. They were faded now, but anyone could see they were pictures of Nora with little Jerry at various stages of his growth. There was Jerry at six months, Jerry at a year, Jerry at four years. And Nora, smiling gently at her son. The love seemed to shine right out of the pictures, Pat thought.

Pat replaced the pictures and put the wallet back in his pocket. He got up from his chair and moved toward the stairway. People who knew him would have been surprised. No one had ever seen Pat when his movements weren't brisk and youthful. He could still go into a tap routine at the drop of a hat, and he always gave the impression that he was on the verge of doing so. Now he moved slowly, almost painfully — a tired old man, with no need to hide it from anyone. There was no one to hide it from; Jerry was missing, Liz was gone.

He climbed to the second floor and turned to the attic door. He opened it, switched on the lights, and climbed up to the area under the eaves. There he opened the wardrobe trunk he'd shown to Haviland. From the left side he took out the cowboy outfit — the chaps, the boots, the vest and shirt and Stetson hat, and the gun belt with the two jeweled six-shooters. Slowly he carried them down to his bedroom on the second floor. There Pat Mahoney proceeded to get into costume.

He stood, at last, in front of the full-length mirror on the back of the bathroom door. The high-heeled boots made him a couple of inches taller than usual. The Stetson was set on his head at a rakish angle. The jeweled chaps and vest glittered in the sunlight from the window. Suddenly old Pat jumped into a flat-footed stance, and the guns were out of the holsters, spinning dizzily and then pointed straight at the mirror.

"Get 'em up, you lily-livered rats!" old Pat shouted. A bejeweled gunman stared back at him fiercely from the mirror.

Then, slowly, he turned away to a silver picture frame on his bureau. Nora, as a very young girl, looked out at him with her gentle smile.

"It'll be all right, honey," Pat said. "You'll see. It'll be another boffo, honey. Don't you worry about your boy.

Don't you ever worry about him while I'm around. You'll see." . . .

It was a terrible day for Clayton, but Gertrude Naylor, the chief operator in the telephone office, said afterward that perhaps the worst moment for her was when she spotted old Pat Mahoney walking down the main street — right in the middle of the street — dressed in that crazy cowboy outfit. He walked slowly, looking from right to left, staying right on the white line that divided the street.

"I'd seen it a hundred times before in the movies," Gertrude Naylor said, afterward. "A cowboy, walking down the street of a deserted town, waiting for his enemy to appear — waiting for the moment to draw his guns. Old Pat's hands floated just above those crazy guns in his holster, and he kept rubbing the tips of his fingers against his thumb. I showed him to Millie, and we started to laugh, and then, somehow, it seemed about the most awful thing of all. Jerry Mahoney had murdered those kids and here was his old man, gone nutty as a fruitcake."

Old Mr. Granger, in the bank, had much the same reaction when the aged, bejeweled gun toter walked up to the teller's window.

"Good morning, Mr. Granger," Pat said, cheerfully.

Mr. Granger moistened his pale lips. "Good morning, Pat."

"You're not too busy this morning, I see," Pat said.

"N-no," Mr. Granger said. The killer's father — dressed up like a kid for the circus. He's ready for a padded cell, Mr. Granger thought.

"Since you're not so busy," Pat said, "I'd like to have a look at the detailed statement of my account for the last three months." As he spoke, he turned and leaned against the counter, staring out through the plate-glass bank window at the street. His hands stayed near the guns, and he kept rubbing his fingertips against the ball of his thumb.

"You get a statement each month, Pat," Mr. Granger said.

"Just the same, I'd like to see the detailed statement for the last three months." Pat said.

"I had to humor him, I thought," Mr. Granger said later. "So I went back in the vault to get his records out of the files. Well, I was just inside the vault door when he spoke again, in the most natural way. 'If I were you, Mr. Granger,' he said, 'I'd close that vault door, and I'd stay inside, and I'd set off all the alarms I could lay my hands on. You're about to be stuck up, Mr. Granger.'

"Well, I thought it was part of his craziness," Mr. Granger said, later. "I thought he meant *he* was going to stick up the bank. I thought that was why he'd got all dressed up in that cowboy outfit. Gone back to his childhood, I thought. I was scared, because I figured he was crazy. So I *did* close the vault door. And I *did* set off the alarm, only it didn't work. I didn't know then all the electric wires into the bank had been cut."

Gertrude and Millie, the telephone operators, had a box seat for the rest of it. They saw the black sedan draw up in front of the bank and they saw the four men in dark suits and hats get out of it and start up the steps of the bank. Two of them were carrying small suitcases and two of them were carrying guns.

Then suddenly the bank doors burst open and an ancient cowboy appeared, hands poised over his guns. He did a curious little jig step that brought him out in a solid square stance. The four men were so astonished at the sight of him they seemed to freeze.

"Stick 'em up, you lily-livered rats!" old Pat shouted. The guns were out of the holsters, twirling. Suddenly they belched flame, straight at the bandits.

The four men dived for safety, like men plunging off the deck of a sinking ship. One of them made the corner of the bank building. Two of them got to the safe side of the car.

The fourth, trying to scramble back into the car was caught in the line of fire.

"I shot over your heads that first time!" Pat shouted. "Move another inch and I'll blow you all to hell!" The guns twirled again and then suddenly aimed steadily at the exposed bandit. "All right, come forward and throw your guns down," Pat ordered.

The man in the direct line of fire obeyed at once. His gun bounced on the pavement a few feet from Pat and he raised his arms slowly. Pat inched his way toward the discarded gun.

The other men didn't move. And then Gertrude and Millie saw the one who had gotten around the corner of the bank slowly raise his gun and take deliberate aim at Pat. She and Millie both screamed, and it made old Pat jerk his head around. In that instant there was a roar of gunfire.

Old Pat went down, clutching at his shoulder. But so did the bandit who'd shot him and so did one of the men behind the car. Then Gertrude and Millie saw the tall figure of Mr. Haviland come around the corner of the hotel next door, a smoking gun in his hand. He must have spoken very quietly because Gertrude and Millie couldn't hear him, but whatever he said made the other bandits give up. Then they saw Liz Deering running across the street to where old Pat lay, blood dripping through the fingers that clutched at his shoulder . . .

Trooper Teliski's car went racing through the dugway at breakneck speed, siren shireking. As he came to the turn-in to the old quarry, his tires screamed and he skidded in and up the rugged path, car bounding over stones, ripping through brush. Suddenly just ahead of him on the path loomed the crane from the new quarry, inching up the road on a caterpillar tractor. Trooper Teliski sprang out of his car and ran past the crane, shouting at the tractor driver as he ran.

"To hell with that!" Teliski shouted. Stumbling and gasp-

ing for breath, he raced out into the clearing where hundreds
of people waited in a grief-stricken silence for the grappling
for bodies to begin.

"Everybody!" Teliski shouted. "Everybody! Listen!" He
was half laughing, half strangling for breath. "Your kids
aren't there! They're safe. They're all safe — the kids, Jerry
Mahoney, everyone! They aren't here. They'll be home before you will! Your kids —" And then he fell forward on his
face, sucking in the damp, loam-scented air.

Twenty minutes later Clayton was a madhouse. People
running, people driving, people hanging onto the running
boards of cars and clinging to bumpers. And in the middle of
the town, right opposite the bank, was a station wagon with
a yellow school bus sign on its roof, and children were spill-
ing out of it, waving and shouting at their parents, who
laughed and wept. And a handsome young Irishman with
bright blue eyes was locked in a tight embrace with Elizabeth
Deering . . .

Haviland's fingers shook slightly as he lit a cigarette. Not
yet noon and he was on his third pack.

"You can't see him yet," he said to Jerry Mahoney. "The
doctor's with him. In a few minutes."

"I still don't get it," Jerry said. "People thought *I* had
harmed those kids?"

"You don't know what it's been like here," Liz Deering
said, clinging tightly to his arm.

Jerry Mahoney turned and saw the newspaper taped over
the broken front window, and his face hardened. "Try and
tell me, plain and simple, about Pop," he said.

Haviland shook his head, smiling like a man still dazed.
"Your Pop is an amazing man, Mr. Mahoney," he said.
"His mind works in its own peculiar ways . . . The disappearance of the bus affected him differently from some others. He saw it as a magic trick, and he thought of it as a
magic trick — or, rather, as *part* of a magic trick. He said it
to me and I wouldn't listen. He said it is a magician's job

to get you to think what he wants you to think and see what
he wants you to see. The disappearance of the children, the
ghastly faking of their death in the quarry — it meant one
thing to your Pop, Mr. Mahoney. Someone wanted all the
people in Clayton to be out of town. Why?

"There was only one good reason that remarkable Pop of
yours could think of. The quarry payroll. Nearly a hundred
thousand dollars in cash, and not a soul in town to protect it.
Everyone would be looking for the children, and all the bandits had to do was walk in the bank and take the money. No
cops, no nothing to interfere with them."

"But why didn't Pop tell you his idea?" Jerry asked.

"You still don't know what it was like here, Mr. Mahoney," Haviland said. "People thought you had done something to those kids; they imagined your Pop knew something
about it. If he'd told his story, even to me, I think I'd have
thought he was either touched in the head or covering up. So
he kept still — although he did throw me a couple of hints.
And suddenly, he was, to all intents and purposes, alone in
the town. So he went upstairs, got dressed in those cowboy
clothes and went, calm as you please, to the bank to meet
the bandits he knew must be coming. And they came."

"But why the cowboy suit?" Liz Deering asked.

"A strange and wonderful mind," Haviland said. "He
thought the sight of him would be screwy enough to throw
the bandits a little off balance. He thought if he started blast-
ing away with his guns they might panic. They almost did."

"What I don't understand," Liz said, "is how, when he
fired straight at them, he never hit anybody!"

"Those were stage guns — prop guns," Jerry said. "They
only fire blanks."

Haviland nodded. "He thought he could get them to drop
their own guns and then he'd have a real weapon and have
the drop on them. It almost worked. But the one man who'd
ducked around the corner of the building got in a clean shot
at him. Fortunately, I arrived at exactly the same minute, and
I had them all from behind."

"But how did you happen to turn up?" Jerry asked.

"I couldn't get your father out of my mind," Haviland said. "He seemed to know what was going to happen. He said they'd be searching for the kids, whether I told them to wait at home or not. Suddenly I had to know why he'd said that."

"Thank God," Jerry said. "I gather you got them to tell you where we were?"

Haviland nodded. "I'm still not dead clear how it worked, Jerry."

"It was as simple as pie à la mode," Jerry said. "I was about a half mile into the dugway on the home trip with the kids. We'd just passed Karl Dickler headed the other way when a big trailer truck loomed up ahead of me on the road. It was stopped, and a couple of guys were standing around the tail end of it.

"Broken down, I thought. I pulled up. All of a sudden guns were pointed at me and the kids. They didn't talk much. They just said to do as I was told. They opened the back of the big truck and rolled out a ramp. Then I was ordered to drive the station wagon right up into the body of the truck. I might have tried to make a break for it except for the kids. I drove up into the truck, they closed up the rear end, and that was that. They drove off with us — right through the main street of town here!"

Haviland shook his head. "An old trick used hundreds of times back in bootleg days. And I never thought of it!"

"Not ten minutes later," Jerry went on, "they pulled into that big deserted barn on the Haskell place. We've been shut up there ever since. They were real decent to the kids — hot dogs, ice cream cones, soda.

"So we just waited there, not knowing why, but nobody hurt, and the kids not as scared as you might think," Jerry laughed. "Oh, we came out of the dugway all right — and right by everybody in town. But nobody saw us."

The doctor appeared in the doorway. "You can see him for a minute now, Jerry," he said. "I had to give him a pretty strong sedative. Dug the bullet out of his shoulder and it hurt a bit. He's pretty sleepy — but he'll do better if he sees you, I think. Don't stay too long, though."

Jerry bounded up the stairs and into the bedroom where Pat Mahoney lay, his face very pale, his eyes half closed Jerry knelt by the bed.

"Pop," he whispered. "You crazy old galoot!"

Pat opened his eyes. "You okay, Jerry?"

"Okay, Pop."

"And the kids?"

"Fine. Not a hair of their heads touched." Jerry reached out and covered Pat's hand with his. "Now look here, Two-Gun Mahoney . . ."

Pat grinned at him. "It was a boffo, Jerry. A real boffo."

"It sure was," Jerry said. He started to speak, but he saw that Pat was looking past him at the silver picture frame on the dresser.

"I told you it'd be all right, honey," Pat whispered. "I told you not to worry about your boy while I was around to take care of him." Then he grinned at Jerry, and his eyes closed and he was asleep.

Jerry tiptoed out of the room to find his own girl.

# As If By Magic

**Julian Symons**

*A brief, brilliant tale by Julian Symons in which a murderer vanishes from a crowded amusement pier.*

THEY SAY that a murder is most easily committed in a crowd, and that was the way it almost proved, for there was a big enough crowd that Bank Holiday Monday at the end of Brightsand Pier.

On the windy side of the pier, people streamed into the Amusement Arcade to play the Kentucky Derby or the Great Brooklands Speedway, to see What the Butler Saw, or to lose pennies on little machines. The Punch and Judy stand was silent. The Brightsand Concert Party had given their afternoon performance and gone home.

In the onion-domed tea pavilion in the middle of the pier, worn-out parents refreshed themselves with nice cups of tea while their clamorous children ate rich fruit cake and ice cream. On the sheltered side of the pier, people sat in deckchairs sunning themselves, sleeping with newspapers over their faces, or looking out at the toy-like boats on the sea.

It was in this cheerful, busy, unobservant Bank Holiday crowd that the murderer saw his chance. His name doesn't matter — he was an inoffensive-looking supremely ordinary little man. His victim, whose name is almost unimportant, was a dark bulky man sleeping in one of the deckchairs, with his feet on the railing. The deckchairs on both sides of the bulky man were vacant.

The inoffensive-looking little man stood over the deckchair, like a man greeting a friend. He pulled a heavy clasp knife from his belt and stabbed downward, once, twice, three times. The bulky man gave a kind of grunt.

The little man then flung away the knife, now gleaming red. It curved in a wide parabola into the blue sea.

The little man then walked quickly but calmly away. The murder did not take more than ten seconds.

This was, as afterward appeared, a quite unpremeditated crime. The murderer simply saw his enemy, his back to him, at his mercy, remembered his clasp knife, and acted almost without thought. The motive? It proved to be grinding, agonizing jealousy. The bulky man had taken away the little man's wife and was living with her. The motive and background of the crime were discovered in the succeeding days and weeks by the slow machinery of the law. What happened on the day of the crime was quicker.

*The murder had been seen.* Miss Slater, a capable middle-aged schoolmistress down on a day trip to Brightsand, actually saw the knife rise and fall. She saw a vivid spurt of red splash onto a brown jacket. For a few moments her mind refused to take in what her senses had recorded. Then she pointed and screamed . . .

At once the scene was changed to one of frantic, slightly purposeless action. People in deckchairs stood up, fishermen abandoned their lines, one of the waitresses ran out of the tea pavilion. There were confused questions and answers.

"It's a thief . . . lady's fainted . . . running this way . . . a little man, she said . . . a boy's fallen in . . . no, somebody's been murdered."

The confusion lasted only a couple of minutes. Then the body was discovered and two plainclothes policemen, stationed on the pier to watch for pickpockets, had cordoned off the top end of the pier and begun investigations.

But in that short time the little man with the bloodstain on his brown jacket had vanished — vanished completely, as if by magic . . .

Francis Quarles had been on the pier for half an hour before the murder, acting as companion to his small nephew, Roger. They had been on the Dodgem Cars, played Skeeball, and spent several shillings in the Amusement Arcade.

Roger had eaten an extraordinary amount of ice cream and candy floss, and had watched the Punch and Judy show, which he characterized as smashing, though really for kids. With some interest Quarles saw the cordoning off at the end of the pier and the arrival of the local inspector, Garrity. He accepted with pleasure the Inspector's suggestion that he might like to see what went on.

Miss Slater's evidence was simple. Yes, she had seen the murderer, but she had not seen his face. He had been standing over the deckchair. She was quite sure she had seen the blood spurt onto the right sleeve of his jacket.

The murderer, said Miss Slater, had been wearing gray flannel trousers, he was of less than medium height, and she thought he had brown hair. He had walked away from her, toward the entrance to the tea pavilion.

She repeated this evidence again and again, and could not be shaken from it.

Had he gone into the tea pavilion? No, said the waitress who had been standing at the door and had then run out — quite positively he had not. Nobody had come in just before or after she heard the scream.

Had he entered the Amusement Arcade next door? The attendant said no. The changing-room behind the concert party stage was locked and padlocked. The Punch and Judy man, who was still in his box, had seen no little man in a blood-stained brown jacket hurry past.

Had he got off the pier, then? The two plainclothesmen, who had been stationed at the point where the bulbous end of the pier narrowed into an ordinary promenade, swore positively that no such little man had passed them just before or after Miss Slater's scream. And Quarles, who had been standing near them, was ready to swear it too.

The police proceeded methodically. Either the murderer had changed his jacket — which meant that he must have had a spare jacket and a place to change in without being noticed — or he had got rid of the jacket in some way. Or he was still wearing it.

You couldn't evade these three all-inclusive conclusions. But somehow the murderer did evade them.

There were more than 300 people at the end of the pier, less than half of them men. Only six of these were jacketless, for there was a nip in the air, and these six were vouched for by friends or relatives. There were a good many brown jackets, but not a single one with blood on.

For good measure Inspector Garrity checked the people in the tea pavilion and in the Amusement Arcade. At the end of an hour he had got precisely nowhere, and the people who had been kept at the end of the pier were extremely restive.

"It's no use," the Inspector said. "The man had no place to hide, no place where he might have changed his coat. He must have passed you somehow, and he's now off the pier."

"On the contrary," Quarles said. "The murderer was the only person on this part of the pier who had a hiding place, and a good reason for being in it. He walked quickly round to his hiding place, entered it, changed into an old jacket, and put his bloodstained jacket into the case in which he carries his professional paraphernalia."

Quarles put his hand upon the shoulder of the inoffensive-looking little man who ran the Punch and Judy show. "What better hiding place and changing-room could you want than the inside of a Punch and Judy box?"

# The Impossible Theft

## John F. Suter

*Some critics contend that the best impossible crime tales are ones in which the solution is simple enough to be revealed in the final sentence of the story. If so, this is one of the best.*

ROBERT CHISHOLM'S PALMS were faintly damp. He had less confidence in his ability to persuade than in the probability of his accomplishing the theft. Still, he hoped that theft would be unnecessary.

Donald Tapp looked up at him sardonically as he turned the second key to the double-locked room.

"Robert," he said in a voice that had been hoarse all his life, "you still haven't told me how you found out about my collection."

Chisholm's shrug was the smooth, practiced action of a man who knows and controls every muscle. He permitted his smile to be open and frank, instead of the faintly diabolical one which his lean face wore on certain occasions.

"I told you," he said. "A mutual friend. He just doesn't want to be identified."

Tapp reached around the metal doorframe and pressed a switch. Fluorescent lights hesitated, blinked, then came on.

He pursed his thick lips. "Mutual friend? I don't advertise what I own. There is always a clamor to have such items as these placed in a museum. Time enough for that when I'm dead." He studied Chisholm quizzically. "Would it have been Perry?"

Chisholm became poker-faced. "Sorry, Don."

Tapp still waited before ushering him into the room.

"Robert, I haven't seen you in — how many years? Even though we played together as boys and went to school together — clear through college. Now you arrive in town for a convention and after all these years you look me up. I'm delighted, Robert, delighted. I don't see old friends much any more. Chiefly my own fault. But, Robert, you arrive and make small talk and then, in the middle of it, you ask to see the collection."

Chisholm said, just a shade too casually, "If you'd rather not —"

*Ask yourself, Don,* he thought; *when you were a kid and*

*somebody asked "Whatcha got?" you'd always hide it, make
a big secret of it.*

Tapp stepped away from the door, lifting a stubby right
hand. "Come in and look. I'll be honest and say I'm particular. Not everybody can get into this room. But you're an
old friend. At least, you were never grabby like the other
kids."

*If you only knew,* Chisholm thought, entering the strongroom which Tapp devoted to his collection of rare historical
documents.

It was a windowless room, about 12 feet by 20, lighted
only by two rows of fluorescent tubes overhead. The only
door was at the end of one long wall. To the left, on entering, the wall was decorated with a large rectangular mirror in
a gilded frame. The borders of the glass itself were worked
in elaborate scrolls and tracery. Ranged against the two long
walls and the far end of the room were nine exhibition cases,
four along each wall, one at the end. The cases were of beau-
tifully grained wood, with glass tops.

Tapp beckoned Chisholm across the room.

"We'll begin here." He snapped a switch on the side of
one cabinet, and the interior became evenly illuminated,
showing a frayed yellowed paper on a background of black
velvet.

As Chisholm bent his lean shoulders to look at the descrip-
tive card, Tapp began to explain, "The last page of a letter
by James Garfield. Identity of recipient unknown, but signature authenticated. Can you read it? It says, *As to your wish
that I make a Fourth of July address in your community, this
would give me the greatest of pleasure. I must defer my answer, however, because I feel that there is some prior com-
mitment which I cannot identify at this moment. Should this
prove to be only faulty memory, I shall be pleased to accept
.  .  .* Of course, when you realize this was written just prior
to that fatal July 2, it makes for interesting speculation,
doesn't it?"

As Chisholm murmured an appropriate reply, Tapp switched off the light and moved to the right. "In this cabinet I have a receipt from William Tecumseh Sherman to Braxton Bragg for money that Bragg asked Sherman to invest for him in San Francisco in 1854, when Sherman was in the banking business. The accompanying letters have great historical significance."

Chisholm stared with a fascination he did not need to pretend as Tapp led him from case to case, showing him exceptionally valuable documents signed by George Washington, Abraham Lincoln, Andrew Johnson, Alexander Graham Bell, John C. Fremont, William H. Seward, and Carry Nation. This last brought a chuckle from Tapp.

"Simple, isn't it? *No truce with Demon Rum! Carry Nation.*"

He snapped off the light in the eighth case and turned toward the last one, at the end of the room. He paused and glanced at Chisholm.

"Robert, what was it you told me you were doing these days?"

"Area man for Shaw and Pontz Lock Company." Chisholm reached toward his left lapel with supple, slender fingers and tapped the identity tag which was stuck to his coat by the adhesive on the back of the tag. "The convention is one of hardware dealers. I'm showing a new line of passage sets."

Tapp shrugged off a faint air of perplexity. "Well! Let's look at my prize exhibit." He illuminated the last cabinet.

In it lay a scrap of paper no bigger than the palm of the average-sized hand. It was even more yellowed than the other documents, the ink slightly more faded. It was charred along the top edge.

Tapp said nothing. Chisholm bent to look closely.

"Some kind of register or ledger?"

"That's right. From an inn."

"Three names. James — Allen? Samuel Green. That one's clear. But — *Button Gwinnett?*"

Tapp rubbed his stubborn chin with his solid-fleshed left hand. The tip of his broad nose wrinkled in amusement.

"You're amazed, Robert. Yes, the rarest of all signatures in United States history. Your amazement is justified. But it's genuine, I assure you — absolutely genuine."

"But how did you — ? Where did you — ?"

Tapp shook his head. "When I am dead, all information on these documents will be released to the museum which will inherit them. In the meantime, that information is my secret."

Chisholm glanced around the room. "I hope you have these well protected. And adequately insured."

"Both, you may be sure."

"What protection, Don? This interests me, since I'm in the lock business." He bent over the case containing the Button Gwinnet signature.

"I'm satisfied with it," said Tapp bluntly.

"Are you?" Chisholm drew a key ring from his pocket. It bristled with keys — and other odd-looking objects. His supple fingers gripped something which Tapp could not see, and he inserted it quickly into the lock on the edge of the glass top. Something clicked and he lifted the lid of the case. "You see?"

Instantly a clamor began somewhere in the big house.

"I see. And do you hear?" Tapp gave his old friend an exasperated look. "Come on. I'll have to shut off the alarm."

"Might I remain here, Don? I'd like to look some more. I promise I won't touch anything."

Tapp shook his head. "Nobody looks unless I'm here. But if you don't want to come with me, you may stand by the door, outside, until I come back."

After Tapp had locked both locks from the outside, Chisholm stood by the door thinking about the strongroom. All the cases were obviously wired to alarms. He had seen no wires. This meant that the wiring probably went through the legs of the cases, where it would be difficult to reach. Did each case activate a separate alarm, or trip a separate indicator, to show exactly which cabinet a burglar had attacked? Probably.

And the mirror on the left wall? What was a mirror doing in a room of this sort?

Tapp came bustling back, his chunky frame still radiating annoyance.

"Now, Robert," he said, unlocking the door for the second time, "I ask you, *please* don't try to sell me any locks — not this time."

"We have some things which would help you, if you'd let me demonstrate," Chisholm said, as he began to scan the room closely on re-entering.

"All right, all right — but show me a little later. In my den or in my office. Of course, I'm always interested in improving my safeguards. But not just now."

Chisholm moved slowly from case to case, keeping up a running conversation to distract Tapp's attention. But he could discover nothing other than the alarms and the puzzling mirror. There were, of course, the two locks in the door — which would be impossible to jimmy, or to pick. Then two tiny air passages, high in the end walls, protected by a fine, strong mesh caught his roving eye; but he dismissed them as irrelevant.

Finally he straightened and looked directly at Tapp.

"There's a lot of money represented here, Don."

Tapp nodded soberly. "I'd hate to tell you how much, Robert."

"And you'll put even more documents in this room, won't you?"

"If something good comes along."

"This, of course, means that you have the money to spend."

Tapp's expression grew pained. "You're being a bit ingenuous, Robert. Of course I have the money."

"Have you ever considered putting some of that money into something more worthwhile?"

Tapp grinned without humor. "I should have known there was more to this visit than a chat with an old friend. Now comes the touch. How much do you need?"

Chisholm shook his head. "The need isn't mine, Don. It's Green Meadows Hospital. A check for $50,000 from you would put their new equipment drive over the top."

Tapp grimaced. "Green Meadows! I've heard their pitch. A corny one, too. Green Meadows — even the name's corny. No, thanks, Robert. Why did you have to spoil our first meeting in years?"

Chisholm said seriously, "I don't consider geriatric problems corny, Don. Are you sure you just don't like to think of the kind of future any one of us might have to face? Look here: I've contributed $20,000 myself, and believe me, it'll hurt for a while. If I could give twenty, surely you can give fifty?"

Tapp grimaced again. "I don't like people telling me what I can or can't give to charity."

"It would be a deduction on your income tax return."

"Thanks. I know all the possible deductions upside down and backwards."

"Is there any way I can reach you on this, Don? Could I tell you some details of their program —"

Tapp shook his head firmly. "No way at all — not even for an old buddy. Especially not for an old buddy. I can't stand corn."

Chisholm's eyes narrowed, and his brows slanted up in a manner familiar to many people who had met him.

"All right, Don. You won't listen to a rational argument, so I'll make you an irrational proposition. Is your gambling blood still what it used to be?"

Tapp's smile was grim. "If it's a sure thing, I'll still bet."

"Would you bet a check for $50,000 that I can't steal something of value from this room?"

Shock and amazement crossed Tapp's heavy features. "Why, that's idiotic. I won't listen."

Chisholm held out a restraining hand. "No, wait. You

have complete confidence in your safeguards. Let's see just how good they are. I don't know a thing about them except there are locks on the door and alarms connected with the cabinets. Yet I am willing to bet I can beat your system.''

Tapp pondered. ''There's nothing in the world which can't stand improvement. But $50,000 —''

Chisholm pressed on. ''Here's what I propose: shut me in this room for fifteen minutes — no more. In that short time I guarantee to steal one of these documents — *and get it out of here in spite of all your safeguards*. If I get that paper *out* of this room, you'll make the contribution to the hospital.''

''And if you fail? What is your stake?''

''I'll guarantee to increase the efficiency of your safeguards one hundred per cent.''

''That's hardly worth fifty thousand.''

''I own a quarter interest in my company. I'll assign it to you.''

Tapp eyed him shrewdly. ''You seem pretty confident.''

''I might be betting on a sure thing, Don. The way you like to do. Or I might be willing to take a bigger risk than you.''

Tapp mused, ''Fifteen minutes. And you have to get it *out* of the room by the end of that time  You know, I could just leave you locked in here.''

''No, you must come and let me out. But I must agree to let you search me or put any reasonable restrictions on me until it's absolutely clear that you've lost.''            ·

''When do you want to do this?''

''Right now.''

Tapp studied Chisholm speculatively. ''Chisel — remember how we used to call you that? — when we were kids a lot of the others had contempt for me because I wouldn't take chances. I've done pretty well in life because of caution. But don't be misled: I *will* take a risk. I'll take this one.''

Chisholm smiled broadly, but this time his smile had a Mephistophelian look. ''Fine. Shall we begin?''

Tapp held out his wrist silently and they compared watches.

"Fifteen minutes from the time you close the door," said Chisholm.

Tapp went out. As he pushed the door shut, he called through the narrowing crack, "Not that I think you have a snowball's chance, Chisel."

The door had scarcely closed before Chisholm was examining the mirror on the long wall with minute attention. He would have to proceed as though it were a two-way mirror, with only a thin layer of silver. He doubted that this was true, but he could not ignore the possibility. Finally he located what he was looking for: a circular loop in the border decoration on the glass. The glass within the loop looked subtly different.

His smile grew even more diabolical. He quickly stripped the convention badge from his left lapel and pasted it over the circle in the glass.

He then turned swiftly to the cases, taking out his keyring. Before he started to use it, he took a pair of thin rubber gloves from another pocket and put them on. Then, at a pace only a little slower than a walk, he went from case to case and opened the locks, which he had studied while looking at the documents the second time.

When he had lifted all the lids, he laughed at the thought of nine alarms ringing simultaneously in Tapp's ears, or nine position lights flashing at one time in Tapp's face. He then went from case to case and reached inside each. All his movements were swift. Most of them were intended as pure misdirection.

Finally he had what he wanted. Now all he had to do was to make sure — doubly sure — that he was not being observed. To provide a cloak, he removed his jacket and slipped it over his shoulders backward, with the back of the jacket hanging in front of him and concealing his hands. His fingers made several rapid movements beneath the protection of the jacket.

Then he suddenly reversed the process and put the coat back in its normal position.

He looked at his watch. Only eight minutes had passed.

For the remainder of the time Chisholm lounged against the doorframe singing slightly ribald songs in a clear, but not overloud, voice.

Precisely at the end of fifteen minutes, first one, then the other of the door locks was opened. The door itself, which was covered with a paneling of steel, swung back.

As Tapp stepped in, his glance already darting around the room, Chisholm clapped him lightly on the back.

"I hope you brought the check with you, Don."

Tapp half turned, and Chisholm felt a hard object bore into his ribs. He looked down. Tapp had shoved a pistol into his side.

"I have the check, Chisel, but you're going to earn it — if you get it at all. Step back."

Chisholm obeyed.

"Now, go over there to the opposite wall and sit on the floor by that first case. Fine. Extend your arms so that one is on either side of the leg of the case. Very good."

Chisholm, from his position on the floor, saw Tapp take a pair of handcuffs from his pocket. Warily, the shorter man approached him.

"Wrists out, Chisel. Good."

Tapp leaned over and snapped the cuffs on Chisholm's wrists. The tall diabolical-looking man had not ceased to smile.

"A lot of trouble, Don, just to find out what I did take. A lot of trouble to keep me from confusing you even more while you look. But I'll be glad to tell you without all this melodrama."

"Just be quiet, Chisel," Tapp said calmly "If you aren't, I'll slug you with the butt of this gun."

"Violence wasn't in our agreement, Don."

"You were not completely honest with me, Chisel. After you put all your misdirections into action, the hunch I'd had about you came out into the open. I remembered your hobby when you were a boy. I made one phone call to a local convention delegate I happen to know, and he told me you still practice your hobby. You're still an amateur magician, aren't you, Chisel?''

Chisholm shrugged. "I do a little routine to catch the buyer's attention, then I work it into a sales talk for our products. It often helps.''

"Spare me," Tapp muttered, peering into cases. His face darkened. "You lied to me, Chisel. You said you would take only one document. I count three of them: the Garfield letter we read, the Seward I mentioned, and the Button Gwinnett.''

"I didn't lie,'' Chisholm replied calmly. "Figure it out for yourself.''

"Misdirection again.'' Tapp turned and stared at him, but it was clear that his thoughts were elsewhere. In a moment he turned back to the cabinets and carefully lifted the velvet in the bottom of each. He found nothing.

He stood in thought for a few more minutes.

"The Garfield and the Alexander Graham Bell are the same size, and so are the Seward and the Lincoln. The Button Gwinnett doesn't match any, but it is *smaller* . . .''

Once more he went from case to case, this time lifting each of the remaining documents. When he had finished, he was smiling. He had found two of the missing papers carefully placed beneath others of the same size. He restored the Garfield and Seward documents to their proper cases.

"That leaves only the Button Gwinnett, Chisel. But this was what you had in mind all along. It's obvious. And if you're worth your salt as a magician, its hiding place won't be obvious. So let's eliminate the commonplace.''

Tapp went over the cases carefully, first lifting out all the documents, then each piece of velvet. When he had replaced everything, he closed and locked the cases. Then he dropped to his knees and inspected the under sides of the cabinets.

He found nothing.

He walked to each end of the room in turn and reached up

to the tiny air passages. The mesh in both was still firmly in place, and he could not budge it at either opening.

Then his eye caught the mirror.

"Oh, and another thing —" He walked to the mirror and stripped off the convention tag. "You're a sharp fellow, Robert."

Chisholm laughed. "Was my guess right? Closed-circuit TV? Did I cover the lens?"

"You put a patch on its eye, I must admit."

"No two-way mirror?"

"I considered it, but with several receivers on the TV, I can be at any one of several places in the house. A two-way mirror would only restrict me."

He walked over and stood in front of Chisholm. "Two possibilities still remain. One is that you might have slipped it into my own pocket at the door. So I'll check that out now."

He searched through all his pockets, but found nothing which had not been in them before.

He now stooped and unlocked the handcuffs, but made no move to take them from Chisholm's wrists.

"Drop the cuffs there, get up, and go to that corner," he said, motioning with the gun to the bare corner farthest away from the door.

Chisholm obeyed. When he had moved, Tapp inspected the area where the magician had been sitting.

"All right. Now take off your clothes — one garment at a time — and throw them over to me."

Chisholm complied, beginning with his coat jacket, until he stood completely stripped.

Tapp went over each item minutely, crushing cloth carefully, listening for the crackle of paper, inspecting shoes for false heels and soles and the belt for a secret compartment. From Chisholm's trousers he extracted a handkerchief and an ordinary keyring. In the pockets of the coat jacket he found a larger collection. The inside breast pocket yielded a wallet and two used envelopes with jottings on the back. The outside pockets contained the unusual keyring, the rubber gloves, a nearly full pack of cigarettes, a crumpled cigarette package, a ballpoint pen, and a rubber band.

Tapp examined all these things with intense concentration. In the wallet he found money, a driver's license, a miscellany of credit and identification cards, and a small receipt for the purchase of a shirt at a local department store. He searched for a hidden compartment in the wallet, but found none. He then shook the cigarettes from the pack, but neither the pack itself nor the individual cigarettes was the least out of the ordinary. Replacing them, he then smoothed out the crumpled pack. Several items inside it he dumped on the top of one of the cases: a twist of cellophane; two wadded bits of brownish, waxy-looking paper; a fragment of wrapper from a roll of peppermints; and part of a burned match. He snorted and swept this trash back into its container.

He drew in his breath with an angry hiss. "All right, Chisel, let's look *you* over. Turn around. Raise your arms. All right, now sit down on the floor and raise your feet."

"Nothing on the soles of my feet except dust from the floor. You should clean this place oftener," said Chisholm, leaning back on his arms.

Tapp's only answer was a growl.

"Have you checked the ceiling?" Chisholm asked.

Tapp looked up involuntarily. The ceiling was bare.

"See, you wouldn't have thought of that, would you?" Chisholm mocked.

Tapp leaned against one of the cabinets and aimed the pistol at Chisholm's midriff.

"Chisel, playtime is over. I want that Button Gwinnett back."

"Or else, eh? You forget a number of things. We haven't yet established whether the paper is in this room or out of it. We haven't exchanged your check for $50,000 for the stolen document. I haven't even put my clothes back on. And, incidentally, I give you my word: the missing paper isn't in my clothing."

Tapp tossed the clothing to Chisholm. "It doesn't matter. You're going to tell me where that piece of paper is."

Chisholm began to dress. "How do you propose to make me tell? Shoot me? On the grounds that I broke into your house to steal? A respected businessman like me — steal? If you killed me, then you'd never find your paper. If you only wounded me, I'd refuse to talk. So where are we, old friend?"

Tapp said grimly, "This bet of yours is just a stall. Once you get out of this room you'll take off with that signature to certain other collectors I could name. Why else won't you admit who told you about my collection? Only a handful of people know about it."

Chisholm was tempted to yield on this point and reveal to Tapp that it was the district manager of Tapp's own insurance company who had mentioned the collection to him in strict confidence. Had he not wished to show even the slightest sign of weakness, he would have told this.

"The whole thing was strictly honorable," Chisholm said. "This stunt was my own idea."

"And my idea," said Tapp heavily, "is to lock you in here without food and water until you return that paper. When you finally get out, I could always claim that I thought you had left the house and had locked you in without knowing."

Chisholm shook his head. "I had more respect for you, Don. If you did that, you'd either have to leave the other documents with me — and risk my destroying them — or take them out and have their absence disprove your story."

Inwardly, Chisholm was beginning to have qualms. If Tapp should abandon reason in favor of a collector's passion, as he seemed about to do, anything might happen. The best course was an immediate distraction.

"How do you know," he said challengingly, "that the paper isn't *already* outside the room?"

Tapp snorted 'Impossible!''

"Is it, now? There is a small trick I often do at dinner gatherings *which depends entirely on the victim's being too close to me to see what my hands are really doing.* I move a handkerchief or tissue from hand to hand near the victim's face, then throw it over his shoulder when my hand is too close for him to see exactly what I've done."

Tapp said warily, "But at no time were you outside this room."

"I didn't have to be."

Suddenly Tapp understood. "You mean when I came in!" He moved back and reached behind him to open the door. "Stay where you are." He stepped out and pushed the door shut again.

Chisholm waited tensely.

The door opened to a pencil-wide crack. "There's nothing out here, Chisel."

Chisholm answered evenly. "I didn't say there was. But if you'll use the brains I've always given you credit for, you'll realize that I don't *want* to steal your precious piece of paper. If I had, why make the bet? Let me out of here and give me the $50,000 check for the hospital, and I'll tell you where the Button Gwinnett signature is."

A silence followed his words. Seconds dragged by. Minutes.

Finally Tapp spoke. "You swear that this will end here? That you won't even tell anyone about this incident? I used to think your word could be relied on, Chisel."

"I'll swear on anything you name."

"That won't be necessary." The door opened wide "Now, where is it?"

Chisholm smiled and shook his head. "First, the $50,000 check."

Tapp eyed him shrewdly. "I don't know that the paper is out of the room. I don't owe you anything unless it *is* outside, and you're still *inside*. But you agreed to tell me where it is."

Chisholm kept smiling. "I'll swear again, if you like. The paper is outside the room, according to the conditions of our bet."

Tapp studied him. "Very well, come up to my den and I'll give you the check. You have my word that I'll keep my part of the bargain. Now — *where is that paper?*"

Chisholm stepped to Tapp's side and clapped him affectionately on the back. Then he held out his right hand.

"Here."

As Tapp all but snatched the document from him, Chisholm fished in his own jacket pocket. He took out the crumpled cigarette pack, opened it, and shook out the contents.

"Remember the convention badge I stuck over your TV camera lens? Such badges are only strips of cardboard coated on the back with a permanently tacky adhesive — the way surgical adhesive tape is coated." From the cigarette pack he took the two scraps of brownish, waxy paper. "That gave me the idea. It's easy to obtain tape with such an adhesive on *both* front and back. This brown paper protects the adhesive until it's peeled off, making the tape ready for use. In this case I kept a small bit of such tape in my pocket, removed the Button Gwinnett signature from the cabinet, exposed the adhesive on one side of the tape, and stuck the Button Gwinnett to that exposed side. Then I made the other side of the tape ready and palmed the whole thing."

Chisholm repeated an earlier gesture. A look of comprehension spread over Tapp's face.

"When you came into the room at the end of the fifteen minutes," Chisholm explained, "I simply put the Button Gwinnett paper in the one place you couldn't see — *on your back!*"

# Mr. Strang Takes a Field Trip

## William Brittain

*Another impossible theft, this one against a museum background and solved by William Brittain's teacher-detective Mr. Strang.*

THE YELLOW BUS with *Aldershot High School* painted on its side in large black letters came to a creaking halt in front of the Central City Natural History Museum. As the driver opened the door, the 27 teen-agers inside shifted excitedly in their seats. Mr. Strang, his battered felt hat perched squarely on the middle of his head to hide a bald spot that was increasing in size at an alarming rate, stood up and hobbled stiffly down the steps of the bus, followed by his biology students who milled about in what looked like utter confusion.

Silently the short slender teacher raised one hand over his head. The shrill yelps of the girls and the raucous comments of the boys stopped abruptly. The students formed themselves into two straight lines that would have done credit to a Marine drill instructor. With a quick nod Mr. Strang then led his class into the building.

"Ouch!" Mr. Strang turned just in time to see the boy at the head of one line clutch the seat of his pants, a distressed look on his face. The teacher glared at the second boy in line and held out his hand.

"The pin, Mr. Grier," he said wryly. "Give me the pin, if you please."

Smirking, Bradley Grier handed Mr. Strang the long map pin with which he had jabbed his fellow student.

"I'd hoped that for just one day you would forego the practical jokes, Bradley," said the teacher. "We go on few enough field trips without having you ruin them with your childish attempts at humor. You and I can discuss your little prank later, but right now the doors of the museum are about to open. We'll be among the first ones inside, and I hope the place won't be in a shambles when we leave."

Inside the museum Mr. Strang ushered his class to the foot of a long curving stairway leading upward. "We'll go straight up to the top floor to The Hall of Mammals and work our way down from there," he announced. "Any questions?"

Seeing no raised hands, the teacher started up the steps. The students broke ranks, pausing from time to time to look at the stuffed animals placed on each landing.

"Git yer hands off that before I report you!" Mr. Strang turned to see Bradley Grier, his arms still wrapped around an enormous grizzly bear which seemed to be embracing him lovingly in return. The boy was looking guiltily at a small man in a leather workman's apron who eyed the group belligerently.

"I been from top to bottom of this building today collecting exhibits for cleaning," snarled the man. "They've had everything on 'em from shoe polish to bubble gum. I just finished brushing down that bear not more'n two hours ago, and there's about twenty more animals in the basement to do. So look, but don't touch!"

Mr. Strang found himself wishing that Bradley had chosen today for one of his numerous absences from school.

The members of the class reached the top floor and found themselves facing two large arched doorways. Bronze letters over the left doorway read INDIANS OF THE WESTERN HEMISPHERE; to the right was the entrance to THE HALL OF MAMMALS. A smaller sheet-metal door at the extreme right end of the hallway had a cardboard sign saying *Employees Only*, and Mr. Strang wondered how long it would be before one of the students pulled the ancient gag of asking to see the stuffed employees.

The Hall of Mammals was devoted almost entirely to unusual types of furred animals. Just inside the doorway a duck-billed platypus lay curled around its egg on top of a glass case filled with small creatures neatly classified as being either carnivorous or herbivorous. Beyond this was the skeleton of a burro supported by hidden braces, and a vampire bat hung from the ceiling, its enormous wings outstretched. Even the mighty sperm whale was represented in the middle of a grouping of aquatic mammals by a single tooth almost twelve inches in length.

While his students dashed from one zoological oddity to

another, Mr. Strang stood in front of a large niche in one wall. At one side of the niche an oppossum and an Australian koala, mounted on polished wooden pedestals high enough to bring them to eye level, were separated from a Tasmanian devil on a similar stand by an empty space of about four feet. The devil, which resembled a small long-tailed bear, had lips curled back to reveal sharp teeth, and Mr. Strang was glad the little monster wasn't alive.

"Mean-looking thing, isn't he?"

The teacher turned to face a tall cadaverous man who wore the gray blazer of a museum attendant. "My name's Talbot," said the man in a soft voice extending his hand, "and you must be Mr. Strang. We were told to expect your class. I'm assigned to The Hall of Mammals, so if you have any questions please feel free to ask."

Mr. Strang shook Talbot's hand and then glanced to one side just in time to see Bradley Grier, accompanied by another student, disappear through a doorway at the rear.

"Where does that lead?" asked the teacher warily, gesturing toward the rear door.

"Just into the next room — the Indian exhibit," replied Talbot. "Don't worry about the boys. Our Mr. Albemarle has charge of that area. He'll look after them."

"It's not the boys I'm worried about. It's —"

Mr. Strang was abruptly interrupted by the roar of a man's voice from the next room. The cry was one of mingled outrage and disbelief. "It's gone!"

As the shout echoed off the museum's marble walls, the babbling of the students stopped abruptly, creating an eerie silence. There was a sound of footsteps tapping across a hard surface, and then a man appeared in the rear doorway.

The man, who wore a blazer similar to Talbot's, stood there a moment, an angry expression on his face. Finally he spotted Mr. Strang and pointed an accusing finger in the teacher's direction.

"One of your kids stole my mask," said the man, striding

purposefully toward Mr. Strang, "and I want it back. Now where is it?"

The teacher stared at the man in amazed silence. It was Talbot who finally spoke up. "Mr. Albermarle," he said stiffly, "this is Mr. Strang. He's here on a field trip with his class, and he hasn't been out of my sight since he got to this floor. Now what's this all about?"

"Well, maybe the teacher hasn't been out of your sight, but you can't say the same for the kids," said Albemarle. "Two of them came through the door back there and were looking at the Indian exhibits. I went to see if I could help them, and that is when I saw the mask was missing."

"What mask?" asked Mr. Strang.

"Come on and I'll show you," said Albermarle. "When are you teachers going to learn how to look after your classes while they're in the museum? That's your job, isn't it — to keep them from stealing and wrecking everything in sight?"

Restraining an impulse to plant a foot in Albemarle's ample backside, Mr. Strang followed the attendant into the next room. As he walked through the doorway, two boys standing next to one wall launched themselves at the teacher and began chattering loudly.

"We didn't do nothin', Mr. Strang!"

"Look, sir, if this man would just tell us what's missing —"

Mr. Strang considered the youth who was standing beside Bradley Grier. "Why, Mr. Pellman," said the teacher with a mocking smile, "imagine meeting you here. Did you and Bradley decide to take a little stroll, or were you planning to escape from the rest of the class?"

"This isn't funny, Mr. Strang," moaned Steven Pellman. "Bradley and me — I — well, anyway, we just wanted to see what was in here. And he hadn't been in this room more than a minute when that museum guard grabbed us and started yelling about how we stole something. I still don't know what he's talking about."

"I'll show you what I'm talking about," growled Albemarle as he motioned for Mr. Strang to follow him.

The room containing the Indian exhibits was divided neatly down the middle by a velvet rope. On one side were displays of North American Indians, featuring cases full of flint arrowheads and other artifacts and a full-sized war canoe and teepee. On the other were the Central and South American Indian exhibits. Albemarle led the teacher across the room and pointed to a spot on one wall behind a high rack of pottery.

Set in a circular pattern on the wall were a group of the most grotesque masks that Mr. Strang had ever seen. Made of wood, stone, and other materials, their bulging eyes, thick, rounded mouths, and oddly colored chins and cheeks made a display which was both fascinating and frightening.

On the wall in the center of the circle was a dark wooden plaque about 18 inches square. But whatever had been mounted on the plaque was now gone.

"It was an Inca burial mask," said Albemarle. "Pre-Columbian, and solid gold, too. That thing was worth a fortune, and one of these two took it. Probably both of them had a hand in it."

"If one of my students took it I'll get it back for you," said Mr. Strang.

"What do you mean, 'if'? They're the only ones who have been in here this morning." Albemarle pointed to the large arched doorway at the other end of the room. "I haven't been more than ten feet from that entrance since I came to work," he said. "Nobody could have come through there without my seeing them. The only other way in here is from The Hall of Mammals next door. And your kids are the only ones who have been on this floor so far today. Most people start their looking downstairs. We don't get much of a crowd here until noon."

"And of my class only these two, Grier and Pellman, came into this room. Is that right?"

"That's right."

"Any possibility that they could have taken the mask out of here — say, into The Hall of Mammals?"

"None at all. I had my eye on them from the moment they came in. Oh, they could have gotten the mask off the wall without my seeing it — that shelf of pottery hides the place where the mask was hanging from the front doorway. But they didn't go back next door. I'm sure of that."

Mr. Strang turned to the two students. "You've heard what the man said, boys," he murmured, "and I think you'll agree the jokes's gone far enough. Now where did you put it?"

Bradley Grier and Steve Pellman were pictures of outraged innocence. Mr. Strang noticed that the rest of his students were now gathering in the rear doorway.

"Keep them in the next room, please, Mr. Talbot," called Mr. Strang. He turned back to the two boys standing at the wall. "If you don't tell me where that infernal thing is," he went on, "I'm going to have to treat this not as a joke but as an attempt to steal museum property. So for the last time, where is that mask?"

Steve Pellman took a step forward. "Honest, Mr. Strang," he began, "we didn't take anything. Sure, we looked at that board on the wall. Brad asked me what I thought was mounted on it. Before I could answer, this man grabbed both of us."

"Mr. String, or whatever your name is," said Albemarle, "that mask was one of the most valuable articles in this museum. Why, the gold in it alone must be worth a lot of money, to say nothing of its archeological value. And if it doesn't turn up I'm just going to have to call the police."

The police! Mr. Strang pictured himself trying to explain to his principal how he took a class on a field trip and got involved with the police. "Wait a minute," he said placatingly. "How big was this mask?"

"Why, it was — well, the size of a mask. Made to fit over a man's face. And real thick. That gold was —"

"Then it's not exactly the type of object one could slip into a pocket and walk off with, is it?" asked the teacher.

"No, I guess not — not unless you had oversized pockets. Even then, there would be quite a bulge."

"Then you'll agree that neither of the boys has it on his person?"

"Why, yes, I suppose so," replied Albemarle, looking closely at the students in their tight-fitting clothing.

"And you admit they didn't leave this room?"

Albermarle nodded.

"Then the mask has to be somewhere in this room. I suggest that you and I search for it. And you might tell Mr. Talbot to keep any other visitors off this floor until we're finished."

Mr. Strang considered his theory to be flawless. But the fact remained that half an hour later he and Albemarle were covered with dust, the exhibit of INDIANS OF THE WESTERN HEMISPHERE had been thoroughly searched — and the mask was still missing.

"It's impossible," said Albemarle, rubbing his hands against his now grimy blazer. "Nobody has it, it isn't here — what could have happened to it?"

Mr. Strang rubbed his hand across his forehead, leaving streaks of dirt over one eye. He set his jaw grimly. "I may have been mistaken about the mask's being still in this room," he said, "but we know for sure the boys haven't been off this floor. Now I'm going to take my class outside to the top of the stairs. Mr. Talbot can stay with them. You and I are going over this entire floor with a fine-tooth comb. And when we've found the mask — which we're certain to do — we'll come back in here and wring the necks of both these boys."

"But Mr. Strang —" began Bradley Grier.

"Shut up," replied the red-faced teacher in a most unprofessional burst of anger. "Right now I want to be left alone with my thoughts — which at present concern slow lingering torture for you and Steve Pellman."

The class was led to the landing at the top of the stairs. After glancing at each student in turn and examining two of the girls' larger handbags, Albemarle announced that he was satisfied that nobody had the mask in his possession. At that, leaving Talbot with the students, he and Mr. Strang went into The Hall of Mammals.

"What about these stuffed animals?" asked Mr. Strang, picking up the koala from its stand and shaking it. "Is there any way one of them could be cut open and —"

"Not a chance," said Albemarle. "The skins are mounted over fiberglass shells. Nothing short of an ax would go through them. Even then there'd be a sound like a bass drum. See?"

The attendant struck his knuckles against a racoon mounted on the branch of a tree. There was a hollow, booming sound. "It would be impossible to do it without somebody seeing or hearing," he concluded.

"Then our search shouldn't take long," said the teacher.

It didn't. In less than half an hour the room was carefully searched, the mask was still missing, and Mr. Strang was considering the possibility that black magic was involved.

"Priapuloidea!" muttered the teacher. "The mask has to be on this floor, doesn't it? I mean, you saw it here earlier, didn't you?"

"That's right. I inspect all my exhibits when I come to work. That mask was in place at least an hour before the museum opened."

"Then it has to be here — but it isn't," said Mr. Strang, walking out of The Hall of Mammals. He glanced at the metal door at the end of the hall. "There's a place we haven't searched. What's in there?"

"An elevator shaft," said Albemarle.

"Oh? Then maybe —"

"Maybe somebody pitched the mask into the shaft? Forget it, Mr. Strang. That door can only be opened from the other side — so nobody will fall through it by accident."

Mr. Strang had to remind himself sternly that teachers must not break down in front of their students.

Tired, dusty, and bedraggled, the teacher walked out to the head of the stairs where Steve Pellman and Bradley Grier were standing near Talbot. Mr. Strang looked at the boys, a forlorn expression on his face.

"Where?" he asked simply.

"Honest, Mr. Strang, we didn't —" Steve began.

"Forget it, Steve," interrupted Bradley. "He's got it all figured out that we did it no matter how much we deny it. He can't think of anything except that we took it. I guess that's what the great Mr. Strang calls 'keeping an open mind.' "

The other students held their collective breath as Mr. Strang glared at Bradley. They were waiting for the verbal explosion which the boy's insolence would undoubtedly trigger off. The teacher clenched his fists, and his eyes flashed. Then the anger died, the thin shoulders slumped wearily, and a low chuckle came from the teacher.

"You're absolutely right, Bradley," he said softly, "although you might have put it a bit more delicately. My procedure up to now has been most unfair and highly unscientific. I'm afraid I've allowed your previous reputation to influence my thinking. Still, the mask is missing. Do you have any suggestions for it?"

"Mr. Strang," replied Bradley, a note of relief in his voice, "you've always told us there's no problem that can't be solved if enough thought is given to it. It seems to me — excuse me, sir — that now's a good time for you to either — er — put up or shut up."

"Umm." Deep in thought, the teacher walked slowly to the entrance of The Hall of Mammals. He paused and scratched his head. Peering through the doorway he could see the opossum and the koala perched innocently on their stands.

And then he remembered something Albemarle had told him.

"Outrageous," he murmured to himself, "and yet there's no other possible —"

"What are you mumbling about?" asked Albemarle. "I'm going to have to call the police and report —"

"Just a minute, please," said Mr. Strang, waving his hand impatiently. "That opossum on the stand, Mr. Albemarle — did you know the opossum is native to North America?"

"What's that got to do with the mask?"

Before answering, Mr. Strang slowly removed his glasses from his inside jacket pocket. After polishing them on his necktie he held them in one hand, making jabbing motions in the air. The other hand was inserted deep into a jacket pocket. Although the ritual was new to Albemarle, the students of Aldershot High School were quite familiar with it.

Mr. Strang, having considered all facets of the problem at hand, was prepared to deliver a Lecture.

"Before I answer your question," he replied, "I'd like you to consider something, Mr. Albemarle. Since you first announced that the mask was missing we've gone on the assumption that it was hidden on this floor. And yet we've searched everywhere and not found it. Isn't it obvious, therefore, that we were wrong — that the mask is somewhere else?"

"But it's got to be here."

"Why?"

"Look, Mr. Strang, Talbot and I came up here at eight o'clock. That was two hours before the museum opened. You and your class got here about ten fifteen. And nobody has left this floor this morning!"

"No?" Mr. Strang turned to Bradley Grier. "On the way up the stairs earlier you had a slight altercation with a museum employee — the man in the leather apron. Do you remember what he said about his work, Bradley, something that might have a bearing on our problem?"

"I don't think so. Hey — wait a minute! He said he'd been from top to bottom of the museum collecting animals for cleaning."

"From top to bottom," repeated Mr. Strang. "And this is the top floor of the museum, isn't it? So we were *not* the only ones up here. That workman came up and left again. I further suggest, Mr. Albemarle, that in collecting the animals he had to use the elevator to take them to the basement where he does whatever repairs are necessary."

"Wait a minute," said Albemarle. "Are you trying to pin this on old Ernie Frye?"

"Frye? Is that the man's name?"

"It is. And he's been working in this museum more than twenty-five years. He takes better care of the exhibits than most people do of their kids. Nobody's going to make me believe that Ernie stole —"

"You said the mask is extremely valuable."

"Sure it is. But Ernie? Impossible! Besides, he never was actually on this floor. He waited inside the elevator while Talbot and I brought him the things to be cleaned."

"What did you send down, Mr. Albemarle?"

"Why, let me see. There was a feather headdress and a llama's hair robe. I guess Talbot sent down a couple of animals. I heard him moving some things around after I got back to my post."

"I see. I don't suppose there's any possibility that you could have sent the mask down with the other things accidentally?"

Albemarle shook his head. "Ernie gave me a receipt for the headdress and the robe," he said. "He'd have spotted that mask right away if I'd had it. Besides, there are seven men working with him in the basement. One of them would have been sure to see something as big as the mask and ask Ernie about it."

Mr. Strang smiled. "Splendid," he said. "We can therefore eliminate Mr. Frye as the thief. I suspect, however, that he was the means by which the mask was taken off this floor."

"But how was it done without anybody seeing it?"

Mr. Strang took Albemarle by the arm and guided him into The Hall of Mammals. There he pointed dramatically to the niche containing the opossum, the koala, and the Tasmanian devil.

"Notice the empty space between the koala and the Tasmanian devil," said the teacher. "That space — about four feet — must have contained one of the animals that Mr. Talbot sent down for cleaning. I suspect that animal carried off the mask."

"You mean it was something alive?" asked Albemarle in surprise.

"Hardly," said Mr. Strang. "But here, in a single group, are an opossum from North America and a koala, found primarily in Australia. Then there's that empty space and the Tasmanian devil on the other side of it. It occurred unlikely to me that the three animals were just placed together haphazardly. If they weren't, then they must have something in common, even though they came from different parts of the world."

"In common? Like what?" asked Albemarle.

"Remember what you said when I asked about the size of the mask? You said nobody could conceal it *unless he had oversized pockets*. Do you know what a marsupial is, Mr. Albemarle?"

"No. Talbot's the animal man around here."

"It's an animal which has a pouch for carrying its young. Or, if you will, an oversized pocket. All three of these animals are marsupials — that's their common factor, the reason the four of them were placed in the same niche. Now what other animal with a pouch would fit into the empty space? It would have to be fairly large since it obviously wasn't set on a stand like the others."

"A kangaroo!" cried Albemarle, snapping his fingers.

"Exactly — a kangaroo. An animal nearly the size of a grown man. The one animal with a pouch or pocket large enough to contain the mask."

"And nobody would notice if the mask were hidden in the pouch," added Albemarle. "But look, the only one who could have hidden the mask there without being noticed is —"

"Mr. Talbot," replied the teacher. "He must have slipped through the rear door into the Indian Hall while you were at the elevator with Frye. After he'd taken the mask from the wall he came back in here, hid the mask in the kangaroo's pouch, then moved the animal out to the elevator door. You suspected nothing because you didn't even realize anything was missing until we got here. You said yourself that except for your one inspection when you first came on the job today, you didn't move from the front door of the Indian Hall."

"Then the mask must be in the basement right now," said Albemarle. "And Talbot's got to get it before somebody down there starts working on that kangaroo."

"If you're looking for Mr. Talbot," said Bradley Grier, who was standing at the front doorway of The Hall of Mammals, "you'd better hurry. He just started downstairs. He said something about calling the police and that we should wait —"

Albemarle looked around excitedly and finally yanked a bone from the skull of the burro's skeleton. Waving the white bone over his head like a club, he dashed through the doorway and down the stairs, calling loudly for Talbot to stop. Mr. Strang, moving more slowly, arrived at the top of the stairs just in time to see Talbot overtaken by his pursuer who brought the bone crashing down on Talbot's head.

Half an hour later the missing exhibit had been retrieved from its unique hiding place. A tired but completely happy Mr. Strang stood with his class and watched Ernie Frye remount the glittering golden burial mask on the wall of the Hall of Indians. He felt a touch on his sleeve and turned to an equally joyful Mr. Albemarle.

"What a day this has been," said the attendant. "For a teacher, you're quite a detective, Mr. Strang."

"And you, Mr. Albemarle, were a veritable Samson," replied the teacher.

"Samson?"

Mr. Strang pointed to the piece of bone which was still clutched in Albemarle's hand. "The burro's skull," said the teacher. "Didn't Samson also defeat his enemy with the jawbone of an ass?"

# No One Likes To Be Played for a Sucker

## Michael Collins

*Private detectives like Michael Collins's Dan Fortune don't usually function in locked room stories. But there have been some notable exceptions — especially in the works of Henry Kane and Bill Pronzini — and here's another.*

It CAN BE a mistake to be too smart. Deviousness takes real practise, judgment of human nature as fine as a hair, and something else — call it ice. The ice a man has inside him.

Old Tercio Osso came to me with his suspicions on a Thursday morning. That alone showed his uneasiness. Old Tercio hadn't been out of his Carmine Street office in the morning for twenty years — not even for a relative's funeral.

"Business don't come and find you," Tercio pronounced regularly.

Osso & Vitanza, Jewelry, Religious Supplies and Real Estate, and if you wanted to do business with Tercio, or pay your rent, you went to his office in the morning. In the afternoon Tercio presided in his corner at the Mazzini Political Club — a little cards, a little *bocci* out back.

Lean old Cology Vitanza, Tercio's partner of thirty years, reversed the procedure, and at night they both held down the office — thieves struck at night on Carmine Street, and there was safety in numbers.

It was Cology Vitanza that old Tercio came to me about.

"We got troubles, Mr. Fortune. I think Cology makes plans."

The old man sat like a solemn frog on my one extra chair. He wore his usual ancient black suit, white shirt, and black tie with its shiny knot so small it looked as if it had been tied under pressure. The shabbiness of my one-room office did not bother Tercio. On Carmine Street, no matter how much cash a businessman has in various banks, he knows the value of a shabby front: it gives the poor confidence that a man is like them.

"What kind of plans?"

Tercio shrugged. "Business it's not good. We make some big mistakes. The stock market, buildings not worth so much as we pay, inventory that don't sell."

"I didn't know you made mistakes, Mr. Osso."

"So?" Tercio said. "Maybe I'm old. Vitanza he's old. We lose the touch, the neighborhood it's change. The new

people don't buy what we got. Maybe we been playin' too
much *bocci,* sit around tellin' too many stories from the old
days.''

"All right," I said. "What plans do you figure Vitanza
makes?"

Tercio folded his plump hands in his broad lap. "For six
years Cology got no wife. He got ten kids what got lotsa kids
of their own. We both gettin' old. We got insurance, big.
We talk about what we do next year and after and we don't
think the same, so? Then I see Cology talking to people."

"What kind of insurance have you got?"

"On the inventory, on both of us, for the partners."

I sat back in the gray light from my one air-shaft window.
"You're saying you think Vitanza is making plans to collect
on the insurance?"

"I see him talk to Sid Nelson yesterday. Three days ago
he drinks coffee alone with Don Primo."

Don Primo Veronese was a lawyer, a member of the Mazzini Club, and, by strong rumor, a fence for small hoods. Sid
Nelson was a hood, not small but not big — sort of in between. A thief, a killer, and a careful operator.

"You and Vitanza talk to a lot of people."

"Sure, I talk to Don Primo myself," Tercio agreed. "I
don't talk to no Sid Nelson. I don't say we should make a
special inventory. I don't take big money from the bank, put
in envelope, carry in my pocket. I don't go to Mass five
times in one week."

"What do you want me to do, Mr. Osso?"

A slow shrug. "In winter the wolf comes into the streets
of the city. The old lion got to learn new tricks or starve.
Maybe I'm crazy, okay. Only you watch Cology. You be a
detective."

"That's my work," I said. "All right, a hundred in advance."

"A horse works on hay," Tercio said, and counted out
two nice crisp fifties. "You tell me nine o'clock every
night."

After old Tercio had gone I rubbed at the stump of my missing arm, then phoned Lieutenant Marx at the precinct. I told him Tercio's story.

"What do you want me to do?" Marx said.

"I don't know," I said. "Tell me that Tercio Osso is a smart old man."

"Tercio is a smart old man," Marx said. "All I can do is stand by, Dan. At least until you get something that can be called reasonable suspicion."

"I know," I said.

"You can check out most of it," Marx pointed out.

That's what I did. I checked out Osso's story.

It checked. Other people had seen Cology Vitanza talking to Don Primo, and, especially, to Sid Nelson. The firm of Osso & Vitanza was in trouble — cash tied up, notes overdue, interest not paid, a few bad deals the other Carmine Street financiers were grinning about, and the jewelry stock not moving at all.

Vitanza had been going to Mass almost every day. He had withdrawn $5,000 in cash. (A teller I knew, and ten bucks, got me that information.) I had to take Tercio Osso's word about the special inventory of the unmoving stock, but I was sure it would turn out true.

I began tailing Cology Vitanza. It wasn't a hard tail. The tall old man was easy to follow and a man of routine. He never took me out of the ten-square-block area of Little Italy. I reported to Osso every night at nine o'clock by telephone.

On Friday I spotted Vitanza talking again to Sid Nelson. The hoodlum seemed interested in what Vitanza had to say.

I ate a lot of spaghetti and drank a lot of wine for two days. I saw one bad movie, and visited the homes of twenty old men. That is, Vitanza visited and I lurked outside in the cold getting more bored every minute. I wore out my knees kneeling at the back of a dim church.

But I was in the Capri Tavern at six o'clock Saturday night when Vitanza stopped to talk to a seedy-looking character in a rear booth. A white envelope passed from Vitanza to the seedy type. I waited until the new man downed his glass of wine and ambled out. Then I switched to tailing him.

I followed the seedy man through Little Italy and across to the East Side. He looked around a lot, and did all kinds of twists and turns, as if he figured he might be followed. That made it hard work, but I kept up with him. He finally headed for the Bowery.

A block south of Houston he suddenly ducked into a wino joint. I sprinted and went in, but he was out the back way and gone. I went around through the alleys and streets of the Bowery for another hour trying to pick up his trail, but I had no luck.

I went back to Carmine Street to find Cology Vitanza. He wasn't at the Mazzini Club, and neither was Osso. I tried their other haunts and didn't find them. The lights were on behind the curtained windows of the shop and office on Carmine Street, but I couldn't go in without tipping my hand, so I took up a stakeout.

Nothing happened for half an hour. Then some people tried to get into the store, but the front door was locked. That wasn't right for a Saturday night. It was almost nine o'clock by then. I made my call to Osso from a booth where I could watch the front door of the store. There was no answer, so I called Lieutenant Marx.

"I don't like how it sounds," Marx said "Too bad you lost that Bowery character. I've done some checking on their insurance. They've got $50,000 on the inventory, $25,000 life on each payable to the other, and $50,000 surviving-partner insurance with option to buy out the heirs."

"A nice haul," I said. "What do we do?"

"Sid Nelson hasn't moved. I put a man on him for you."

"The Commissioner wouldn't like that."

"The Commissioner won't know," Marx said, and then was silent a few seconds. "We've got no cause to bust in yet."

"And if nothing's wrong we tip off Vitanza."

"But they shouldn't be locked up on Saturday night," Marx said. "The patrolman on the beat ought to be suspicious."

"I guess he ought to," I said.

"I'll be right over," Marx said.

Marx arrived with two of his squad inside three minutes. He'd picked up the beat patrolman on the way. I joined them at the door to the store. We couldn't see anything through the curtains.

"Pound the door and give a call," Marx instructed the beat patrolman.

The patrolman pounded and called out. Nothing happened. Marx chewed his lip and looked at me. Then, as if from far off, we heard a voice. It was from somewhere inside the store, and it was calling for help.

"I guess we go in," Marx said.

He kicked in the glass of the door and reached inside for the lock.

At first we saw nothing wrong in the jewelry store. Then Marx pointed to the showcases where the expensive jewelry was kept. They were unlocked and empty.

In the office in the back a rear window was open. A man lay on the floor in a pool of not-quite-dry blood. A .38 caliber automatic was on the floor about five feet from the body, toward the right wall of the office. There was a solid door in the right wall, and behind it someone was knocking and calling, "What's happen out there? Hey, who's out there?"

Marx and I looked at each other as one of his men bent over the body on the floor. It was not Tercio Osso, it was Cology Vitanza. Marx's second man swung the door of the safe open. It had been closed but not locked. It was empty.

Marx went to the solid door. "Who's in there?"

"Osso! He knock me out, lock me in. What's happen?"

Marx studied the door. There was no key in the lock. I went and searched the dead man. I shook my head at Marx — no key. One of Marx's men pointed to the floor.

"There."

The key was on the floor not far from the gun. I picked it up. It was one of those common old house keys, rough and rusted, and there would be no prints. Marx took the key and opened the door.

Tercio Osso blinked at us. "Mr. Fortune, Lieutenant. Where's Cology, he —"

Osso stepped out into the office and saw his dead partner. He just stood and stared. Nothing happened to his face. I watched him. If anything had shown on his face I would have been surprised. Everyone knew he was a tough old man.

"So," he said, nodding, "he kill Cology. It figure. The crazy old man! Crazy!"

"You want to tell us what happened?" Marx said.

"Sure, sure," the old man said. He walked to his desk and sat down heavily. I saw a trickle of blood over his left ear. He looked at Vitanza's body. "He come in maybe hour, two hours ago. What time is it?"

"Nine twenty," Marx said.

"That long?" Osso said. "So two hours since. Seven thirty, maybe. One guy. He comes in the front. I go out to see. He got a mask and a gun. He push me back to office, me and Cology. He makes us go lock the front door, clean out the cases and then the safe. He work fast. He shove me in storeroom, knock me out."

The old man touched his head, winced. "I come to I don't know what time. I listen. Nothing, no noise. I listen long time, I don't want him to come back for me. Nothing happen. I hear phone ring. So I start yelling. Then I hear you bust in."

Osso looked around. "He got it all, huh? Out the window. Only he don't keep the deal, no. Cology a crazy man. A guy like that don't keep no deals."

There was a long silence in the office. Sirens were growing in the cold night air outside as the police were arriving at Marx's summons. Marx was chewing his lip and looking at me. I looked at Osso.

"You're telling us you figure Vitanza hired a guy to rob the store for the insurance, and then the guy killed him? Why?"

Osso shrugged. "Who know? Maybe the guy don't want to split with Cology. Maybe the guy figures the jewels are worth more than a cut of the insurance. They fight, Cology's dead. How do I know, I'm locked inside the storeroom."

The Assistant Medical Examiner arrived, the fingerprint team, and two men from Safe and Loft. I went into the storeroom. It was small and windowless. There was no other door. The walls were white and clean, and the room was piled with lumber, cans, tools, and assorted junk. I found a small stain of blood on the floor near the door. The walls seemed solid.

When I went back out Marx's men had finished marking the locations of the body, the gun, and the key. The M.E. stood up and motioned to his men to bring their basket.

"Shot twice in the back," the M.E. said. "Two hours ago, maybe more, maybe a little less. Rigor is just starting. He's a skinny old man. Died pretty quick, I'd say. The slugs are still in him — .38 caliber looks about right."

"The gun's been fired twice," one of Marx's men said, "not long ago."

"Prints all over the place, all kinds," the fingerprint man said. "It won't be easy to lift them clean."

Marx growled, "Prints won't help. What about you Safe and Loft guys?"

A Safe and Loft man said, "Rear window opened from inside. Some marks on the sill could have been a man climbing out. The yard is all concrete, no traces, but we found this."

The Safe and Loft man held up a child's rubber Halloween Mask. Marx looked at it sourly.

"They all use that trick now. The movies and TV tell 'em how," Marx said, and came over to me. He lit a cigarette. "Well, Dan?"

"Everything fits," I said. "Just about what I was supposed to figure that Vitanza was planning — except for his killing."

"Neat," Marx said.

"Too neat," I said. "Let's talk to Osso."

While his men and the experts went on working, Marx took Osso into the storeroom. I went with them. The old man watched us with cold, black eyes.

"This is just what you expected when you went to Fortune," Marx said to the old man.

"I got a hunch," Osso said.

"What does Cology figure on getting out of it, Tercio?" I said. "The insurance on the stock, no more. Maybe he figures on keeping most of the jewels, too, okay. But figure what you get out of it. You get the whole works — stock insurance, life insurance on Cology, partnership insurance, option to buy it all."

"So?" Osso said, watching me.

"So if Cology was going to set up a risky deal like this it ought to be you who's dead, not him. The thief should have killed you and knocked Cology out. Then there's a big pie to split with Cology."

"You think I set this up?"

I nodded. "It smells, Tercio. We're supposed to figure that Vitanza hired a punk to fake a holdup, but not kill you when there was more riding on you than on the stock? Then the hired hood kills Cology for some reason and leaves his gun here on the floor? Leaves his mask out in the yard to prove he was here? Leaves the key on the floor so we know you were locked in?"

Osso shrugged. "You figure I set it up, take me down and book me. I call my lawyer. You find the guy I hire. You do that. I tell the truth. I hire no one, you won't find no one. I'm inside the storeroom, so how I kill Cology?"

Marx said, "It's too neat, Osso. You practically told Fortune how it was going to happen."

"So book me. I get my lawyer. You find the man I hire."
And the old man smiled. "Or maybe you figure I kill from
inside a locked room?"

Marx snapped, "Take the old man down, book him on
suspicion. Go over the place with a vacuum cleaner. Send
anything you find to Technical Services."

They took Osso. Marx followed and I left with him.

The police had gone, except for a patrolman posted at the
broken door in front, when I jimmied the back window and
went in. I dropped into the dark office and flicked on my
flashlight. I focused the beam on the marks that showed
where the gun, the key, and the body had been.

I heard the steps too late. The lights went on, and I turned
from pure reflex. I never carry a gun, and if I'd had a gun I
couldn't have pulled it with my flash still in my lone hand.
I was glad I didn't have a gun. I might have shot by reflex,
and it was Lieutenant Marx in the doorway. That's the trouble with a gun, you tend to depend on it if you have one.

I said, "You, too, Lieutenant?"

"What's your idea?"

"The old man seemed too confident," I said. "He just
about begged you to book him on suspicion of having hired
a man to fake the robbery and kill Vitanza."

"Yeah," Marx said, "he did. You think he didn't hire
anyone?"

I nodded. I didn't like it, but unless Cology Vitanza had
set it up after all, which I didn't believe, there had to be
another answer. Marx didn't like it either. "You know what
that gives us," Marx said.

"I know," I said, "but Tercio's too smart to hire a killing
and have a monkey on his back the rest of his life. No, he'd
do it himself."

"You got more than a hunch, Dan?"

"The gun," I said. "It's the flaw in the setup. It sticks
out. A thief who kills takes his gun away with him. Osso
would know that."

"So?"

"So the gun's being in the office has to be the clue to the answer," I said. "It was here because Osso couldn't do anything else with it. The jewels are gone, the mask was out in the yard, the front door was locked on the inside out in the shop. If Osso had had a choice he'd have taken the gun away and the key too. He didn't. Why?"

Marx rubbed his jaw. "So if he did it, it reads like this: he took the ice and stashed it; he planted the mask and left the rear window open; he killed Vitanza; and then he got into that storeroom, somehow got locked in with the key outside and a long way from the door."

"Yes and no," I said. "If he killed Vitanza *before* he got into that room, he could have disposed of the gun to make it look more like an outside killer. He didn't. So, somehow, he must have killed Vitanza from *inside* the locked storeroom."

"And then got the gun and key out?"

"That's it," I said.

Marx nodded. "Let's find it."

We went to work. The locked room is an exercise in illusion — a magician's trick. Otherwise it's impossible, and the impossible can't be done, period. Since it *had* been done, it must be a trick, a matter of distracting attention, and once you know what you're really looking for, the answer is never hard.

When we had dismissed the distraction — the hired robber-and-killer theory — the rest was just a matter of logic. I sighted along the line from the body to the seemingly solid wall. The line pointed directly to a light fixture set in the wall. Sighting the other way, the line led to Vitanza's desk and telephone.

"Vitanza came in," I said. "Osso was already inside the locked room. Vitanza went to his desk. He probably always did that, and Osso could count on it. Or maybe he saw that the jewels were gone and went to his desk to telephone the police. Osso probably knew he would be sure to do that, too. They'd been partners thirty years.

"And Osso shot him in the back," Marx said. "That's why the shots were in the back, the desk faces the other way."

"Let's look at that light fixture," I said.

It was one of those small modern wall-lamps with a wide circular metal base. It had been attached to the wall recently and was not painted over. The wall behind it sounded hollow, but we could not move the lamp.

"It doesn't come off, Dan," Marx said.

"Not from this side," I said.

We went into the storeroom. I measured off from the door to exactly where the light fixture was attached on the other side of the wall. We studied the wall. The whole wall had been recently painted. The cans of quick-drying paint were among the litter in the storeroom. On the floor there were a few crumbs of dried plaster.

"Quick-drying plaster," I said to Marx.

Marx found a hammer and chisel in the storeroom. There were flecks of plaster on the chisel. He opened a hole directly behind the light fixture — it opened easily. The back of the light fixture was clearly visible about two inches in, between vertical two-by-fours. The fixture had a metal eye on the back. It was held in place by a metal bar that passed through the eye and was angled to catch the two-by-fours.

"That's it," I said. "Simple and clever."

Marx had two hands. He reached in with his left, turned the metal bar, and held the fixture. He pushed the fixture out and to the left and aimed his pistol through the hole with his right hand. He had shot at the desk five feet away — in direct line with where the body of Cology Vitanza had fallen.

I said, "He had this hole open on this side. He heard Vitanza come in and head for the desk. He pushed out the fixture. It didn't matter if Vitanza heard or not — Osso was ready to shoot.

"He shot Vitanza, tossed the gun and key through the hole, pulled the fixture back and refastened it, plastered up the hole, and painted it. He knew no one would break in until after I called at nine o'clock. He hid here and waited.

"If we believed that Vitanza had set it up, fine, we'd be looking for a non-existent thief and killer. If we think Osso hired a man, fine, too. We're still looking for a non-existent thief and killer, and in a few weeks Osso cleans up this storeroom, and the new plaster sets so it can't be told from the old plaster. Maybe he fixes the light fixture so it's permanent in the wall. All the evidence is gone, and he's in the clear."

"Only now the lab boys should be able to prove some of the plaster is newer," Marx said, "the fixture moves out, and the evidence is in this room. We've got him!"

Marx called in Captain Gazzo of Homicide, and Chief of Detectives McGuire got a judge to order the office and storeroom sealed. The D.A. would want the jury to see the office and storeroom just as they were when Vitanza was killed.

I gave my statement, Marx made his report, and Gazzo faced the old man with it. Osso was a tough old bird.

"I want my lawyer," Osso said.

He got his lawyer, they booked him, and I went home to bed. I felt good. I don't get many locked rooms to play with, so I was pleased with myself.

Until morning.

"It's not the gun," Captain Gazzo said.

I was in Gazzo's office. So was Marx. Gazzo held the .38 automatic that had been on the office floor — the gun that had been the tipoff, the weak link, the key to it all.

"This gun didn't kill Vitanza," Gazzo said. "Ballistics just reported. Vitanza was killed with a .38, but not this one."

I said nothing. Neither did Marx.

"A locked room," Gazzo said sarcastically. "Clever, very clever."

I said it at the start: it can be a mistake to be too smart. A locked-room murder is an illusionist's trick, a matter of the misdirection of attention. And the one who had been too smart was me.

"All he threw out was the key," I said. "That was all he had to throw out all along. The rest was to distract us."

There had never been any reason why Osso had to kill from inside the storeroom, only that he lock himself in from the inside and get the key out. The whole locked room had been just a trick to distract us. A gun on the floor by a dead man; the right caliber and fired recently and the right number of times. Who would dream it was the wrong gun?

"The key," Gazzo said. "First he's brought in on suspicion of having hired a man to fake a robbery and kill his partner. Next he's booked for having killed his partner from inside a locked room with a trick scheme. Now he killed his partner outside the room, switched guns, locked himself in, and just tossed the key out. What next?"

"He killed Vitanza," Marx said. "I'm sure he did."

"I'm sure too," Gazzo agreed, "but what jury will believe us now with the speech his lawyer'll make about dumb cops and police persecution? You guys like fairy tales? How do you like the one about the man who cried wolf? The D.A. is bawling on his desk thinking about facing a jury against Osso now."

"We'll find out what he did," Marx said. "We'll find the right gun and the jewels."

"Sure we will," Gazzo said. "Some day."

"And I bet it won't do us any good," I said.

It didn't. Three days after the killing the superintendent of a cheap rooming house on the Lower East Side reported that a tenant hadn't come out of his room for three days. The police broke in and found the man dead. It was the seedy character I had followed and lost.

He had been shot in the shoulder. The bullet was still in the wound. But that was not what had killed him. He had died from drinking whiskey with lye in it. The bottle was in the room. The police found some drinking methyl alcohol with a lot of the missing jewels in the room, but not all. They also found a .38 caliber automatic that had been fired twice.

"It's the gun that killed Vitanza," ballistics reported.

"Only the bum's prints on the gun," fingerprinting said.

"It's certain he died four or five hours *after* Vitanza died," the M.E. said. "The bad whiskey killed him. He might have been unconscious most of the time, but after three days we'll never prove it. He lost blood from that shoulder wound."

Ballistics then added the final touch. "The bullet in the bum's shoulder came from the gun you found on the floor of Osso & Vitanza's office. The gun was registered to Cology Vitanza himself."

With my statement and report on what I had observed Cology Vitanza do, on the actions Osso had reported and I had checked out, the evidence logically added up to only one story: the seedy character had been hired by Cology Vitanza to rob the jewelry store. For some reason there had been a fight while Osso was unconscious in the locked room. (Osso stated he had plastered the hole in the storeroom the day before; with the evidence against the bum his story was better than Marx's and mine.)

Vitanza had wounded the bum, and the bum had killed Vitanza. Then the wounded bum had run for his room carrying the loot, hiding some of it. In his room, weak from his wound, he had drunk the bad whiskey, passed out, and died. It was just the way a wounded bum would die.

I had a different story. The day after they dropped all charges against Tercio Osso I went to his office. He didn't try to evade me.

"I owe you a couple days and expenses," Osso said.

"You hired me in the first place just to make me and Marx suspicious," I said. "You figured I'd talk to the police and you knew we'd suspect a trick. You wanted us to accuse you right away of hiring someone to kill Vitanza."

Osso said nothing.

"You arranged all those suspicious acts of Vitanza's. It wouldn't be hard. You were partners, old friends, and he'd do anything you asked him to do if you said it was business. You asked him to talk to Sid Nelson about something innocent, to take out $5,000 in cash for you, to meet the bum with a note, even to go to a lot of Masses."

The old man was like a fat black frog in the chair.

"You played us like trout. It was too easy and not smart for you to have hired a killer. We were sure to look for more. That's when you handed us the locked room and the gun on the floor."

Osso smiled.

"That gun would have made any cop wonder, and you expected us to figure out the locked-room trick. You wanted us to charge you with it, and you wanted time. You needed at least a few hours to be sure the bum was dead, and the locked room would keep us nice and busy for at least a few hours."

The old man began to light a thin black cigar.

"You killed Vitanza while I was tailing the bum. You took the jewels, locked up, went out the back window. You went to the bum's room and filled him with the bad whiskey, then shot him with Vitanza's gun. A wound that would bleed but not kill.

"Then you planted the gun that had killed Vitanza in the bum's room with some of the jewels. You knew no one would look for the bum for days. You went back to the office and laid out Vitanza. You put the gun that had shot the bum on the office floor. You locked yourself in the storeroom from the inside and tossed out the key through the light fixture hole in the wall.

"Then you sat back and led me and Marx into being too smart for our own good. You got the time you needed. You kept us away from the bum until it was too late. You've got what you were after, and you're safe." I stopped and looked at the old man. "One thing I want to know, Osso. Why did you pick me?"

Tercio Osso blew smoke and looked solemn. He shrugged. He took the black stogie from his mouth and studied it. Then he laughed loudly.

"You got one arm," Osso said, grinning at me. "You're easy to spot. I got to know where you are all the time to make it work, see? I got to make it easy for that bum to spot you and lead you a chase before he loses you. And I got to make it easy for the man watching you all the time."

"You had a man watching me?"

"Sure, what else? Good man, a relative, never talk." Osso studied his cigar some more. "You got good friends on the cops, and you're a real smart man, see? I mean, I know you figure out that locked room."

And Osso laughed again. He was very pleased with his shenanigans. I said nothing, just stared at him. He studied me.

"I got to do it, see?" Osso said at last. "I'm in trouble. Vitanza he don't agree with me no more. He was gonna ruin me if I don't stop him. So I stop him. And I fix it so you smart guys outsmart yourselves."

I stood up. "That's okay, Osso. You see, you made the same mistake Marx and I made."

"So?" he said, his black eyes narrowing.

"That's right. You forgot other people can be as smart as you. You fixed it good so that no one can prove in court what you did, but everyone knows you did it. You made it too complicated, Osso. You're the only one who could have worked it all. What I figured out, and just told you, I also told Vitanza's ten kids, and the members of the Mazzini Club. They're smart, too."

"I kill you too!" Osso croaked.

"You couldn't get away with it twice, not with everyone knowing what you did. You're too smart to try. Bad odds, and you always play the odds."

I left him chewing his lip, his shrewd mind working fast. Who knows, he's a smart man, and maybe he'll still get away with it. But I doubt it. As I said, other men are smart, too, and Vitanza's kids and the Mazzini Club boys believed the story I had figured out.

I read the newspapers carefully now. I'm waiting for a small item about an old man named Tercio Osso being hit by a truck, or found in the river drowned by accident, or maybe the victim of an unfortunate food poisoning in a restaurant that just happens to be run by a member of the Mazzini Club.

Nothing fancy or complicated this time, just a simple, everyday accident. Of course, everyone will know what really happened, but no one will ever prove it. Whoever gets Tercio Osso won't even have to be particularly careful. A reasonably believable accident will do the trick.

After all, we're all human and have a sense of justice, and no one likes to be played for a sucker

# The Arrowmont Prison Riddle

## Bill Pronzini

*Sometimes the problem posed by an impossible crime story is so bizarre that it seems to defy explanation. Such is the case in this excellent period tale by Bill Pronzini.*

I FIRST MET the man who called himself by the unlikely name of Buckmaster Gilloon in the late summer of 1916, my second year as warden of Arrowmont Prison. There were no living quarters within the old brick walls of the prison, which was situated on a promontory overlooking a small winding river two miles north of Arrowmont Village, so I had rented a cottage in the village proper, not far from a tavern known as Hallahan's Irish Inn. It was in this tavern, and as a result of a mutual passion for Guinness stout and the game of darts, that Gilloon and I became acquainted.

As a man he was every bit as unlikely as his name. He was in his late thirties, short and almost painfully thin; he had a glass eye and a drooping and incongruous Oriental-style mustache, wore English tweeds, gaudy Albert watch chains and plaid Scotch caps, and always carried half a dozen looseleaf notebooks in which he perpetually and secretively jotted things. He was well read and erudite, had a repertoire of bawdy stories to rival any vaudevillian in the country, and never seemed to lack ready cash. He lived in a boarding house in the center of the village and claimed to be a writer for the pulp magazines — *Argosy, Adventure, All-Story Weekly, Munsey's.* Perhaps he was, but he steadfastly refused to discuss any of his fiction, or to divulge his pseudonym or pseudonyms.

He was reticent about divulging any personal information. When personal questions arose, he deftly changed the subject. Since he did not speak with an accent, I took him to be American-born. I was able to learn, from occasional comments and observations, that he had traveled extensively throughout the world.

In my nine decades on this earth I have never encountered a more fascinating or troubling enigma than this man whose path crossed mine for a few short weeks in 1916.

Who and what was Buckmaster Gilloon? Is it possible for one enigma to be attracted and motivated by another enigma? Can that which seems natural and coincidental be the result instead of preternatural forces? These questions have plagued me in the sixty years since Gilloon and I became involved in what appeared to be an utterly enigmatic crime.

It all began on September 26, 1916 — the day of the scheduled execution at Arrowmont Prison of a condemned murderer named Arthur Teasdale . . .

Shortly before noon of that day a thunderstorm struck without warning. Rain pelted down incessantly from a black sky, and lightning crackled in low jagged blazes that gave the illusion of striking unseen objects just beyond the prison walls. I was already suffering from nervous tension, as was always the case on the day of an execution, and the storm added to my discomfort. I passed the early afternoon sitting at my desk, staring out the window, listening to the inexorable ticking of my Seth Thomas, wishing the execution was done with and it was eight o'clock, when I was due to meet Gilloon at Hallahan's for Guinness and darts.

At 3:30 the two civilians who had volunteered to act as witnesses to the hanging arrived. I ushered them into a waiting room and asked them to wait until they were summoned. Then I donned a slicker and stopped by the office of Rogers, the chief guard, and asked him to accompany me to the execution shed.

The shed was relatively small, constructed of brick with a tin roof, and sat in a corner of the prison between the textile mill and the iron foundry. It was lighted by lanterns hung from the walls and the rafters and contained only a row of witness chairs and a high permanent gallows at the far end. Attached to the shed's north wall was an annex in which the death cell was located. As was customary, Teasdale had been transported there five days earlier to await due process.

He was a particularly vicious and evil man, Teasdale. He had cold-bloodedly murdered three people during an abortive robbery attempt in the state capital, and had been anything but a model prisoner during his month's confinement at Arrowmont. As a rule I had a certain compassion for those con-

demned to hang under my jurisdiction, and in two cases I
had spoken to the governor in favor of clemency. In Teasdale's case, however, I had conceded that a continuance of
his life would serve no good purpose.

When I had visited him the previous night to ask if he
wished to see a clergyman or to order anything special for
his last meal, he had cursed me and Rogers and the entire
prison personnel with an almost maniacal intensity, vowing
vengeance on us all from the grave.

I rather expected, as Rogers and I entered the death cell at
ten minutes of four, to find Teasdale in much the same state.
However, he had fallen instead into an acute melancholia; he
lay on his cot with his knees drawn up and his eyes staring
blankly at the opposite wall. The two guards assigned to him,
Hollowell and Granger (Granger was also the state-appointed
hangman), told us he had been like that for several hours. I
spoke to him, asking again if he wished to confer with a
clergyman. He did not answer, did not move. I inquired if he
had any last requests, and if it was his wish to wear a hood
for his final walk to the gallows and for the execution. He
did not respond.

I took Hollowell aside. "Perhaps it would be better to use
the hood," I said. "It will make it easier for all of us."

"Yes, sir."

Rogers and I left the annex, accompanied by Granger, for
a final examination of the gallows. The rope had already been
hung and the hangman's knot tied. While Granger made certain they were secure I unlocked the door beneath the platform, which opened into a short passage that ended in a narrow cubicle beneath the trap. The platform had been built
eight feet off the floor, so that the death throes of the condemned man would be concealed from the witnesses — a hu-
mane gesture which was not observed by all prisons in our
state, and for which I was grateful.

After I had made a routine examination of the cubicle, and
relocked the door, I mounted the thirteen steps to the platform. The trap beneath the gibbet arm was operated by a

lever set into the floor; when Granger threw the lever, the trap would fall open. Once we tried it and reset it, I pronounced everything in readiness and sent Rogers to summon the civilian witnesses and the prison doctor. It was then 4:35 and the execution would take place at precisely five o'clock. I had received a wire from the governor the night before, informing me that there wasn't the remotest chance of a stay being granted.

When Rogers returned with the witnesses and the doctor, we all took chairs in the row arranged some forty feet opposite the gallows. Time passed, tensely; with thunder echoing hollowly outside, a hard rain drumming against the tin roof, and eerie shadows not entirely dispelled by the lanternlight, the moments before that execution were particularly disquieting.

I held my pocket watch open on my knee, and at 4:55 I signaled to the guard at the annex door to call for the prisoner. Three more minutes crept by and then the door reopened and Granger and Hollowell brought Teasdale into the shed.

The three men made a grim procession as they crossed to the gallows steps: Granger in his black hangman's duster, Hollowell in his khaki guard uniform and peaked cap, Teasdale between them in his grey prison clothing and black hood. Teasdale's shoes dragged across the floor — he was a stiffly unresisting weight until they reached the steps; then he struggled briefly and Granger and Hollowell were forced to tighten their grip and all but carry him up onto the gallows. Hollowell held him slumped on the trap while Granger solemnly fitted the noose around his neck and drew it taut.

The hands on my watch read five o'clock when, as prescribed by law, Granger intoned, "Have you any last words before the sentence imposed on you is carried out?"

Teasdale said nothing, but his body twisted with a spasm of fear.

Granger looked in my direction and I raised my hand to indicate final sanction. He backed away from Teasdale and rested his hand on the release lever. As he did so, there came from outside a long rolling peal of thunder that seemed to shake the shed roof. A chill touched the nape of my neck and I shifted uneasily on my chair.

Just as the sound of the thunder faded, Granger threw the lever and Hollowell released Teasdale and stepped back. The trap thudded open and the condemned man plummeted downward.

In that same instant I thought I saw a faint silvery glimmer above the opening, but it was so brief that I took it for an optical illusion. My attention was focused on the rope: it danced for a moment under the weight of the body, then pulled taut and became motionless. I let out a soft tired sigh and sat forward while Granger and Hollowell, both of whom were looking away from the open trap, silently counted off the passage of sixty seconds.

When the minute had elapsed, Granger turned and walked to the edge of the trap. If the body hung laxly, he would signal to me so that the prison doctor and I could enter the cubicle and officially pronounce Teasdale deceased; if the body was still thrashing, thus indicating the condemned man's neck had not been broken in the fall — grisly prospect, but I had seen it happen — more time would be allowed to pass. It sounds brutal, I know, but such was the law and it had to be obeyed without question.

But Granger's reaction was so peculiar and so violent that I came immediately to my feet. He flinched as if he had been struck in the stomach and his face twisted into an expression of disbelief. He dropped to his hands and knees at the front of the trap as Hollowell came up beside him and leaned down to peer into the passageway.

"What is it, Granger?" I called. "What's the matter?"

He straightened after a few seconds and pivoted toward me. "You better get up here, Warden Parker," he said. His voice was shrill and tremulous and he clutched at his stomach. "Quick!"

Rogers and I exchanged glances, then ran to the steps,

mounted them, and hurried to the trap, the other guards and the prison doctor close behind us. As soon as I looked downward, it was my turn to stare with incredulity, to exclaim against what I saw — and what I did not see.

The hangman's noose at the end of the rope was empty.

Except for the black hood on the ground, the cubicle was empty.

Impossibly, the body of Arthur Teasdale had vanished.

I raced down the gallows steps and fumbled the platform door open with my key. I had the vague desperate hope that Teasdale had somehow slipped the noose and that I would see him lying within, against the door — that small section of the passageway was shrouded in darkness and not quite penetrable from above — but he wasn't there. The passageway, like the cubicle, was deserted.

While I called for a lantern Rogers hoisted up the rope to examine it and the noose. A moment later he announced that it had not been tampered with in any way. When a guard brought the lantern I embarked on a careful search of the area, but there were no loose boards in the walls of the passage or the cubicle, and the floor was of solid concrete. On the floor I discovered a thin sliver of wood about an inch long, which may or may not have been there previously. Aside from that, there was not so much as a strand of hair or a loose thread to be found. And the black hood told me nothing at all.

There simply did not seem to be any way Teasdale — or his remains — could have gotten, or been gotten, out of there.

I stood for a moment, staring at the flickering light from the lantern, listening to the distant rumbling of thunder. *Had* Teasdale died at the end of the hangman's rope? Or had he somehow managed to cheat death? I had seen him fall through the trap with my own eyes, had seen the rope dance and then pull taut with the weight of his body. He *must* have expired, I told myself.

A shiver moved along my back. I found myself remembering Teasdale's threats to wreak vengeance from the grave, and I had the irrational thought that perhaps something otherworldly had been responsible for the phenomenon we had witnessed. Teasdale had, after all, been a malignant individual. Could he have been so evil that he had managed to summon the Powers of Darkness to save him in the instant before death — or to claim him soul *and* body in the instant after it?

I refused to believe it. I am a practical man, not prone to superstition, and it has always been my nature to seek a logical explanation for even the most uncommon occurrence. Arthur Teasdale had disappeared, yes; but it could not be other than an earthly force behind the deed. Which meant that, alive or dead, Teasdale was still somewhere inside the walls of Arrowmont Prison.

I roused myself, left the passageway, and issued instructions for a thorough search of the prison grounds. I ordered word sent to the guards in the watchtowers to double their normal vigilance. I noticed that Hollowell wasn't present along with the assembled guards and asked where he had gone. One of the others said he had seen Hollowell hurry out of the shed several minutes earlier.

Frowning, I pondered this information. Had Hollowell intuited something, or even seen something, and gone off unwisely to investigate on his own rather than confide in the rest of us? He had been employed at Arrowmont Prison less than two months, so I knew relatively little about him. I requested that he be found and brought to my office.

When Rogers and Granger and the other guards had departed, I escorted the two civilian witnesses to the administration building, where I asked them to remain until the mystery was explained. As I settled grimly at my desk to await Hollowell and word on the search of the grounds, I expected such an explanation within the hour.

I could not, however, have been more wrong.

The first development came after thirty minutes, and it was nearly as alarming as the disappearance of Teasdale from the gallows cubicle: one of the guards brought the news, ashen-faced, that a body had been discovered behind a stack of lumber in a lean-to between the execution shed and the iron foundry. But it was not the body of Arthur Teasdale.

It was that of Hollowell, stabbed to death with an awl.

I went immediately. As I stood beneath the rain-swept lean-to, looking down at the bloody front of poor Hollowell's uniform, a fresh set of unsettling questions tumbled through my mind. Had he been killed because, as I had first thought, he had either seen or intuited something connected with Teasdale's disappearance? If that was the case, whatever it was had died with him.

Or was it possible that he had himself been involved in the disappearance and been murdered to assure his silence? But how could he have been involved? He had been in my sight the entire time on the gallows platform. He had done nothing suspicious, could not in any way I could conceive have assisted in the deed.

How could Teasdale have survived the hanging?

How could he have escaped not only the gallows but the execution shed itself?

The only explanation seemed to be that it was not a live Arthur Teasdale who was carrying out his warped revenge, but a dead one who had been embraced and given earthly powers by the Forces of Evil . . .

In order to dispel the dark reflections from my mind, I personally supervised the balance of the search. Tines of lightning split the sky and thunder continued to hammer the roofs as we went from building to building. No corner of the prison compound escaped our scrutiny. No potential hiding place was overlooked. We went so far as to test for the presence of tunnels in the work areas and in the individual cells, although I had instructed just such a search only weeks before as part of my security program.

We found nothing.

Alive or dead, Arthur Teasdale was no longer within the walls of Arrowmont Prison.

I left the prison at ten o'clock that night. There was nothing more to be done, and I was filled with such depression and anxiety that I could not bear to spend another minute there. I had debated contacting the governor, of course, and, wisely or not, had decided against it for the time being. He would think me a lunatic if I requested assistance in a county or statewide search for a man who had for all intents and purposes been hanged at five o'clock that afternoon. If there were no new developments within the next twenty-four hours, I knew I would have no choice but to explain the situation to him. And I had no doubt that such an explanation unaccompanied by Teasdale or Teasdale's remains would cost me my position.

Before leaving, I swore everyone to secrecy, saying that I would have any man's job if he leaked word of the day's events to the press or to the public-at-large. The last thing I wanted was rumor-mongering and a general panic as a result of it. I warned Granger and the other guards who had come in contact with Teasdale to be especially wary and finally left word that I was to be contacted immediately if there were any further developments before morning.

I had up to that time given little thought to my own safety. But when I reached my cottage in the village I found myself imagining menace in every shadow and sound. Relaxation was impossible. After twenty minutes I felt impelled to leave, to seek out a friendly face. I told my housekeeper I would be at Hallahan's Irish Inn if anyone called for me and drove my Packard to the tavern.

The first person I saw upon entering was Buckmaster Gilloon. He was seated alone in a corner booth, writing intently in one of his notebooks, a stein of draught Guinness at his elbow.

Gilloon had always been very secretive about his note-books and never allowed anyone to glimpse so much as a word of what he put into them. But he was so engrossed when I walked up to the booth that he did not hear me, and I happened to glance down at the open page on which he was writing. There was but a single interrogative sentence on the page, clearly legible in his bold hand. The sentence read:

*If a jimbuck stands alone by the sea, on a night when the dark moon sings, how many grains of sand in a single one of his footprints?*

That sentence has always haunted me, because I cannot begin to understand its significance. I have no idea what a jimbuck is, except perhaps as a fictional creation, and yet that passage was like none which ever appeared in such periodicals as *Argosy* or *Munsey's*.

Gilloon sensed my presence after a second or two, and he slammed the notebook shut. A ferocious scowl crossed his normally placid features. He said irritably, "Reading over a man's shoulder is a nasty habit, Parker."

"I'm sorry, I didn't mean to pry —"

"I'll thank you to be more respectful of my privacy in the future."

"Yes, of course." I sank wearily into the booth opposite him and called for a Guinness.

Gilloon studied me across the table. "You look haggard, Parker," he said. "What's troubling you?"

"It's . . . nothing."

"Everything is something."

"I'm not at liberty to discuss it."

"Would it have anything to do with the execution at Arrowmont Prison this afternoon?"

I blinked. "Why would you surmise that?"

"Logical assumption," Gilloon said. "You are obviously upset, and yet you are a man who lives quietly and suffers no apparent personal problems. You are warden of Arrowmont Prison and the fact of the execution is public knowl-

edge. You customarily come to the inn at eight o'clock, and
yet you didn't make your appearance tonight until after
eleven.''

I said, "I wish I had your mathematical mind, Gilloon.''

"Indeed? Why is that?''

"Perhaps then I could find answers where none seem to
exist.''

"Answers to what?''

A waiter arrived with my Guinness and I took a swallow
gratefully.

Gilloon was looking at me with piercing interest. I avoided
his one-eyed gaze, knowing I had already said too much. But
there was something about Gilloon that demanded confidence. Perhaps he could shed some light on the riddle of
Teasdale's disappearance.

"Come now, Parker — answers to what?'' he repeated.
"Has something happened at the prison?''

And of course I weakened — partly because of frustration
and worry, partly because the possibility that I might never
learn the secret loomed large and painful. "Yes,'' I said,
"something has happened at the prison. Something incredible, and I mean that literally.'' I paused to draw a heavy
breath. "If I tell you about it, do I have your word that you
won't let it go beyond this table?''

"Naturally.'' Gilloon leaned forward and his good eye
glittered with anticipation. "Go on, Parker.''

More or less calmly at first, then with increasing agitation
as I relived the events, I proceeded to tell Gilloon everything
that had transpired at the prison. He listened with attention,
not once interrupting. I had never seen him excited prior to
that night, but when I had finished, he was fairly squirming.
He took off his Scotch cap and ran a hand through his thin-
ning brown hair.

"Fascinating tale,'' he said.

"Horrifying would be a more appropriate word.''

"That too, yes. No wonder you're upset.''

"It simply defies explanation," I said. "And yet there has to be one. I refuse to accept the supernatural implications."

"I wouldn't be so skeptical of the supernatural if I were you, Parker. I've come across a number of things in my travels which could not be satisfactorily explained by man or science."

I stared at him. "Does that mean you believe Teasdale's disappearance was arranged by forces beyond human ken?"

"No, no. I was merely making a considered observation. Have you given me every detail of what happened?"

"I believe so."

"Think it through again — be sure."

Frowning, I reviewed the events once more. And it came to me that I had neglected to mention the brief silvery glimmer which had appeared above the trap in the instant Teasdale plunged through; I had, in fact, forgotten all about it. This time I mentioned it to Gilloon.

"Ah," he said.

"Ah? Does it have significance?"

"Perhaps. Can you be more specific about it?"

"I'm afraid not. It was so brief I took it at the time for an optical illusion."

"You saw no other such glimmers?"

"None."

"How far away from the gallows were you sitting?"

"Approximately forty feet."

"Is the shed equipped with electric lights?"

"No — lanterns."

"I see," Gilloon said meditatively. He seized one of his notebooks, opened it, shielded it from my eyes with his left arm, and began to write furiously with his pencil. He wrote without pause for a good three minutes, before I grew both irritated and anxious.

"Gilloon," I said, "stop that infernal scribbling and tell me what's on your mind."

He gave no indication of having heard me. His pencil continued to scratch against the paper, filling another page. Except for the movement of his right hand and one side of his mouth gnawing at the edge of his mustache, he was as rigid as a block of stone.

"Damn it, Gilloon!"

But it was another ten seconds before the pencil became motionless. He stared at what he had written and then looked up at me. "Parker," he said, "did Arthur Teasdale have a trade?"

The question took me by surprise. "A trade?"

"Yes. What did he do for a living, if anything?"

"What bearing can that have on what's happened?"

"Perhaps a great deal," Gilloon said.

"He worked in a textile mill."

"And there is a textile mill at the prison, correct?"

"Yes."

"Does it stock quantities of silk?"

"Silk? Yes, on occasion. What — ?"

I did not finish what I was about to say, for he had shut me out and resumed writing in his notebook. I repressed an oath of exasperation, took a long draught of Guinness to calm myself, and prepared to demand that he tell me what theory he had devised. Before I could do that, however, Gilloon abruptly closed the notebook, slid out of the booth, and fairly loomed over me.

"I'll need to see the execution shed," he said.

"What for?"

"Corroboration of certain facts."

"But —" I stood up hastily. "You've suspicioned a possible answer, that's clear," I said, "though I can't for the life of me see how, on the basis of the information I've given you. What is it?"

"I must see the execution shed," he said firmly. "I will not voice premature speculations."

It touched my mind that the man was a bit mad. After all, I had only known him for a few weeks, and from the first he had been decidedly eccentric in most respects. Still, I had never had cause to question his mental faculties before this, and the aura of self-assurance and confidence he projected was forceful. Because I needed so desperately to solve the riddle, I couldn't afford *not* to indulge, at least for a while, the one man who might be able to provide it.

"Very well," I said, "I'll take you to the prison."

Rain still fell in black torrents — although without thunder and lightning — when I brought my Packard around the last climbing curve onto the promontory. Lanternlight glowed fuzzily in the prison watchtowers, and the bare brick walls had an unpleasant oily sheen. At this hour of night, in the storm, the place seemed forbidding and shrouded in human despair — an atmosphere I had not previously apprehended during the two years I had been its warden. Strange how a brush with the unknown can alter one's perspective and stir the fears that lie at the bottom of one's soul.

Beside me Gilloon did not speak; he sat erect, his hands resting on the notebooks on his lap. I parked in the small lot facing the main gates, and after Gilloon had carefully tucked the notebooks inside his slicker we ran through the downpour to the gates. I gestured to enter, and then quickly closed the iron halves behind us and returned to the warmth of the gatehouse. I led Gilloon directly across the compound to the execution shed.

The guards I had posted inside seemed edgy and grateful for company. It was colder now, and despite the fact that all the lanterns were lit it also seemed darker and filled with more restless shadows. But the earlier aura of spiritual menace permeated the air, at least to my sensitivities. If Gilloon noticed it, he gave no indication.

He wasted no time crossing to the gallows and climbing the steps to the platform. I followed him to the trap, which still hung open. Gilloon peered into the cubicle, got onto all fours to squint at the rectangular edges of the opening, and then hoisted the hangman's rope and studied the noose. Finally, with surprising agility, he dropped down inside the cubicle, requesting a lantern which I fetched for him, and spent minutes crawling about with his nose to the floor. He located the thin splinter of wood I had noticed earlier, studied it in the lantern glow, and dropped it into the pocket of his tweed coat.

When he came out through the passageway he wore a look mixed of ferocity and satisfaction. "Stand there a minute, will you?" he said. He hurried over to where the witness chairs were arranged, then called, "In which of these chairs were you sitting during the execution?"

"Fourth one from the left."

Gilloon sat in that chair, produced his notebooks, opened one, and bent over it. I waited with mounting agitation while he committed notes to paper. When he glanced up again, the flickering lanternglow gave his face a spectral cast.

He said, "While Granger placed the noose over Teasdale's head, Hollowell held the prisoner on the trap — is that correct?"

"It is."

"Stand as Hollowell was standing."

I moved to the edge of the opening, turning slightly quarter profile.

"You're certain that was the exact position?"

"Yes."

"Once the trap had been sprung, what did Hollowell do?"

"Moved a few paces away." I demonstrated.

"Did he avert his eyes from the trap?"

"Yes, he did. So did Granger. That's standard procedure."

"Which direction did he face?"

I frowned. "I'm not quite sure," I said. "My attention was on the trap and the rope."

"You're doing admirably, Parker. After Granger threw the trap lever, did he remain standing beside it?"

"Until he had counted off sixty seconds, yes."

"And then?"

"As I told you, he walked to the trap and looked into the

cubicle. Again, that is standard procedure for the hangman. When he saw it was empty he uttered a shocked exclamation, went to his knees, and leaned down to see if Teasdale had somehow slipped the noose and fallen or crawled into the passageway.''

"At which part of the opening did he go to his knees? Front, rear, one of the sides?''

"The front. But I don't see —''

"Would you mind illustrating?''

I grumbled but did as he asked. Some thirty seconds passed in silence. Finally I stood and turned, and of course found Gilloon again writing in his notebook. I descended the gallows steps. Gilloon closed the notebook and stood with an air of growing urgency. "Where would Granger be at this hour?'' he asked. "Still here at the prison?''

"I doubt it. He came on duty at three and should have gone off again at midnight.''

"It's imperative that we find him as soon as possible, Parker. Now that I'm onto the solution of this riddle, there's no time to waste.''

"You have solved it?''

"I'm certain I have.'' He hurried me out of the shed.

I felt dazed as we crossed the rain-soaked compound, yet Gilloon's positiveness had infused in me a similar sense of urgency. We entered the administration building and I led the way to Rogers' office, where we found him preparing to depart for the night. When I asked about Granger, Rogers said that he had signed out some fifty minutes earlier, at midnight.

"Where does he live?'' Gilloon asked us.

"In Hainesville, I think.''

"We must go there immediately, Parker. And we had better take half a dozen well-armed men with us.''

"Do you honestly believe that's necessary?''

'I do,'' Gilloon said grimly. "If we're fortunate, it will help prevent another murder.''

The six-mile drive to the village of Hainesville was charged with tension, made even more acute by the muddy roads and the pelting rain. Gilloon stubbornly refused to comment on the way as to whether he believed Granger to be a culpable or innocent party, or as to whether he suspected to find Arthur Teasdale alive — or dead — at Granger's home. There would be time enough later for explanations, he said.

Hunched over the wheel of the Packard, conscious of the two heavily armed prison guards in the rear seat and the headlamps of Rogers' car following closely behind, I could not help but wonder if I might be making a prize fool of myself. Suppose I had been wrong in my judgment of Gilloon, and he *was* daft after all? Or a well-meaning fool in his own right? Or worst of all, a hoaxster?

Nevertheless, there was no turning back now. I had long since committed myself. Whatever the outcome, I had placed the fate of my career firmly in the hands of Buckmaster Gilloon.

We entered the outskirts of Hainesville. One of the guards who rode with us lived there, and he directed us down the main street and into a turn just beyond the church. The lane in which Granger lived, he said, was two blocks further up and one block east.

Beside me Gilloon spoke for the first time. "I suggest we park a distance away from Granger's residence, Parker. It won't do to announce our arrival by stopping in front."

I nodded. When I made the turn into the lane I took the Packard onto the verge and doused its lights. Rogers' car drifted in behind, headlamps also winking out. A moment later eight of us stood in a tight group in the roadway, huddling inside our slickers as we peered up the lane.

There were four houses in the block, two on each side, spaced widely apart. The pair on our left, behind which stretched open meadowland, were dark. The furthest of the two on the right was also dark, but the closer one showed light in one of the front windows. Thick smoke curled out of its chimney and was swirled into nothingness by the howling wind. A huge oak shaded the front yard. Across the rear, a copse of swaying pine stood silhouetted against the black sky.

The guard who lived in Hainesville said, "That's Granger's place, the one showing light."

We left the road and set out laterally across the grassy flatland to the pines, then through them toward Granger's cottage. From a point behind the house, after issuing instructions for the others to wait there, Gilloon, Rogers, and I made our way downward past an old stone well and through a sodden growth of weeds. The sound of the storm muffled our approach as we proceeded single-file, Gilloon tacitly assuming leadership, along the west side of the house to the lighted window.

Gilloon put his head around the frame for the first cautious look inside. Momentarily he stepped back and motioned me to take his place. When I had moved to where I could peer in, I saw Granger standing relaxed before the fireplace, using a poker to prod a blazing fire not wholly comprised of logs — something else, a blackened lump already burned beyond recognition, was being consumed there. But he was not alone in the room; a second man stood watching him, an expression of concentrated malevolence on his face — and an old hammerless revolver tucked into the waistband of his trousers.

Arthur Teasdale.

I experienced a mixture of relief, rage, and resolve as I moved away to give Rogers his turn. It was obvious that Granger was guilty of complicity in Teasdale's escape — and I had always liked and trusted the man. But I supposed everyone had his price; I may even have had a fleeting wonder as to what my own might be.

After Rogers had his look, the three of us returned to the back yard, where I told him to prepare the rest of the men for a front-and-rear assault on the cottage. Then Gilloon and I took up post in the shadows behind the stone well. Now that my faith in *him,* at least, had been vindicated, I felt an enormous gratitude — but this was hardly the time to express

it. Or to ask any of the questions that were racing through
my mind. We waited in silence.

In less than four minutes all six of my men had surrounded
the house. I could not hear it when those at the front broke
in, but the men at the back entered the rear door swiftly.
Soon the sound of pistol shots rose above the cry of the
storm.

Gilloon and I hastened inside. In the parlor we found
Granger sitting on the floor beside the hearth, his head buried
in his hands. He had not been injured, nor had any of the
guards. Teasdale was lying just beyond the entrance to the
center hallway. The front of his shirt was bloody, but he had
merely suffered a superficial shoulder wound and was cursing
like a madman. He would live to hang again, I remember
thinking, in the execution shed at Arrowmont Prison.

Sixty minutes later, after Teasdale had been placed under
heavy guard in the prison infirmary and a silent Granger had
been locked in a cell, Rogers and Gilloon and I met in my
office. Outside, the rain had slackened to a drizzle.

"Now then, Gilloon," I began, "we owe you a great debt,
and I acknowledge it here and now. But explanations are
long overdue."

He smiled with the air of a man who has just been through
an exhilarating experience. "Of course," he said. "Suppose
we begin with Hollowell. You're wondering if he was bribed
by Teasdale — if he also assisted in the escape. The answer
is no: he was an innocent pawn."

"Then why was he killed? Revenge?"

"Not at all. His life was taken — and not at the place
where his body was later discovered — so that the escape
trick could be worked in the first place. It was one of the
primary keys to the plan's success."

"I don't understand," I said. "The escape trick had already been completed when Hollowell was stabbed."

"Ah, but it hadn't," Gilloon said. "Hollowell was murdered *before* the execution, sometime between four and five o'clock.''

We stared at him. "Gilloon," I said, "Rogers and I and five other witnesses *saw* Hollowell inside the shed —''

"Did you, Parker? The execution shed is lighted by lanterns. On a dark afternoon, during a thunderstorm, visibility is not reliable. And you were some forty feet from him. You saw an average-size man wearing a guard's uniform, with a guard's peaked cap drawn down over his forehead — a man you had no reason to assume was not Hollowell. You took his identity for granted.''

"I can't dispute the logic of that," I said. "But if you're right that it wasn't Hollowell, who was it?''

"Teasdale, of course.''

"Teasdale! For God's sake, man, if Teasdale assumed the identity of Hollowell, whom did we see carried in as Teasdale?''

"No one," Gilloon said.

My mouth fell open. There was a moment of heavy silence. I broke it finally by exclaiming, "Are you saying we did not see a man hanged at five o'clock this afternoon?''

"Precisely.''

"Are you saying we were all victims of some sort of mass hallucination?''

"Certainly not. You saw what you believed to be Arthur Teasdale, just as you saw what you believed to be Hollowell. Again let me remind you: the lighting was poor and you had no reason at the time to suspect deception. But think back, Parker. What actually *did* you see? The shape of a man with a black hood covering his head, supported between two other men. But did you see that figure walk or hear it speak? Did you at any time discern an identifiable part of a human being, such as a hand or an exposed ankle?''

I squeezed my eyes shut for a moment, mentally re-examining the events in the shed. "No," I admitted. "I discerned nothing but the hood and the clothing and the shoes. But I *did* see him struggle at the foot of the gallows, and his body spasm on the trap. How do you explain them?''

"Simply. Like everything else, they were an illusion. At a preconceived time Granger and Teasdale had only to slow their pace and jostle the figure with their own bodies to create the impression that the figure itself was resisting them. Teasdale alone used the same method on the trap.''

"If it is your contention that the figure was some sort of dummy, I can't believe it, Gilloon. How could a dummy be made to vanish any more easily than a man?''

"It was not, strictly speaking, a dummy.''

"Then what the devil was it?''

Gilloon held up a hand; he appeared to be enjoying himself immensely. "Do you recall my asking if Teasdale had a trade? You responded that he had worked in a textile mill, whereupon I asked if the prison textile mill stocked silk.''

"Yes, yes, I recall that.''

"Come now, Parker, use your imagination. What is one of the uses of silk — varnished silk?''

"I don't know," I began, but no sooner were the words past my lips than the answer sprang into my mind. "Good Lord — balloons!''

"Exactly.''

"The figure we saw was a *balloon?*''

"In effect, yes. It is not difficult to sew and tie off a large piece of silk in the rough shape of a man. When inflated to a malleable state with helium or hydrogen, and seen in poor light from a distance of forty feet or better, while covered entirely by clothing and a hood, and weighted down with a pair of shoes and held tightly by two men — the effect can be maintained.

"The handiwork would have been done by Teasdale in the relative privacy of the death cell. The material was doubtless supplied from the prison textile mill by Granger. Once the sewing and tying had been accomplished, I imagine Granger took the piece out of the prison, varnished it, and returned it later. It need not have been inflated, naturally, until just prior to the execution. As to where the gas was obtained, I would think there would certainly be a cylinder of hydrogen in the prison foundry.''

I nodded.

"In any event, between four and five o'clock, when the three of them were alone in the death annex, Teasdale murdered Hollowell with an awl Granger had given him. Granger then transported Hollowell's body behind the stack of lumber a short distance away and probably also returned the gas cylinder to the foundry. The storm would have provided all the shield necessary, though even without it the risk was one worth taking.

"Once Granger and Teasdale had brought the balloon-figure to the gallows, Granger, as hangman, placed the noose carefully around the head. You told me, Parker, that he was the last to examine the noose. While he was doing so he inserted into the fibers at the inner bottom that sharp sliver of wood you found in the trap cubicle. When he drew the noose taut, he made sure the sliver touched the balloon's surface so that when the trap was sprung and the balloon plunged downward the splinter would penetrate the silk. The sound of a balloon deflating is negligible; the storm made it more so. The dancing of the rope, of course, was caused by the escaping air.

"During the ensuing sixty seconds, the balloon completely deflated. There was nothing in the cubicle at that point except a bundle of clothing, silk and shoes. The removal of all but the hood, to complete the trick, was a simple enough matter. You told me how it was done, when you mentioned the silvery glimmer you saw above the trap.

"That glimmer was a brief reflection of lanternlight off part of a length of thin wire which had been attached to the clothing and to the balloon. Granger concealed the wire in his hand, and played out most of a seven- or eight-foot coil before he threw the trap lever.

"After he had gone to his knees with his back to the witness chairs, he merely opened the front of his duster. No doubt it made something of a bulge, but the attention was focused on other matters. You did notice, Parker — and it was a helpful clue — that Granger appeared to be holding his stomach as if he were about to be ill. What he was actually doing was clutching the bundle so that it would not fall from beneath his duster. Later he hid the bundle among his belongings and transported it out of the prison when he went off duty. It was that bundle, incidentally, that we saw burning in the fireplace in his cottage.''

"But how did *Teasdale* get out of the prison?''

"The most obvious way imaginable,'' Gilloon said. "He walked out through the front gates.''

"What!''

"Yes. Remember, he was wearing a guard's uniform — supplied by Granger — and there was a storm raging. I noticed when we first arrived tonight that the gateman seemed eager to return to his gatehouse, where it was dry. He scarcely looked at you and did not question me. That being the case, it's obvious that he would not have questioned someone who wore the proper uniform and kept his face averted as he gave Hollowell's name. The guards had not yet been alerted and the gateman would have no reason to suspect trickery.

"Once out, I suspect Teasdale simply took Granger's car and drove to Hainesville. When Granger himself came off duty, I would guess that he obtained a ride home with another guard, using some pretext to explain the absence of his own vehicle.

"I did not actually *know,* of course, that we would find Teasdale at Granger's place; I merely made a logical supposition in light of the other facts. Since Granger was the only other man alive who knew how the escape had been worked, I reasoned that an individual of Teasdale's stripe would not care to leave him alive and vulnerable to a confession, no matter what promises he might have made to Granger.''

"If Teasdale managed his actual escape that easily, why did he choose to go through all that trickery with the balloon?

Why didn't he just murder Hollowell, with Granger's help, and then leave the prison *prior* to the execution, between four and five?''

"Oh, I suppose he thought that the bizarre circumstances surrounding the disappearance of an apparently hanged man would insure him enough time to get clear of this immediate area. If you were confused and baffled, you would not sound an instant alarm, whereas you certainly would have if he had simply disappeared from his cell. Also, the prospect of leaving all of you a legacy of mystery and horror afforded him a warped sense of revenge.''

"You're a brilliant man," I told him as I sank back in my chair.

Gilloon shrugged. "This kind of puzzle takes logic rather than brilliance, Parker. As I told you earlier tonight, it isn't always wise to discount the supernatural; but in a case where no clear evidence of the supernatural exists, the answer generally lies in some form of illusion. I've encountered a number of seemingly incredible occurrences, some of which were even more baffling than this one and most of which involved illusion. I expect I'll encounter others in the future as well.''

"Why do you say that?''

"One almost seems able after a while to divine places where they will occur," he said matter-of-factly, "and therefore to make oneself available to challenge them.''

I blinked at him. "Do you mean you *intuited* something like this would happen at Arrowmont Prison? That you have some sort of prevision?''

"Perhaps. Perhaps not. Perhaps I'm nothing more than a pulp writer who enjoys traveling.'' He gave me an enigmatic smile and got to his feet clutching his notebooks. "I can't speak for you, Parker," he said, "but I seem to have acquired an intense thirst. You wouldn't happen to know where we might obtain a Guinness at this hour, would you?''

One week later, suddenly and without notice, Gilloon left Arrowmont Village. One day he was there, the next he was not. Where he went I do not know: I neither saw him nor heard of or from him again.

Who and what was Buckmaster Gilloon? Is it possible for one enigma to be attracted and motivated by another enigma? Can that which seems natural and coincidental be the result instead of preternatural forces? Perhaps you can understand now why these questions have plagued me in the sixty years since I knew him. And why I am continually haunted by that single passage I read by accident in his notebook, the passage which may hold the key to Buckmaster Gilloon:

*If a jimbuck stands alone by the sea, on a night when the dark moon sings, how many grains of sand in a single one of his footprints? .*

# *Box in a Box*

## Jack Ritchie

*Since Jack Ritchie's detective stories aren't quite like anyone else's, it's not surprising that this locked room story isn't quite like any other.*

WHEN RALPH AND I reached the scene, the large bedroom was noisy with uniformed policemen, technicians, medics, and photographers fussing around the perimeter of the body.

Ralph put two fingers into his mouth and whistled.

Damn, I thought, I've never been able to do that.

A silence of sorts ensued and then a short round man in his early fifties spoke up. "I'm innocent. I've been framed."

I regarded him sternly. "You will have your opportunity to speak later."

"What's wrong with right now?"

I conceded the point. "Very well, who are you?"

"The murderer." He quickly amended that. "I mean everybody *thinks* that I murdered my wife Hermione but I didn't. My name is Eustis Crawford."

Ralph and I took Eustis Crawford into an adjoining room where we found a tall thin man wearing a hearing aid and a dark-haired woman in her thirties waiting.

The tall thin man made the introductions. "I am Oglethorpe Wesson. And this is my sister Genevieve." He regarded Eustis Crawford coldly. "Eustis murdered his wife, who is, or rather was, our aunt. He and Hermione were the only people in their bedroom when she died. The windows and the doors were bolted from the inside. When Genevieve and I finally succeeded in entering, we found Hermione dead on the floor and Eustis unconscious on the floor beside her with a revolver in his hand. Obviously he had fainted after he shot her."

"I did not faint," Eustis Crawford said stiffly. "I definitely did not faint."

Oglethorpe snorted. "You're always fainting, Eustis. Last week you passed out in the garden when you thought you'd been stung by a bee. And yesterday, when you tweaked your finger in the liquor-cabinet door. You faint whenever you are under any kind of stress and I submit that murder is a shock to the nervous system, even that of the murderer's."

Eustis's eyes were reflective. "The last thing I remember is sitting up in bed reading and listening to my tape recorder. And then for some reason I found myself on the floor beside Hermione with Oglethorpe shaking me awake." He stifled a yawn. "Very possibly I simply dozed off and fell out of bed."

"Nonsense," Oglethorpe said. "If you had fallen out of bed, surely your thud on the floor would have wakened you. And furthermore, you were at least twelve feet from the bed when I found you. Face it, Eustis, you shot Hermione and then fainted."

I turned to Genevieve. "You heard the shot?"

She nodded. "We were just outside their bedroom door. Oglethorpe and I had finished listening to the ten o'clock TV news and we were in the hallway going to our respective rooms when we heard the shot. We knocked at the door and asked if there was anything wrong, but we received no answer. We tried the doorknob, but the door was bolted."

"How did you get in?"

Oglethorpe touched his hearing aid for a moment. "We went through my bedroom out onto the balcony till we got to the French doors, but they were bolted from the inside."

Genevieve corroborated that. "Oglethorpe finally had to take one of the balcony chairs and break a glass pane in one of the doors. He reached inside and unbolted it."

"Are you positive that *all* of the French doors were bolted from the inside?"

"Positive," Genevieve said. "And the bedroom door to the hallway was bolted from the inside too."

I nodded thoughtfully. "You and your brother spent the evening watching television?"

"No," Oglethorpe said. "Frankly, I don't care for television except for the news programs. I was downstairs in my workshop turning table legs most of the evening."

I turned to Eustis. "Did you have a quarrel with your wife?"

He put his right hand over his heart. "We were happily

married for nearly eight months. We never exchanged so
much as a harsh word.''

Genevieve reluctantly agreed. ''Come to think of it, Eustis
never *did* quarrel with Hermione. I think that's a little unnatural.''

''If we should rule out murder as the result of a quarrel,''
I said, ''would there be any other reason Mr. Crawford
would want to murder his wife?''

Oglethorpe adjusted something on his hearing aid. ''For
her money, of course. Hermione was rather wealthy, in a
lower-upper-class sort of way, and she kept Eustis on a strict
allowance.''

I drew Ralph to one side, ''Well, Ralph, we've finally got
one.''

''Got one what?''

''A closed-room murder mystery.''

''There's no mystery about it. Eustis shot his wife. He's
the only one who could have done it. The room was locked
from the inside.''

''Exactly,'' I said. ''But, Ralph, if Eustis was going to
murder his wife — especially for money — would he have
arranged to lock himself in the same room with her body?''

''All right, maybe it wasn't for money. They just had their
first spat, he lost his temper, and shot her. Then he fainted.''

''Ralph,'' I said. ''This is a rather large house and it has
many rooms. Doesn't it strike you as rather a coincidence
that Oglethorpe and Genevieve should just *happen* to have
been outside the door at the exact moment the shot was
fired?''

We drew Genevieve Wesson to a private corner of the
room. ''You say your Aunt Hermione had quite a bit of
money?'' I asked.

''Quite a bit.''

''And Eustis?''

''Nothing, really. Eustis was the chief accountant at the
Performing Arts Center. Hermione was on the Board of
Sponsors and she met Eustis when she came to him to discuss

the financial arrangements for an appearance of the Bulgarian National Ballet Company. One thing led to another and they were married.''

"Ah," I said. "And after she married Eustis, did she not change her will so that he would get the major portion of her estate in the event of her death?''

"Hermione never made out a will in her life. She was one of those people who believe they will die immediately if they do.''

"If Hermione had died of natural causes, her husband would have gotten her estate?''

"I suppose that's what would have happened.''

"However, your aunt did not die of natural causes, did she? And so if Eustis is convicted of her murder he cannot inherit any part of her estate, since a murderer may not profit from his crime.''

Genevieve smiled. "I'm counting on that.''

I returned to Eustis who had yawned again and now appeared to be looking for a place to sit down. "Could you give me your version of this unfortunate incident?''

He sighed. "Well, there really isn't much to tell. Hermione and I went upstairs at about ten. We usually read in bed for a while before turning out the light. The last thing I remember is reading Edgar Allan Poe's *The Purloined Letter* and listening to the *Pavan for a Dead Princess* on my tape recorder.'' He frowned in thought. "Or did I play *The Pines of Rome?* For some reason I keep confusing the two compositions.''

"Mr. Crawford," I said, "do you take pills — I mean sleeping pills?''

"Goodness no. I have no trouble at all getting to sleep once I close my eyes.''

"Before you and your wife went up to your bedroom, did you have anything to eat or drink?''

"I had a brandy and soda downstairs. I usually do before I go to sleep. It helps me to relax.''

"Who made the drink for you?''

"I made it myself."

"Who owns the revolver used to kill your wife?"

"I really don't know. I never saw it before in my life."

Ralph and I took Eustis back to the bedroom where the murder had been committed. I spoke to Dr. Tanner, the chief medic. "I'd like you to take a sample of this man's blood."

Tanner nodded. "Am I supposed to look for anything in particular?"

"Barbiturates," I said. "Or anything in the sleep-inducing category."

I left Eustis with Tanner and took Ralph to one side. "We've got to examine this room thoroughly, Ralph. I want to be absolutely certain that this was indeed a locked chamber at the time of the murder. Search for any openings, no matter how small. Hot-air registers, bell ropes."

"Bell ropes?"

"Those things used for summoning servants. Snakes have been known to crawl up and down bell ropes and fatally bite people."

Ralph looked at the ceiling. "Well, now, Henry, snakes and bell ropes are tricky things. Personally, I think that if a snake started down from the top of a bell rope, he'd just lose his grip and flop down and maybe fracture a vertebra. And if he tried to get back up, I don't think he could make it either. Bell ropes are just too vertical, Henry. Now if you could find one that's off-center about forty-five degrees, maybe, just maybe —"

"Ralph," I said patiently, "why must you rattle on about the prehensility and gripping strength of vipers? Hermione Crawford was shot. Not bitten by a snake." I rubbed my hands. "Now let us examine the room for any apertures."

After fifteen minutes, we rejoined each other.

"Not one damn aperture, Henry. No bell ropes or hot-air registers. The room is heated by radiant baseboard. As far as I can see, this place was airtight when Hermione Crawford was shot and Eustis was alone with her when it happened."

"Ralph," I said, "look at this tape recorder on the night-stand."

He looked. "So?"

"It doesn't have any tape in it," I said.

"It's right next to the recorder, Henry."

"I know. But it shouldn't be." I inserted the tape, turned on the recorder, and listened. Was it *The Pines of Rome* or the *Pavan for a Dead Princess?* I shrugged and turned it off.

I went back to Eustis Crawford, who was now having his hands tested for the presence of gunpowder grains. "Mr. Crawford, you say that the last thing you remember is being in bed with your wife and reading while listening to your tape recorder?"

"Yes."

"Did you hear out the tape to the end and then remove it from the tape recorder?"

"No. I fell asleep while it was playing."

I left Eustis yawning and took Ralph to the French doors. "Look at this, Ralph. Each of these panes of glass is held into place by four small slats of wood." I pointed to the frame which had been broken to gain access to the room. "You will notice that there are some light scratches here, as though perhaps a screwdriver had been used to remove the slats at one time."

Ralph peered closer and said, "Hm."

I nodded. "I must speculate to some degree, but I believe I have the answer to this entire riddle. We will start from the beginning. This evening someone in this household slipped barbiturates into Eustis Crawford's bottle of brandy. Unless the bottle has been destroyed or hidden, I think that we'll find it in the liquor cabinet downstairs. And after consuming his drink, Eustis went upstairs with his wife."

Ralph rubbed his jaw. "And once they got inside, they bolted the bedroom door and also the French doors?"

"Not necessarily, Ralph, though it's possible. But they did get into bed and Eustis picked up a book and turned on his tape recorder. Meanwhile, the murderer waited somewhere out in the darkness of the balcony until he saw Eustis lapse into his drugged sleep.''

"Murderer?"

"Or murderess. I will use the word murderer merely for convenience at the moment. And once Eustis was asleep, the murderer entered the room via the French doors. Or, if they were bolted, all he had to do was tap on the glass to gain Hermione's attention, smile sweetly, and ask to be let in because he wanted to talk with her for a moment. And since the person she saw was either her nephew or her niece, she had no reason to suspect foul play. But when Hermione let him in, he produced the revolver and shot her.

"He then dragged the unconscious Eustis out of his bed and placed him beside his dead wife. He replaced the cartridge he had fired with another one and then formed Eustis's hand around the revolver. He fired the gun again, this time through the open French door and into the night. He did that so that we would be certain of finding gunpowder grains on Eustis's hand.''

"How come nobody heard the shots, Henry?"

"Because the murderer used a silencer."

Ralph thought about it. "In that case, though shouldn't the murderer have powder grains on his hand too?"

"I doubt it. If he knew enough about powder grains to put them on Eustis's hand, then surely he must have been intelligent enough to take pains that none of them appeared on his own person. Very likely he wore gloves and some other protective device to prevent the powder grains from getting on his hands or clothing."

I noticed that Eustis had fallen asleep in his chair. "And then the murderer removed the *Pavan for a Dead Princess* — or whatever — from Eustis's tape recorder and substituted a tape of his own. This tape was entirely blank, except for the sound of one pistol shot."

Ralph raised an interested eyebrow.

I nodded. "Timing was incredibly important here, of

course. He knew the precise moment the tape would reach
the point of the shot, which would be within a minute or two
of ten-forty. He turned on the recorder, with the volume undoubtedly high, and then bolted the bedroom door from the
inside — if it was not bolted already. And then, probably
with a screwdriver, he removed one of the panes from a
French door — the one which we now see broken.

"He stepped out onto the balcony, closed the door after
him, reached back inside, and ran the bolt home. Then he
replaced the windowpane and the slats, went down to the
drawing room, and remained there listening to the ten o'clock
news. At ten-thirty, as usual Oglethorpe and Genevieve went
upstairs, putting them in the vicinity of Hermione's bedroom
door at the moment the tape reached the sound of the shot.
When the murderer gained access to the room from the balcony later, it was a simple matter to slip the tape back into
his pocket — he has probably managed to dispose of it by
now."

Ralph scratched his neck speculatively. "Who's your can-
didate for the murder? Oglethorpe or Genevieve?"

"Oglethorpe."

"Why Oglethorpe?"

"Because of the hearing aid."

"What does the hearing aid have to do with it?"

"I haven't quite pinpointed that yet, but it's probably the
key to this entire case. Every time I've looked at Oglethorpe,
he's been fiddling with that hearing aid. That's got to be significant somehow."

"Why?"

"Ralph," I said, "do you remember the Gillingham murder case? One of our prime suspects, Elmer Bjornson, appeared to be confined to a wheelchair, but we discovered that
he could really walk. That taught me to always be suspicious
of murder suspects in wheelchairs and by extension I think I
can safely apply that to people who wear hearing aids."

"Henry," Ralph said, "it's true that Bjornson could walk,
but that didn't have anything to do with the murder of Gil-

lingham. We just stumbled across that before we arrested the real murderer.''

I rubbed my jaw. "You mean that Oglethorpe's hearing aid has *nothing* to do with this murder?''

"I'm afraid not, Henry.''

I pulled myself together. "Ah well, nailing the true murderer in this case is just a matter of perseverance. We will come up with the culprit or culpritess soon. But at least, for the time being, we have succeeded in preventing an innocent man from being sent to prison.'' I smiled modestly. "Actually, I suppose almost any reasonably competent detective would eventually have come up with all the glaring inconsistencies in this case.''

Ralph nodded. "That's right, Henry.''

There was a rather long silence and I began to feel uneasy. "What is it, Ralph?''

He sighed. "This case reminds me of the purloined letter.''

"How does it remind you of the purloined letter?''

"Henry, the best place to hide a murder is inside a murder. Suppose you want to kill your wife for her money. No matter how cleverly you plan the thing, you know that you will still be the most logical suspect. The police would dig and dig and the chances are good that they would come up with something that would trip you up. So you decide to take the bull by the horns. Since you are going to be suspected anyway, why not go all out? Make it seem at first glance that only you could possibly have killed her.''

I closed my eyes.

Ralph continued. "When you go upstairs with your wife, you shoot her, using a silencer on the gun. Then you leave the room and get rid of the silencer and the spent cartridge and replace it with a fresh one. You return to the room and wait until you hear Oglethorpe and Genevieve coming up the stairs. You let them get just outside the door and then you fire the pistol out of the open French door into the night air.

"And while Oglethorpe and Genevieve are knocking at the

bedroom door, you simply close and bolt the French doors —
one of whose window frames you have previously tampered
with. Then you swallow a few barbiturates and lie down beside your dead wife. You pretend that you are unconscious
when Genevieve and Oglethorpe break into the room and that
is that.''

Ralph sighed again. ''You then sit back and let the police
do their work. They will realize that the situation is just *too*
pat, *too* overwhelming. Point by point, they will unravel the
frame-up and feel noble while they are doing it. Even if, by
some remote chance, you are actually brought to trial, any
good lawyer could point out the holes in the case and get you
an acquittal.''

I stared at Eustis, asleep in his chair with a smile on his
face.

Damn, I thought, Ralph's right. And he's going to get
away with it.

We carried Eustis to headquarters, but without any great
optimism.

Then Ralph and I dropped in at the nearest tavern.

The bartender recognized me. ''What'll it be, sergeant?
Tomato juice or sherry?''

''Sherry.''

''Oh?'' he said. ''That bad a day?''

I nodded glumly. ''That bad a day.''

He filled my glass to the brim and gave me water for a
chaser.

# The Number 12 Jinx

## Jon L. Breen

*Yes, there can even be an impossible disappearance at a baseball game, as in this fine story by Jon L. Breen.*

BEFORE I TELL YOU about the impossible disappearance at Surfer Stadium, a little anecdote might be appropriate.

In a game at one of the midwestern ball parks last season, I'm umpiring behind home plate — my name is Ed Gorgon, and I've been a major-league umpire for close to three decades. Anyway, in this particular park you can't see all of the bullpen from home plate. You can tell when a relief pitcher is warming up, but you can't see who he is because he's hidden by a fence.

On this occasion I see the bullpen catcher hunker down and start to receive warmup pitches from a reliefer, and I casually say to the batter coming up to hit, "I see ol' Spook Durkin is heatin' up out there." The batter, a rookie and not the smartest guy in the league, looks at me like I'm Sherlock Holmes in a chest protector and says, "Ed, how can you tell that? How do you know who's warming up?"

It's so simple, I'm ashamed to explain it. "The bullpen catcher has his mask on. These masks aren't so comfortable you wear 'em without a reason, and you don't warm a guy up with a mask on unless he's a knuckleballer who has no idea where the ball he's throwing is going. And the only knuckler out there is Spook Durkin. Strike!"

The kid shakes his head in wonder before getting back in the box. "It's simple when you explain it, Ed."

"Yeah," I say. "Strike two!" The kid better get his mind on the game or he'll be back in the Coast League before he knows what hit him.

Anyway, that little story just shows how a man's acumen can be overrated, and it leads into the story I really want to tell you — about "Honey" Reed and his short career with the Los Angeles Surfers.

John "Honey" Reed, who could play six positions well and two others adequately, who could hit with power and run like your basic deer, came to the Surfers from Chicago with a reputation as a troublemaker. He seemed to need an excuse to live up to it, and he found it over the simple matter of choosing a number for his uniform.

The number Honey Reed wanted was the one he'd worn throughout his career — in high school, college, the minors, the majors — the number 6. And there was the problem. Although no L.A. Surfer was wearing number 6 when Reed came to the club, he was told he couldn't wear it.

Six had been retired by the Surfers, having been worn by the great ballplayer of years ago, Fritz Krieg, who had played for the Surfers back when they were the Bronx Lions, long before they moved west. Though nobody in L.A. had ever seen Krieg play, he was one of the greats who, if he hadn't had the misfortune of being the only Major Leaguer killed in World War II, might have been greater still.

The controversy raged throughout spring training. Reed reported and agreed reluctantly to train wearing number 7, but he swore that if he couldn't wear 6 on opening day he would not play ball with the Surfers. The papers and TV had a field day with it, making Fritz Krieg into a local hero on the order of Sandy Koufax, and reviving the old rumor that Krieg had actually met his death in a bombed brothel.

The long rhubarb came to a climax when the Surfers returned to town from Arizona for two exhibitions in their home park prior to the opening of the season. A meeting was called in the office of Frances Gabrielson, owner of the Surfers, and present besides Honey Reed were Surfer player-representative Mort Fredericks; Florence Krieg, the widow of Fritz; team publicist Terry Takomoto; general manager Roy Giddings; and field manager Barney Dunlap.

The way the meeting was described to me later, everybody there except Fredericks is trying to get Reed to knuckle under and wear another number. Mrs. Gabrielson, a cool and elegant elderly lady, tries sweet reason and an appeal to team tradition, a tough case to make since the name Lions had been dropped for Surfers when the team came to L.A. Bar-

ney Dunlap's method of argument is loud and red-faced incredulity and an apparently genuine inability to comprehend
anyone else's arguments.

The widow underlines the necessity she feels for keeping
Fritz's memory alive, and Roy Giddings makes reference to
Krieg's war record. At this point Takamoto, whose Nisei parents were interred during World War II, blows his top,
swearing that Reed said under his breath, "On which side?"
Reed denies the charge but apologizes to Mrs. Krieg and tells
her he never believed the rumors about Fritz's death. Mrs.
Krieg, white-faced, claims she doesn't know what rumors
he's referring to.

One point of discussion is whether the Bronx Lions that
Krieg played for and the Los Angeles Surfers are really the
same organization for number-retiring purposes. Giddings
claims they are, regardless of the move of several thousand
miles, and Reed surprisingly backs him up. He says, "I've
done a lot of research into the history of this club, and it is
for sure the same organization." Is there some implied threat
in Reed's voice, a slight chilling of the atmosphere for a moment? My informants disagree on that point.

Anyway, after much more discussion and replowing of the
same ground, with Mort Fredericks halfheartedly defending
Reed's right to the number he wants, the slugger suddenly
decides to give in, to give up number 6.

There are smiles all around and mutual congratulations until general manager Giddings asks, "So what number do you
want, John?"

"Well, if I can't wear 6, I'll make it twice 6. I'll be number 12."

Barney Dunlap groans, and there is an awkward silence.

Reed breaks it by asking his teammate, "Mort, there's nobody on the club wearing 12, is there?"

"No," Fredericks admits, "there isn't."

"We don't wear 12 on the Surfers," says Barney Dunlap
flatly. "We just don't."

In a low voice Honey Reed inquires, "Is it retired, too, in

memory of some Bronx Lion who died in World War I in a —"

Mrs. Gabrielson breaks in quietly on Reed's offensive crack, and it's possible not everyone in the room even hears it. "Mr. Reed," she says, keeping her cool, "you must believe me that there are good and sound reasons for our unwillingness to have you wear number 12 and that they spring from nothing so much as a concern for your own well-being."

Reed will not be brought down, however. He blows up. "Look, I've gone out of my way to cooperate with you people on this. I wanted 6 and you said I couldn't have 6 and I said okay. Now I want 12 and for some reason you say I can't have 12 either. Well, I'm gonna have 12. If I play baseball for this club, that is. I don't need to play this game another day, you know — I have a restaurant, I have a bowling alley, and I have three offers to broadcast ball games. I can announce my retirement right here and now, and it won't hurt me one bit."

"Cool off, Honey," says Barney Dunlap. "Let us explain it." Barney, though, seems disinclined to start.

Finally, rather embarrassed, Terry Takamoto says, "Number 12 is jinxed."

"Jinxed? Look, I know most ballplayers are superstitious, but I'm not."

"Why were you so attached to number 6 then? Isn't that superstition?"

"No. It's a sentimental thing with me, but I don't really think 6 is particularly lucky —"

"John, I'm not superstitious either," says Mrs. Gabrielson, "but the history of number 12 on this club is really quite remarkable — horrible, actually — and I wouldn't want to take any chances with it. Tell him about it, Roy."

"Right," says Giddings. "You remember Alvin Hudspith?"

"Sure I do. Second baseman. Didn't he die . . . ?"

"Of a beanball thrown by a Chicago pitcher named Abramowicz. One of only two men in baseball history to die as the result of a thrown ball.''

"I was on that club with Abramowicz,'' says Barney Dunlap. "It ruined his career, too. Lost all heart for the game.''

"Anyway, Alvin Hudspith was number 12 for the Bronx Lions. The next guy to wear number 12 was Ingemar Lundquist, a rookie first baseman for the Lions who could have been another Lou Gehrig. But one night he was out after curfew, had too much to drink, and wandered in front of a subway train. Nobody wore number 12 again until after the team moved west. Mort can tell you about the next guy to wear number 12. You were a rookie catcher with the club the year Willie Washington came up, weren't you, Mort?''

"Yeah, we came up together through the minor-league system. I caught nearly all his games, minors and majors. He won eight in a row wearing number 13 — ol' Willie's not a superstitious dude, you see. But one day on the road his uniforms got lost in transit, so he wore number 12 instead. That day something popped in his arm, and he was never the same again. Two years later he was making a living tending bar.''

Reed laughs and that doesn't endear him to Mort Fredericks. "An old story. Pitchers are just freaks anyway, and I don't think Willie Washington was cut out for great things. Damned if you need a curse to explain a sore-armed pitcher.''

Fredericks looks fighting-mad for an instant, but Reed laughs again, disarmingly. "Do you really believe in it, Mort?''

They look at each other for a few seconds, challengingly some think, then Mort laughs too, with an effort. "No, not really. I think it's pretty silly.''

"I don't,'' Barney Dunlap mumbles.

Reed adds, "Anyhow, at least Washington lived. Maybe the curse is wearing off.'' He laughs again, and those who were there swear it has a hollow sound, echoing off the walls of the office. "I'm wearing 12. Take it or leave it.''

After a few moments of pensive silence Mrs. Gabrielson

decrees that they take it. Maybe because, after that meeting, nobody in the room cares too much if the number 12 jinx keeps working or not.

Of course the papers pick it up, and they like the curse angle even better than they did the Fritz Krieg controversy. By the next night, when Reed is scheduled to make his debut in Los Angeles in the last exhibition game of the season, all L.A. and all baseball are waiting to see what terrible fate is going to befall John "Honey" Reed in his indifference to the number 12 curse.

All the parties to the meeting I described are there, too. Fredericks, of course, on the field; Barney Dunlap in the dugout; Roy Giddings and Terry Takamoto in the press box; and even Florence Krieg, as a guest in owner Frances Gabrielson's private box.

The game goes along in orderly fashion until the top half of the fifth inning. I'm umpiring at first base, and Joe Bidwell, a rookie ump, is behind the plate. Mort Fredericks is catching for the Surfers, who lead in the game 8 to 1, and Honey Reed, wearing number 12 and with a homer and single in defiance of the curse already, is playing first.

On a one-ball and two-strike count, the Surfer pitcher misses the outside corner of the plate with his pitch and Joe Bidwell calls it a ball. Fredericks, thinking the guy has struck out, is all ready to throw the ball around the infield and reacts violently to Joe's call. He tears off his mask, throws it into the dirt, gets red in the face, and starts jumping up and down. No call for it, as far as I can see. The pitch was close, but not that close, and Fredericks' team is leading by seven runs. The Surfer pitcher just stands there watching, as much puzzled by the theatrics as I am.

"That rookie ump's got a lot to learn, Ed," Honey Reed says to me at first base.

"You just play your position," I tell him, and I start toward home plate to make sure things don't get out of hand. As senior ump, I have to watch out for Bidwell.

When he sees me coming, Fredericks turns to me. Bidwell should have chased him already, and I'm determined not to take any guff from him.

"You saw it, Ed. We had him struck out."

"You can't appeal to me on a called strike, Mort, and you know it. Now this is just an exhibition game, and I don't want to toss anybody, but one more word from you and you are gone."

"Well, if the league's gonna recruit blind umpires —"

"That's it. Take a hike." I speak softly but give him the thumb so everybody in the ball park gets the message.

With an angry snort Mort picks his mask up from the dirt and goes storming toward the Surfer dugout. Barney Dunlap is still there, looking more puzzled at his catcher's behavior than mad at me. Of course, he knows if he comes out to argue a called strike, he'll be gone too.

I return to my position behind first. Honey Reed says, "That's a cheap shot, Ed."

"You do your job and I'll do mine," I say, baffled by all this fuss and rancor in an 8-to-1 exhibition game.

The batter hits the next pitch deep to shortstop. The Surfer infielder makes a great stop on the ball, but he's too far back and can't get enough on the throw, and on a close play I call the runner safe. All of a sudden Honey Reed is all over me.

"Ed, I had him and you know it!"

"Shut up and play ball," I say, beginning to run short of patience.

"It wasn't even close, damn it!"

"Reed, if you want to join Fredericks for an early shower just keep on talking."

This time Barney Dunlap comes out and starts jawing at me too, mainly to save his first baseman from ejection. I have the feeling Dunlap's heart isn't in his protest, and he's as baffled by his players' antics as I am.

Barney's intervention does Reed no good. He can't stay away from me and before long I have no choice. He, too, gets a decisive thumb. Like Fredericks, he doesn't stick around once he's been bounced — why make the fine bigger? He just turns around and walks toward the Surfer dugout.

Barney gives me a last managerial glare, but his eyebrows do a sort of nothing-personal shrug, and he waddles back to the dugout. I suspect now we can play ball, and for a couple of innings I am right.

But around the end of the seventh, Barney Dunlap calls me over to the dugout.

"Ed," he says, "the damnedest thing has happened. Honey Reed has disappeared."

"Probably just went home early. Something was eating him, and I don't think it was just my calls."

"You don't understand, Ed. I mean he's vanished. Between the dugout and the clubhouse. He started down the tunnel, but he never got to the other end. It's impossible, Ed. It couldn't happen."

"Better get on the phone and tell Roy Giddings," I say.

"Ed, you're the big detective. Won't you sort of look into it?"

"I can't till after the game. I'm sure nothing happened to Reed, and there's a simple explanation for whatever seems to have happened."

"There's an explanation all right. He was wearing number 12 — that's the explanation." Barney's fat face looks comically but sincerely terrified.

Of course, it's none of my business what happens to a player after he leaves the field, and I have no choice but to keep the game going. But all the way to the ninth inning the little puzzle of how Honey Reed could have disappeared on his way from the dugout to the locker room niggles at me.

After the game is over, I walk back to the locker room through the Surfers' tunnel, though the umps have our own route to our cramped dressing-room facilities. The one important point about the tunnel is that it makes two turns along the way, so that you can't see the whole tunnel from the dugout to the locker room. I'm pretty sure the walls of the tunnel are innocent of secret panels — there's no excuse for gothic trappings in a new baseball park. (Or in an old one, come to think of it.)

When I get to the end of the tunnel, Roy Giddings approaches me.

"Found him?" I ask the worried-looking general manager.

"No, we haven't. Ed, it's unreal. I can't figure it."

Naturally, it has occurred to me the whole thing may be a publicity stunt dreamed up by the Surfer management, but Giddings' look of worry appears genuine to me. Gradually, with unwelcome help from Barney Dunlap and other players, Giddings gives me the details of the mystery.

Gus Brend, the clubhouse attendant, was sitting in the doorway to the Surfer locker room when the ejected Mort Fredericks came storming through. Fifteen minutes later the team trainer came back for a forgotten piece of equipment, and at this time the tunnel was empty. Gus swears that between the time Mort came through and the time the trainer did, *no one came through the tunnel*. The ballplayers in the dugout are just as sure Honey Reed walked down the tunnel and never came back. Thus, number 12 has vanished with not so much as a puff of smoke.

A nice little problem, but surely still a joke of some sort, not a police matter just yet. I yield to the flattery of Giddings about my detective prowess and agree to do a little investigation of my own.

First I interview Mort Fredericks.

"What did you do when you came back to the clubhouse?"

"What I normally do — took a shower. I felt like breaking up the place, you guys had me so steamed, but I like old Gus and didn't want to make extra work for him."

"Gus didn't follow you into the clubhouse?"

"No, I motioned him to stay put in his chair. I didn't need anything and he looked kind of worn out."

"What was he doing? Did he have the game on the radio?"

"Naw, old Gus is stone-deaf. He just sat there — oh, I think he had the morning paper.''

"Could he have missed anybody coming through the tunnel?''

"Not old Gus. He's sharp-eyed. If he says nobody came through the tunnel after me, I have to believe nobody came through the tunnel.''

"And you never saw Honey Reed?''

"Hell, no. I was still in the shower when the excitement started. First time I heard Honey was missing I had a towel wrapped around me and was wringing wet.''

Next I have a word with Gus Brend. Gus looks right at my lips when I talk and doesn't miss a word.

"You're sure nobody came down the tunnel after Mort Fredericks?''

"Sure I'm sure.''

"You were reading the paper though?''

"Off and on. Mostly just sittin', smoking my pipe.''

"Weren't you curious about what happened when Fredericks came back?''

"Yeah, but his way of walkin' looked angry to me, and he motioned to me to just stay in my chair, so I did. I let 'em alone when they're that mad.''

"You say he walked angry. How did his face look?''

"Didn't see it. He had his catcher's mask on.''

"Does Fredericks usually smash up the place when he's mad?''

"Been known to. Not this time, though.''

"Were you sitting in your chair all the time between the beginning of the game and the time Fredericks came storming through the tunnel?''

"Nope, I had my work to do, keeping the locker room and the clubhouse tidy.''

"Nobody back there but you?''

"Nope.''

When I'm through with Gus, I'm summoned again by Roy Giddings and Barney Dunlap, demanding amazing deduc-

tions. I'm a little short with them — of course, I have it figured out now, as you will too, and I decide my time's been
wasted with something purely silly. Sick of playing games,
I retreat to the umps' room, where my three colleagues
haven't even started getting dressed, so fervently are they
discussing the foibles of major-league ballplayers.

I strip off my uniform and step into the shower room, and
at that moment the shoddy, publicity-smelling vanishing of
Honey Reed becomes police business. He's lying dead on the
floor of the umpires' shower, blood drying on a vicious
wound on his skull.

A few hours later I'm sitting in Mrs. Gabrielson's private
box, more an apartment really, overlooking a darkened ball-
field. I'm nursing a drink and feeling a little uneasy — a man
of my position as neutral arbiter fraternizing with the officials
of a major-league club. Still, we've all been of interest to the
police the last few hours and thrown together that way. So I
sit sharing a drink with the publicist, the general manager,
the field manager, and the owner of the L.A. Surfers. I'm
telling them a little story. The police have left, taking the
killer of Honey Reed with them.

"So when I went back to the dugout, leaving my fellow
umps to watch over the body, I got Roy here to call the
police and I immediately told Mort what had happened. What
Mort told me then convinced me I knew who had killed
Honey Reed and how the killing tied in with his disappearance."

"But Mort didn't tell you anything," Roy Giddings says.

"That's right — he didn't tell me anything," I reply, sip-
ping my drink and enjoying myself. My Sherlock Holmes
qualities may be overrated, but that doesn't mean I don't play
them to the hilt when I'm in the mood.

"The meeting in my office," muses Mrs. Gabrielson.
"That should have warned us something like this could happen. Reed seemed to have a threat in every word he said, as
if he knew all sorts of terrible things about the Surfers organization and about all of us. Did he really?"

"I don't know how many terrible things there are to
know," I say. "But basically I don't think so. He'd just
heard a lot of rumors, and he was in a really nasty mood
from the way you described it to me. It was easy for one of
you to infer he knew something he really didn't."

"The disappearance," says Mrs. Gabrielson. "How did
that work?"

"Simple. Did it ever occur to you that the catcher and the
plate umpire are the only two people who appear on the ball-
field in *disguise?* When Mort gets to that point halfway
through the tunnel, where he can't be seen from either end,
he stops and strips off his jersey, his chest protector, his shin
guards, everything that identifies him as a catcher. His mask
is already off. He leaves them there in a little pile and goes
on down the tunnel. Old Gus isn't in his chair yet. If he was,
Mort would have to do something to distract him and sneak
by. At any rate, he goes into the clubhouse unseen. He
doesn't have to worry about deaf Gus hearing him, of course.

"Then, when Honey Reed gets himself tossed out — like
Mort, quite intentionally — he goes halfway through the tunnel, picks up the jersey and puts it on over his own, plus the
chest protector, shin guards, and mask. Of course, he has to
make sure Gus is in the chair before he comes storming past
him, motioning him to stay there and going into the clubhouse. The key to it is that he has the mask on — no catcher
goes around with his mask on except in the game, unless of
course he aims to *disguise* himself — which is just what
Reed was doing, pretending to be Fredericks.

"There's another tipoff about the mask. Why would a guy
as mad as Fredericks is supposed to be when I kick him out
even bother to pick up his mask out of the dirt, unless he has
some particular use for it?

"If old Gus could hear and was listening to the game on
the radio, the whole illusion could never work, because he'd
know the different times of the ejections, and the time of
'Fredericks' passing him would be too late."

"Then," says Terry Takamoto, "the whole vanishing was

just a practical joke worked out between Fredericks and Reed?''

"Right. Mainly by Reed, I think. It couldn't have been anything more important than a joke, because too many things could go wrong for anything really important to be riding on it. Gus could have seen Fredericks sneak into the clubhouse. Or he could have left his chair later and left the tunnel unviewed, blowing the whole illusion. The players all know Gus is in the habit of sitting there during the game, after an hour or so of working in the clubhouse, but it's not something you can absolutely count on. For a while I thought you were behind this, Mr. Takamoto — more space in the papers couldn't hurt the Surfers.''

"I hope we have a classier operation than that, Mr. Gorgon," says Takamoto.

"And that we take the number 12 jinx more seriously, as well," says Mrs. Gabrielson. "Reed mocked it, and it punished him."

"In a way I suppose it did," I reply. "Anyway, I knew that as soon as Mort heard what happened to Reed, he'd own up right away to his part in the prank unless —"

"— he was the murderer," Takamoto finishes.

"Right, though I don't know if murderer is the precise term. Maybe manslaughterer, or anyway, for now, suspect. Fredericks apparently hoped, stupidly, that the vanishing trick wouldn't be seen through and we'd think the curse had reached out and struck Honey Reed down. He confessed readily enough with a little questioning from the police. Not any kind of premeditated murder, I'm sure of that.

"Reed goes to hide in the umps' dressing room, and after Fredericks gets out of the shower, before the game is over, Fredericks goes down there probably to help Reed escape to some safer hiding place. They know we'll be back there when the game is over. The two of them get into a quarrel. Maybe Reed makes a crack about Mort's friend Willie Washington that hits too close to home. It seems for all these years Mort has felt guilty about the end of Washington's career.

Washington really hurt his arm roughousing in a hotel room with Fredericks, and the two of them kept it a secret from the club. Mort was afraid that Reed, with his act of knowing everything, had found out all about it and would tell the club officials, though what Mort thought you folks would do to him for it I can't imagine. Anyway, the fear of Reed's giving him away is what persuaded him to go along with the joke in the first place.

"Anyhow, in the umps' room, Fredericks for whatever reason takes a poke at Reed who, says Mort, hits his head hard on a sharp corner in the shower room and dies. Mort decides to brazen it out. But if the vanishing trick is figured out, he's the obvious suspect — only he would know that Reed hid out in the umps' room."

There is a short silence. Then Mrs. Gabrielson speaks up grimly. "No Surfer," she says, "will ever again wear number 12."

# The Magician's Wife

## J. F. Peirce

*It's fitting that this story by J. F. Peirce, published here
for the first time, should take place on stage during a
magician's act. Locked room and impossible crime stories owe much to the world of magic, as Clayton Rawson recognized so well.*

$T$HIS IS a locked room puzzle with a difference. When Mildred Hanks disappeared from a coffin, it was in front of a hundred policemen.

Merlin, the Magician, sawed his wife Mildred in half every night, using a coffin to make the trick more ghoulish. The circular saw whirred, and the whirr became a scream as the blade tore through the coffin.

Some of the audience covered their ears to shut out the scream. Others who didn't swore they could hear the tearing of flesh, the splintering of bone, though that seems impossible.

Merlin claimed to be a descendant of King Arthur's Merlin. Certainly his hoary tricks suggested that it might be true. In his one original trick, he offered a hundred dollars to anyone who could pull a sword from a stone as Arthur had pulled his sword Excalibur. None could! But after uttering the usual abracadabra, Merlin unsheathed the sword easily.

However, the climax of his performance was sawing his wife in half, and as he helped her into the coffin, he told a continuous stream of one-line jokes that had earned him the sobriquet "The Henny Youngman of Magicians."

"Take half my wife, *please!*

"Half a wife is better than one.

"If your wife has a weight problem, this is one way to cure it." And so on.

It's not surprising that he had been reduced to performing for benefits.

One night he was playing a benefit for the Police Retirement Fund, and over half of the force and their families were in the audience.

That night, when Merlin's assistant screamed *murder,* there was a blinding flash, followed by an explosion, and a cloud of smoke spread over the stage, hiding the hideous spectacle from view.

When the smoke cleared, the coffin was empty. Merlin's

wife had disappeared, and his assistant on stage was screaming, "He killed his wife! *He killed her!*" The police rushed
onto stage and secured the exits immediately.

And Captain Zachary — a tall, lean, hungry-looking homicide officer — took charge.

Some hours later, when after a search neither Merlin's
wife nor her body had turned up, the members of the audience were permitted to go home.

Zachary faced the magician, his assistant, and the stage
crew seated in the front row of the auditorium.

Lieutenant Joyce was taking notes, as were several reporters.

"Okay, what's your real name?" the captain asked the
magician.

"Hanks. Charles Hanks."

"And your wife's name?"

"Mildred. Find Milly for me, *please!*"

"We'll do our best, Mr. Hanks. Where are you from?"

"Bristol, England."

His assistant snorted. "He's from hunger," she said. "He
hasn't even been able to earn enough so we can return
home."

Zachary turned to her. "And you are?" he said.

"Ellen Simms. I'm his sister-in-law. Milly's my sister."

She'd proved to be a disappointment, the captain felt.
There were life-sized cutouts of the performers in the lobby.
Hers displayed melon-shaped breasts exploding from a low-
cut blouse. In the flesh, she was less attractive. Her hair was
a garish red; her face, a mask of makeup, and her bulging
bosom was concealed by a dickey.

Though in the cutouts there was a marked resemblance between the two women, Mildred Hanks apparently had none
of her sister's brassy hardness. Her hair was platinum, and
she, at least in the picture, wore almost no makeup.

The magician looked to be forty. He had patent-leather
black hair worn in a pompadour which accentuated his Sa-
tanic features.

"Now, would *you* tell me just what happened?" Zachary asked Merlin.

"I don't *know*," the magician answered. "I *wish* I did. Everything was going along as usual until the explosion and the smoke. When Milly disappeared, I was struck dumb."

"Too bad it wasn't permanent!" his sister-in-law said.

Zachary started to tell her to shut up, then thought better of it. He might learn more by pitting them against one another.

"Where could your wife have disappeared to?" Zachary asked.

"I've no idea."

"How did you and she get along?"

"Like two love birds."

Ellen Simms snorted.

"What happened?" Zachary asked her.

"Like he said, Milly screamed. Then there was the flash, the explosion, the smoke, and she was gone — just like a real magician had done it."

"Where could she have disappeared to?"

"I don't know. I'd never have guessed he was that good."

"Why do you think he killed her?"

"Because of the way they was actin' tonight."

"What were they doing — fighting?"

"No. Just glarin' at one another. 'If looks could kill!' I've never seen such hate as was in their eyes. It proper shook me."

"Why weren't you on stage for the final number?"

She said she had assisted Merlin during his first series of tricks. Then Merlin had performed alone, doing sleight-of-hand and spouting his one-liners. After that he had been joined by Mrs. Hanks and had levitated her with the aid of a broom. When his wife left the stage, the stagehands had rolled on the sword and stone, and Merlin had again worked alone.

Next had followed a series of illusions, during which Ellen

Simms had assisted Merlin. Shortly after she left the stage, the stagehands brought on the coffin.

Merlin was joined by his wife, and he had helped her into the coffin, which Zachary had examined carefully. Mrs. Hanks had extended her head, her feet, and her arms through openings in the ends and sides of the coffin. Curtains at each of the openings prevented the audience from seeing into the coffin once it was closed.

The table on which the coffin rested was a hollow box large enough to hold a body. There was a hole in its top, directly beneath the foot of the coffin, which had a hinged door that swung upward when pushed from below.

Mrs. Hanks had worn filmy harem pajamas. Her face, except for her hair and her eyes, had been concealed by a veil that also hid the top half of her torso. The make-up smeared veil had been found in the coffin.

"Why weren't you on stage for the final number?" Zachary asked the assistant again.

She turned so that he could see a tear in her blouse that was fastened together with pins. "I caught my blouse on something and went back to the dressing room to pin it. When I came out, the coffin was already on stage. Milly was stepping into it.

"I was supposed to be inside the table top. I push up the trapdoor with my feet and stick them out the end of the coffin as Milly curls into the fetal position and sticks out her head and hands.

"Milly and Merlin *thought* I was inside the table. Milly must have discovered I wasn't when I didn't respond to her rap to stick out my feet. She must have stuck her own feet out of the coffin, hoping no one would see her withdraw them when she curled up as Merlin began to saw. That's when she screamed — everyone probably was looking at her face, not her feet."

Zachary nodded. "And what do you think happened to your sister?"

"I don't know. I'd say Merlin made her disappear, but he's not that bloody clever."

"He didn't know you weren't inside the table?"

"I don't see how he could've. He was on stage when the coffin was rolled on."

"Then why did you accuse him of murdering your sister?"

Ellen Simms looked down. If she flushed, the flush was hidden by her makeup. "I guess because I felt responsible for whatever happened to her — guilty!

"I wasn't where I was supposed to be. It didn't matter that my blouse was torn while I was in the table. I was thinking of the curtain calls later." She put her fist to her mouth. "I'm not feeling well. Could I possibly leave?"

Zachary nodded. "Give the lieutenant your address. And don't leave the city before I say so."

The redhead turned to Merlin. "And I'm quitting," she said. "You can take your bloody act and stuff it!"

Merlin shrugged. "Then you'd better tell me where I should send your money. It may be several days 'fore I have it."

"You can stuff your money too! . . . When I leave, you'll never see or hear from me again!"

Merlin rose and made a pass near the captain's ear, seeming to take a one hundred dollar bill from it. The lower left-hand corner of the bill was missing.

"At least take this," the magician said.

Ellen Simms hesitated, then took the bill. After giving her address to the lieutenant, she disappeared into the wings.

Zachary turned to "Pops" Warner, the stage doorman. Pops was retired from the police force and had taken the job as doorman to supplement his retirement income. Zachary remembered him as a good cop.

"What can *you* tell us, Pops?" Zachary asked.

"Not much, Captain. Merlin and his wife came in an hour before the performance to set up their props and work on light cues. They were both carrying suitcases, and they both gave me a big 'Hi.' "

"How did they act?"

"Pleasant enough. They didn't talk while they were setting up, but they didn't need to. They both knew what to do."

"When did Ellen Simms come in?"

"About three-quarters of an hour later. She brushed past me, almost bumping me with her suitcase. She just had time to change into her costume and dash on stage."

"Was anyone else backstage during the evening?"

"Other than the stagehands and the stage manager, no one."

"Did you leave the door at any time?"

"Once to go to the john. I asked Mike to keep an eye on it."

Zachary turned to the stage manager.

"No one came in while Pops was gone," the stage manager said.

"Where were you when Mrs. Hanks disappeared?"

"By the lightboard. I was looking at Merlin. Then there was the flash and the explosion. The flash blinded me. By the time my eyes refocused, there was smoke all over the stage."

"Could Merlin have set off the flash powder and the smoke bomb?"

"I don't see how. I was looking right at him."

"Even when Mrs. Hanks screamed?"

"I see what you mean. I was looking at her then."

"Did you see Ellen Simms go on stage?"

"No. I rushed to get a fire extinguisher. By the time I got back, she was already on stage yelling 'Murder!' "

Zachary turned to the two stagehands. "Where were you during the flash and the explosion?"

"In the Prop Room putting up the sword and the stone," one of them said.

Zachary turned back to the stage manager. "The flash powder was sprinkled in the footlight trough. Who could have done it?"

"Any of us — while pretending to check the footlights."

"The wires and detonator have disappeared. What could have happened to them?"

"You can search me. *Literally.*"

"How could Mrs. Hanks have disappeared?"

"When it happened, I thought she might have gone through one of the trapdoors, but you saw they haven't been used in years. Then I thought maybe someone had tied a wire around her like Peter Pan and pulled her up into the flies, but you checked them and the light bridge."

Zachary nodded, then dismissed the stage crew before turning to Merlin. "You can change and leave," he said. "Just give the lieutenant your address before you do. And don't leave the city."

"What do you make of it, Captain?" one of the reporters asked once Merlin had gone.

Zachary shrugged. "Though Mrs. Hanks screamed, there's no blood in the coffin, no evidence she was hurt. I'm betting that she disappeared of her own volition — even though it seems there's no way she could have."

"Could the stage crew have helped her?"

"Not without Pops being in on it. And I'll stake my reputation on him."

"Then how'd she do it? She couldn't have come through the auditorium. We'd have seen her. She was in costume."

Zachary's face lit up. "Her street clothes were in the dressing room when I checked it." He turned to Lieutenant Joyce. "Go see if they're still there. And look for an extra suitcase. Let Merlin wonder what you're after."

The lieutenant had hardly left before the box office manager came running down the aisle from the direction of the lobby. "There's a call for Merlin," he said. "From his wife!"

"Where is she?" Zachary demanded. "What happened to her?"

"That's what I asked her. She claims she doesn't know. She says she's in her hotel room, that she's got amnesia."

"Did you see her or Merlin earlier tonight?"

"No, but I caught a glimpse of Ms. Simms."

"At what time? Where?"

"About twenty minutes before the performance — in the lobby."

"Did you get a good look at her?"

"No, but who could mistake that red hair, those knockers?"

"Was she leaving or coming in?"

"Leaving."

"Did she have a suitcase with her?"

The box office manager nodded.

"Didn't you think it strange she was leaving just before a performance?"

"No, she and the Hanks are staying at the hotel across the street. It's not unusual for a performer to run across to the hotel to get something."

Lieutenant Joyce appeared from the wings. "Merlin's packing the only suitcase," he reported. "Mrs. Hanks's street clothes are missing. He started packing after I entered."

"Roust out Judge Haynes," Zachary commanded. "Get warrants to search the Hanks's and Ellen Simms's hotel rooms on suspicion there's been a murder."

"Mrs. Hanks's?"

"No. Ellen Simms's."

The lieutenant whistled, then quickly departed.

Zachary turned to the box office manager. "Give Merlin his wife's message," he said, "but don't say anything else."

The manager nodded.

"How could Ellen Simms have been murdered?" a reporter asked. "We saw her leave not fifteen minutes ago."

"You saw Mrs. Hanks leave. Ellen Simms was never in the theater."

"But I saw both of them."

"You saw a red head with big knockers and a platinum blonde with not too much in that department. Right?"

The reporter nodded.

"That's what we all saw. Why we thought there were two

women. It was an illusion, a classic case of a magician's misdirection. Not once did we see the two together. Even if Pops and the box office manager had looked at Ellen Simms more closely, the family resemblance and the thick makeup would probably have fooled them.''

"But what happened?''

"Either Merlin or his wife murdered Ellen Simms. Then they both conspired to cover up the murder by having Mrs. Hanks disappear on stage. It almost worked.

"When Mrs. Hanks came to the theater tonight, she had Ellen Simms's street clothes, a red wig, and a pair of over-sized falsies in her suitcase. After helping Merlin set up, she dressed as Ellen Simms, left the theater by the lobby, then reentered via the stage door. After that, she changed from one woman to the other while Merlin performed onstage alone.

"When she came onstage for the final number, she was wearing a veil that covered the lower half of her face and her upper torso. We saw only her eyes and her platinum hair. Under the veil was a made-up face and a well-padded body. The red wig was already in the coffin.

"While everyone was distracted by Mrs. Hanks's scream, Merlin set off the flash powder and the smoke bomb. Then, hidden by the smoke, Merlin concealed the wires and deto-nator in his tailcoat, and Mrs. Hanks transformed herself into Ellen Simms. All she had to do was remove her veil, put on the wig, and step from the coffin. She left the make-up smeared veil in the coffin. And if you'll remember, Mrs. Hanks wore little makeup.

"It was a brilliant idea — to have her disappear before an audience of policemen, then reappear suffering from amnesia. Now she can claim she doesn't know how she got from the theater to her hotel room. She'll be dressed in her harem costume, yet no one will have seen her enter the hotel wearing it. They'll only have seen Ellen Simms with a suitcase. More magic!

"And we'll have to testify that Ellen Simms, who can't be

found, told Merlin that he'd never *see* or *hear from her* again. Normally, we wouldn't even have looked for her since Mrs. Hanks has reappeared.''

"Then how will you be able to prove what happened if they've gotten rid of Ellen Simms's body?''

"Mrs. Hanks made a mistake when she carried away her street clothes and her suitcase. And hopefully she won't have gotten rid of the wig and falsies. She may want Ellen Simms to be seen again elsewhere, buying a plane or a bus ticket. In any case, she won't have destroyed the hundred dollar bill that Merlin gave her. I'll be able to identify it because its lower left-hand corner's missing.''

Merlin appeared from the wings and hurried up the aisle, followed by the box office manager, to disappear into the lobby.

"Aren't you going to arrest him?'' a reporter asked.

"Not till he's talked to his wife. There'll be less chance of her getting rid of the wig and falsies if she thinks we don't suspect them.''

"Which of them did it?''

"Merlin could have gotten her pregnant and killed her when she demanded he divorce her sister, marry her. Or Mrs. Hanks could have caught them in the act. But they both tried to cover up the murder.''

"What tipped you off to it?''

Zachary smiled. "A dickey that concealed a bosom that should have been falling out to distract us from Merlin's magic!''

# The Problem of the Covered Bridge

### Edward D. Hoch

*Among the classic types of impossible crime problems are the tracks in the snow which mysteriously come to an end.*

YOU'RE ALWAYS hearin' that things were better in the good ol' days. Well, I don't know about that. Certainly medical treatment wasn't better. I speak from experience, because I started my practice as a country doctor up in New England way back in 1922. That seems a lifetime ago now, don't it? Heck, it *is* a lifetime ago!

"I'll tell you one thing that was better, though — the mysteries. The real honest-to-goodness mysteries that happened to ordinary folks like you an' me. I've read lots of mystery stories in my time, but there's never been anything to compare with some of the things I experienced personally.

"Take, for instance, the first winter I was up there. A man drove his horse and buggy through the snow into a covered bridge and never came out t'other end. All three vanished off the face o' the earth, as if they'd never existed!

"You want to hear about it? Heck, it won't take too long to tell. Pull up your chair while I get us — ah — a small libation."

I'd started my practice in Northmont on January 22, 1922 (the old man began). I'll always remember the date, 'cause it was the very day Pope Benedict XV died. Now I'm not Catholic myself, but in that part of New England a lot of the people are. The death of the Pope was a lot bigger news that day than the openin' of Dr. Sam Hawthorne's office. Nevertheless, I hired a pudgy woman named April for a nurse, bought some second-hand furniture, and settled in.

Only a year out of medical school, I was pretty new at the game. But I made friends easily, 'specially with the farm families out along the creek. I'd driven into town in my 1921 Pierce-Arrow Runabout, a blazin' yellow extravagance that set my folks back nearly $7,000 when they gave it to me as a graduation gift. It took me only one day to realize that families in rural New England didn't drive Pierce-Arrow Runabouts. Fact is, they'd never even seen one before.

The problem of the car was solved quickly enough for the

winter months when I found out that people in this area lucky enough to own automobiles cared for them during the cold weather by drainin' the gas tanks and puttin' the cars up on blocks till spring arrived. It was back to the horse an' buggy for the trips through the snow, an' I figured that was okay by me. In a way it made me one of them.

When the snow got too deep they got out the sleighs. This winter, though, was provin' unusually mild. The cold weather had froze over the ice on Snake Creek for skatin', but there was surprisin' little snow on the ground and the roads were clear.

On this Tuesday mornin' in the first week of March I'd driven my horse an' buggy up the North Road to the farm of Jacob an' Sara Bringlow. It had snowed a couple of inches overnight, but nothin' to speak of, and I was anxious to make my weekly call on Sara. She'd been ailin' since I first come to town and my Tuesday visits to the farm were already somethin' of a routine.

This day, as usual, the place seemed full o' people. Besides Jacob and his wife there were the three children — Hank, the handsome 25-year-old son who helped his pa work the farm, and Susan an' Sally, the 16-year-old twin daughters. Hank's intended, Millie O'Brian, was there too, as she often was those days. Millie was a year younger than Hank, an' they sure were in love. The wedding was already scheduled for May, and it would be a big affair. Even the rumblings 'bout Millie marryin' into a non-Catholic family had pretty much died down as the big day grew nearer.

"'Lo, Dr. Sam," Sally greeted me as I entered the kitchen.

I welcomed the warmth of the stove after the long cold drive. "Hello, Sally. How's your ma today?"

"She's up in bed, but she seems pretty good."

"Fine. We'll have her on her feet in no time."

Jacob Bringlow and his son entered through the shed door, stampin' the snow from their boots. "Good day, Dr. Sam," Jacob said. He was a large man, full of thunder like an Old

Testament prophet. Beside him, his son Hank seemed small and slim and a bit underfed.

"Good day to you," I said. "A cold mornin'!"

"'Tis that. Sally, git Dr. Sam a cup o'coffee — can't you see the man's freezin'?"

I nodded to Hank. "Out cuttin' firewood?"

"There's always some to cut."

Hank Bringlow was a likeable young chap about my own age. It seemed to me he was out of place on his pa's farm, and I was happy that the wedding would soon take him away from there. The only books an' magazines in the house belonged to Hank, and his manner was more that of a fun-lovin' scholar than a hard-workin' farmer. I knew he and Millie planned to move into town after their marriage, and I 'spected it would be a good thing for both of 'em.

Millie always seemed to be workin' in the kitchen when I made my calls. Maybe she was tryin' to convince the family she could make Hank a good wife. By the town's standards she was a pretty girl, though I'd known prettier ones at college.

She carefully took the coffee cup from young Sally an' brought it to me as I found a place to sit. "Just move those magazines, Dr. Sam," she said.

"Two issues of *Hearst's International?*" It wasn't a magazine frequently found in farmhouses.

"February and March. Hank was readin' the new two-part Sherlock Holmes story."

"They're great fun," I admitted. "I read them a lot in medical school."

Her smile glowed at me. "Mebbe you'll be a writer like Dr. Conan Doyle," she said.

"I doubt that." The coffee was good, warming me after the cold drive. "I really should see Mrs. Bringlow an' finish this later."

"You'll find her in good spirits."

Sara Bringlow's room was at the top of the stairs. The first time I went in, back in January, I found a weak, pale woman in her fifties with a thickened skin and dulled senses, who might have been very close to death. Now the scene was different. Even the room seemed more cheerful, an' certainly Sara Bringlow was more vividly alive than I'd ever seen her. Sittin' up in bed, with a bright pink shawl thrown over her shoulders, she welcomed me with a smile. "See, I'm almost all better! Do you think I can git up this week?"

Her illness today would probably be classed as a form of thyroid condition called myxedema, but we didn't use such fancy words back then. I'd treated her, an' she was better, an' that was all I cared about. "Tell you what, Sara, you stay in bed till Friday an' then you can get up if you feel like it." I winked at her 'cause I knew she liked me to. "If truth be known, I'll bet you been sneakin' out of that bed already!"

"Now how would you know that, Doctor?"

"When Sally met me at the door I asked how you were and she said you were up in bed but seemed pretty good. Well now, where else would you be? The only reason for her sayin' it like that was if you'd been up and about sometime recently."

"Land sakes, you should be a detective, Dr. Sam!"

"I have enough to do bein' a doctor." I took her pulse and blood pressure as I talked. "I see we had some more snow this mornin'."

"Yes indeed! The children will have to shovel off the ice before they go skatin' again."

"The wedding's gettin' mighty close now, isn't it?" I suspected the forthcomin' nuptials were playin' a big part in her recovery.

"Yep, just two months away. It'll be a happy day in my life. I s'pose it'll be hard on Jacob, losin' Hank's help around the farm, but he'll manage. I told him the boy's twenty-five now — got to lead his own life."

"Millie seems like a fine girl."

"Best there is! Catholic, of course, but we don't hold that again' her. 'Course her folks would rather she married Walt

Rumsey on the next farm, now that he owns it an' all, but Walt's over thirty — too old for a girl like Millie. I 'spect she knowed that too, when she broke off with him.''

There was a gentle knock on the door and Susan, the other twin, came in. "Momma, Hank's gettin' ready to go. He wants to know about that applesauce for Millie's ma.''

"Land sakes, I near forgot! Tell him to take a jar off the shelf in the cellar.''

After she'd gone I said, "Your daughters are lovely girls.''

"They are, aren't they? Tall like their father. Can you tell them apart?''

I nodded. "They're at an age where they want to be individuals. Sally's wearin' her hair a mite different now.''

"When they were younger, Hank was always puttin' them up to foolin' us, changin' places and such.'' Then, as she saw me close my bag, her eyes grew serious for a minute. "Dr. Sam, I *am* better, aren't I?''

"Much better. The thickenin' of your skin is goin' away, and you're much more alert.''

I left some more of the pills she'd been takin' and went back downstairs. Hank Bringlow was bundled into a fur-collared coat, ready for the trip to Millie's house. It was about two miles down the windin' road, past the Rumsey farm and across the covered bridge.

Hank picked up the quart jar of applesauce and said, "Dr. Sam, why don't you ride along with us? Millie's pa hurt his foot last week. He'd never call a doctor for it, but since you're so close maybe you should take a look.''

Millie seemed surprised by his request, but I had no objection. "Glad to. I'll follow you in my buggy.''

Outside, Hank said, "Millie, you ride with Dr. Sam so he doesn't get lost.''

She snorted at that. "The road doesn't go anywhere else, Hank!''

But she climbed into my buggy an' I took the reins. "I hear tell you've got yourself a fancy yellow car, Dr. Sam.''

"It's up on blocks till spring. This buggy is good enough for me." Mine was almost the same as Hank's — a four-wheeled carriage with a single seat for two people, pulled by one horse. The fabric top helped keep out the sun and rain, but not the cold. And ridin' in a buggy during a New England winter could be mighty cold!

The road ahead was windin', with woods on both sides. Though it was nearly noon, the tracks of Hank's horse an' buggy were the only ones ahead of us in the fresh snow. Not many people came up that way in the winter. Before we'd gone far, Hank speeded up and disappeared from sight round a bend in the road. "Hank seems so unlike his pa," I said, making conversation.

"That's because Jacob is his stepfather," Millie explained. "Sara's first husband — Hank's real father — died of typhoid when he was a baby. She remarried and then the twins were born."

"That explains the gap."

"Gap?"

"Nine years between Hank and his sisters. Farm families usually have their children closer together."

Hank's buggy was still far enough ahead to be out of sight, but now the Rumsey farm came into view. We had to pause a minute as Walt Rumsey blocked the road with a herd of cows returnin' to the barn. He waved and said, "Hank just passed."

"I know," Millie called back. "He goes so fast we can't keep up with him."

When the cows were gone I speeded up, still following the track of Hank's buggy in the snow. As we rounded the next corner I thought we'd see him, 'cause the road was now straight and the woods on both sides had ended. But there was only the covered bridge ahead, and the empty road runnin' beyond it to the O'Brian farm.

"Where is he?" Millie asked, puzzled.

"He must be waitin' for us inside the bridge." From our angle we couldn't yet see through it all the way.

"Prob'ly," she agreed with a chuckle. "He always says that covered bridges are kissin' bridges, but that's not true at all."

"Where I come from —" I began, and then paused. The interior of the bridge could be seen now, and no horse an' buggy were waitin' inside. "Well, he certainly went in. You can see the tracks in the snow."

"But —" Millie was half standing now in her seat. "Something's there on the floor of the bridge. What is it?"

We rode up to the bridge entrance and I stopped the horse. There were no windows cut into the sides of this covered bridge, but the light from the ends and from between the boards was enough to see by. I got down from the buggy. "It's his jar of applesauce," I said. "It smashed when it fell from the buggy."

But Millie wasn't lookin' at the applesauce. She was starin' straight ahead at the unmarked snow beyond the other end of the fifty-foot bridge. "Dr. Sam!"

"What is it?"

"There are no tracks goin' off the bridge! He came into it, but he didn't leave it! Dr. Sam, *where is he?*"

She was right, by gum! The tracks of Hank's horse an' buggy led into the bridge. Fact is, the damp imprint of the meltin' snow could be seen for several feet before it gradually faded away.

But there was no horse, no buggy, no Hank Bringlow.

Only the broken jar of applesauce he'd been carrying.

But if he hadn't disturbed the snow at the far end of the bridge, he must be — he *had* to be — still here! My eyes went up to the patterned wooden trusses that held the bridge together. There was nothing — nothing but the crossbeams and the roof itself. The bridge was in remarkably good shape, protected from weathering by its roof. Even the sides were sturdy and unbroken. Nothin' bigger than a squirrel could've fit between the boards.

"It's some sort of trick," I said to Millie. "He's got to be here!"

"But *where?*"

I walked to the other end of the bridge and examined the unmarked snow. I peered around the corner o' the bridge at the frozen surface of Snake Creek. The skaters had not yet shoveled off the snow, and it was as unmarked as the rest. Even if the horse an' buggy had passed somehow through the wooden floor or the sides o' the bridge, there was no place they could've gone without leavin' a mark. Hank had driven his buggy into the bridge with Millie an' me less than a minute behind him, dropped his quart jar o' applesauce, and vanished.

"We've got to get help," I said. Instinct told me I shouldn't disturb the snow beyond the bridge by goin' forward to Millie's house. "Wait here an' I'll run back to Rumsey's farm."

I found Walt Rumsey in the barn with his cows, forkin' hay out of the loft. " 'Lo, Doc," he called down to me. "What's up?"

"Hank Bringlow seems to have disappeared. Darnedest thing I ever saw. You got a telephone here?"

"Sure have, Doc." He hopped down to the ground. "Come on in the house."

As I followed him through the snow I asked, "Did Hank seem odd in any way when he went past you?"

"Odd? No. He was bundled up against the cold, but I knew it was him. I kept my cows to the side o' the road till he passed."

"Did he say anything?"

"No, just waved."

"Then you didn't actually see his face or hear his voice?"

Walt Rumsey turned to me. "Wa-el, no. But hell, I've known Hank mosta my life! It was him, all right."

An' I s'pose it had to be. No substitution o' drivers could've been made anywhere along the road, and even if a substitution had been made, how did the substitute disappear?

I took the phone that Walt Rumsey offered, cranked it up, and asked for the Bringlow farm. One of the twins answered. "This is Dr. Sam. We seem to have lost your brother. He didn't come back there, did he?''

"No. Isn't he with you?''

"Not right now. Your pa around?''

"He's out in the field somewhere. You want Momma?''

"No. She should stay in bed.'' No need to bother her yet. I hung up an' called the O'Brian farm with the same results. Millie's brother Larry answered the phone. He'd seen nothin' of Hank, but he promised to start out on foot toward the bridge at once, searchin' for buggy tracks or footprints.

"Any luck?'' Rumsey asked when I'd finished.

"Not yet. You didn't happen to watch him after he passed, did you?''

Rumsey shook his head. "I was busy with the cows.''

I went back outside and headed for the bridge, with Rumsey taggin' along. Millie was standin' by my horse an' buggy, lookin' concerned. "Did you find him?'' she asked.

I shook my head. "Your brother's on his way over.''

While Rumsey and I went over every inch of the covered bridge, Millie simply stood at the far end, watchin' for her brother. I guess she needed him to cling to just then. Larry O'Brian was young, handsome, an' likeable — a close friend of both Hank Bringlow an' Walt Rumsey. My nurse April told me that when Walt inherited the farm after his folks' death, both Larry and Hank helped him with the first season's planting. She'd also told me that despite their friendship Larry was against Hank marryin' his sister. P'raps, like some brothers, he viewed no man as worthy of the honor.

When Larry arrived he had nothing new to tell us. "No tracks between here an' the farm,'' he confirmed.

I had a thought. "Wait a minute! If there aren't any tracks, how in heck did you get over here this mornin', Millie?''

"I was with Hank at his place last night. When the snow started, the family insisted I stay over. We only got a couple of inches, though.'' She seemed to sense an unasked question, and she added, ''I slept with the twins in their big bed.''

Larry looked at me. ''What d'you think?''

I stared down at the smashed quart of applesauce which everyone had carefully avoided. ''I think we better call Sheriff Lens.''

Sheriff Lens was a fat man who moved slowly and thought slowly (Doctor Sam continued). He'd prob'ly never been confronted with any crime bigger than buggy stealin' — certainly nothin' like the disappearance from the covered bridge. He grunted and rasped as he listened to the story, then threw up his hands in dismay. ''It couldn'ta happened the way you say. The whole thing's impossible, an' the impossible jest don't make sense. I think you're all foolin' me — maybe havin' an April Fool joke three weeks early.''

It was about then that the strain finally got to Millie. She collapsed in tears, and Larry and I took her home. Their pa, Vincent O'Brian, met us at the door. ''What is this?'' he asked Larry. ''What's happened to her?''

''Hank's disappeared.''

''Disappeared? You mean run off with another woman?''

''No, nothin' like that.''

While Larry helped Millie to her room, I followed Vincent into the kitchen. He wasn't the hulkin' ox of a man that Jacob Bringlow was, but he still had the muscles of a lifetime spent in the field. ''Hank wanted me to come along,'' I explained. ''Said you'd hurt your foot.''

''It's nothin'. Twisted my ankle choppin' wood.''

''Can I see it?''

''No need.'' But he pulled up his pants leg reluctantly and I stooped to examine it. Swellin' and bruisin' were pronounced, but the worst was over.

''Not too bad,'' I agreed. ''But you should be soakin' it.''

Glancing around to be sure we weren't overheard, I lowered

my voice and added, "Your first thought was that Hank Bringlow had run off with another woman. Who did you have in mind?"

He looked uneasy. "Nobody special."

"This may be serious, Mr. O'Brian."

He thought about it and finally said, "I won't pretend I'm happy about my daughter marryin' a non-Catholic. Larry feels the same way. Besides, Hank fools around with the girls in town."

"For instance?"

"For instance Gert Page at the bank. Wouldn't be surprised he run off with her."

I saw Millie comin' back downstairs and I raised my voice a bit. "You soak that ankle now, in good hot water."

"Has there been any word?" Millie asked. She'd recovered her composure, though her face still lacked color.

"No word, but I'm sure he'll turn up. Was he in the habit of playin' tricks?"

"Sometimes he'd fool people with Susan an' Sally. Is that what you mean?"

"Don't know what I mean," I admitted. "But he seemed anxious for you to ride with me. Maybe there was a reason."

I stayed for lunch, and when no word came I headed back to town alone. The Sheriff an' some others were still at the covered bridge when I rode through it, but I didn't stop. I could see they'd gotten nowhere toward solvin' the mystery, and I was anxious to get to the bank before it closed.

Gert Page was a hard-eyed blonde girl of the sort who'd never be happy in a small New England town. She answered my questions 'bout Hank Bringlow with a sullen distrust she might have felt towards all men.

"Do you know where he is, Gert?"

"How would I know where he is?"

"Were you plannin' to run off with him before his marriage?"

"Ha! Me run off with him? Listen, if Millie O'Brian wants him that bad, she can have him!" The bank was closin' and she went back to countin' the cash in her drawer. "B'sides, I hear tell men get tired of married life after a bit. I just might see him in town again. But I sure won't run off with him and be tied to one man!"

I saw Roberts, the bank's manager, watchin' us and I wondered why they kept a girl like Gert on the payroll. I 'spected she was most unpopular with the bank's lady customers.

As I left the bank I saw Sheriff Lens enterin' the general store across the street. I followed and caught him at the pickle barrel. "Anything new, Sheriff?"

"I give it up, Doc. Wherever he is, he ain't out by the bridge."

The general store, which was right next to my office, was a cozy place with great wheels of cheese, buckets o' flour, an' jars o' taffy kisses. The owner's name was Max, and his big collie dog always slept on the floor near the potbellied stove. Max came around the counter to join us and said, "Everyone's talkin' about young Hank. What do you think happened?"

"No idea," I admitted.

"Couldn't an aeroplane have come over an' picked up the whole shebang?"

"I was right behind him in my buggy. There was no aeroplane." I glanced out the window and saw Gert Page leavin' the bank with the manager, Roberts. "I hear some gossip that Hank was friendly with Gert Page. Any truth to it?"

Max scratched the stubble on his chin and laughed. "Everybody in town is friendly with Gert, includin' ol' Roberts there. It don't mean nothin'."

"I guess not," I agreed. But if it hadn't meant anything to Hank Bringlow, had it meant somethin' to Millie's pa an' brother?

Sheriff Lens and I left the general store together. He promised to keep me informed and I went next door to my office.

My nurse April was waitin' for all the details. "My God, you're famous, Dr. Sam! The telephone ain't stopped ringin'!"

"Hell of a thing to be famous for. I didn't see a thing out there."

"That's the point! Anyone else they wouldn't believe — but you're somethin' special."

I sighed and kicked off my damp boots. "I'm just another country doctor, April."

She was a plump jolly woman in her thirties, and I'd never regretted hirin' her my first day in town. "They think you're smarter'n most, Dr. Sam."

"Well, I'm not."

"They think you can solve this mystery."

Who else had called me a detective that day? Sara Bringlow? "Why do they think that?"

"I guess because you're the first doctor in town ever drove a Pierce-Arrow car."

I swore at her but she was laughin' and I laughed too. There were some patients waitin' in the outer office and I went to tend to them. It was far from an ordinary day, but I still had my practice to see to. Towards evening, by the time I'd finished, the weather had turned warmer. The temperature hovered near 40 and a gentle rain began to fall.

"It'll git rid o' the snow," April said as I left for the day.

"Ayah, it'll do that."

"Mebbe it'll uncover a clue."

I nodded, but I didn't believe it. Hank Bringlow had gone far away, and the meltin' snow wasn't about to bring him back.

The telephone woke me at four the next mornin'. "This is Sheriff Lens, Doc," the voice greeted me. "Sorry to wake you, but I gotta bad job for you."

"What's that?"

"We found Hank Bringlow."

"Where?"

"On the Post Road, about ten miles south o' town. He's sittin' in his buggy like he jest stopped for a rest."

"Is he — ?"

"Dead, Doc. That's what I need you for. Somebody shot him in the back o' the head."

It took me near an hour (Doctor Sam went on) to reach the scene, drivin' the horse an' buggy fast as I could over the slushy country roads. Though the night was mild, the rain chilled me to the bone as I rode through the darkness on that terrible mission. I kept thinkin' about Millie O'Brian, and Hank's ma only just recoverin' from her lengthy illness. What would the news do to them?

Sheriff Lens had some lanterns out in the road, and I could see their eerie glow as I drove up. He helped me down from the buggy an' I walked over to the small circle of men standin' by the other rig. Two of them were deputies, another was a farmer from a nearby house. They hadn't disturbed the body — Hank still sat slumped in a corner o' the seat, his feet wedged against the front o' the buggy.

I drew a sharp breath when I saw the back of his head. "Shotgun," I said curtly.

"Can you tell if it happened here, Doc?"

"Doubtful." I turned to the farmer. "Did you find him?"

The man nodded and repeated a story he'd obviously told 'em already. "My wife heard the horse. We don't git nobody along this road in the middle o' the night, so I come out to look around. I found him like this."

In the flare of lantern light I noticed somethin' — a round mark on the horse's flank that was sensitive to my touch. "Look here, Sheriff."

"What is it?"

"A burn. The killer loaded Hank into the buggy an' then tied the reins. He singed the horse with a cigar or somethin' to make it run. Could've run miles before it stopped from exhaustion."

Lens motioned to his deputies. "Let's take him into town. We won't find nothin' else out here." He turned back to me "At least he's not missin' any more."

"No, he's not missin'. But we still don't know what happened on that bridge. We only know it wasn't any joke."

The funeral was held two days later, on Friday mornin', with a bleak winter sun breakin' through the overcast to throw long March shadows across the tombstones of the little town cemetery. The Bringlows were all there, 'course, and Millie's folks and people from town. Afterwards many of us went back to the Bringlow farm. It was a country custom, however sad the occasion, and many neighbors brought food for the family.

I was sittin' in the parlor, away from the others, when the bank manager, Roberts, came up to me. "Has the Sheriff found any clues yet?" he asked.

"Nothin' I know of."

"It's a real baffler. Not just the *how*, but the *why*."

"The *why?*"

He nodded. "When you're goin' to kill someone you just do it. You don't rig up some fantastic scheme for them to disappear first. What's the point?"

I thought about that, and I didn't have a ready answer. When Roberts drifted away I went over to Sara Bringlow and asked how she was feelin'. She looked at me with tired eyes and said, "My first day outta bed. To bury my son."

There was no point arguin' with a mother's grief. I saw Max bringin' in a bag of groceries from his store and I started over to help him. But my eye caught somethin' on the parlor table. It was the March issue of *Hearst's International*. I remembered Hank had been reading the Sherlock Holmes story in the February and March issues. I located the February one under a stack o' newspapers and turned to the Holmes story.

It was in two parts, and called *The Problem of Thor Bridge*.

Bridge?

I found a quiet corner and sat down to read.

It took me only a half hour, and when I finished I sought out Walt Rumsey from the next farm. He was standin' with Larry O'Brian on the side porch, an' when he saw me comin' he said, "Larry's got some good bootleg stuff out in his buggy. Want a shot?"

"No, thanks, Walt. But you can do somethin' else for me. Do you have a good stout rope in your barn?"

He frowned in concentration. "I s'pose so."

"Could we ride over there now? I just read somethin' that gave me an idea about how Hank might've vanished from that bridge."

We got into his buggy an' drove the mile down the windin' road to his farm. The snow was melted by this time, and the cows were clustered around the water trough by the side of the barn. Walt took me inside, past empty stalls an' milk cans an' carriage wheels, to a big shed attached to the rear. Here, among assorted tools, he found a twelve-foot length of worn hemp.

"This do you?"

"Just the thing. Want to come to the bridge with me?"

The ice of the creek was still firm, though the road had turned to mud. I handed one end o' the rope to Rumsey and played out the other end till it reached the edge of the frozen creek. "What's this all about?" he asked.

"I read a story 'bout a gun that vanished off a bridge by bein' pulled into the water."

He looked puzzled. "But Hank's buggy couldn'ta gone into the crick. The ice was unbroken."

"All the same I think it tells me somethin'. Thanks for the use o' the rope."

He took me back to the Bringlow house, puzzled but un-questioning. The mourners were beginning to drift away, and I sought out Sheriff Lens. "I've got an idea about this mystery, Sheriff. But it's sort of crazy."

"In this case, even a crazy idea would be welcome."

Jacob Bringlow, tall and unbent from the ordeal of the funeral, came around the corner o' the house with one of the twins. "What is it, Sheriff?" he asked. "Still searchin' for clues?"

"We may have one," I said. "I got an idea."

He eyed me up an' down, p'raps blamin' me for what happened to his stepson. "You stick to your doctorin'," he said with a slur, and I knew he'd been samplin' Larry's bottle. "Go look at my wife. She don't seem right to me."

I went inside and found Sara pale and tired-looking. I ordered her up to bed and she went without argument. Max was leavin', and so was the O'Brian family. The banker had already gone. But when I went back on the porch, Jacob Bringlow was still waitin' for me. He was lookin' for trouble. Maybe it was a mixture of grief and bootleg whiskey.

"Sheriff says you know who killed Hank."

"I didn't say that. I just got an idea."

"Tell me. Tell us all!"

He spoke loudly, and Larry O'Brian paused with Millie to listen. Walt Rumsey came over too. In the distance, near the buggies, I saw Gert Page from the bank. I hadn't seen her at the funeral, but she'd come to pay some sort of last respects to Hank.

"We can talk about it inside," I replied, keepin' my voice down.

"You're bluffin'! You don't know a thing!"

I drew a deep breath. "All right, if you want it like this. Hank was reading a Sherlock Holmes story before he died. There's another one he prob'ly read years ago. In it Holmes calls Watson's attention to the curious incident of the dog in the night-time. I could echo his words."

"But there was no dog in the night-time," Sheriff Lens pointed out. "There's no dog in this whole danged case!"

"My mistake," I said. "Then let me direct your attention to the curious incident of the cows in the daytime."

It was then that Walt Rumsey broke from the group and ran towards his buggy. "Grab him, Sheriff!" I shouted. "He's your murderer!"

I had to tell it all to April, back at my office, because she hadn't been there and wouldn't believe it otherwise. "Come on, Dr. Sam! How did the cows tell you Walt was the killer?"

"He was bringin' them back to the barn, across the road, as we passed. But from where? Cows don't graze in the snow, and their waterin' trough is next to the barn, not across the road. The only possible reason for the cows crossin' the road in front of us was to obliterate the tracks of Hank's horse an' buggy.

"Except for those cows, the snow was unbroken by anything but the single buggy track — all the way from the Bringlow farm to the covered bridge. We know Hank left the farm. If he never reached the bridge, whatever happened to him had to happen at the point where those cows crossed the road."

"But the tracks to the bridge! You were only a minute behind him, Dr. Sam. That wasn't long enough for him to fake those tracks!"

I smiled, runnin' over the reasonin' as it first came to me. "Roberts the banker answered that one, along with Sherlock Holmes. Roberts asked *why*—why did the killer go to all that trouble? And the answer was that he didn't. It wasn't the killer but Hank Bringlow who went to all the trouble.

"We already knew he'd fooled people with his twin sisters, confusin' their identities. And we knew he'd recently read *The Problem of Thor Bridge,* which has an impossible suicide of sorts takin' place on a bridge. It's not too far-fetched to imagine him arrangin' the ultimate joke — his own disappearance from that covered bridge."

"But *how,* Dr. Sam?" April wanted to know. "I read that Sherlock Holmes story too, an' there's nothin' in it like what happened here."

"True. But as soon as I realized the purpose o' those noonday cows, I knew somethin' had happened to those tracks at the barn. And only one thing could've happened —

Hank's buggy turned off the road and went *into* the barn. The tracks from the road to the bridge were faked.''

"How?'' she repeated, not yet ready to believe a word of it.

"*When* is the more important question. Since there was no time to fake the tracks in the single minute before we came along, they had to have been done earlier. Hank and Walt Rumsey must've been in cahoots on the scheme. Walt went out that mornin', after the snow had stopped, with a couple o' old carriage wheels linked together by an axle. On his boots he'd fastened blocks o' wood a couple o' inches thick, with horseshoes nailed to the bottoms.

"He simply trotted along the road, through the snow, pushin' the pair o' wheels ahead of him. He went into the bridge far enough to leave traces o' snow, then reversed the blocks o' wood on his boots and pushed the wheels back again. The resultin' tracks looked like a four-footed animal pullin' a four-wheeled buggy.''

"But —'' April started to object.

"I know, I know! A man doesn't run like a horse. But with practise he could space the prints to look good enough. And I'll bet Hank an' Walt practised plenty while they waited for the right mornin' when the snow was fresh but not too deep. If anyone had examined the tracks o' the horse carefully, they'd've discovered the truth. Careful as he was, Walt Rumsey's prints comin' back from the bridge woulda been a bit different, hittin' the snow from the opposite direction. But they figured I'd drive my buggy up to the bridge in his tracks, all but obliteratin' them, which is what I did. They couldn't really be examined then.''

"You're forgettin' the broken jar o' applesauce,'' April said. "Don't that prove Hank was *on* the bridge?''

"Nothing of the sort! Hank knew in advance his ma planned to send the applesauce to Mrs. O'Brian. He prob'ly suggested it, and he certainly reminded her of it. He simply gave Walt Rumsey a duplicate jar a day or two earlier, an' it was that jar Walt broke on the bridge. The jar Hank was carrying went with him into Walt's barn."

"What if it hadn't snowed that mornin'? What if someone else came along first to leave other tracks?"

I shrugged. "They would've phoned one another and postponed it, I s'pose. It was only meant as a joke. They'd have tried again some other day, with other witnesses. They didn't really need me an' Millie."

"Then how did it turn from a joke to murder?"

"Walt Rumsey had never given up lovin' Millie, or hatin' Hank for takin' her away from him. After the trick worked so well, he saw the perfect chance to kill Hank and win her back. Once I knew he was in on the trick, he had to be the killer — else why was he keepin' quiet 'bout his part in it?

"Hank had hidden his horse an' buggy in that big shed behind the Rumsey barn. When we all went back to town, an' Hank was ready to reappear an' have a good laugh on everyone, Walt Rumsey killed him. Then he waited till dark to dispose of the body on the Post Road. He drove the buggy part way, turned the horse loose to run, and walked home.

"This mornin' after the funeral I made an excuse of wantin' a piece of rope so I could see the inside of Rumsey's barn again. He had spare carriage wheels there, and the shed was big enough to hold a horse an' buggy. That was all the confirmation I needed."

April leaned back and smiled, convinced at last. "After this they'll probably give the you the Sheriff's job, Dr. Sam."

I shook my head. "I'm just a country doctor."

"A country doctor with a Pierce-Arrow car!" . . .

"That's the way it happened, back in '22. I've often thought I should write it up now that I'm retired, but there's just never enough time. Sure, I've got other stories. Lots of 'em! Can I get you another — ah — small libation?"